ANOTHER LIFETIME AGO

BEN MARNEY

Copyright © 2019 by Ben Marney

All rights reserved.

No part of this book may be reproduced in any form or by any electronic or mechanical means, including information storage and retrieval systems, without written permission from the author, except for the use of brief quotations in a book review.

❦ Created with Vellum

SPECIAL OFFER

Writing is a lonely job, so meeting and getting to know my readers is a thrill and one of the best perks of being an author. I would like to invite you to join my Private Readers' Group and in return I'll give you a FREE copy of *Lyrics Of My Life*. This is a collection of autobiographical short stories about my crazy life.

I think you'll like this book; it's been quite a ride so far and I really would like to meet you. Please join my readers group here: www.benmarneybooks.com

SPECIAL THANKS

Once again, thanks to Susan Jordan for the incredible job she did editing this book.

You make me look so much smarter…

Dedication

For my family, mom, dad and Ron. I miss you…

*And of course, for my wife Dana.
My girl with the beautiful turquoise eyes.*

"In the end, it's not the years in your life that count. It's the life in your years."

— Abraham Lincoln

1

SAVANNAH

School was out for the summer and as usual I was playing on the railroad tracks that ran behind my house, that's when I saw the moving truck pull up next-door and stop. I ran to my tree house built out of old scrap lumber I had salvaged around town. It was nestled between four large spreading limbs of a massive 60 foot tall Coastal Live Oak tree, and for the next four hours, I watched them move in, paying close attention to the beautiful girl with the long blonde hair, blowing in the wind.

She eventually saw me in the treehouse and walked over, looked up, and smiled. "Hello, I'm Savannah. Do you live here?" I climbed down out of the tree house and walked over to her. She towered over me by almost six inches. "Hi, I'm Travis. Yeah, I live here."

"Cool!" she said, "we're gonna be next door neighbors. What grade are you in?"

I was only 8 years old, but I can still remember having trouble forming my words that day, staring into her beautiful face and sparkling eyes the color of turquoise. It took me a few seconds to remember, but finally I said, "when school starts I'll be in the third grade."

"Me too!" She yelled excitedly, reaching out her arms and hugging me.

Feeling her arms around me caused my heart to race in my chest. It wasn't the first time I had been hugged by a girl, but it was the first time it took my breath away and made me blush. My cheeks turned a bright shade of crimson. She flashed her amazing smile at me again, and without asking, began climbing up into my treehouse, yelling for me to follow her. That was the first of thousands of times I followed her up that tree...

I've tried for years to forget that day, the day I lost my heart and fell in love with Savannah. But like an old tattoo that has faded with time, if you look close...it's still there like an ugly scar.

2

MATADOR

Thirteen years later...

I was lying on my bunk in the barracks in Beirut, Lebanon when I heard someone yell my name. "Lance Corporal Travis Lee?" It was a First Lieutenant. I jumped to my feet to attention and saluted, "I'm Lee, sir."

"Lance Corporal, you are to report to the CO, ASAP. He wants to talk to you."

"Major General Britton wants to talk to me? What did I do?"

The lieutenant frowned. "I have no idea Marine, I was just told to come get you. So move your ass and report to him, NOW!" he ordered.

It was the first time I'd ever been ordered to report to the CO in the three years I had been in the Marines. As I walked there, I racked my brain trying to figure out what I could have possibly done to get called up on the carpet like this. When his assistant opened the door Major General William Britton, from Knoxville, Tennessee, was sitting behind his desk. The chaplain was standing next to him on his right side.

"You wanted to see me Sir?" I asked.

He looked up at me with a somber face. In a slow Tennessee drawl he said, "Yes Travis I did. Have a seat son." When he said those words, I knew it must be something personal, because he addressed me by Travis, instead of by my rank and last name.

"What is it Sir?"

He shot a glance at the Chaplain, who immediately took the seat next to me.

The chaplain leaned over toward me, "I'm afraid we have some bad news from home. Your mother," He paused and looked down, "She...she passed away yesterday. I'm so sorry for your loss."

They both stared at me, waiting for my expected emotional response, but it never came. I just sat there quietly, not moving.

"Did you hear what the Chaplain said?" He asked. "Your mother has died." I nodded, "Yes Sir, I heard him. Is that all Sir? Can I go back to my platoon now?"

With stunned faces they looked at each other. "No, Lance Corporal Lee, you may not go back to the barracks. Your mother's funeral is scheduled in two days. I have just signed papers for your 4 week leave and I've made special arrangements for you to fly out of here in a few hours."

I stood up. "I really appreciate it sir, but I have no desire to go to that funeral. I don't want to leave my platoon here in Beirut."

Major General Britton jumped to his feet. "SIT BACK DOWN IN THAT CHAIR MARINE!" He yelled.

I sat down and dropped my head, staring down at my feet. "I'm sorry sir, but she wasn't much of a mother." He stood up again. "Follow me!" He ordered as he walked out his door. I followed him to the mess hall. We both got coffee and settled across from each other at a table in the private officer's section.

He took a long sip of his coffee, looked me in the eyes and leaned back in his chair. "Travis, we have something in common. My father was a grunt in the Marines. He never even made it to Private 1st Class" he began, "He served in WWII, he was a mean son of a bitch that used to get drunk and take out his anger on my mother, and sometimes me. When I was 17, I couldn't take it anymore, so one day when he swung at me, I fought back. I beat the shit out of him that night and joined the

Marines the next day. I hated him and never talked to him again as long as he lived."

I didn't know how to respond, so I just sat there, silent.

"He died three years after I joined the Marines and like you, I didn't want to go to his funeral either, but my CO ordered me to go. He told me the same thing I'm going to tell you. Travis, you are a Marine, and that's a life long pledge. Your fellow Marines are your family now and as long as you live your brother and sister Marines will be there for you if you need them. Whatever happened in your life before you became a marine has nothing to do with who you are now and who you have become. Your life back then is nothing more than just old baggage. Go to your mother's funeral and bury all of those bad memories and never think of them again. I'm not saying forget your mother, I'm just saying to forget all the bad memories you have of her and only remember the good ones."

He took another sip of his coffee and stared at me across the table. In his Tennessee southern accent, he smiled at me and said, "Think you can do that son?"

I nodded, "I'll try sir, but honestly I don't have many good memories of her."

He leaned forward. "What about your father?"

I chuckled and said. "Huh…I never got the chance to meet him, but I believe he was probably worse than my mother. He never wanted to have children and three days after I was born, he left us. I know that, because my mother never let me forget it. She blamed me for him walking out my whole life. Don't get me wrong, she didn't beat me or anything like that, she just…well…never showed me any love.

She fed me, put a roof over my head and gave me clothes, but she never once hugged me…or even touched me for that matter. Even when I was a little kid and fell down and scraped my knees, she wasn't there like other moms with kind loving words as she cleaned and put on the bandage. She would just yell at me for getting blood on the rug."

I sat back and took a sip of my coffee. "I realize Sir, it may sound petty now, but when I was a little kid, six or seven years old, it had a profound effect on me that I can't seem to get over. I grew to hate her more and more through those years. She was so cold and hateful and it got worse as she got older."

He shook his head. "So you joined the Marines as soon as you could to get away from her."

"No sir, I didn't join the Marines because of my mother. That would have meant that I cared about what she thought and I haven't given a shit about that since I was 13. No sir, I joined the Marines to get away from someone else. And she's another reason I don't want to go back home to the funeral. I never want to see her again!"

He smiled. "Travis, I don't mean to make light of this, but I'm talking to you here man to man, friend to friend, not as your Commanding Officer. Let me give you some friendly advice. Son, you were what, 17 or 18? You were still a kid. Your childhood sweetheart broke your heart and you're still hurting. Travis, that was another lifetime ago. You are no longer that 18 year old boy, you are a man now, a Marine. Trust me son, she won't be the only woman who will break your heart in your life. I don't know what she did to you, but it's time you put that behind you too. Forgive her son and move on."

I nodded, "I've been trying to Sir, for almost 3 years now, but what she did to me... to us...I don't think I'll ever be able to forgive".

When I walked back into the barracks, everyone in my platoon turned and stared.

Lying in his bunk, Hag looked up and asked, "What did you do? What'd the Old Man want?"

I had known Hag for almost three years. We met in boot camp and had been through a few tight scrapes together in Beirut during our time stationed there. He had saved my ass more than once and he was my one real friend. His real name was Gary Smith, but because he was from Muskogee, Oklahoma we all called him Hag, short for Merle Haggard. He constantly drove us all nuts when, without warning, he would start singing "I'm Proud To Be An Okie From Muskogee." It wasn't because we hated the song...it was because Hag couldn't sing for shit, but sang every verse anyway.

Straight out of Boot Camp, all 15 of us had been stationed in Beirut for the last 22 months. There was a two year maximum limit for our deployment, so we only had about eight more weeks to go before we could get out of that hell hole. The excited anticipation of finally going home was building inside all of us. We had been sent there by President Reagan, when he agreed to be part of a multi national United Nations peace-keeping force.

While I was there, I achieved the rank of Lance Corporal and was appointed platoon leader over 14 men. I knew every one of them since boot camp, and because of that, when I was promoted to platoon leader......I caught a lot of grief from a few of them. Although we all knew each other's real name, we never used them. Instead we called each other by the nicknames our drill sergeant came up with on our first few days of boot camp back in San Diego.

Jim Reed from Alabama was called 'Gomer', Walter Anderson from Chicago was called 'Capone' (after the famous Chicago gangster Al Capone), Jimmy Wilkerson from Florida was called 'Orlando' and on and on it went. I was from a small beach community in Texas, named Matagorda and although it was a long way from Mexico, the drill sergeant branded me with the name of 'Matador'. He explained that it meant 'to kill' in Spanish. I didn't like that name much but unfortunately it stuck.

I pulled out my duffel and began filling it with my clothes and gear.

"Going somewhere Matador?" Hag asked.

I shrugged. "My mother died. The old man gave me a four weeks leave. I don't want to go, but I'm under orders to attend her funeral."

Hag was the only person on earth, besides Savannah, who knew about my mother and how she had treated me. Through the years since boot camp we had spent hours talking about our lives to each other. I knew everything about him and his dreams, and he knew everything about me and mine.

Hag had his whole life all planned out. When he got out of the Marines he planned to go back to Muskogee, marry his high school sweetheart and go to college at Oklahoma State University. After that he hoped he'd get a job coaching high school football somewhere in Oklahoma.

Before the Marines, I had my life planned out as well, but now those plans were sort of vague. All of those plans had changed suddenly.

∼

Savannah's father was a violent angry drunk, who used to smash things against the walls and beat up her mother. When he would come home drunk, Savannah would run out her back door to my house and scratch on my window to wake me up.

On those violent, horrific nights, as quietly as I could, trying not to wake my mother, I would slip out my window and Savannah and I would ride our bicycles the 10 miles to the beach on Matagorda Peninsula.

Lying on the beach in the sand, listening to the crashing waves, staring up at the stars, we would talk until the sun came up about the life we were going to build together when we finally grew up and got married. Over those ten years during the late night bike trips to that beach escaping her father's drunken wrath, we planned out every single detail.

When we graduated high school we were going to leave Matagorda behind. I was going to become a lawyer and she was going to teach kindergarten until we had our first child. After that, she going to be a stay home mother raising our three children…two boys and one girl. And I planned to hug each one of those children every single day, showing them what love felt like. Our plans never changed all the way through high school.

It wasn't a secret plan, our parents, all our friends and most of the people in the small community of Matagorda knew about it as well. And everyone believed it would surely come true someday. But then 'Savannah did what she did' and all those dreams disappeared into the salty, humid Texas air.

∼

Hag climbed out of his bunk and walked over to me. "Sorry, Matador, but I think the old man's right on this one. You need to get on that plane and leave this God forsaken place for a while. Go back to Texas and go to that funeral. When you're there, bury your mother and put all that crap she put you through in that casket with her."

I didn't respond and just kept packing my duffel bag.

Hag looked down and shuffled his feet. "You think you'll see Savannah when you're there? Maybe at the funeral?"

I stared back at him. "I hope not. I'm not sure what I'd do or say if I saw her."

When I finished packing, I went around the room shaking hands on my way out. When I got to the door I stopped, turned around and looked at my platoon. "Try not to fuck up too bad while I'm gone. See you in four weeks."

3

EVERY ONE OF THEM

When I walked into the back of the church, I could see my mother's casket, at the end of the center isle, covered with flowers positioned below the pulpit.

I was shocked to see the turnout. Matagorda only had a population of a little over 500 and it looked like half of the town was there. The sanctuary was almost full, every pew packed with mourners, sitting quietly, hands folded in their laps with their heads bowed. I had expected to see an empty church, except for her two sisters and my uncles, but apparently, my mother actually had friends. Of course she wouldn't have told me about them. We hadn't had a conversation of any substance in years.

When everyone realized I had entered the church, the entire congregation turned to watch me walk down the isle. As I walked, I scanned the faces in the crowd and was relieved not to see Savannah......she wasn't there.

With every eye in the chapel watching, I slowly made my way down the isle to the third row, a few feet from the casket and took a seat.

I purposely hadn't told any of my friends or relatives I had joined the Marines. I didn't want anyone to know, or for them to have anyway to contact me. I had simply packed a bag, walked to the terminal, got on the bus, and left town without saying a word to anyone.

When the congregation saw me walking down the isle in my Dress Blues with my brass and ribbons glistening in the light, there was an audible gasp.

I chose to sit alone in the third row behind my aunts and uncles. Truthfully, I barely knew them, they had rarely visited us during my childhood and never once offered any help to her...or me. I assumed they were only there to rummage through her house and search for anything of value. The thought of that made me smile, because I knew that they would leave town disappointed; all she had was some old worn out furniture and some old clothes. Mother didn't even own the house she had lived in all those years, she rented it.

I sat there erect and silent behind them, never once acknowledging them or showing any signs of emotion during the ceremony.

After the funeral, they opened the casket for viewing. I had no desire to see her dead body and didn't rise with the rest of the family to line up. Mistakenly assuming I was too distraught to stand, the pastor walked to where I was sitting and took my arm, pulling me up to my feet.

"Lean on me Travis," He said, "I'll help you."

I wanted to jerk my arm back and yell, "I don't need your help!" But instead, I stood and let him lead me over to her casket.

In the three years since I had seen her, she had lost a lot of weight due to the cancer. She was wearing a dark blue dress with a white lace collar. Her skeleton thin hands were clasped together at her waist, her shockingly stark white hair was combed smoothly framing her emaciated face. Her eye lids were closed, but seemed to be several inches further back in deep sunken sockets. If I didn't know for sure it was my mother, I would never have recognized her. She showed no resemblance of the angry, hateful woman I grew up with.

Without emotion, I leaned over her casket and whispered, "Mother, I'm going to do my best to forget everything you did to me and maybe, one day, I'll be able to forgive you....but I'm not there yet. I do sincerely hope you Rest In Peace. Goodbye."

I walked out of the church nodding at a few familiar faces on the way. I passed on my relatives invitation to ride to the grave side service in the family limo. Instead I slowly followed close behind them in the rental car I had picked up at the Houston airport. I also turned down their offer to sit under the canopy in one of the green cloth covered folding chairs, lined up in a sad row, a few feet away from the freshly dug grave. I elected to stand alone, at military attention, several feet away.

When the graveside service was over, I found myself surrounded by several of my old high school friends offering me their condolences. They slowly walked and talked with me as I made my way back to my car.

When we made it to the car, leaning against the hood smiling, was Kelly Smith. Kelly was without a doubt my closest friend in Matagorda. We had grown up together. He lived a few blocks over, we had met in kindergarten and he had helped me drag old scraps of lumber from all over town and helped build that tree house. He also knew Savannah almost as well as I did.

"Well look at you all dressed up spit shined in your fancy uniform," He said grinning wide. "Where the hell have you been General?"

"It's Lance Corporal, you ignorant civilian red neck!" I reached out and grabbed him, pulling him into a bear hug, "Kelly, It's good to see you again. Did you ever find a woman dumb enough to go out with you?"

He held up his hand, showing me a wedding band on his ring finger. "Remember Betty Joe Duff?"

"No way!" I yelled, "BJ, the one with the giant boobs? She married you? Was she drunk or something?"

"How dare you to talk about my wife's giant boobs" He grinned and wiggled his eye brows, "You should see em' now, she's six months pregnant. We got married last year. She's having a rough time of it and didn't feel very well this morning, so she couldn't come, but she wants to see you. Maybe you could drop by the house before you leave."

"Maybe next time. Unfortunately, I've got to catch a plane in Houston in a few hours," I said with a straight face, lying. Actually I didn't have anything to do, or anywhere to go for three and a half weeks, but I wasn't going to stay there in Matagorda. I didn't want to take the chance of running into Savannah and wanted to get out of town as fast as I could.

Kelly nodded his head, "She'll be sorry she didn't get to see you, but I understand." He shifted his eyes from one side to the other. I could tell he was searching to find the correct words. "I guess you know about Savannah?"

"Know what?" I asked.

He shuffled his feet and looked down. "She and Levi got married a few months after you left."

I frowned and shrugged my shoulders. "Sounds about right," I said gritting my teeth. "They deserve each other."

Kelly lowered his brow and glared at me. "Why would you say something like that? Levi Cruz has always been, and still is, a self centered, spoiled, rich, arrogant prick! He's not right for Savannah and you know it! What the hell happened between you two? I always thought that you two would..."

I held up my hand to stop him. "Kelly, don't say it...that's what I always thought too, but she..." I caught myself, "I don't want to talk about it. It's over between us, that's all you need to know!"

I hugged Kelly goodbye, promising to stay in touch and drove away.

I had planned to head south and spend the rest of my leave on Padre Island and knew I should have just kept driving, but instead, I turned off the highway and headed to my old house. There was nothing there I wanted, but for some reason I had to see it one last time. Maybe to just say goodbye to the train tracks I had played on so many times in my childhood, or to take one last look at that old treehouse.

When I pulled onto my street, I saw two cars backed into the driveway of my mother's house, so I pulled to the curb and killed the engine. I sat there watching them, like vultures picking and cleaning the bones of a dead animal. My aunts and uncles stripped that house, carting out all the furniture, dishes, pictures, pots and pans and clothes. "Good riddance," I said to myself. "Take it all you greedy bastards!"

When they finished and finally left, I cranked the car and slowly drove down the street and pulled in the driveway.

When I opened the front door and looked around, the place was a wreck. My greedy kinfolks had trashed it in their rush to collect their bounty. The floors were littered with old magazines and newspapers. Large rectangular shapes of clean unsoiled floors dotted the room where the oriental rugs had once laid. All the windows were bare, the curtains and drapes had all been yanked down and carried away. The doors of the kitchen cabinets were standing open, revealing the empty shelves inside.

In the two small bedrooms, the floors had piles of apparently unwanted articles of clothing, some still attached to the old bent wire hangers wadded up in the corners. My old bedroom was stripped clean, no bed, no dresser or end table. They had even taken the old rickety typewriter stand I used to have as my desk. The only thing that remained was the three, two by six foot plywood boards nailed to the wall covered with the mural. Although it wasn't what anyone would call a great work of art, it showed Savannah's artistic potential as a 12 year old child. She was always drawing or painting something. She had painted the mural for me as a surprise for my 12th birthday.

∼

Every summer, in June, my birth month, my mother sent me away to camp, to Garner State Park. I always loved going to summer camp when I was younger, I thought it was something my mother did for me, one of her rare nice gifts. And although she never said it, I always thought it was my birthday present. But one year, when I caught influenza and couldn't go, I realized that she wasn't doing it for me, she was doing it for her.

I knew this, because she told me. "I can't believe you did this now, of all times," She ranted every time she came into the room, "I'm supposed to be rid of you and all of your needy crap for three glorious weeks. I should be in Austin with my sisters, but oh no, I'm stuck here with you contaminating the entire house with your nasty germs. I'm so angry at you for doing this to me!"

I spent my birthday in that bed, but my mother never mentioned it one time, but Savannah didn't forget.

She waited until she saw my mother drive away before she scratched on my window and raised it up. With the window opened, she pushed the three large, painted plywood sections through and climbed in after them.

"Don't get out of bed," She said smiling, "I brought you something for your birthday." She lined the three plywood boards up side by side, nailed them to the wall and then stepped back admiring her work.

"What do you think?" She asked, grinning.

I slowly raised up in my bed and stared at the mural, covering almost the entire wall. It was a painting of the railroad tracks that curved through the thick green woods in my back yard, with Fall's golden leaves covering the ground on each side of the tracks disappearing into the woods.

"Savannah, this is amazing!" I shouted, "How long did it take you to paint this?"

She turned her head and smiled at me. "Do you really like it? I've been painting it for almost a year."

She walked to the mural and pointed at the track. "Did you see this?"

I sat up further and squinted my eyes to see what she was pointing to. It was two quarters laying side by side on the track. "That's so cool!" I yelled.

She walked to my bed and sat on the edge. "This way you don't have to get out of bed to see outside! Happy Birthday Travis!"

∼

I stared at the mural for a long time, remembering that day, then I took my fingers and tried to pull one of the panels away from the wall, but it was nailed solid and didn't budge. I thought about calling Kelly to come over and help me take them off the wall, but changed my mind. If I did take it down, what would I do with it?

I looked at it one last time and walked out of the room, hoping that the new tenant would appreciate it's beauty and keep it, instead of yanking it down or painting over it.

The only piece of furniture that remained in the entire house was in my mother's bedroom. It was an old shabby, unpainted night stand that used to sit next to her now, missing bed. There was an 8 by 10 picture frame laying face down on the old night stand. I walked over, picked up the frame, and looked at the photo under the glass. When I saw it, my eyes filled with tears and I dropped to my knees.

I had no idea how or where she could've gotten that picture, but there it was, framed in gold. It was a picture of me, with a wide smile in my uniform, taken the day I had gotten out of boot camp.

I held it in my hand staring at it a long time, fighting back my emotions, but they eventually won the battle. Kneeling in the floor of her bedroom, I began to cry. For the first time, since I'd heard of her death, I allowed myself to grieve. For almost twenty minutes, on my knees in that empty bedroom, I cried, letting go of all that baggage and felt the pain in my heart go away. Finally, after all those years...I forgave my mother.

I heard the train coming, so I ran to the tracks behind the house and placed two quarters on the rail. When it passed, I picked up the two now flattened quarters, the size of sand dollars, put them in my pocket, thinking about the mural in the bedroom and all the thousands of times Savannah and I had done that before in our childhood.

When I turned around to walk back to the house, standing next to the large oak under the treehouse...was Savannah.

"Hi there," She said softly, "I thought I might find you here."

When I saw her I froze. Her sudden vision and hearing the sound of her voice again made my heart skip in my chest.

I opened my mouth to speak, but couldn't think of anything to say to her. So I just stood there staring at the woman who had destroyed all of my hopes and dreams.

I could see tears rolling down her face and her wet turquoise eyes glistening in the sunlight. Her long blonde hair was moving gently with the wind, exactly as it had done the day I had first seen her, all those years ago. She was even more beautiful now than she was then. She was wearing a long, soft flowing sun dress, that exposed her tan shoulders and neck.

"Say something Travis. Please talk to me. We need to talk!"

She reached out to touch me, but when I saw the large diamond wedding ring on her left hand, sparkling in the sunlight, it felt like my heart had shattered inside of my chest.

I turned and ran toward the front of the house. I could hear her tearful cries and shouts behind me as I ran. When I reached my rental car, I hurriedly fumbled for my keys, but she ran up to me before I could open the door and grabbed my arm.

"Why did you leave me?" She screamed, gasping for air, "What about all of our dreams? I thought you loved me! How could you have gotten on that bus and left me like that? Without telling me goodbye, without telling me why? How could you?"

She fell to her knees on the driveway, bawling, the front of her yellow sundress soaked with her tears. "Please Travis, tell me," She whispered, "What did I do?"

Before I could answer, a black car pulled up in front of the house and a Marine Lieutenant stepped out and walked up to me. "Are you Lance Corporal Lee?"

I snapped to attention and saluted. "Yes sir. I'm Lance Corporal Travis Lee."

Another Lieutenant got out of the car, walked up and stood next to him. They both looked down curiously at Savannah crying on her knees on the driveway, but looked back at me and said, "Lance Corporal Lee, we have been sent here from the commanding officer of the Corpus Christi Naval Base to collect you. Your leave has been canceled and you are ordered to come with us immediately."

The Lieutenant took my arm and began pulling me toward the car. "What about my rental car sir?"

He let go of my arm and thought for a moment. "My orders are to bring you back with me, so leave it here, we'll send someone to return it."

"May I have a second sir?" I said motioning toward Savannah, still on her knees crying in the driveway.

"You have two minutes," He said, walking away to his car.

I walked back and stood above Savannah. She lifted her head and looked at me in the eyes. "What did I do?"

For three years I had thought about what I would say to her if I ever got the chance, but at that moment looking down into her beautiful, pleading turquoise eyes...I couldn't say those hurtful words. All I could think to say was, "Savannah, I loved you with every ounce of my being, but I saw you with Levi. You know what you did."

I turned to walk away, but stopped and looked back. "Tell Levi if I ever see him again...I will kill him."

∽

I had asked several times during the trip, but neither of the two Lieutenants would tell me what was going on. When we finally made it to the Naval Base in Corpus Christi, they took me to the base commanding officer. It was there...I learned of the horrible, incomprehensible news.

It was October 21st, 1983 when I had boarded the plane to fly home. Two days later, October 23rd, while I was sitting in the third row of the First Baptist Church listening to the preacher pray for my mother's soul...a suicide bomber detonated a truck bomb in Beirut a few yards from the building serving as the barracks for the 1st Battalion 8th Marines of the 2nd Marine Division...my division.

The bomb killed 220 men and women. It was the deadliest single-day death toll for the United States Marine Corps since the Battle of Iwo Jima in World War II.

With only seven weeks left of their deployment, Gomer, Capone, Orlando, Major General William Britton and the rest of my platoon had all died in the blast. Every one of them.

The first to go, whose bunk was closest to the bomb...was private 1st class...Gary 'Hag' Smith.

4

THE AIRSTREAM

Savannah slowly raised up off her knees in the driveway. Blood was trickling down her right leg from a small cut she had received from the sharp gravel when she collapsed at Travis's feet, but she didn't feel it, her body was numb.

Her face was streaked with mascara from tears that were flowing down her face as she watched the black car drive away with Travis in the back. She waved, but he didn't wave back.

The front door of his rental car was standing open, so she got in and sat in the driver's seat. Gently, she ran her fingers over the wheel, hoping that she might somehow feel the energy left behind where he had touched it.

In Travis's haste to pull his duffel out of the passenger seat, the gold picture frame he had stuffed in the top, had fallen out and was lying face down on the floorboard.

When she saw it, she leaned over, picked it up, and turned it around. When she saw Travis's handsome face smiling back at her, she burst into tears, rocking back and forth in the seat, hugging the photo tightly against her chest.

"Oh Travis, my love," She whispered through her tears, "You are wrong about me!   I didn't betray you, I would never have done that. I love you! I know what I did, and maybe it was wrong,...but I did it for you...for your dreams...for us."

∼

The next morning I boarded a Navy jet that flew me to Washington DC. When we landed, I was taken to a helicopter and flown to Joint Base Andrews to meet the plane carrying the 14 caskets of my platoon, as well as the casket of Major General Britton.

I stood silent, at attention, waiting with the families and what appeared to be most of the top brass in Washington. In the crowd, I noticed a tiny, maybe five foot tall redhead with freckles running across her nose. She was standing a few feet away from me, staring forward with her head held high, constantly wiping the tears from her cheeks. The moment I saw her, I knew who she was, and who she was waiting for.

"Belinda?" I asked softly.

She turned and looked at me. "Yes?" She said, her eyes searching my face for recognition.

"I'm Travis Lee. Hag was my friend."

For a beat she didn't seem to recognize my name, then her eyes widened. "Matador?"

I shook my head and smiled, "Yeah, that's me," I said softly, "I thought it was you. Hag has shown me your picture about a million times. You're all he ever talked about. I hope you know how much he loved you."

"With big tears rolling down her face, she smiled and said, "Yes, I know."

She stared at me for a long time with a strange look in her eyes. Finally she whispered, "Matador...why weren't you...I mean...how are you still alive?"

I dropped my head. "I wasn't there. I was in Texas."

With understanding eyes, she took my hand and gave me a gentle smile. "Gary would be happy you weren't there. He wrote about you often in his letters...and he loved you too."

I tried to respond, but I couldn't speak, so I clenched my jaw, fighting back my emotions, nodded and turned back to watch the plane roll to a stop on the tarmac behind her.

It took over an hour for the six Marine honor guards to unload the flag draped caskets, taking them one step at a time off the plane, with well practiced sharp moves and small steps, with military precision carrying them to the waiting black Cadillac hearses. It was the longest and most difficult 60 minutes of my life.

Over the next ten days, I flew to nine different states and served as part of the honor guard for all 14 of their funerals. After attending Major General Britton's funeral, I was ordered back to Washington. When I arrived, I was taken to the Pentagon to meet with some of the top brass there and a team of public relation officers.

In that meeting, I sat silent listening as they filled me in on how the loss of so many Marines in one day, the most since WWII, had been a public relations disaster for the Marine Corps' image. They had the next six months of my life planned out for me.

First, I was being promoted to a full corporal. Next, since I was one of the only surviving members of the entire division, they wanted to give me a medal, presented to me at a highly publicized ceremony that would be covered by all the major news networks. Then I was scheduled to appear on all of the cable news shows talking about the members of my platoon who had been killed in the blast.

"Talk about their personal lives," they told me, "maybe tell a few stories about their girlfriends back home or their families. We need to divert the public's attention away from Beirut and the bombing. You know what to do."

At one time, I had thought that maybe I would make the Marine Corps my career, but that day, in that meeting, I instantly changed my mind and abruptly put an end to my military career when I stood up and told a Brigadier General to take that medal and promotion that I did not earn or deserve, and shove them up his ass.

∼

Twenty two months and three weeks later, I signed my discharge papers, took off my uniform for the last time, and left the Marine Corps behind.

I had saved most of the money I had earned the last three years, so I bought an old truck, threw my duffel in the back and headed to Texas. I was headed to Lubbock, 553 miles and eight and a half hours away from Matagorda and Savannah.

When I got to Lubbock I found a job bussing tables at a Mexican restaurant, and taking advantage of the US Government's offer to pay for my college, I enrolled in Texas Tech University.

I was a few months away from my 22nd Birthday when I moved into the Freshman dormitory. My new roommate had just turned 18. He was a nice enough guy, but he, like everyone else in that place was a very young 18, and I was a very old 22. I had absolutely nothing in common with anyone there, so after a few months, I moved out.

I found a good deal on a used 25 foot Airstream camp trailer and set it up in the K O A camp grounds 10 miles off campus, just off the loop. It was a quiet, peaceful place to live. The office had a small store, a large bathroom/shower area and even had a heated pool and hot tub.

Living there turned out to be the best decision I could have made. My trailer was parked in between two other trailers occupied by two elderly retired couples, who sort of adopted me. In return for some minor help with repairs on their trailers or cars, they supplied me with homemade cookies and brownies.

I lived in that trailer at the K O A campground for the next three years, taking as many hours as I could year round at Texas Tech and eventually graduated with a Bachelor of science in English.

Over the three years, I had studied hard and had graduated with honors near the top of my class and had also worked my way up from bussing tables to assistant manager at the Mexican restaurant.

During those years, I had gone out with a few of the waitresses at the restaurant, and even had a few dates with several of my college classmates, but never had more than one date with any of them. Although they were all pretty and usually very nice, not one of them sparked anything inside of me or held my interest long.

I will admit at times I was lonely and would have enjoyed talking to someone, but I learned how to survive the solitude by sticking to a daily routine. Each morning, rain or shine, snow on the ground or hot sand, before class I ran three miles, swam 10 laps in the indoor pool, then took a shower. After my classes, I usually worked as many hours as they would let me at the restaurant and then read and studied until bedtime.

I had a small television, but rarely watched it. If I found myself with free time, I usually spent it reading novels. I had learned not to allow my mind idle time, because when I did, all I ever thought about....was Savannah.

∼

I had kept my promise and had stayed in touch with Kelly Smith back home in Matagorda, often writing him long letters. At least once a month he would write me back with news of his life with his wife Betty Joe and their children. Although in my letters I never asked about her, Kelly always added a few paragraphs in his, telling me about Savannah. It had taken Kelly three letters to get up enough courage to call me on the phone and tell me about something he felt was too important to say in a letter.

"Travis, I wanted to tell you about this the day I saw you at your mother's funeral, but I just couldn't get it out. I know I should have, but I just couldn't do that to you then."

"Must be bad news," I said.

I could hear him breathing hard in the receiver. "I'm not sure what you would call it, but it's something you need to know about. I think you need to sit down for this."

I lowered myself into the chair, "OK, I'm sitting…tell me. What is it?"

"Ahh…well…ahh" he stammered, "when you left and Savannah and Levi got married…well…ahh…umm…ahh…"

"Come on Kelly, just say it."

"A few months after that…Savannah got pregnant and she gave birth to a child."

I could feel my heart thumping in my chest, pulsing through my body, and I felt light headed.

"Did you hear me?" Kelly asked.

"Yes," I whispered.

"It was a little boy she named Alexander."

I didn't speak, I couldn't, because my mind was consumed with images of Levi and Savannah having sex making that baby. I tried to push them out of my head, but they wouldn't go away. Clenching my jaw and grinding my teeth, I sat silent holding the phone up to my ear for a long time.

"Travis, I'm so sorry to have to tell you all this, but you needed to know. Are you alright? Say something."

I took a deep breath. "Yeah, I'm OK. I'm just trying to process it. Don't worry about it, I appreciate you telling me, and you're right I needed to know. I bet he's a beautiful baby."

"Yes, he's a beautiful little boy. He has Levi's dark skin and Savannah's turquoise eyes and blonde hair."

I started to respond, but I couldn't think of anything to say, so I just sat there.

After a few seconds of awkward silence, Kelly asked, "Did you hear about Levi's father?"

"No, what about him?"

"He passed away three months ago. Levi inherited everything and now he's running all of the dealerships. As you might expect, he's flaunting his money worse than ever. The ass hole is building a huge three story ocean front beach house out on the Matagorda Peninsula."

∽

Levi's father, a Mexican immigrant, had opened the dealership in Bay City when we were all in the ninth grade. His father opened five more dealerships up and down the upper Texas Coast from Corpus Christi to Houston before he was through, and as a result was very wealthy.

While the rest of us rode the school bus the 30 miles from Matagorda to the Bay City High School each day, Levi drove his brand new Mustang convertible, blowing his horn at us as he passed each morning.

Like me, Savanna and Kelly lived in a small two bedroom, flat roofed, ranch style house near the railroad tracks, 10 miles from the ocean. Levi lived in a beautiful three-story house perched on the beach overlooking the Gulf of Mexico.

We were all poor, but Levi was rich, and from the first grade through high school, he never let us forget it. But that was not why I had always disliked him, I wasn't jealous of his money, but I will admit I was a little jealous of his looks. He was Latino, a tall, dark and very handsome Latino, and I didn't like the way he looked at Savannah. Everybody in school knew that Savannah was my girl, but Levi didn't seem to care and constantly flirted with her.

I had always despised Levi for that and had never trusted him. But what bothered me the most, were the times I had caught Savannah smiling and flirting back.

5

OLIVIA

I had applied to three law schools, hoping to get accepted to at least one, so when I received the letter back from the University Of Texas I was shocked but excited.

All those years when Savannah and I would ride our bicycles to the beach at night and lay on the sand talking about my dreams of going to law school...the law school in those dreams was always the University of Texas.

Two weeks later, I hooked my Airstream behind my truck, said my goodbyes and headed out to the University Of Texas in Austin.

I found a nice campground close to the campus, landed a new job at another Mexican restaurant and started my first, very difficult year of law school.

That first year was a bitch...Torts, Contracts, Civil Procedure, Property, Criminal Law, Constitutional Law, Legal Methods, etc....all crammed into my head in the first year.

Between my classes, my impossible reading load, and working part time at the restaurant, I had little time to sleep, but somehow I survived.

The next two years were difficult as well, but nothing like the first one, so I had actually gotten back into a daily exercise routine again.

During my second year, the owners of the Mexican restaurant had offered me the assistant manager's position, but I declined, because I had enough on my plate with law school. Also I needed to make as much money as I could in the least amount of time, so I continued on as a waiter. The hourly rate wasn't much, but on a good night I could pull in two or three hundred in tips, which helped pay the bills.

I was so busy with law school and work, the three years seemed to just fly by and before I knew it, it was over and I was considering offers from several law firms and studying for the bar exam.

I had hoped to get an offer from a firm in Austin, because I had fallen in love with the city and with the friendly people who lived there. Austin is located in the middle of the Texas hill country and is surrounded with beautiful lakes. And although in the entire three years I had only been able to spend a few days swimming and waterskiing on a few of those lakes, it was enough to convince me that Austin was where I wanted to settle.

Unfortunately, the only offers I had received were from large firms in Houston and Dallas. I contacted a few Austin firms inquiring, but none were hiring, so reluctantly I took the best offer I had received from a large firm in Houston.

I had spent all the years of my life living in Texas, except for the three years I had been in the Marines, but had only been in Houston one other time. It was the day I flew in from Beirut on my way to my mother's funeral seven years earlier. All I had actually seen of the city that day was the bumper to bumper traffic on the freeways. It had taken me over two hours to get out of the city limits and to be honest, my first impression of Houston was not good.

When I arrived and checked into my hotel, my first big challenge was locating a nice, safe place to setup my trailer to live. I had a week before I had to report to work, so I began searching.

After three days and driving way too many hours in that impossible traffic, I gave up and decided to rent an apartment, only a few miles away from my new office and move my trailer to a beautiful spot on Lake Travis, a few miles north of Austin. My plan was to drive back to

Austin every other weekend or so and use my trailer as my weekend getaway.

In theory, it was a good plan, but in reality, it didn't work out that well. I had underestimated the number of hours I would be expected to work at my new law firm as a first year associate. And when I added the hours I had to spend studying for my bar exam, well, I didn't see that trailer again for 18 months.

The first two years at that firm, I didn't actually do much lawyering, I spent most of my time researching case studies backing up the other more experienced associates or the partners with their cases.

Finally in my second year, they started assigning me a few small cases, that I did my best to settle out of court as I had been encouraged to do by the firm partners. After a few more years, I had become an expert at talking the clients into taking the settlements whether it was the right thing to do or not.

On several of these cases, I had gone to the partners trying to convince them to let me fight for the client and take the case to court.

"I realize I'm only a third-year associate with no trial experience," I said, "but how am I supposed to get that experience if you won't let me at least try?" I said to Archer Goodman, the senior partner of the firm, "Archer, this settlement offer is a joke. The man is going to be in a wheelchair the rest of his life! I can win this, I know I can."

Archer smiled. "Travis, you remind me of myself when I was about your age and I appreciate your passion for your client, I really do, but a million dollar offer is no joke. That's a guaranteed $300,000 in revenue for the firm and $700,000 to your client. If you go to trial and lose, then this firm is out $100,000 or more in expenses, and your client gets nothing, not a penny. It's a huge risk for all of us. What does your client say about it?"

I shrugged my shoulders. "So the possibility of me going to trial and winning 20 or 30 million isn't part of your thought process?"

Archer frowned. "You didn't answer my question. What does your client think about the offer?"

Fighting back my frustration, trying to stay calm, I leaned back in my chair and said, "I just got the call with the offer, he doesn't know."

"He doesn't know!" He yelled. "Travis, when I hired you I saw a lot of promise. You were smart as a whip, top of your class at UT, head of the law review, a decorated Marine, on and on. Your resume was very impressive and that's why I put you in that office. None of the other first year associates got a window, but you did. I put you there, because I had a feeling you were going to be our new rainmaker and up to now, you haven't disappointed me."

Losing control of my temper, I jumped up and glared over the desk. "Disappointed? Coming to you wanting to fight for my client is a disappointment? This is the sixth time I've come to you trying to do what I thought a good lawyer was supposed to do, and every time you shoot me down. I thought that promise you saw in me was because you saw the potential of a great lawyer, not just a rainmaker. For three years I have outperformed every associate in this firm by five times. I have been your rainmaker and I'm sick of it. This case should go to trial and you know it!"

Archer stood up and looked me in the eyes. "Travis, I've been doing this for 35 years against your three. It's called a bird in the hand and if you weren't so naïve you'd understand. If you take this to trial and win 20, 30, even 50 million it doesn't matter, because it will be years before anyone sees any money. They will appeal and appeal again. In the mean time this firm will be out hundreds of thousands of dollars and your client will still be in that wheelchair...with nothing, not a penny."

He sat back down behind his desk. "You will get the trial experience you want so badly I promise, but first you start as second chair on a few trials and then someday I will let you move over to the first chair...but not now, not on this case. Don't be naïve Travis, call your client and convince him to take the settlement. That's the way we do things around here, and if you want to continue working here...make that call."

I wanted to say, "What you call 'naïve' is what I call, 'doing the right thing,' but I didn't. Instead, I walked back to my office and made the call. I wanted to pack up my office and walk out, but burning that bridge would have followed me through my entire career. And, I was just an associate attorney with no actual trial experience, so I wouldn't have much to offer another firm. However, it was very apparent to me that they weren't actually interested in helping their clients, all they cared about were the fees. That wasn't why I had worked so hard all those years to become a lawyer and was not what I had dreamed about my entire life, but I was trapped and couldn't leave and stayed there for two more years. The only good thing to come of my angry meeting was, showing Archer Goodman my building frustrations apparently sped up his plans for me. The following month I was assigned second chair on my first court trial. Six months and three trials later, I was allowed to sit in the first chair and lead my first real trial...that I won easily.

Although they offered me a Jr. Partnership to keep me, two years later, I began putting out some feelers, looking for a new firm.

On a whim, I made a few calls to several small firms in Austin. But his time when I called I wasn't an idealistic, fresh out of law school kid who hadn't even passed his bar exam on the phone, but rather a licensed lawyer with five years experience under my belt working with the largest law firm in Houston. This time, each firm eagerly took my calls and I garnered the attention of three firms there and all three seemed very interested.

My first interviews were with the two largest law firms in Austin, and they both made me good offers, but I was leery of joining another large firm, with a huge overhead, layers of ridiculous interoffice politics, and a very tall ladder to climb to make full partner. What I really wanted was to join a small boutique firm with only a few lawyers to deal with.

My last interview was with Bachman, Turner, Bachman and Associates.

"Mr. Lee," James Bachman, the founder and senior partner began, "It's a pleasure to meet you, and I must say I'm very impressed with your resume. I just hung up talking to Archer Goodman, with Goodman and Associates in Houston, and he tells me that he believes you would make a perfect fit for my firm."

I smiled. "That's good to hear, but I'm a little surprised that Archer is saying good things about me."

James laughed. "Well, he did say that you are bit headstrong, and a little hardheaded."

I smiled and nodded. "If caring more about my client than the fee we will earn is headstrong and hardheaded, then he is correct. Mr. Bachman, If you're only interested in a 'yes' man, someone who can settle cases to bring in fees and create billable hours we can stop this interview now. That's why I'm leaving Archer's firm."

He grinned. "Call me James. May I call you Travis?"

"Of course."

"Travis, I'm looking for a great lawyer, period. That's my only prerequisite. I started this firm in 1978, because I had become dissatisfied working for large firms as well. A few years later, Henry Turner, one of my oldest friends joined the firm and in 1989, my daughter, Olivia joined after she graduated from Yale. If you have done any research on us you should know that we rarely settle a case. We are trial lawyers and damn good at it. To be honest with you, I wasn't considering bringing on a new associate at this time, but when you called and I did some checking up on you, I realized that you are exactly what we need around here."

He picked up an envelope from his desk and handed it to me. "This is my offer. It's a good one, and non negotiable. If you're interested, we'd love to have you. If not, it was a pleasure to meet you."

He stood and held out his hand to shake mine. "I'm due in court. Look over the offer and let me know."

I followed James out of his office, walked to my car and opened the envelope. It didn't matter to me what the offer was, I had already made up my mind. I *had* done my research and knew his firm's reputation of fighting hard for the little guy. They rarely settled a case out of court and had landed some of the largest jury awards in the US, earning their clients and their firm hundreds of millions in the process. Although they were one of the smallest firms in Austin, they were one of the richest. And having James Bachman as my mentor was worth more than any offer he could make. But when I read the offer, all I could think to say was, "Wow!"

∼

My new office was located in a large historic house that had been remodeled to accommodate the firm, only a few blocks away from the court house. The job came with a beautiful office with a large Mahogany desk, surrounded with walls of oak paneling and bookshelves filled with law books. It also came with a legal secretary and a paralegal, and the three of us took up all of the third floor space.

James' wife, Amelia, was Italian and had passed on her dark skin, brown eyes and black hair to her daughter, and my new partner, Olivia. She was slim and very tall. She had graduated from Yale one year before I had graduated from the UT Law School. She was 36, I was 35, she was divorced, I was single. I was 6 foot two and she stood almost six foot in heels. Almost every day, when people would see us together, someone would say, "You two make such a beautiful couple."

More than once, those words had come from her mother and father. "You two would make beautiful babies," Amelia, Olivia's mother said the first time I met her.

James smiled wide, obviously agreeing. "They would be beautiful and smart too."

"Mom! Dad! Please," Olivia shouted, "We haven't even gone out on our first date!"

I assumed that was their way of letting me know that interoffice fraternization was not frowned on in their firm, and any interest I may develop for their daughter was just fine with them.

The first time it happened, I smiled and didn't respond, but that didn't stop them from dropping their hints.

"Travis, I have two tickets to the symphony I'm not going to use," James said one morning after a staff meeting, "and Olivia loves the symphony. It's about time you two went on an official date."

When he said it, Olivia glanced at me, smiled, and blushed.

Fortunately, I was booked to go out of town that day to take a deposition in Denver, so I couldn't go, but that didn't stop them from their matchmaking attempts.

For several months, I did my best to ignore their blatant hints and the awkward situation it put me in. When it happened, I would smile and quickly escape up the three flights of stairs to my office.

~

I had tried to move my trailer from Lake Travis back to the camping area near downtown Austin, but the new park owners told me that my trailer was too old. They didn't allow anything older than 10 years in the park. The old Airstream 'was' getting a little shabby, so I traded her in on a new 40 footer, with three pull-outs, an electric awning, a fireplace and a 50 inch flatscreen TV.

When I got it all set up with all the walls pulled out, it was slightly bigger than the apartment I had lived in for five years in Houston.

On my second weekend in my new trailer, the office had surprised me with a house warming party. They covered my kitchen cabinets with food and booze and it turned out to be quite a night. Everyone, including Olivia, showed up bearing gifts at my new home.

It was midnight before they all finally left. They had trashed the place, so I started picking up the paper plates and cups. I filled the plastic garbage bag, walked to the dumpster and threw it away. When I got back to my trailer, I saw Olivia's car in my driveway and she was sitting on my front steps.

I smiled, "Hey, I thought you left."

She smiled back, "I did, but when I got a few miles away, I realized that I wasn't in any condition to get on the freeway. I guess I had more to drink than I thought. Would you mind making me some coffee? I think I need to sober up a little before I drive again."

"Of course," I said with a chuckle, "Come on in and we can try out my new coffee maker."

Inside, she kicked off her shoes and laid down on the couch. It took me a few moments to figure out my new coffee machine, but eventually I hit the button and it started making noises. When it finished, I poured two cups and walked to the couch, but Olivia was sound asleep when I got there.

I nudged her arm with my knee. "Hey, wake up. The coffee's ready." She didn't move.

I sat the cups down on the table and gently touched her face. "Wake up sleeping beauty." I whispered, brushing her hair away from her eyes with my hand. I shook her gently and whispered again, "Wake up, your coffee is getting cold." Without opening her eyes, she rolled onto her side and cuddled my hand against her chest in her arms.

I knew then that she was not going to wake up anytime soon. She was lying half on, half off of the love seat which was too short for her body. Her dress had ridden up, exposing her beautiful long, tanned legs, her small bare feet and her perfectly manicured toes, that were dangling awkwardly off the couch.

Not knowing exactly what to do, I picked her up in my arms, walked her to the bedroom and laid her gently on the mattress. I placed her head on a pillow, worked the covers out from under her, and covered her up with a blanket.

The love seat actually pulled out to make a bed, so I opened it up, grabbed a spare blanket and pillow and tried my best to fall asleep. After an hour of tossing and turning, I gave up on sleep and sat up dangling my legs over the side of the bed. My mind had been whirling and no matter how hard I tried to think of something else to stop it from spinning, nothing worked.

All I could think of was how amazing it had felt holding Olivia in my arms and how incredibly sexy the sight of her tanned long legs looked.

I tried to think of how long it had been since I'd held a woman in my arms. I had dated a few women when I was at Texas Tech, I even had sex with a few, but it was always quick with no hugging or cuddling. I didn't date at all the entire three years I was in law school, there was just no time for that, and had only gone out with a few women in Houston, but again it was just unemotional sex. After racking my brain I realized that the last time I had actually felt a woman in my arms that I had cared about, had been the last time I had made love to Savannah. The memory of holding her tightly afterward and kissing her flashed in my mind and instantly, the familiar searing pain in my heart came with it. It was a pain I thought I had finally buried.

I cussed and shook my head, trying to force Savannah's memory out of my mind and the horrible pain out of my chest.

"So...what's her name?"

I looked up to see Olivia standing in the doorway. Apparently, she had woken up and taken off her dress, because in the dark it looked like all she had on was her bra and panties.

I stared at her image standing there in the dark for a long time before I spoke. "Savannah," I whispered, "Her name is Savannah."

She slowly walked up and sat down next to me on the pull out bed. "You said 'is' Savannah, not 'was'. Is she still in your life?"

I nodded, "Not for a long time...years. She's married and has a son."

Olivia took my hand, "But she's still in your heart, right?"

I shrugged and dropped my head. "I don't know how to get her out. I keep trying, but..."

She squeezed my hand. "I know it may not feel like it now, but you're lucky and I envy you."

"Lucky?" I yelled, "she broke my heart, betrayed me, and screwed my life for years. Why would you envy that?"

Her eyes filled with tears. "At least you know what true love feels like. I've never felt that before, from anyone."

"What about your ex-husband?" I asked.

She wiped her eyes. "He loved my body and my money, not me."

I scanned her body and grinned. "I'm not sure about the money part, but the part about loving your body...I can relate."

She laughed. "It's good to hear you say that. I was beginning to think you were gay. How hard does a girl have to try with you?"

I smirked. "No, I'm not gay...I'm just damaged...broken. And I'm not sure I'm ever gonna heal. That's why I've been so stand offish. I'm not sure what, if anything, I would have to offer. It wouldn't be fair to you."

She leaned over and kissed me. "Travis, you're a good man...but I'm a big girl...a grown woman."

She laid back on the bed, pulling me with her, "Let me worry about what is fair to me. You may not ever love me the way you love her, but I'm OK with that, Just give me a chance. Let me try to repair some of the damage Savannah has done to you. I promise, I will never hurt you."

∽

Over the next three years of my life, my law practice grew substantially, my relationship with Olivia continued to develop and for the first time in years I was relatively happy. Unfortunately, my feelings along with the pain I felt for Savannah, had not waned. I often caught myself, when I was alone, thinking about her.

The long monthly letters back and forth between Kelly and me, had been long replaced by frequent e-mails. It wasn't unusual to hear from him several times a week.

I had seen him several times through the years when he would bring his family to San Antonio or Austin for a visit. He and BJ had three kids, two boys and one girl, ranging from 13 down to 5. He had done very well with his insurance agency and had finally built his dream house on the beach at Matagorda Peninsula, only a few houses down from Levi and Savannah's.

Even though it was, totally unsolicited by me, he kept me up on Savannah and her life through the years.

Even with all of their wealth, Levi and Savannah had not lived a happy marriage. According to Kelly, they constantly bickered in public and had actually caused many loud and violent scenes in several of the restaurants in town.

That violence had escalated even further a few times. Each time it happened, Kelly would wake me up, calling me on the phone to fill me in on the details.

The first time, she just had bruises around her neck...the second, Levi had apparently broken her arm, the third time, it was her leg.

At each occurrence, the neighbors had called the police and while Savannah was taken away in an ambulance, Levi was being arrested for domestic abuse and taken to jail.

"Travis, It's a bad situation, "Kelly said over the phone, "BJ and I have tried to talk some sense into her. We keep telling her that she needs to leave him, to run away and file for a divorce, but she always ignores us, bails him out, drops the charges and takes him back. This time, he broke her damn leg! But I'd bet my new house that as soon as she's out of the hospital, she's going to drop the charges again."

I shrugged my shoulders on the other end of the phone. "I wouldn't take that bet, because I think you're right. But there's not much anyone can do. I've seen it many times in my practice. In fact, my firm won't take a Domestic violence case any longer, because the wife always ends up dropping the charges and moving back into the house. I just hope Levi doesn't kill her one day, because that's usually how these things end."

"I don't suppose you'd be willing to talk to her," Kelly asked, "Travis, she might listen to you."

"I...I don't know if I could do that...or what good it would do," I said. "We haven't talked in years."

There was a long pause on the phone, but finally Kelly broke the silence. "Travis, I haven't told you everything in my letters. The whole truth is, Savannah's never been the same since you left. She stopped painting. I don't think she's sketched anything in years and you know that's not like her. To tell you the truth, I haven't seen her smile in years. She is...I really can't explain it, but she's just...just sad all the time. I guess depressed would be the correct word. I've never told you this before, but she's been in and out of the psychiatric ward in a hospital in Corpus Christi several times over the years. They've kept that a secret, because you know how it is in a small town . I only know this, because I sold them their medical insurance and have seen the claims."

Kelly paused and took a breath, "This is none of my business, because I don't know what happened between you two, but I believe her mental health problems and what ever it was that made you leave so suddenly...are connected."

I didn't respond.

"Travis, whatever happened that day...it's been years and years, you just need to forgive her. Call her, it might save her life."

The following day, with her right leg in a full cast...before I had a chance to try to call her...Savannah dropped the Domestic Violence charges against Levi and took him back.

6

ALEXANDER

I landed a huge case that required me to spend the next few months flying from one end of the country to the other taking depositions. It ended up being a long and difficult trial, but the day before my closing, the other side, realizing they were probably going to lose, offered a substantial cash settlement that my client accepted. When our firm won a multi million dollar case like that, there was always an 'after hours' celebration in our office, with catered food and champagne.

The case had taken almost a year of every second of my time and had taken its toll on my mind and body. I was completely spent and exhausted when I finally made it back to the office that night. When I opened the door, the party was in full swing and when they saw me, the room broke into applause and cheers.

I smiled and took a glass of champagne, but it was the last thing I wanted. My body was aching and my head was pounding with a throbbing pain in my temples from the headache I'd had most of the day.

I was in no mood for a party, so after a few congratulatory slaps on the back and making my way around the room, I slipped up the stairs to the peace and quiet of my office and laid down on my couch.

I hadn't looked around the room when I walked in, so I didn't see him sitting in my chair by my desk.

"Mr. Lee?" I heard a young male voice say softly.

I raised my head and tried to focus my eyes in the direction of the voice. The only light in the room was from the small bankers lamp glowing softly on my desk, so I couldn't actually see his face.

"Who's there?" I asked, raising up on the couch.

"You don't know me, we have never met," he said. "I'm Alexander Cruz, Savannah Cruz was my mother."

I stood and walked over to him, holding out my hand. He stood and shook it. "It's nice to meet you Alexander. I'm very fond of your mother."

I sat down behind my desk and studied the young man's face. I could see Levi's deep cleft in his sharp chiseled chin. I could also see Savannah's long thick golden hair covering his forehead, streaming to his shoulders. I could also see concern in his turquoise eyes that Savannah had passed to him.

"You said, 'Savannah Cruz *WAS* my mother," I said softly, "Has something happened to her?"

His eyes filled with tears, "Yes sir," he said in a whisper.

"Oh my God. Is she dead? What happened?"

Alexander dropped his head and shrugged. "I don't know, but I think so."

I frowned, wrinkling my forehead. "What do you mean, you don't know. Is she dead or alive? It's a simple question."

He raised his head and looked me in the eyes. "Everybody thinks she's dead, but…nobody really knows for sure."

I shook my head. "Alexander, I'm trying my best to understand what you're saying, but you've lost me. First, who is everybody…and second, how could they not know for sure?"

"The police, they are convinced she's dead, but nobody knows for sure because she's missing."

I jumped to my feet. "Savannah is missing?" I yelled, "For how long?"

"Five days. Dad came home from work last Friday night and she wasn't there. We've searched everywhere, but we can't find her," he dropped his head again and stared at the ground, "That's one of the reasons why I hitchhiked here. I thought...maybe..."

Stunned, I plopped back down in my chair. "Alexander, I haven't seen your mother in years. Why would you think she would be here?"

Suddenly, my office door swung open and Olivia staggered in, holding two flutes of champagne in her hands. "What are you doing up here? You're missing your party!"

When she saw Alexander sitting in the chair in front of my desk, she tilted her head and smiled at him. "I'm sorry, I didn't realize you were with a client."

I looked up at her and nodded. "He's not a client. This is Alexander Cruz, Savannah's son."

Olivia's lips parted and I could see the surprised shock in her eyes. She had just enough champagne in her to disconnect her normal filter. "Your Savannah?" She yelled, looking at me, "Holy shit!"

I glared at her. "Why don't you go back to the party," I said firmly, "Alexander and I have a lot to talk about. I'll be down in a little while."

Unfortunately, she didn't take the hint. Instead, she put the champagne flutes down on my desk and sat down in the chair next to Alexander.

"Hello, I'm Olivia, Travis's partner," she said holding her hand to him.

Shyly, he took her hand and shook it, but didn't speak.

"How did you get up here?"

He shrugged and said, "The stairs."

She laughed. "I mean, how did you get past the receptionist?"

I had wondered the same thing. "Olivia." I said sternly, "That really doesn't matter, he's here because his mother is missing."

Her eyes widened. "Oh my God! Savannah is missing? What happened?"

Alexander glanced at me and then looked at Olivia. "You knew my mother?"

Olivia had the ability to somehow instantly sober to the situation, no matter how much she had had to drink. I had experienced it a few times before, but it still amazed me.

She reached over and took his hand. "No, I've never actually met your mother, but I've heard so many stories about her from Travis. So many, it seems like I knew her well and I'm very concerned about her. So, if you don't mind, from the beginning, tell me what has happened and why you are here."

Alexander gave her a small smile and began filling her in with everything he had told me.

While he was talking, she had walked to my sitting area and made some coffee. "Would you like some?" She asked him, "or would you rather have a coke or water?"

"I'll take a coke. I'm only 16. Mom says I'm too young for coffee." His eyes filled with tears again, "I'm sorry, it's just that..."

"It's Ok, "she said gently, "but you need to remember that she's just missing. She may be alive. Don't ever lose hope."

I leaned over my desk and said, "Alexander, you've now said it twice. Coming here searching for your mother was *ONE* of the reasons you hitch-hiked here...what was the other reason?"

He sat up erect in his chair. "Mr. Lee, I've heard about you for my entire life. My mother has talked about you as long as I can remember. She even made a scrap book with all kinds of pictures and newspaper clippings about you. She looked at that book almost every day of her life. I know that you were a great football player in high school, and a hero in the Marines. You were on the Deans list every year you were at Texas Tech University and graduated Summa Cum Laude. You were head of the Law Review and one of the Chancellors, 'Keeper of the Peregrines' which meant you graduated the 4th highest grade point average in your Law School class at UT. You were one of the top lawyers in the largest law firm in Houston and as of three months ago, you are a full partner here at this firm."

Olivia stared over the desk at me and raised her eyebrows. "Keeper of the Peregrines?"

I smiled. "I came in fourth, so it's not really that impressive."

"Yes it is sir," Alexander said, "It's one of the highest honors you can receive."

I smiled at him. "Thank you Alexander. I worked very hard for that."

I was a bit stunned to find out that Savannah had been keeping up with me and my career all these years. I wasn't exactly sure what to say next. "So...let me guess. Your mother found all this out about me from Kelly Smith?"

He nodded. "I'm not sure, but Uncle Kelly, Aunt BJ and mom have always been close friends."

"Your Uncle Kelly has always had a big mouth," I said with a chuckle, "but I need to clear something up. I 'was' in the Marines, but I was no hero. I was honored, however, to know 14 men that were."

Olivia stood and walked to the coffee pot. "You still haven't told us your second reason. Why you hitchhiked all this way here."

With her cup refilled, she walked back and sat down facing him. "It must be an important reason," She said.

Alexander took a deep breath and looked at me. "It's for my Dad. I came here for my dad. They have arrested him for murdering my mom. He didn't do it Mr. Lee, I know he didn't do it, he would never do something like that!"

He covered his face with his hands and cried. "He's in real trouble this time and he needs your help."

I stood up and stared down at him. "Are you saying...you want 'me' to represent him?"

He looked up at me with pleading eyes. "Yes sir. You know him. You grew up with him and you have to know that he couldn't have done something like this. He loves my mother!"

Olivia had heard all the stories and knew about Levi's multiple arrests for domestic violence. She locked eyes with me and held up her hand, signaling me not to respond.

"Alexander, I don't think you realize what you're asking of Travis. First of all, Travis is not a criminal defense lawyer, that is not his specialty. And second, because of his closeness to your mother...it would be a serious conflict of interest. Can't you see that?"

He jumped to his feet. "No!" He yelled, "I don't see that!"

He walked around my desk and stood close, looking me in the

eyes. "Mr. Lee, I may only be 16 years old, but I am not stupid or naïve. I know that you and my mother were boyfriend and girlfriend from little kids and all through high school. And I know something happened to end that...that's when you left to join the Marines. But I also know that my mother has never stopped loving you. Yes, I know she loves dad too, but it wasn't the same thing.

You were all she ever talked about and the reason mom and dad fought all the time. He knows it too. It was very confusing to me for a long time, but now that I'm older I understand. My mother loves my father, but she's, *'In Love'*, with you. She's always been in love with you, and I'm sure she will be...until the day she dies."

He wiped his eyes. "I don't know what it was that broke you two up, and I don't care. But I think you need to know that you crushed her heart that day and she's still hurting after all these years because of it. Mr. Lee, I don't know if my mother is alive or dead, but I do know that my father had nothing to do with any part of it. I know that for a fact. I tried to tell the police, but they didn't believe me because I'm his son. Mr. Lee he's in jail...right now. He's been arrested for something he didn't do. I know you're not a criminal lawyer, but you are a brilliant lawyer and dad needs your help to prove he's innocent. Please, Mr. Lee."

I put my hand on his shoulder. "Alexander, I would like to help you, but I've been keeping up with your mother too," I dropped my hand and looked him in the eyes, "I know about your father's domestic violence arrests. I know about the bruises, about her broken arm and her broken leg. You're a very intelligent boy, so how can you just ignore what he's done to your mother in the past? The police arrested him because...well...this is the usual way domestic violence ends. Somebody dies. I know you love your father, but how can you be so sure he's innocent after all he's done to her?"

He raised his eyes up to mine, they were full of tears. "It's because of that...of what everyone thinks he's done to mom...that's how I know for sure he's innocent." He walked back, sat in the chair and started crying.

Confused, I glanced at Olivia. She shrugged her shoulders, equally confused. I sat down in my chair and stared across the desk at him. "Alexander, you've lost me. What are you trying to say?"

Olivia handed him a Kleenex and took his hand. "Are you saying that your father wasn't the one who hurt your mother?"

He shook his head. "Ok..If it wasn't your father, then who was it?" She asked gently. "Was it you?"

Again he shook his head, but didn't answer.

"Then who was it? I asked. Alexander, if you want my help, you have to tell me the truth. Who hurt your mother?"

He looked down at the floor. "I promised dad I would never tell."

"Alexander listen to me. If you know who hurt her, you have to tell. If it wasn't your father, the police need to know. They believe he is a wife beater and trust me, they are not treating him well in that jail. For God's sake son, your mother is missing and the police believe your father killed her. You came all this way asking me for my help. If you really want that, you have to tell me everything. It may be the only way I can save your father."

Alexander raised his head and wiped his eyes. "You're gonna help him?"

I glanced over at Olivia and she nodded. "Yes," She said, "We will help him, but only if you tell us the truth," She turned in her chair, facing him, "Alexander, look at me."

He raised his head up and stared into her eyes. "Who was it...who hurt Savannah?"

He took a deep breath and let it out slowly. "No one," Tears were rolling down his cheeks, soaking his shirt, "She did it to herself, because...because she wanted to die."

Olivia jerked her head up and stared at me with shocked eyes.

"Suicide?" I shouted, "Are you saying that her injuries were...were all caused from her attempts to kill herself?"

He didn't speak, but nodded his head yes.

"How do you know this for sure?" Olivia asked, "Were you there?"

He stood up and began pacing the room. "When I was seven years old, I got real sick at school one day and the nurse took me home. When I opened the door, the house was dark, all the drapes were closed and the lights were off. That was real strange, because mom always opened all the drapes, especially in the living room, so I knew something was wrong. I started yelling her name, but she didn't answer. This was in our old house, before we moved to the beach. It was a lot smaller and I knew she would have heard me yelling."

He stopped pacing and sat back down in the chair. "I started running through the house searching for her, but couldn't find her. Then I heard a noise in the bathroom. When I opened the door, she was hanging from a scarf she had tied around the shower head." His tears were back, soaking his face. He tried to wiped them away with the back of his hand, "I pulled her down and laid her on the floor, but she wasn't moving. I didn't know what to do, so I ran to the phone and called dad. When I ran back to the bathroom, she was curled into a ball, crying."

"That's when your father took her to the psychiatric hospital in Corpus Christi the first time?" I said.

He looked up at me. "How did you know about that?"

I gave him a gentle smile. "I told you I've been keeping up with her. I know she's been to that hospital three or four times over the years. Don't worry, I've never told anyone about that, not even Olivia."

"How long was she there?" Olivia asked.

"Only a few weeks the first time. When she got home she seemed great. She was always smiling and singing around the house. Dad and I thought she was going to be okay after that. We moved into the beach house a few years later, but I don't think dad could really afford it, because I heard them talking about money things a lot after that. He was trying to get her to go shopping with her friends. He was trying to get her to leave the house and to go have fun with her friends, but she would just say things like, 'You know we can't afford that.'"

"Really?" I said shocked, "I thought Levi was wealthy. I heard that he inherited all of your grandfather's dealerships?"

"Yes he did, but he also inherited all of the debt that went with them. He's had to close five of the seven over the years. Dad told me once that Grandpa was a great car salesman, but a terrible business man. When grandpa died and dad took them over, they were all losing money."

"Then why did he buy that beach house?" I asked, "You guys moved in right after your grandfather died, right?"

"I was too young to understand anything about financial problems back then, but now I believe he did it trying to cheer mom up. She had stopped singing and smiling, and she never left the house. All she ever did was stare at the pages of that scrapbook she had made about you."

"What did Levi do when he saw her looking at the book?" Olivia asked, "Did it make him angry?"

Alexander nodded. "Yeah, they fought about it a lot. They always tried to hide it from me, but I used to listen outside their bedroom door. I was too young to really understand what they were fighting about, so I would just sit there in the floor behind their door, listening to them screaming at each other and cry.

"But when I was 10 or 11 I figured it out. One night dad said, 'No matter what I do, no matter how hard I try to please you, even though you know he will never forgive you for what we did...you still love him and you'll never love me the way you love him.'"

When he said those words he lifted his head and looked me in the eyes. "Mr. Lee, why did you leave my mother? What did they do?"

7
THE AWFUL TRUTH

I wasn't sure how to answer his question. It was obvious he didn't know, and I couldn't tell him. Although he was very mature for 16, he was too young to hear the truth.

"Alexander, your mother and I were very young and very much in love. I wasn't much older than you are now, but I wasn't as mature as you are. What she did wasn't really that important," I lied, trying not to show any emotion in my face, "Let's just say that I was too young to handle it and I didn't have the courage to confront her, so instead, like a coward...I just left. If I had known the damage I would do to Savannah..."

I paused, trying to think of the words that might explain my actions without telling him the truth. but there weren't any. "Alexander, all I can tell you now is that I'm sorry for what I've done to your mother...and you. I hope that someday you'll forgive me for it."

I glanced at my watch, it was almost 9 pm. "Have you eaten today?"

He shook his head shyly. "No sir."

I grinned at him. "I haven't either, and I'm starving. You like Mexican food?"

He smiled for the first time that night, "You bet I do!"

Olivia and I slowly picked at our plates while we watched in amazement at how much food Alexander could eat. He went through three full baskets of chips, four enchiladas, three tacos and a chimichanga.

When he finally put down his fork, I asked, "Would you like some desert?"

"Sure!" He said, "What do they have?"

After dinner, I drove to the downtown Marriott and checked him in. We could tell he was completely exhausted, nodding off a few times in my back seat on the way to the hotel, so we walked him to his room, told him to stop worrying, get some sleep and we would meet him for breakfast in the morning.

∼

After we left Alexander's hotel room, Olivia and I walked to the lobby bar, found a quiet table, ordered two double Chevas Regal's and sat quietly staring at each other for almost 15 minutes before either one of us said a word.

"You think she finally did it?" Olivia asked setting her glass down on the table. "Maybe somewhere away from the house, so no one could stop her?"

I emptied my glass and waved at the waiter for another round. "That's what I'm thinking."

When the waiter brought the new round, I picked mine up and took a small sip, then sighed. "I just hope she didn't do it somewhere deep in the woods. If she did, we may never find her."

Olivia sipped her scotch slowly, staring at the Austin skyline through the window. "Do you really think you can represent Levi fairly...after what he did?"

I nodded, "I don't know, but for Alexander's sake, I think I have to at least talk to him and try. I don't have to forgive him, or even like him, but I think I have to represent him. If you were listening to Alexander carefully, I assume you caught the fact that apparently, Levi is broke. He doesn't have the money to hire a defense lawyer. So...I guess that leaves me."

Olivia smiled at me across the table. "No offense counselor, but I don't think that would do Levi much good. Like I told Alexander, you are not a criminal defense lawyer...but I am."

I shook my head. "No way! I couldn't ask you to do that. I'm sorry I've already gotten you this involved. It has to be weird to you, hearing all this about Savannah and...you know."

She reached across the table and took my hand. "Travis, I got into this relationship with my eyes wide open. I've known about your feelings for Savannah from the first night I seduced you."

I raised my head and grinned. "Seduced me? I thought I seduced you?"

She rolled her eyes. "Of course you did," she smirked, "I was there remember?"

She took another sip of her drink and looked at me. "This last year has been great. It couldn't have been better and I guess you know that I care about you...a lot, maybe even love you a little."

I squeezed her hand and smiled. "I...I ahh..."

"Don't worry, I'm not expecting you to say the L word. Maybe someday, but I know you can't do that right now. I know you care about me too, but I also know it's not with all your heart. You can't do that, because Savannah still holds most of it ."

I let go of her hand and looked down. "I'm sorry."

"Travis there's nothing to be sorry about. I knew what I was getting into. I will admit that somewhere in the back of my mind, I had hoped that maybe, just maybe in the past year, I had been able to help you put some of those feelings you have for Savannah away, but your eyes are telling me that I'm wrong."

I shrugged. "I don't know what you want me to say."

"You don't have to say anything. I will say it for both of us. I have to take Levi's case. I'm not doing it for 'YOU'...I'm doing it, for me. But I want you to know...no matter what happens from here on between us....I think you are a wonderful, loving, amazing man and I hope and pray that we have a future, but if we don't... I will never regret one single moment I've spent with you."

I leaned over the table and kissed her gently on the lips. "I think you are amazing too."

I leaned back and took another long drink of my scotch. "So, where do we go from here?"

She thought for a few moments. "I don't think we need to put Alexander through anymore. He's in a fragile state and I certainly don't want to cause him any more damage. I think the next move on our agenda is to drive to the Matagorda County Jail and interview our new client. After that...we have to try to find Savannah. Because...until we find her, one way or the other, alive or dead...we have no case...and no one, including you, me, or Levi has a future until we do."

∼

The Matagorda county jail was located in Bay City, 21 miles North of Matagorda Bay. It was a gloomy, one story brick structure with few exterior windows. We were taken to a small, dismal room with a long stainless steel table in the center with two chairs on one side and one on the other. There were no windows and the only sound inside was the air conditioner whistling through the vents above our heads.

We heard the clanking of his shackles behind the large steel door before the guards opened it. The shock and surprise in his eyes, when he saw me sitting behind the interview table was obvious.

I hadn't seen Levi in years and had wondered how he would look. After they unlocked his shackles and seated him in the chair across from me, I realized that the years had been good to him. There were no deep lines around his eyes or across his forehead like mine. We were exactly the same age, but other than the sprinkles of gray hair peeking through the black on his temples, he didn't look a day older.

He squinted his eyes, trying to focus on my face, wrinkling his forehead, "Travis? Is that you? What are you doing here?"

I nodded my head. "Yes, its me. Alexander came to see me in Austin yesterday and told me you needed my help."

His eyes lit up and beamed with pride. "Alexander did that? Austin? How did he get there?"

"He hitch-hiked." I said.

He grinned and shook his head. "He's a good boy, but I wish he hadn't done that, and I'm sorry you've come all this way. I can't afford to hire a lawyer like you. I don't have that kind of money anymore."

I was having trouble listening. The vision of him with his arms around Savannah that day, was flashing like a strobe light in my head. I wanted to reach across the table, grab a hand full of his black hair and smash his handsome face down hard on the stainless steel.

"There will be no charge for our representation Mr. Cruz," Olivia said, "Our firm is taking your case Pro bono...for Alexander and for Savannah."

"Really?" He said stunned, "Travis, I thought you hated me. Why would you do this?"

I stood up behind the table. "I'll never forgive you for what you did, but I've never hated you. All I want to know is...when did it start? How long had it been going on behind my back?"

Levi lifted his head. "What are you talking about? How long had what been going on?"

I sat down hard in my chair and glared at him. "How long had you been fooling around with Savannah?"

His eyes flew open. "Are you talking about sex? You thought Savannah and I were having sex back then? No way! We were just good friends! She was your girl, everyone knew that. Travis, I swear, I never touched her back then."

It sounded like an explosion echoing off the walls when I slammed my fist down hard on the metal table. "Don't you lie to me you son of a bitch! I saw you with my own eyes walking into that abortion clinic. And then I saw you, holding her in your arms walking out! She was bawling! I saw you Levi, so don't ever lie to me again, or we're walking out of here and you can keep your court appointed attorney!"

The door swung open and two guards rushed in. "Is everything Ok in here?" They shouted.

Olivia held up her hand. "Everything's fine officers. Just a little yelling. We'll keep it down from now on," She said, glaring at me. "Isn't that right, counselor!"

When they closed the door, I looked back at Levi. "Are you really going to look me in the eyes and deny it was you and Savannah at that clinic?"

"No, you're right, it 'WAS' Savannah and me that day," He said, leaning forward in his chair, "I drove her there and paid for it, but you are wrong about 'WHY' we were there."

I tilted my head unbelieving. "Are you saying that it wasn't your baby?"

Levi began nodding his head up and down. "It all makes sense now," he said more to himself than to me, "I can't believe it, you two, both of you have been so wrong all these years." He lifted his head and stared at me, "Why didn't you say something? Confront me, beat me up, anything. How could you just leave without knowing the truth."

"What truth?" I growled. "I saw you with my own eyes. That was all the truth I needed."

He shook his head. "No it wasn't. There was something else you needed to know. Something that would have changed all of our lives."

I had no idea where he was going, so I remained silent, sitting there staring at his face.

"Think about it Travis. Remember how it was back then? You were 'Mr. Popular', big time football star and I was the arrogant, spoiled rich kid that everyone despised. But the truth was...I wasn't trying to be arrogant, I was just trying to get people to like me. So I drove a new Mustang to school. If your father had given you a new Mustang, are you telling me that you would have ridden the bus? But because I didn't ride that bus and drove to school, everyone hated me and thought I was just showing off.

The only person in our entire class that was nice to me was Savannah. She was the only person who would talk to me...my only friend.

I knew you didn't like it when you saw us talking, but again she was all I had. Didn't you know that? Didn't she tell you over and over that we were just friends?"

I frowned and nodded. "Yeah, she did, but I didn't believe her. I always thought there was more to it."

"But you were wrong. I would never have done anything to risk my friendship with her. Never!"

"So How did it happen?" I asked, "How did she wind up pregnant and with you that day at the abortion clinic?"

He frowned. "You still don't get it? I thought you were supposed to be really smart. Are you serious? Can you not figure out why she was there that day?"

I shrugged my shoulders and glared at him. "I assumed she was there to have an abortion, so I wouldn't find out that she was pregnant."

"Yes, that's why she was there," he said staring directly into my eyes, "But it's not what you think. It wasn't my baby. Travis, it was yours!"

Suddenly, I felt light headed and I broke into a sweat. I couldn't seem to talk, but I finally forced out, "It was...my baby? Why didn't she tell me."

"Because if you had found out she was pregnant, you would've abandoned all of those plans and dreams you two had made all those years together. She knew you Travis. You would have insisted on doing the right thing; getting married and finding some mundane job, so you could support them. You had always dreamed of becoming a lawyer, like you are now. Travis, she was going to have the abortion for 'you'...and for all of your dreams."

The awful truth was coming too fast to comprehend. My brain started searching my memories for signs. How could I not have noticed that Savannah was pregnant? But worst of all, how could I have instantly jumped to that incredibly wrong conclusion? How could I have been so stupid? What made me believe she could have betrayed me? I had no answers.

"Do you remember the last time you saw her?" Levi asked, "the day of your mother's funeral? "You told her you saw us at the clinic together, and then you told her the next time you saw me, you would kill me! When you said that, she thought that somehow, you had found out about the abortion and left her, because she had killed your son."

"I lifted my head. "It was a boy?"

Levi looked down. "Yes, it was a boy. Savannah has never forgiven herself for having that abortion. To her, it was an unforgivable sin. And all these years she has believed that's why you left, why you hated her."

I looked away and sighed. "I've never hated her. To be honest, I've never stopped loving her, but couldn't forgive her either. That's why I left and have stayed away all these years.

When I found out about you two getting married, it convinced me that I had been right all along. I was angry, but I figured she'd gotten what she wanted and would be OK."

I took a deep breath and looked at him across the table, "God, Levi…I don't know what to say. Have I ruined all of our lives?"

Levi didn't respond for a few moments. Then he sighed and said, "She was devastated and confused when you left, I was the only one she could talk to. I knew she didn't really love me…not like she loved you, but I didn't care. She was so damaged and I wanted to see if I could help her. I honestly thought I could eventually make her love me, and I think she did, but it's not the same kind of love she had for you. She tried to hide it from me, but I always knew. She never got over you."

The door swung open again and the guard yelled, "You have five minutes. Wrap it up."

"Levi, we will come back tomorrow," Olivia said, "We haven't had time today to talk about your case, but you need to know that I will be your lead counsel. My specialty is criminal defense, Travis will be my second chair on your trial. But I need to ask you a few questions before we leave…and I need to know the truth. Are any of the Domestic Violence allegations that you were arrested for true?"

He shook his head no.

"Ok, one last question," Without any emotion in her voice she asked, "did you kill Savannah?"

His eyes instantly filled with tears. "No, God no! She may not have loved me like she loved Travis, but that didn't matter to me. I loved her with every part of my heart and soul. No, I've never laid a hand on Savannah in my life, and I swear, I did not kill her."

I stood up, reached out and shook his hand. "I've been a fool. I know this doesn't mean much now, but I'm sorry I didn't get to know you back then. I have misjudged you all these years. I'm sorry I didn't trust you and screwed up our lives. I just hope it's not too late to make it up to you and Savannah. I promise you, we're going to get you out of here, but to do that, we have to find her. Do you have any idea where she is?"

8
THE DISTRICT ATTORNEY

After we left Levi, we drove to a restaurant and had lunch. During our meal, Olivia called the office and found out that Jerry Johnston, the Matagorda County District Attorney, had called and requested that we come to his office to discuss Levi's case.

The bright, modern designed courthouse looked out of place. It reminded me more of a library on a college campus than a courthouse in a small historic town square. We found his office on the third floor, introduced ourselves to his receptionist, and we were escorted into his office.

The D.A. was older than I had expected, mid 60's. He was short, balding with an ample belly hanging over his straining belt. He stood up and introduced himself, smiling wide, holding out his hand to shake ours. Then he motioned for us to sit in the two leather chairs facing his desk. "I really appreciate ya'll coming," He said with his deep Texas drawl, "I wanted to meet you and see if there's anyway we could speed all this up and save the taxpayers some money by avoiding a trial. I thought that maybe, due to all the incriminating evidence against your client, we might come to some kind of plea agreement on Mr. Cruz's case. I just wanted to let you know that I'm willing to work with you on this."

We were at a disadvantage, because all the office had been able to dig up so far, was Levi's arrest report, so we had no real idea of what incriminating evidence he was referring to, but we were assuming it was all circumstantial based on his prior domestic violence arrest records. As far as we knew, there was no body, no crime scene, no real motive, just their mistaken belief that Levi was a serial wife beater.

I started to say something, but Olivia touched my knee and shot me a hard look. It was her subtle way of telling me to keep my mouth shut and let her do her job.

Olivia flashed her smile at him and said, "Would it be OK if I call you Jerry?" She said using a slow Texas drawl I'd never heard before.

Jerry broke into a wide grin. "Well, sure you can, little lady. And before we get started, I want to tell you that I'm a big fan of your father. I've had the honor of meeting him a few times. He's a true legal legend in Texas. Please give him my regards. And, when I found out his firm was representing Mr. Cruz, I had my staff do some research on you. It sure looks like you are following in your father's footsteps. I understand that you've done really well for a..." He caught himself, "Ahh, I mean for a young lawyer."

Although it was 1999 and that year there were more female graduating law students than males, Jerry had unfortunately shown his ignorance and prejudice to Olivia.

"Were you about to say...for a woman?" She asked indignant.

His face flushed, as he squirmed in his seat. "I guess I was, but Miss Olivia I didn't mean any disrespect. It's just that there's only a few women lawyers in Matagorda county and I'm a bit old fashioned. Again I apologize."

"Apology accepted, but in the future you can call me Olivia or Miss Bachman, but please don't ever call me 'Little Lady or Miss Olivia' again. That's degrading and chauvinistic. Are we clear on that?"

He nodded. "Yes ma'am, I mean, Miss Bachman...crystal clear."

It was obvious he didn't like being scolded, because his demeanor quickly changed from good ole boy to all business. "I'm willing to consider dropping the charges down from murder one to manslaughter. That's 10 to 20. It's his first real offense, so I'm sure the judge will go along with my recommendations and give him the minimum; he'll be out in seven or eight years with good time."

She glanced at me and then turned towards Jerry and smiled. "Seriously? That's why you wanted us to come see you today?" She asked, "Unless I've missed something important, from what I see of your case...well...to be honest with you Jerry, I don't see much of a case. Is there a body? No, I'm pretty sure there's not. Is there any physical evidence of a crime? Again, no I don't think there is," She reached into her briefcase, pulled out a document and handed it to him. "This is your copy of my brief that I will be filing to suppress any mention of Mr. Cruz's past arrests in the trial. They are inadmissible and you know it! Without his past arrests for domestic violence, you have no case."

She flashed her smile again. "Jerry we both know that the police jumped the gun when they arrested Levi. You have no incriminating evidence against my client and we both know that. Everything you have is circumstantial. He shouldn't have been arrested in the first place. The only thing we all know for a fact is that Levi's wife, Savannah, is missing. And as far as I can tell, no one is searching for her. And that brings me to my last question. Why in the hell has your police chief called off the search for one of your citizens that is missing?"

The tips of Jerry's ears were glowing bright red matching the rest of his face burning with his anger. I expected him to return Olivia's fire with a loud and long retort, but that didn't happen. Instead, he began flipping the pages of a yellow pad on his desk. When he found what he was looking for, he looked up and smiled. "Actually, they're still looking, but I don't think they'll find anything. I'm afraid that Savannah is, pardon my crudeness, but I believe she's fish food, out there a few miles away in the Gulf."

"Why would you think that?" I asked.

He grinned, "Well sir, there's a couple of reasons. First, did you know that Levi owned a boat? Yes he does, and it's a pretty good one too. A 36 foot Sea Ray," He turned his gaze away from me and stared at Olivia, "And Miss Bachman, guess what? Somebody took that boat out the day Mrs Cruz went missing. It was found, abandoned, floating a few miles off of Matagorda peninsula."

Olivia looked at me, then turned towards the D.A. "Jerry, we have evidence we wanted to talk to you about that proves Savannah had tried to commit suicide three times in the past. This fits with our theory that she must have finally done it, and that explains why she's missing. She must have jumped off the boat, and that's why it was found abandoned."

Jerry broke into a grin. "This evidence you wanted to talk to me about that proves her previous suicide attempts...I don't suppose you got that from Levi's son, did you?"

Olivia nodded. "As a matter of fact, yes. Alexander was the one who found her on her first attempt."

"Do you have any physical evidence of collaborating witnesses to these supposed suicides besides Levi and Alexander?" He lifted his eyebrows, "If not, how exactly were you planning on proving that this isn't just some story Alexander made up, trying to get his father out of jail? Cause...that's sort of what we thought he was doing when he told us that same story."

"Then how do you explain the abandoned boat?" Olivia asked, "So rather than believing Alexander, you choose to believe that Levi slipped away from his dealership without being seen, drove to Matagorda, killed Savannah, loaded her into his boat, dumped her body at sea, swam to shore, drove back to his dealership and slipped back in...all without being seen, in broad daylight? That's what you believe? Really?"

Jerry shook his head. "I'll admit that's a lot to accept, but let me ask you this. If Savannah had planned on committing suicide by jumping off the boat in the ocean, then why would the lab boys find traces of her blood in the bilge of that boat. What do you think, she stabbed herself, then washed the blood off the deck, and then jumped overboard. Do you see my problem? Is that what you were talking about earlier...you know, something you might have missed?"

Fuming in her chair, Olivia didn't answer him.

"And there's one other reason I'm pretty sure she's fish food. Of course, you being his lawyers and all, I figure you already know that Levi is flat broke. If you didn't know that, well, if I was you, I'd try to get my fee up front."

He smiled and looked at his notes on the yellow pad. "In fact, he's real broke. When you add up everything he owes to his creditors at the car dealership and what not, it comes to a little over two million dollars."

"What possible difference does that make to this case?" Olivia asked.

"Well, my psychologists tell me that financial problems are the number one cause of domestic squabbles. And I figure a two million dollar problem just might have caused quite a fight between them."

Olivia sighed, "More unfounded speculation."

Jerry nodded, "Yeah, could be, but I'm betting they had more than a few fights over that. But like you said, that's just speculation on my part and something I couldn't bring up in a trial...unless," he raised his eyebrows and smiled, "I had something more that connected it, something that just might show a motive."

He reached under the yellow pad, pulled out a document and handed it to Olivia. "I realize now you must not have had a chance to read the discovery documents I sent to your office, or this wouldn't be such a surprise."

After Olivia read it, she gave me a serious look and handed me the papers. It was an insurance policy. A TWO MILLION DOLLAR life insurance policy...on Savannah.

We both knew instantly, meeting with the D.A. without reading the discovery documents and knowing all the facts had been a huge mistake. We had underestimated this old man and had just gotten our asses kicked. We had nothing to bargain with, not one damn thing, so we left quickly with our tails tucked between our legs and found a bar where we could at least drink, lick our wounds, and figure out our next move.

After we got a few drinks down to calm our nerves, we ordered some food and ate it slowly, both of us carefully contemplating everything we had just learned from the D.A.

"What's your thoughts on the insurance policy?" I asked Olivia.

She nervously drummed her fingers on the table as she thought. "If you were two million in debt and decided to kill your wife to collect on her insurance policy, why only take out a two million policy? That would just cover your debt. If it was me, I would have made it ten or twenty million...at least five.

"You're right," I said. "That doesn't make much sense. Although I hate coincidences, this could very well be one. It's not unusual these days for people to take out one or two million dollar life insurance policies on each other. Maybe this isn't as diabolical as the D.A. assumes."

Olivia raised her eyebrows. "I sure hope so, but we're going to have to find some way to maneuver around that policy. That leaves us with the blood in the bilge," She said, setting her glass on the table, "If Levi *is* innocent, how do we get around *that* evidence?"

"I've been thinking about that. We need to talk to a forensic expert to see if there's anyway to prove how long that blood has been there. If there's no way to precisely date it, then we can argue that it was blood from some other time she had been in that boat. And that's something else, we need to know, how long they've owned that boat and where they docked it."

After our meal, we checked into a hotel and called it a night. Without asking Olivia, I told the desk clerk we needed two separate rooms. She had no obvious negative response, but I could tell she was surprised.

When I handed her the key to her room I said, "I...I hope you understand. I'm just not..."

She held up her hand. "Travis, you don't have to explain anything. I get it. See you in the morning for breakfast."

I followed her down the hall to our rooms, waved goodbye, opened my door, and stepped inside.

I searched the room, but unfortunately there wasn't a mini-bar, so I took off my clothes and stepped into the shower. The hot water felt amazing, running down my neck and aching back. I toweled myself dry and slipped under the crisp cool sheets.

It had been a very eventful 48 hours. I was exhausted and hoped I would immediately fall to sleep, but of course that didn't happen. My mind was spinning, bouncing between the vision of Savannah jumping into the water, trying to kill herself, to the last time I saw her...crying on her knees in my mother's driveway 14 years ago. I tried to remember what I had said to her that day, but I couldn't recall my exact words. All I could remember was looking in her eyes as I said them. I had been cruel to her and I was ashamed of myself.

After tossing and turning a few hours, I gave up on sleep, threw on some clothes and walked to the vending machines. I bought a Coke and a Snickers bar and walked outside to the pool. I had forgotten my watch, so I had no idea what time it was, but I knew it had to be two or three in the morning. When I reached the deck, I was shocked to see Olivia in the pool swimming laps. When she saw me she looked up and smiled. "I'm sorry ma'am, but the pool closed," I said, smiling back.

"Sue me," She said, turning around, swimming another lap.

I sat there, sipping my coke, eating my Snickers watching her swim. When she finished, she wrapped a towel around her and sat in the chair next to me. "Couldn't sleep either?" I asked.

"No, She said, "Too much information to sort out I guess," She wiped her face dry with the corner of the towel, "And I can't stop wondering about something. How well do you know Levi?"

I offered her a sip of my coke. While she was drinking it I said, "I didn't know him very well. We weren't exactly friends in school."

She handed me back the can. "I think that's what's bothering me the most. Travis, I know you well. You like everybody and everybody likes you. What exactly was it about Levi that made you not like him?"

I shrugged. "I don't really know, but from the first time I laid eyes on him in the first grade, I didn't like him. I've just never felt like I could trust him."

"Then what made you believe him today?"

I lifted my head and stared at her. "I'm not sure I do believe him. Maybe for Alexander's sake, I just want to believe him."

She took another sip of my coke. "Do you realize it's only been two days since Alexander came to your office. We sort of jumped into this without much thought. Do you think it's possible that Levi is playing us somehow? That this is just some elaborate scheme he's come up with to get away with Savannah's murder?"

I shook my head. "I'm sorry, but I'm not following you."

"I'm just thinking out loud, it's what I do when I'm working a case that doesn't add up. It's probably nothing."

"Maybe, but maybe it's not, go on, what are you thinking?"

She stood up, took the towel and wrapped it around her head, like an Indian headdress and sat back down. "For now, let's forget everything Levi told us in the jail today and consider the facts we know. First, you and Savannah were a couple in school and everyone knew that. Second, the only guy you didn't like or trust was the one guy who seemed to hit on her constantly. From an outsider looking in, it seems like he was obviously interested in Savannah and would have loved to see you two break up."

I nodded, agreeing. "Yeah, I guess he would have."

"There's something that has always bothered me about your story. The part about you seeing them walking into that abortion clinic. Did you go there often?"

I shook my head. "No. I knew it was there, but I'd never been there before."

"Then why were you there that day, at the exact time they were walking in? What were you doing there?"

"I was delivering flowers to the office across the street. It was my summer job, I was working for a florist."

"Did you make that delivery?" She asked.

I rubbed my hand over my face thinking back. Then my eyes

widened. "No," I yelled, "I remember now. They said it must have been a mistake. No one had ordered flowers." I stared at Olivia.

"I assumed it was something like that," She said, "Then it wasn't just a coincidence that you were there at that exact time. Someone wanted you there, to see them...and my money's on Levi."

"I guess that makes sense, but we were just kids, 17 years old. Do you honestly believe he could have been that diabolical at that age? And, if that was his plan, why didn't he tell me that today? He told me everything else, why not that?"

She shrugged. "I don't know. It's possible we're wrong about all of this and it was just a coincidence that you were there."

"Assuming we're right, and it was his big plan back then, so what? He won, he broke us up and got Savannah years ago. What does any of that have to do with what's going on now, with this case?"

"You got me," She said smiling, "that's why I'm swimming laps at three in the morning, but my woman's intuition is telling me that somehow it does."

She reached across the table and took my hand, "Travis, something doesn't feel right to me. I realize we've already agreed to take the case and I'm now his attorney of record, but I think we need to slow down a little and see what we can dig up on this case before we make our next move. I would like to know more about who Levi is now".

~

I arranged for us to meet with BJ and Kelly for dinner that evening after Olivia and I had spent all afternoon reading the discovery documents on Levi's case. Fortunately there were no more surprises in the paperwork. As we had assumed, their entire case was all circumstantial, lacking any actual physical forensic evidence other than the small amount of blood that was found in the bilge of the boat.

Due to the small amount of blood found in that bilge, and relying on our forensic expert's opinion that there was no empirical way to estimate the time the blood was put there, we were confident we could successfully get over that hurdle. But the two million dollar life insurance policy would be our major challenge.

∼

Kelly glanced at BJ and smirked. "We 'are' talking about Levi Cruz here, right?"

I nodded. "I know it doesn't sound like the guy we knew back then, but...I believe he was telling me the truth and maybe I've been wrong about him all these years. That's why I wanted to talk to you two. What do you think of him now? You've known him a lot longer than I have. What kind of man is he?"

"As far as I'm concerned," Kelly said, "he's the same arrogant ass hole he's always been."

"What makes you say that?" Olivia asked, "Other than buying the beach house, what has he done lately to make you think that?"

He shrugged. "It's not anything in particular, it's just..." Kelly looked over at BJ, "can you think of something?"

She shook her head. "Honestly, I haven't talked to Levi much over the years. I've spent a lot of time with Savannah, but Levi was never there."

"Where was he?" I asked.

"He was rarely home, always at one of his dealerships," she said, "always working."

"What about you Kelly?" Olivia asked, "you two ever hang out, maybe play golf or have a drink together?"

He shook his head. "No. I've only seen him a few times and that was usually business. Even then, he was rarely there and not very friendly when he was. He let Savannah handle all of their insurance."

I took a sip of my iced tea, leaned back in my chair and sighed. "So you're like me. You have no idea if he's changed or not, but you still don't like him."

He lowered his brow and thought for a moment. "I guess you're right. I've never really thought about it. I couldn't stand him in high school, so I guess I've avoided getting to know him."

"You said you handled their insurance," Olivia said, "so you sold them the two million dollar policy on Savannah?"

Kelly picked up one of his fried shrimp, dipped it in the red sauce and took a bite. "No," he said as he chewed, "It wasn't me, I didn't sell it to him," he washed down the shrimp with a sip of his beer. "She wouldn't have made it through underwriting with my company with her medical record. What's the name of the insurance company?"

Olivia opened her briefcase, took out the policy and handed it to him. He scanned the document and flipped through the pages. "You're right. It's for two million and Levi is the beneficiary. It's a Grand Life policy and that company was handled by Larry Grisham in Corpus Christi. Unfortunately, Larry passed away last year. I know his wife Martha. I could introduce you if you'd like me to."

I nodded. "I'd appreciate that, but for now my big question is, what about suicide. If Savannah did kill herself...will that policy still pay off?

He flipped the pages again, read it for a few minutes, and then he looked up at me and raised his eyebrows. "Interesting timing," he said.

"What are you talking about?"

He handed me the policy and pointed at the date it was issued. "Now read this," he flipped the pages and pointed at a paragraph. My eyes widened.

"What is it?" Olivia asked.

I shook my head and stared at her. "This policy was purchased exactly two years and two weeks ago. It has a two year wait period on suicide. Savannah disappeared the exact day...the wait period was over."

We all sat silently finishing our meal. When Kelly was done, he pushed his plate away and looked over at me. "Travis, what do you think this means?"

I shrugged my shoulders. "It means Levi is lying to me and killed Savannah for the money...or...Savannah has been planning her suicide for two years."

"So what are you going to do?" Kelly asked.

I stood and looked across the table at him. "I promised Alexander I would help his father. I don't have to believe him to represent him, so that's what I'm going to do. Hopefully I can at least get him one of his parents back."

Kelly looked away. "So you believe she's dead?"

"Kelly, I'm praying for a miracle, but Savannah has been missing for almost two weeks and it's time I face some difficult truths. I have no idea what she felt for Levi, but I know that she loved her son and would never just walk away and leave him alone. If Savannah is alive...then where is she?"

9
THE MERMAID

She opened her eyes, but closed them again quickly, because of the bright sun. Slowly she opened them again, blocking the sun with her hand. She scanned the room, but nothing looked familiar. "Where am I?" She whispered.

Brushing her hair back from her eyes, she felt something on her head. With both of her hands, she gently touched the edges of the bandage. "What is this?" She whispered trying to think, but she had no memory of how or why it was there.

Slowly, she rose up and hung her legs off the edge of the bed, touching the cold wooden floor with her bare feet. She was dizzy and confused. "Hello?" She yelled, "Is anyone there?"

The door opened and a nun, wearing a traditional headdress, with the white veil across her forehead and the black veil running down her back, walked in. "Estás despierto?" (Are you awake?) She said in Spanish excitedly, "Cómo te sientes?" (How do you feel)

She stared back at her. "I'm sorry, but I don't understand. Do you speak English?"

The nun shook her head no, and rushed out of the room. A few moments later, she returned with another, much older nun. She smiled wide and said, "Estoy muy feliz de ver que estás despierto!" (I'm glad to see that you are awake)

Frustrated, she shook her head and yelled, "I can't understand you! Do you speak English? Where am I? How did I get here?"

The older nun shook her head. "No yo no hablo inglés," (I do not speak English) The two nuns looked at each other, not knowing what to do. The younger one tried again, "¿Cómo se llama?"

She wanted to scream, "I don't understand!" But instead, she tilted her head and looked at the young nun, "What did you say?"

The nun smiled and said, " "¿Cómo se llama?"

She had no idea how, but she understood those words. "¿Cómo se llama? What is my name?" She said softly, "Is that what you said?"

The two nuns clapped their hands excited. "Si! What name?" The old one asked.

Finally, she thought smiling back at them. "My name is..." She thought for a moment, "Ahh...my name is..." She had no idea. Her mind was completely blank.

She tried again. "My name is...is..." She could think of nothing, "Oh my God," she screamed, "I don't know! How could I not know my own name?"

She fell back on the bed crying, covering her face with her hands. The older nun reached out and gently brushed her hair. "No llores Todo estará bien. Dios está contigo." (Don't cry. Everything will be fine. God is with you). They rushed out of the room, leaving her alone crying on the bed.

A few moments later, another nun walked in carrying a tray of food. "¿Tienes hambre?"

This time she guessed the nun was asking if she was hungry. When the aroma filled the small room, she realized that she was. She was starving.

She didn't know exactly what she was eating, but there was tortillas, beans, rice and something she hoped was chicken. Whatever it was, it tasted delicious and she cleaned her plate using a tortilla to sop up every single bite.

"Thank you," She said to the nun when she came back to get the tray, "It was delicious!"

"De Nada. You...are...welcome," She said in slow broken English.

"Do you speak English?" She asked her.

"Muy Poco," She said, looking down. (Very little)

Savannah smiled at her. "Can you tell me where I am?"

The nun thought for a moment. "Tecolutla."

"Tecolutla?" She repeated, "Mexico?"

The nun smiled. "Si, Tecolutla, Veracruz, Mexico."

"Veracruz?" She whispered, "Do you know how I got here?"

The nun thought again, searching for the words. "Fishermen caught you. You Sirena."

"Sirena?" What is Sirena?

"Fish maid...Mer..." She couldn't come up with the right words.

Savannah whispered the words, "Fish maid?" Then it hit her, "Mermaid? Are you trying to say mermaid?"

The nun smiled wide. "Si. Sirena, Mermaid. You Mermaid."

"What? Me, a mermaid? What are you talking about?"

The door swung open and a young priest walked in. He was laughing. "Don't mind sister Maria, she's just repeating what she' has heard around town. You are very famous in Tecolutla."

It took her a few seconds to realize he was speaking English to her. "Oh, thank God! You speak English!" she shouted.

He smiled back and held out his hand. "I'm Father Julio Alvarez. You can thank God if you want, but I choose to thank the public schools in San Antonio for my English."

The nun bowed to him, picked up the food tray and walked out of the room.

"Please sit," he motioned for her to sit on her small bed, while he sat in the chair across from her, "Sister Katherine and Sister Alissa are telling me that you can't remember your name. Is that true?"

She sat on the bed and looked at him. "Yes Father. I can't seem to remember anything. How did I get here? And where is here exactly? I've never heard of Tecolutla."

He smiled. "I'm not surprised. We're just a small fishing village on the Gulf Of Mexico about 500 miles south of Harlingen, Texas. You are in my Church, 'Capilla Del Sagrado Corazon'. That means *Chapel of the Sacred Heart*."

She nodded, "Ok, but how did I get here, and why did Sister Maria call me a Mermaid?"

"You were brought here by fishermen, shrimpers. They told me you were in their net when they dumped their catch onto the deck. At first they thought you were dead, but you moved and started coughing. They took you below, gave you water and did the best they could bandaging your head."

She touched the bandage with her hand. "What was wrong with my head?"

"You had a large gash in the back and you were bleeding pretty bad. They applied pressure and got it to stop. Then they brought you here to me. We have a small clinic and we take care of the locals as best we can. But they didn't bring you here just for that. The captain knew you weren't a mermaid, but he couldn't figure out how you could not have drowned in that net? He thought it had to be some kind of a miracle, so he brought you to this church. But unfortunately, his crew members weren't so sure and started telling the story of how they caught a beautiful mermaid, with long blonde hair with eyes the color of turquoise, in their net."

She lifted her hand again and touched the bandage on the back of her head. "Was it a bad cut? You think someone hit me in the head and threw me in the water?"

He nodded. "Either that, or you cut your head when they dropped you on the deck. There's no way to really know. And yes, it was a bad cut. The nuns had to give you several stitches to close it and you needed blood."

"How long have I been here?"

"A little over two weeks," Father Alvarez said, "The shrimpers found you Friday afternoon, 15 miles off the coast of Texas. It took them a few days to get back. They brought you here last Sunday night. It's Saturday now."

She shook her head slowly from side to side. "I have no memory of any of that," Her eyes filled with tears, "Why can't I remember, Father? What's wrong with me?"

"He stood, touched

her head and said a prayer. "I have summoned a doctor from Mexico City. He should be here in a few days. Hopefully he will have some answers for you. In the mean time, I think I will call you...Ariel. Wasn't that the name of the mermaid in the Disney film?" he said with a chuckle. "Have faith my child, God has saved you and brought you to me for a reason. When he's ready he will reveal everything to you. Try to get some rest. That will help heal your body and hopefully...your memory."

10

BODY LANGUAGE

Again, Olivia and I heard the clanking of Levi's shackles rattling long before the guard opened the door and led him into the room.

The shoulders of his orange jumpsuit were spotted from the water dripping from his wet, slicked back hair. His chiseled chin and neck was covered with his new two week growth of his salt and pepper beard.

"What happened to his eye?" Olivia shouted to the guard.

"I have no idea ma'am," he said grinning, "I guess he must have run into a door or fallen down...something like that."

Olivia pulled out her phone and took a picture of Levi's face. Then she turned and took a picture of the guard. "Let's see if the judge thinks it's as funny as you do." She pulled out her yellow pad and looked up at him, "I need your name."

The guard recoiled backwards. "What for?"

Olivia smiled wide. "So I'll know who to file the law suit against."

"What law suit? I'm just a guard here, you can't sue me? I'm not even a real police officer."

"What is your name officer?" Olivia repeated firmly, "And yes I 'can' sue you."

The guard looked at me with frightened eyes. "Can she really do that?"

I shrugged. "I'm afraid so. She's a lawyer, that's what she does. Better give her your name."

"It's Jerry Franks," he said, "But I swear I didn't lay a hand on him."

Olivia wrote down his name and underlined it. "Mr. Franks, I believe you, but unfortunately you were the last person I saw with Mr. Cruz yesterday and then again this morning. During those few hours, my client has mysteriously been injured."

She held up her phone and scrolled to the picture she had taken of Levi on our last visit and then she showed him the picture she had taken of him leading Levi through the door. "As you can see, I have photographic proof. This evidence may or may not hold up in court, but if I do sue you, you will have to hire a lawyer and respond. Most good lawyers charge three to five hundred dollars an hour. And trust me Mr. Franks, you'll need a good one, because I'm not just good, I'm really good. To defend a case like this would take..." She looked over at me and winked, "what do you think counselor, 10 to 20 billable hours?"

I nodded at Jerry. "At the very least," I said.

"So you see Jerry," Olivia continued, "even if you win the case, it will cost you several thousand dollars."

His face went white and his hands started trembling. "I..I don't have any money. Please don't sue me."

Olivia tilted her head and thought for a moment. "Tell you what Jerry. I'm gonna wait to file the suit. And as long as my client doesn't run into any more walls or fall down accidentally I won't file it, but if he has so much as a cut on his chin from shaving..." she paused and stared into his eyes, "do we have an understanding Jerry?"

"Yes ma'am," He said, "Don't worry about that. I'll make sure nothing happens to him."

"Great," she said with a wide smile, "now go away and leave us alone."

When he left, Levi looked at Olivia and said, "Thank you, but it wasn't Jerry who did this."

"I know, but I'm pretty sure it won't be anyone from now on."

"I hope not," Levi said.

He touched his bruised, swollen eye with his hand. "Could you really sue him?"

Olivia looked up over her glasses. "Probably not, but let's just keep that between us."

We spent the next few minutes slowly going over the discovery evidence file with Levi, explaining what it meant, and how we were planning to defend against each piece of evidence.

"Is that it," Levi asked, "that's all they have?"

I shook my head. "No. We've saved the worst for last." I pulled the life insurance policy out of my briefcase and laid it in front of him.

"What's this?" he asked.

"Read it."

Olivia and I sat quietly, watching Levi slowly read the policy, flipping through the pages. When he finished, he looked up. "Where did you get this?"

"We didn't," Olivia said, "the D.A. discovered it. Why did you take this policy out on Savannah? And why two million? That's a random amount?"

"I didn't do this!" He yelled, "Ask Kelly Smith, he takes care of all our insurance. He'll tell you I didn't buy this policy."

I leaned in toward him. "Levi, are you saying that you had no knowledge of this policy until now?"

"Yes!" He screamed, "I've never seen this before. I had no idea."

"Well unfortunately, the D.A. thinks you knew about it, and to be honest with you, it's very incriminating."

"What are you talking about? Incriminating? I'm telling you the truth! I didn't buy this policy!"

Olivia shot me a quick glance. "Levi, you are the sole beneficiary and..." she paused and flipped through the pages. She held up the page and pointed at a highlighted paragraph, "There was a two year waiting period on suicide. Savannah went missing on that exact day."

"Levi, look at me," I said, "this policy will have a paper trail. If you had anything to do with it, that information will come to the surface. You can't hide from this."

"I'm not hiding anything!" He shouted, again staring down at his fidgeting hands.

The reason I had accepted his case and was willing to believe what he had told us in the first interview, was because of his body language. I had taken a few Kinesics classes in college. That's the study of body language; facial expression, posture, gestures and eye movements. I even took a class on Oculesics, an advanced study of eye movements. With only a few classes I certainly wasn't an expert, but I did understand how to read the clues and up to this point, I had seen no obvious signs. The most surprising thing I had learned from those classes, especially in Oculesics, was that there was no real way to tell from eye movements alone if someone was lying. I had always heard that if someone looked up and to the left, that meant they were creating a story and lying, but I found out that's just a myth. After all of the thousands of studies, they have discovered that it was not the eyes, but usually the hands that gave them away. But without question the best way to tell if someone was lying was to simply trust your own instincts, your gut feelings. And for the first time, his hands were fidgeting and my guts were screaming at me. He was lying.

"Levi, I've known you most of my life, but the truth is, I really don't know you at all. I wish I did, because I have no way to read you. I can only pray that you are telling me the truth, because if you had anything to do with this, even if you were just aware it existed, aware Savannah was even considering it... you need to tell us now. Levi, this is their smoking gun. There is no way around this. This is their entire case and trust me, they'll know everything about this policy."

I leaned back, took a deep breath and stared sharply into his eyes. "Levi, if this blows up in our face at trial...we will certainly lose...and you will more than likely spend the rest of your life in prison, or worse...you could get the death penalty."

That seemed to rock him back in his chair. "Travis I swear I knew nothing about the policy, but..."

Olivia shot me a quick glance and leaned toward him. "But what?"

He dropped his head. "I may have given her the idea."

"What are you trying to say?" I shouted.

He sighed deeply and leaned back in his chair. "I didn't mean it. It was just something I said in anger."

"Levi, what did you say?" Olivia asked.

"It was a few years ago," He said softly just above a whisper, "I was so tired of living with all her crap. Knowing that she didn't really love me was...was so hard. I knew I should have left her years ago, but she was unstable and I was afraid of what she might do. It was after her last three week stay in the psychiatric hospital in Corpus Christi. Like all the times before, when she got out of the hospital she was great. She seemed happy and was always smiling and singing around the house. She started drawing and painting again, but when I saw what she was painting...I lost it."

He lifted his head and looked at me. "They were all of you...10 or 15 paintings of your face."

I had no idea what to say or how to respond, so I just sat there, silently studying him carefully.

"I went into a rage," Levi's eyes flared, as he recalled his anger, "I threw all of the paintings in the floor and stomped on them, smashing the wooden frames of the canvases. She was screaming at me, crying."

He took a deep breath. "It had been a bad day for me. I had just left my accountants office and found out that I was about to lose everything. She was crying on the floor picking up the paintings..."

He leaned over and covered his face with his hands, "I didn't mean it, "He whimpered, "I swear I didn't mean it."

"Damn it Levi! What did you say?" I shouted!

"I told her that I was through. Then I... I told her that I'd appreciate it if she would hold off trying to kill herself again for a couple of years, so I could at least buy some life insurance on her to pay off our debts when she did it."

The room grew silent. Olivia stared at me with stunned eyes. None of us said a word for several long minutes.

"I was at the end of my rope, I'd had enough, sick of living in the shadow of Travis. I know it was a horrible thing to say, but I swear I didn't mean it," he wiped his eyes with his sleeve, "I tried to take it back and apologize for saying it, but she just gathered up the paintings, stood up and walked away. She moved into the guest bedroom that night. That was a few years ago and we didn't talk much after that."

He sat quietly for a long time, staring at his fidgeting hands. Then he looked Olivia in the eyes. "I read somewhere that in many murder trials, the attorneys don't care, or even need to believe their client is innocent to represent them. Is that true?"

Olivia lifted her eyebrows and nodded her head. "Yes," she said, "An attorney doesn't have to believe their client is innocent to represent them. The burden of proof, for the guilt of the accused falls on the prosecution. My job is not to prove my client's innocence, it's to convince the jury that there is some doubt of his or her guilt. And the law says, if there is any doubt at all, they cannot convict. So believing if my client is guilty or innocent has nothing to do with how I build my case."

He turned and looked at me. "I know you are struggling to believe me, because you can't forget who I used to be. I'm sure you don't believe someone can grow up and change...but I have.

"I know you didn't buy my story yesterday about being that poor insecure child that nobody liked. Especially the part about Savannah just being my friend, because I'm a terrible liar."

He motioned toward Olivia. "She may not care if I'm innocent or not, but I'm pretty sure that you do. And I believe the only way to convince you that I didn't kill her...is to stop lying."

I nodded and said, "That might help a lot. So what have you lied to me about?"

He dropped his head and stared down. "Truthfully, I've had a thing for Savannah since the first day I saw her way back in elementary school. But of course, she was your girl. That's what everybody told me, hands off Savannah."

He raised his eyes and looked at me. "I was so full of myself back then. I kept thinking, who were you? Just some dirt poor rag tag kid living out by the railroad tracks with the rest of the white trash. What did you have that I didn't? I was rich, with all of the toys, cars and fancy clothes that came with it. But no matter what I did, Savannah just looked through me at you, like I was invisible. I hated you so much back then."

"The only time she ever talked to me was when you guys had a fight, or she was mad at you for something you said or did. It wasn't much, but at least I got to spend some time with her, so I took full advantage of it.

The best part was when you saw her talking to me, I knew it pissed you off. The worst part was, all those times you saw us together talking, all she was talking about was you."

He frowned and took a sip of his water. "She told me all about your plans of leaving Matagorda after high school; about you two getting married and you becoming a lawyer. And she was constantly talking about your three kids, two boys and one girl."

He took another swallow of his water and shook his head. "Listening to her go on and on about your dreams drove me crazy, but she was so beautiful I couldn't look away no matter what she was talking about. It was the only time I got to be near her, so I let that friendship go on."

He leaned back in his chair and ran his hand through his wet hair. "I was so frustrated she couldn't see me as anything other than a friend, just some one to talk to, I gave up even trying to flirt with her, and my hatred for you continued to build inside of me. And because of that flaming hatred, I made the worst decision of my life, a decision that changed and destroyed everything, a decision I will always regret."

He was staring directly into my eyes and his hands were still. I leaned forward. "What was that decision?"

He looked away and dropped his head. "Rather than being the friend she thought I was and giving her the support she needed, I decided to hurt you instead."

I frowned. "Hurt me? In what way?"

"She came to my house one day. She was out of her mind distraught. It was only a few weeks after we had all graduated from high school. She told me that she had missed two of her periods and had bought one of those pregnancy tests from the drugstore. She didn't want to take the test alone, so she came to me," he held up his hands, making air quotes, "her good friend, for help, and advice.

The test was positive. Her first thought was to immediately run and tell you, but," he frowned and shook his head slowly, "I talked her out of it. I convinced her that a child would change everything and completely destroy your lives."

He lifted his head and made eye contact with me. "I told her that getting an abortion was the only thing to do, the only way to get her life back, the only way to live out all of those dreams you two had planned."

"Travis, she never wanted to have that abortion," He said, wiping his eyes, "She didn't believe in them. She wanted to tell you she was pregnant, but I stopped her. But that's not the worst part. I called that florist you were working for and waited until I saw your car before I walked her into the clinic. I wanted you to see us there and was hoping you would do exactly what you did when you saw us...leave."

I glared back at him. "Olivia figured that out a few days ago, and you are right, it was a terrible thing to do. But Levi, that's just water under the bridge. You got what you wanted, you got Savannah, you won. I'm glad you're finally telling me this, I'm glad you're telling me the truth, and I'll have to deal with all of that later, but right now that has nothing to do with this case and why we're here today."

"You're wrong!" he shouted, "It has everything to do with it. Savannah never got over that abortion. She was a Christian and to her it was the ultimate unforgivable sin, 'Thou Shall Not Kill.' In the hospital, they told me that she used to mumble that commandment to herself all the time. Don't you see? She was never going to stop trying. She wanted, no it was more than that, she 'needed' to die to pay for what she had done. But when she realized that she could die and help me and Alexander with our financial problems too, she bought that policy and has been planning her suicide for two years. She waited until the suicide clause was over and then she did it. You have to admit that explains everything."

I shrugged. "Yeah, I guess it could."

"Travis you have to believe me. I may have gotten very, very tired, even infuriated and extremely angry trying to make Savannah love me instead of you all these years. And I'm sure you will discover that I've even talked to a lawyer about divorcing her. And yes I may have always been a selfish, arrogant jerk, a bad businessman and have gotten myself into some serious debt, but you have to believe me...I am not a killer! I did not kill Savannah. She killed herself!"

As he said that, I studied his hands. They were calm and very still.

11

REASONABLE DOUBT

It was the highest profile case the D.A. had ever had in Matagorda county, so everything was moving fast.

At the pretrial, the following day, before we had a chance to even begin developing our defense, the D. A presented the life insurance policy to the judge, and the precise timing of her disappearance. That was all it took, the judge felt, based on that evidence alone, there was enough evidence to proceed to trial, and to keep Levi locked up.

We had to argue for the extra time, but eventually the judge gave in and set the trial to start at 9:00 am, Monday morning, exactly four weeks later. Normally, we had several months to prepare for a trial, but this time we had no choice but to take what we could get and go to work.

First we tried, unsuccessfully, to have Levi's previous arrests for domestic violence blocked from the trial. Any other judge in Texas would have granted our request preventing any mention of them in the trial, because they had absolutely nothing to do with this case and we had included the case law to back it up. But unfortunately, it was a very small town and the judge didn't seem to care about being overturned in an appeals court, so he ruled in favor of his old fishing buddy, the D.A.

Olivia and I agreed that we had gotten all we could get from Levi, so we began going down our list of potential witnesses to interview. First on the list was Alexander.

"He's innocent, right?" He asked, looking up at us wistfully, "You believe him now, right?"

I glanced at Olivia. "What we believe is there is a good chance we can get him out of there," she said, with a gentle smile.

His eyes widened. "You think he killed my mother?"

I looked at him. "Alexander, honestly I don't know. I want to believe him, but that really doesn't matter at this point. What does matter is that there is a real possibility that your mother is missing, because she finally succeeded in committing suicide. You are the only one who has witnessed one of her attempts in the past. If you're willing to testify to that and we can convince the jury that she was suicidal, that should be enough to get your father acquitted."

"But that won't prove to everyone that he's innocent!" He shouted.

Olivia took his hand. "That's not how this works. It's not our job to prove he is innocent, it's our job to convince the jury that there is no absolute, beyond a shadow of a doubt proof that he's guilty. It's called reasonable doubt. And we can't do it without your testimony."

"Why do you think a jury will believe me? The cops sure didn't."

"They may not," Olivia told him, "but you are the only eye witness to your mother's suicide attempts."

"Alexander," I said, "I think they'll believe you. Even if they don't, we have to try. Are you willing to testify?"

He gave me a subtle nod.

"Great," I said, "Ok, let's move on. There's something we need to clear up I'm confused about."

He wrinkled his forehead. "Confused?"

I shook my head. "Yeah. You told us that you used to listen to your parents fight behind their door, right?"

He nodded. "Yeah. What about it?"

"Was it behind your mother's door or your father's door?"

He tilted his head and looked at me confused. "I don't understand your question."

I frowned at him. "Alexander, your father told us that Savannah had been sleeping in another bedroom for several years. Is that not true?"

He clinched his jaw and pressed his lips together. "Won't that make dad look bad?"

"So it's true?" Olivia asked.

He dropped his head. "For almost two years."

"Alexander, you can't hold that kind of stuff from us. We need to know everything," she said, "even if it makes your dad look bad. Do you understand?"

He shrugged. "I guess."

"If something like that came up at the trial," I said, "and we didn't know about it. It could be very damaging to our case. So please, tell us the whole truth. Olivia and I will decide if it needs to come out or not. And, hopefully, because we would already know about it, when something like that comes up, we'll have an explanation ready to defend it. So, is there anything else you haven't told us?"

He thought for a while. "Did I tell you that I didn't see the other suicide attempts? I wasn't there when she did it."

I turned my head and stared at Olivia. "Then how did you know about them?"

"Dad called me and I ran home."

"You saw the after effects, but not her actual attempts?"

"Yeah, she was always sort of out of it when I got home. Telling me she was going to be OK."

"Did you go see your mother in the hospital?"

"No, dad told me not to. He said seeing me would just upset her more."

"So Alexander, you can't testify that you witnessed her last two suicide attempts?" I asked.

He shook his head. "I guess not, but I know she did it."

"OK," Olivia said, "I won't ask you much about the other two attempts, but the D.A. might. When he asks, tell him the truth."

"Tell us more about the boat," I said, "How often did you go out on it? "

"Only a few times."

"How long has he owned it?" Olivia asked.

"Not long, only four or five months."

"Ok," I said, "Now think hard, this is very important. How many times did your mother go out in it?"

He thought for a moment, then lifted his shoulders. "I'm not sure she ever did. Mom got sea sick."

"Think hard, this is very critical to your dad's case. Had Savannah ever been on that boat before she disappeared?"

He closed his eyes trying to pull up memories. After a few moments he yelled, "Yes! I'm not exactly sure when, but I remember them talking about having to pull a fishing hook out of her thumb."

"That's exactly what we needed!" I said, patting him on his shoulder, "I want you to try to remember as much as you can about that. On the stand, Olivia will ask you about it. Just tell the truth about what you remember."

I stood and walked to the bookshelf. "Do you have a recent photograph of your mother?"

He walked to the bookshelf, stood next to me and pointed at a framed photograph. It was a close up of Levi and Savannah smiling on the beach. "I took that one of them last year."

"That afternoon, Olivia and I drove to Corpus Christi. Kelly Smith had set up an appointment with, Martha Grisham, the wife of the insurance agent who had written the application for Savannah's life insurance policy."

Martha was a beautiful, dark complected, small hispanic woman in her mid sixties. She told us that her maiden name had been Martinez and that she had married her husband, Larry Grisham right after they had graduated high school. They opened their insurance agency a few years later and had worked together, Larry as the salesman, Martha as the secretary, bookkeeper, and notary public for over 45 years. Unfortunately, Larry had lost his hard fought battle with cancer eight months earlier. After he died, she sold the agency and retired.

"We had a long, wonderful life together," Martha said with bright smiling eyes, "Larry was a good man and a great father. We weren't rich, mind you, but he was a hard worker and the agency was very successful. It provided us with a comfortable life for years, allowing us to put both of our boys through college and paid the mortgage off on this house."

"So sorry for your loss," Olivia said, "I know that must still be hard for you."

Martha nodded. "Yes, I miss him, but he was in a lot of pain. It was his time and it comforts me to know that he's with God now." She lifted her tea cup gracefully and took a sip. "So what exactly can I do for you today?"

Olivia smiled. "Your husband sold a large life insurance policy a few years ago and we were wondering if, by chance, you would remember anything about that."

She set her cup down on the coffee table. "How large?"

"Two million."

Martha's eyes widened. "Oh yes. I remember that one well. It was the biggest personal policy Larry ever sold."

"Do you remember who he sold it to?" I asked excited.

"Of course I do," She said, "I notarized her signature."

"Was there any problem getting it approved? I would assume a policy that large would require substantial medical research for the underwriting."

"Oh yes. Larry and I had our fingers crossed because it was a good commission, but it went through without any problems."

I pulled out the photograph of Levi and Savannah and showed it to her. "Is this the couple who bought the policy?"

She looked up at me with concerned eyes. "Is there a problem with the policy? We've already spent the commission. I don't have that much..."

"No." I said, stopping her, holding up my hand, "There's nothing wrong with the policy. Don't worry, that's not why we're here."

I held up the picture again. "Is this the couple?"

She shook her head. "It wasn't a couple. Just her," She touched her finger to Savannah's face.

Olivia took the picture out of my hand and placed her finger on Savannah's image. "Are you absolutely positive it was this woman?"

"Yes, I'm sure it was her. I remember that little brown birthmark there above her lip. We even talked about it, because it was just like the one Cindy Crawford has. She said that she had often thought about having it removed, but decided to leave it. Yes, I remember her well. She was so pretty and had a pretty name too."

"Savannah," I said

"Yes, Savannah. That was it," She said, smiling, "I told her that her name was almost as beautiful as she was. And she really was beautiful. I even kidded Larry a little about staring at her." She said with a chuckle, "Oh yes, this is definitely her."

"What about the man in the photograph?"

She picked up the picture and studied it carefully, adjusting her glasses. "No, he wasn't here. I've never seen this man before. Who is he?"

Olivia laid the picture down next to her on the couch. "His name is Levi Cruz. He is her husband and our client. He has been arrested for Savannah's murder and we are representing him."

"Oh my Lord!" Martha shouted. "This beautiful sweet creature is dead? How awful."

"We're not sure she's dead," I said, "but unfortunately she *is* missing."

"Martha, we need to prove that it was Savannah, not Levi who purchased the policy from your husband. Would you be willing to come to the courthouse in Bay City and testify to that fact?"

She considered it a few moments. "Will it help this poor girl?"

Olivia nodded. "Not directly, but it could help her in the long run."

"Ok then. I'll do it for Savannah."

∼

We met with the judge and he reluctantly issued a subpoena for Savannah's medical records from the Corpus Christi Medical Center. We were shocked to discover that Savannah had never been admitted there for anything other than elective plastic surgery, no mention of anything to do with her mental health.

I immediately called Kelly Smith. "I thought you told me that Savannah had been admitted, several times, to the psychiatric ward at the Corpus Christi Medical Center."

"I did," he said.

"I'm looking at her medical records from The Corpus Christi Medical Center," I said, "and that's not what it says."

"What does it say?"

"It says that she was in there three different times for, and I quote, *'elective plastic surgery.'* Why did you think she was in the psychiatric ward?"

Kelly was silent for a beat, thinking before he spoke. "First of all, that's what Alexander told us, but that wasn't the only reason. Travis, I've been doing this a long time. I don't actually get a client's medical files, just an accounting of what their policy has paid out. When I saw the amounts, and the length of her stays, I made an assumption. Trust me, no one stays in the hospital three weeks for plastic surgery. The insurance company would have never approved that. Long stays are usually for serious medical rehab or mental health problems in the psychiatric wing. That report has to be wrong."

"No shit," I said.

"Let me do some checking and make some calls and see if I can get to the bottom of this," Kelly said.

"No, don't do that."

"Why not?" He asked. "I'm telling you Travis, I can pull up my files and show you that she was there for several weeks at a time."

"I have no doubt that you can, but that won't help me with Levi's case. We are basing everything on the fact that Savannah was suicidal and she's missing because she finally did it. That it wasn't Levi who caused her injuries in the past that he was arrested for, but rather it was Savannah with her suicide attempts. Our entire case rests on that. It's the only way to explain why she's missing. And because those medical files are missing, I think it's best to ignore that fact and not stir the pot, giving the D.A. something else to beat us over the head with."

"I understand and I'm not trying to tell you how to do your job, but if it was me, I would want to find out who changed those records. We know Savanna didn't have the computer skills to do it, and neither does Levi. But whoever did this...has those skills and access to that computer. And, whoever it was had a connection to either Savannah or Levi. If it's Levi, then he's guilty as hell!"

I didn't respond.

"Travis, don't you think the D.A. has the same medical records?"

I sighed. "I'm sure he does."

"Well, if he does, how are you going to respond when he asks the jury, 'Why would someone have plastic surgery three times if they were planning on committing suicide?'"

∽

"When Savannah came back from the hospital, was she taking any prescription medicines?" I asked.

Levi shook his head. "No, never. She wouldn't take any prescription drugs. She didn't believe in them. She only took holistic medicine."

"Seriously?" I asked, "Never?"

"Never, not even an aspirin. She wouldn't let Alexander take any either. She was all into that natural healing crap."

I looked at Olivia. "Now we know why there wasn't any antipsychotic prescriptions in her data base."

"It has to be the damn D.A." Levi yelled, "He could have removed the records easily."

I frowned. "Think about it Levi. These records had to be changed over two years ago, before the D.A. ever heard of you. Otherwise the insurance company would have discovered that she was suicidal and rejected the policy."

"Oh yeah," he said, "that makes sense."

"Whoever did this has to be someone who knows you, or knows Savannah, and is a computer expert and had access to the hospital computer," Olivia said, "Can you think of anyone that fits that description?"

Levi stared down at his hands and thought for a few minutes. Cracking his knuckles he said, "Now that I think about it, there was this young good looking doctor that seemed to pay a lot of attention to Savannah."

"What do you mean by that?" I asked, "Was she his patient?"

"There were several doctors, but yeah, he was one of them."

"What made you think he was paying too much attention to her?" Olivia asked.

"I don't know. Nothing specific. It just seemed like he was always there, hanging around her. He didn't do that with his other patients," He leaned forward, "I bet that's it. She had him do it for her, change the records. He certainly had access. Yeah, that has to be it. She must have had him to do it so she could buy the insurance."

"Levi, he could lose his medical license if he got caught. Why would he do that?" I asked.

"Because they had a thing going. Don't you see? That's why he was always hanging around. Yeah, that explains everything."

I watched him crack his knuckles, one finger at a time. "Possibly," I said, "What was his name?"

He immediately shook his head. "I can't remember. That was years ago."

"Levi, this is critical. Try to remember his name. If we can find this doctor, or any of her doctors for that matter we can prove she was there. Do you remember any of their names? What about the nurses?"

He shook his head again. "I only visited her a few times. They didn't want me to come there during her rehab, so I didn't have the chance to get to know them. I'm sorry, but I can't remember any of their names."

Olivia shot me a hard look, motioning that it was time for us to leave.

"Why would he lie about this?" She asked as we walked to the car.

I shook my head. "I don't know, but he is, that was all a load of bullshit. No one, including Levi, has ever insinuated that Savannah was ever unfaithful. Why would he be so ready to accept her being unfaithful with her doctor? It's all bull shit. He's hiding something."

"Travis, I know I shouldn't say this," Olivia said, staring into my eyes, "but if he's lying to us about this, I can't help but wonder what else he's lying about. I'm beginning to think he's guilty. What do we do now?"

I cranked the car and pulled out of the parking lot. "I don't know, but to quote you, 'Whether he's guilty or not has nothing to do with how we build our case.' So, I guess we'll just keep building that case."

She reached over and took my hand. "If he's guilty...and we get him acquitted..."

I nodded. "I know. Double Jeopardy. But trust me, if that's the way this turns out, what I do to him won't have anything to do with a jury."

∼

Before we knew it, the trial date was on us. We weren't completely satisfied with our case, but believed we could convince the jury with enough reasonable doubt to prevent a guilty verdict. At that point, we would have celebrated a hung jury. That would at least give us some time to gather evidence before the retrial.

We had conducted several more interviews with Levi at the jail, leaving us more confused of his innocence or guilt. Honestly, if we could have withdrawn and walked away we would have, but we both knew the judge wouldn't allow it. So we reminded each other that our judicial system was based on the simple truth that everyone, guilty or innocent, deserved to get a fair trial. So we put our growing suspicions away and concentrated on building the best case we could.

We tried our best, but didn't have time to track down the elusive doctors and nurses that had treated Savannah in the psychiatric ward. In the end, we decided to ignore Savannah's medical records all together.

I did find several cases where someone had done strange things, including having plastic surgery and committed suicide a few weeks, or even a few days later. Apparently, there is no real explanation of suicide.

We had lined up several of Levi's coworkers and friends, to testify to his character, had three separate documents from forensic experts saying that they could not put an exact date of the blood discovered in the bilge of the boat. We also had several of their neighbors lined up to testify to Savannah's apparent constant state of depression.

We had Martha Grisham's testimony that she notarized Savannah's signature on the insurance policy and had rehearsed Alexander's testimony of his mother's attempted suicide.

We wished we had more, but with our heads held high, we walked into the courthouse and began the battle of Levi Cruz versus The State Of Texas.

∽

Father Alvarez had reported her to the local police, but after six weeks he still hadn't discovered the identity of the beautiful blonde woman the fisherman had brought to his church. Her legend had continued to spread throughout the country side and as a result, attendance for his services had grown substantially, filling the pews at each mass with hundreds of the curious, hoping to get a glimpse of the beautiful blonde mermaid with turquoise eyes.

After a few weeks, the nuns removed the stitches from her head and helped her wash her long blonde hair.

"It"s beautiful," Sister Mary said handing her a towel.

"Gracias," She said, using the touch of Spanish she had picked up during the past weeks.

When he had time, Father Alvarez had been trying to teach her Spanish and was impressed at how quickly she was picking it up. In return, she had been teaching the sisters English.

The doctor from Mexico City had come and gone. He had given her a clean bill of health, but had no answers to give her about the amnesia. He was confident that it was a result of her head injury, but had no idea when, if ever, she would get her memory back.

To keep her mind occupied and her hands busy, she began spending her days helping the nuns in the clinic taking care of the locals with their minor injuries.

In the evenings, after she had dinner with the nuns, she would take a pencil and paper and draw. She started by drawing the many statues of Jesus and Mother Mary in the chapel, then began to draw the faces of the sisters with such amazing accuracy, it astonished everyone, especially Father Alvarez.

"Ariel, I wonder if perhaps you are a famous artist?" He said studying her drawing of his face. "You are very good at this. This is better than any picture I've ever had taken of me."

"Thank you Father," She said. I don't really understand how I do it. It just seems to flow from my fingers."

He smiled. "It's one of God's gifts to you. I will try to find more supplies, more pencils, paints and some canvas. I think you need to continue to do this. It's part of you and obviously part of your past. Perhaps it will spark something to help you with your memory."

12

THE TRIAL

The Matagorda County District Attorney, Jefferson Davis Johnston concluded his opening statement, laying on his thick Texas accent with a few more 'Good Ole Boys', jabs at Olivia's Ivy League pedigree.

"All I'm asking of you today ladies and gentlemen," he began, "is to use that common sense all us Texans are born with and use so proudly. Don't let this 'Connecticut' educated *YALE* lawyer's fancy words cloud your judgement. That man, Levi Cruz was arrested THREE TIMES!" He held up three of his fingers to visualize his words. "Not once, not twice, but THREE TIMES, the police, with their blue lights flashing and sirens blaring rushed to his home. He had beaten up his poor defenseless, 110 pound, beautiful wife, breaking her arm and shattering her leg in the process."

He shook his head in disgust as he slowly paced in front of the jury. "And now," he held up an 8 x 10 photograph of a smiling Savannah, "this helpless, beautiful creature has vanished off the face of this earth...nowhere to be found."

He handed the photograph of Savannah to a jury member to pass around to the others. "I may be wrong, but to me it's not that hard to figure out what happened to her," He turned and pointed at Levi, "He finally did it. Now, you may be asking yourself why would he kill her this time? He only beat her up before. Why kill her now? To folks like you with good common sense, you're thinking, if he didn't want to be married to her any more why didn't he just leave her, get a divorce...why kill her...especially why kill her now?"

He walked to his table, picked up a document and held it up. "This is why. He did it for money, for two million dollars. This is her life insurance policy, but hang on, there's more you need to know about this piece of paper. When this fancy Ivy League lawyer gets up here in a minute," he spat out the words, Ivy League like they left a bad taste in his mouth, "she's going to try to convince you that Mr. Cruz did not kill Savannah, but rather Savannah...killed herself. She's gonna tell you that Savannah is missing, because she has gone off somewhere and committed suicide!"

He smiled and chuckled. Then he stopped pacing and raised his eyebrows. "Wait a minute!" he shouted, "If she committed suicide, then the insurance company won't have to pay the two million, right?"

Several of the jury members nodded their heads in agreement. "That's what I thought too, but come to find out if you wait for two years after you buy the policy...it *will* pay off."

He backed away from the jury box a few feet and slowly looked each member of the jury in the eyes. "Would you like to guess what happened exactly two years to the day after this policy was purchased?" He paused and shook his head for more effect, "That was the exact day Savannah Cruz disappeared. Now that's quite a coincidence, don't you think?"

Olivia stood up, looked at me and smiled, then quickly walked to face the jury. "Hello everyone, I'm Olivia Bachman. If you don't mind, before I start talking about my client, Mr. Cruz, I'd like to spend a few minutes telling you a little about myself. First, I would to like let you know that I was born and raised 160 miles from here in New Braunfels. I currently live in Austin and am a partner in my father's law firm."

She walked closer to the jury box and gave them all a smile. "To be honest with you, this is the first time in my career I've felt the need to have to do something like this. I worked hard enough in high school to graduate valedictorian, even harder at the University of Texas to graduate Cum Laude and finally, to be one of the three students in the entire state of Texas to be accepted into Yale law school, located in Connecticut...of all places. Now...this is somehow, according to our esteemed District Attorney... a bad thing."

She lifted her hands and shrugged. "Do you think it's a bad thing? I sure hope not." She turned and smiled at the D.A.

"Now that we are all caught up on my fancy Ivy League education, lets get to the reason I am standing before you today.

First, let's talk about these three arrests. We do not deny that Mr. Cruz was arrested three times at his home on suspicion of domestic violence. But what Mr. Johnston didn't tell you...is that after every single arrest, his wife Savannah told the police that Levi was not responsible for her injuries. In fact it was *she* who had caused them. It's in the police records and you'll get to see them for yourself. He also left out the part that Savannah had immediately dropped the charges against him," She held up three fingers, mocking the D.A.'s earlier gesture, "Not once, not twice, but...All THREE TIMES!"

She began pacing in front of the jury. "Mr. Johnston made a big point to make sure I didn't use my fancy words to cloud your," she made air quotes, "Texas common sense. So lets try to use that common sense now. What if I told you that I could prove, and I will, that Mr. Cruz had no knowledge of the two million dollar life insurance policy. That changes things, doesn't it? What if I told you that you will be hearing from Savannah's son who will testify that he witnessed one of his mother's suicide attempts. Again, that knowledge changes things as well, doesn't it?"

She slowly looked each jury member in the eyes, like the D.A. had done. "I will also be asking you to use that Texas common sense when you begin to deliberate this case. Here are the simple facts. There is no evidence of any kind of a struggle, but most importantly, there is no body. There is absolutely no evidence that Savannah Cruz is even dead. All anyone knows for sure is that she's missing and that she was suicidal. My client, Levi Cruz is on trial for her murder," She lifted her eyebrows, "What murder? And even though there is no proof of this supposed murder...you could sentence him to prison for the rest of his life or worse...you could actually sentence him to die by lethal injection. That's what the D.A. is going to ask you to do. And yet...he has zero proof that Savannah is even dead. Everything he will present to you in this trial is purely circumstantial. Not one ounce of evidence that can't be easily explained away. He has nothing but speculative, circumstantial, theories, but nonetheless he's going to ask you to stick a needle in Levi's arm and kill him, because he believes he is guilty. Does that make any *common sense* to you? It doesn't to me."

She backed up and stood in the exact place the D.A. had stood a few moments before. "Ladies and gentlemen all I ask of you is to remember that a coincidence...is just that...a coincidence. When Mr. Johnston brought up that coincidence, I probably should have jumped up and objected and had that stricken from the record, but that's something I rarely do during opening statements. It wouldn't have help anyway, because, you all know that once you hear something...you can't really un-hear it. So rather than object, I thought I would just wait and close my statement today by telling you the way things are supposed to work in a trial like this. And trust me, Mr. Johnston knows this very well. A coincidence...is not evidence. In fact, and again Mr. Johnston knows this. A coincidence is something that you, as a jury, can not even consider. I don't know about you, but it makes me wonder why he even brought it up?"

She smiled at the jury, walked back to our table and sat down.

The judge looked at his watch and turned toward the jury. "Ladies and gentlemen, I think this would be a good time to take a 15 minute recess. When we return Mr. Johnston will call his first witness and we will begin hearing the evidence."

The first day of the trial revealed no surprises. The D.A.'s first three witnesses were the police officers who had arrested Levi for suspicion of domestic violence and assault. On her cross examination, Olivia had gotten all three officers to admit that on each arrest, Alexander and Savannah had insisted that Levi had not touched her and that, in fact, Savannah had caused the injuries herself.

"If everyone at the scene was telling you that Mr. Cruz was innocent," Olivia asked, "then why did you arrest him?"

"It's not unusual for victims of domestic violence to deny what has happened to them," The officer responded, "they lie, because they are afraid that their spouse will retaliate when we leave."

"So are you saying that no matter what the facts are when you arrive at the scene, you arrest the husband and take him to jail anyway?"

The officer nodded. "Yes ma'am. If there is a serious injury to the spouse that's the usual procedure."

Olivia glanced at the jury and shook her head. "Officer Reynolds how many domestic violence calls have you personally worked?"

"I don't know the exact number, but a lot."

"Ok, I understand that it may be hard to remember them all," Olivia said, "perhaps you'll be able to remember *this* number. In all of those domestic violence calls...what was the percent of the times you *didn't* arrest someone? Would you say... 50, 40, 25...10 percent? And remember you're under oath and this can be verified."

He looked down. "I'm pretty sure I made an arrest at each one."

"Officer Reynolds, have you ever heard the term...innocent till proven guilty?"

"Objection!" The D.A. yelled.

"I withdraw my question," Olivia said, returning to her chair. Before she sat down, she turned and looked at the officer, "Officer Reynolds, do you know how this case was resolved?"

He nodded. "The charges were dropped and Mr. Cruz was released."

"Who dropped the charges?"

"Mrs. Cruz."

Olivia took her seat. "No more questions."

After the three police officers' testimony, the judge recessed for lunch.

Because Alexander was our witness he couldn't watch the trial, so at lunch we filled him in on what had gone down so far.

"I hate not being able to watch," he said, "I would have loved seeing those cops squirm in their seats."

Olivia smiled. "They didn't actually squirm, they held up pretty well, but hopefully I made my point to the jury that Levi's arrests were just standard procedure and not based on any real proof."

In the afternoon session, Mr. Johnston called two forensic experts; the first was the local coroner who testified how he matched the blood found in the boat to Savannah. His testimony was a long and boring explanation of how D.N.A. is used.

The second expert was from the Houston crime lab and he testified to the procedure used to discover the exact time the blood was left on the boat. His very long and thorough technical explanation almost put the jury to sleep, with many of them obviously restless, shifting in their seats, yawning.

On each expert, Olivia kept her cross examination short and to the point, but sticking in a few jabs at the same time.

The next day, the D.A. only called two more witnesses, before he rested his case and turned it over to Olivia to present our defense.

The D.A's first witness was an executive from Great Life Insurance company. He testified to the extent they went to underwrite the two million dollar policy. As we had expected the D.A. submitted Savannah's medical records into evidence.

"Mr. Levine, can you explain how the two year suicide clause works?"

"Well, there's not much to explain," he said, "It's simple really. If the policy holder commits suicide before the two-year wait period, then the policy is invalid, but if it's after two years it is valid."

"What would happen if someone disappeared on that exact date, never to be found and only assumed that they had committed suicide. Would it pay the beneficiary then?"

"No, not until the policy holder is officially declared dead. It varies from state to state, but that usually takes five to seven years."

"But eventually, maybe in only 5 years, the beneficiary will be paid, correct?"

"Correct."

The next witness was a psychologist. "So doctor, in your opinion, would someone who had three different plastic surgeries done to their face, to reduce the size of their nose, enhance their cheekbones and then their chin...all within a two year period be considered suicidal?"

"Objection!" Olivia shouted, jumping to her feet, "With all due respect to the doctor's impressive credentials, there is no way he could know Savannah's mental health and make this judgement without interviewing her."

"Overruled," The judge said, "I believe the doctor has more than enough experience in his field to answer this question."

And so it went, with the judge overruling every one of her objections. After the D.A. had rested his case, instead of letting Olivia begin her defense, the judge called for a recess until the following morning. It was obvious to us that he wanted to let the jury ponder the prosecution's witnesses testimony overnight. He wasn't even trying to hide his obvious bias.

The next morning, Olivia asked the judge to make a directed verdict, dropping all charges against Levi, because the prosecution had failed to prove their case. Of course, he denied that and she began.

The judge's bias soon became apparent to everyone in the courtroom, including the jury. He sustained every objection the D.A. shouted during Olivia's attempts at questioning her witnesses. But through it all, Olivia showed no signs of frustration and always got her point across to the jury.

Battling through all the objections and sustains, Alexander remained calm on the stand answering her questions with clarity and maturity beyond his age.

Eventually, after noticing the glares coming at him from the majority of the jury, the D.A. gave up and stopped his objections and let Alexander talk.

"After you found her in the bathroom and she recovered," Olivia gently asked him, "did you ever talk to her about it?"

He lowered his head. "Yes. I asked her why she wanted to die?"

"What was her answer?"

He wiped his eyes with his hand. "She said...she didn't deserve to live, but couldn't tell me why."

"Did she say anything else?"

He shook his head. "She just asked me to forgive her."

"Alexander, what do you think happened to your mother? Why is she missing?"

"Objection!"

"Sustained!"

"I think she finally did it." He said looking at the jury.

"Objection! Your honor!" the D.A. screamed.

The judge turned toward the jury. "Ladies and gentlemen, that was an improper answer from the witness. That answer will be stricken from the record and you are now instructed to forget what he said and not to consider his words in your deliberations."

Olivia turned and walked to her chair. "Your witness."

The next few minutes were actually enjoyable. Olivia had anticipated the D.A.'s cross examination questions well and had rehearsed them several times with Alexander.

His frustration became obvious after Alexander instantly fired back at him with well thought out answers to his questions.

"Ok, let's talk about the day you supposedly found your mother hanging in the bathroom," Johnston began again, "That's pretty convenient timing don't you think? You coming down sick and getting home just in the nick of time."

Alexander nodded. "Yes sir. I was lucky to have arrived when I did. My preacher told me that he believed it was divine intervention. He told me that God had brought me there to save her."

Several members of the jury smiled and nodded approvingly, as Mr. Johnston stammered trying to think of an appropriate response that wouldn't piss off the 12 Christians staring at him in the jury box and the three alternates sitting in the seats behind him.

"Ahh...well I guess that is one explanation." he said, "I don't suppose you have any proof of you getting sick that day."

"No sir, but the nurse who treated me that day and drove me home is sitting over there behind my father. I guess you could ask her if I was really sick."

∼

District Attorney Johnston cussed himself under his breath. He was getting killed up there, but he had no choice, he had to continue. He'd screwed up and completely underestimated this 16 year old boy, so he was forced to continue asking questions he didn't know the answers to, something a first year law student knew not to do.

∼

"When you found your mother," Johnston continued, "what was she wearing?"

"White jeans and a blue blouse," He said.

"You said she had used a scarf and was hanging from the shower head, right?"

"Yes sir."

"What color was the scarf?"

"Objection! Your honor, he was seven years old. What difference does it make what color the scarf was?"

"Sustained! The witness will answer the question."

"I thought it was yellow, but when I got her down and removed it from her neck, I saw that it was multi colored with patterns of butterflies."

Hiding his frustration, Johnston asked, "Alexander, it's my experience that a scarf makes a tight knot. With her weight pulling down on it, how could you have untied her so easily?"

"I didn't untie her, I used a knife."

"Oh really," Johnston said, thinking he'd finally trapped him, "Where did you get a knife? Did you carry a switchblade in your pocket when you were seven years old?"

"No sir, it wasn't a switchblade, it was my Boy Scout knife. I always carried it with me back then. I still do, but the guards on the front doors have it now. They said I couldn't take it inside the court house."

Finally loosing it, he yelled, "Alexander, you seem very well rehearsed. Have you and your attorney been practicing this? You seem to have amazing recall for something that happened nine years ago!"

Alexander (as rehearsed) turned and looked at the jury. "If you came home and found your mother hanging from the shower, wouldn't you remember everything too? I'll never forget that image."

"Young man, do not address the jury," the judge shouted, "address your answers to Mr. Johnston."

"Sorry your honor," he said, glancing at the jury.

"Let's move on," Johnston said, trying to recover some control, "I'd like to hear more about this supposed fish hook in your mother's hand you remember. That's a little convenient don't you think?"

"Convenient?" Alexander said, tilting his head, confused, "I don't understand."

"Your father's attorney, Ms Bachman has just spent two hours of our time talking to a forensic scientist trying to convince the jury that there was no way to date the blood we found in your father's boat, and now, a few minutes later you tell us that you remember a time when she bled in that boat on a different day. Like I said, that's a rather convenient memory, don't you think?"

Alexander shrugged. "I've been out in the hall. They wouldn't let me watch the trial, so I had no idea who Ms Bachman was questioning. Mr. Johnston, I'm a Christian and I put my hand on the Bible and swore to tell the truth. If the truth sounds *convenient* to you, I don't know what else to say, but I'm sorry."

He finally threw in the towel and gave up. "No more questions for this witness," he said slumping back in his chair.

The rest of the air escaped out of the states case when Olivia called

Martha Grisham to the stand. When she picked Savannah's face out of a collection of 16 pictures and swore she was the person who had purchased the two million dollar life insurance policy and then swore under oath that she had never laid eyes on Levi before this day, everyone, including the judge knew that the case was over.

District Attorney Johnston did his best to tie all of his circumstantial evidence into a nice neat bow and gave a very convincing closing, but when Olivia got up, she quickly untied that bow.

For almost 20 minutes, step by step, she highlighted the entire case, reminding the jury of our evidence that countered every piece of the prosecutions circumstantial theories.

"I'll leave you today with one simple question," she said, holding up her index finger, "one very critical question each and every one of you has to answer before you can possibly begin your deliberations of this case.

That question is...have you heard, or seen anything from Mr. Johnston, or heard or seen anything even from me," she paused for effect, "that has convinced you beyond a shadow of a doubt that Savannah Cruz...is even dead."

She backed up and looked at each one of them in the eyes. "Ladies and gentlemen...If you're not convinced that Savannah is dead," she lifted her hands and gave them a smile, "and you can't be, because there is no proof she is...then how can you convict Levi of murdering her?"

After Olivia's close, the judge once again revealed his obvious bias when he charged the jury, reminding them that they could only consider evidence that was admitted into the official record and that they could not consider any testimony they had heard, but had been stricken from the record.

"I know it can be a very hard thing to do," the judge told them, "it's like if I told you'll not to think about an elephant right now, all you can think about is an elephant. But ladies and gentlemen it's your duty to remove those elephants from your mind and only consider the testimony that was allowed into the official record. And one more thing," he said with a smile, "we've heard a whole lot about reasonable doubt in this case. I just want to remind you that *REASONABLE* doubt...is not *ANY* doubt. Just go back there and use you common sense and I'm sure you'll make the correct decision."

With weak stomachs and mixed feelings of Levi's guilt or innocence, Olivia and I didn't talk as we waited silently in the lobby for the jury to return.

Olivia believed that if they came back quickly, it would be a not guilty verdict, but if they deliberated into the next day, it would more than likely mean we had lost.

Honestly, I was hoping for a long deliberation, but the jury was out for less than an hour.

The clerk took the verdict from the jury foreman and handed it to the judge. He opened it and read it carefully with a stone face.

"Was this a unanimous decision?" He asked.

The foreman nodded, "Yes, your honor."

The judge handed the verdict back to the clerk and she returned it to the foreman.

"Will the defendant please rise." the judge barked. We stood, with Levi between us. "Mr. Foreman, you may read the verdict."

With nervous, shaking hands, the foreman opened the paper and said, "We find the defendant, Levi Cruz...NOT guilty."

Olivia looked at me and shrugged. I felt exactly the same, so I shrugged back.

There was no loud eruption from the gallery, only soft mumbles. Levi, who was standing between us, turned and looked back into the gallery and smiled.

I followed his gaze and saw a short, rather robust round woman with curly brown hair smiling back at him.

I'd never seen the woman before, but apparently she knew Levi and was elated with the not guilty verdict.

"Members of the jury," the judge said, "this court dismisses you and thanks you for a job well done," he slammed down his gavel, glaring at the district attorney, "this court is adjourned."

When I looked back at the mysterious woman, she saw me staring at her and quickly looked away. Then she jumped up and hurried out the door. She was wearing hospital scrubs, but not the typical matching light blue top and pants you see doctors wearing. Her top had a multi color paisley pattern, like a nurse would wear. She was overweight and sort of waddled side to side as she hurried out the door.

"Thank you Travis."

I turned and saw Levi holding out his hand. I shook it quickly and said, "You're welcome."

"So it's over?" Levi asked Olivia, "they can't come at me again, right?"

She shot me a curious glance. "No they can't, not for Savannah's murder. You're free to go."

Alexander ran up and hugged Levi, then me, then Olivia. "You guys were amazing. You were right dad, they are the best!"

I turned and stared at Levi. "You knew all along. You sent him to Austin, you told him to hitch hike there."

Levi shrugged his shoulders and looked down. "I don't know what to say. Yes, I asked him to see if he could find you. I was desperate. I needed a great lawyer, but I couldn't afford one," he looked me in the eyes, "you never would have helped me, but I figured you might do it for Alexander. And I was right, wasn't I?"

I wanted to slug him, but instead I just looked away and began packing my briefcase.

"The judge said that you can go home. I have the car out front," Alexander said, excited, "I'll drive you."

Levi smiled at him, shaking his head. "Thanks for the offer kid, but I'd rather drive myself if you don't mind. I just got out of jail, I don't want to get killed on my way home."

Obviously disappointed, Alexander handed him the keys, thanked us, and walked away.

"Again, thank you," Levi said to us smiling, then he turned, twirling the key chain in his fingers and walked out of the court house.

That was the first interaction I had ever witnessed between Levi and Alexander. It seemed very harsh and rude, controlling. Considering the celebratory moment, Levi had just been acquitted of murder, you would have thought that he would have just smiled and allowed Alexander to drive him home. But instead he acted like a jerk.

After I packed my leather satchel, I rushed out of the courtroom, trying to get another look at the mysterious woman, but she was gone.

Across the street, I saw Levi and Alexander get into a car and drive away; Levi behind the wheel and Alexander, looking very sad and upset in the passenger seat.

On the way to the nearest bar, I told Olivia about the mysterious woman. "Maybe it was someone you went to high school with," she said, "and that's why she looked so familiar."

I shook my head. "If that was it, why did she jump up and run away when she saw me looking at her? If it was someone I knew, she would've just waved."

"She had to remind you of someone or you wouldn't have run after her. Who did she look like?"

I pulled into the parking lot, turned off the ignition and turned to look at her. "No, she didn't remind me of anyone. I ran after her because I wanted to ask her how she knew Levi. Don't ask me why, because I'm not sure myself. Something inside me told me that I needed to know."

Olivia sighed, opened the car door and stepped out.

Inside the bar, we slowly sipped our drinks listening to the music playing on the jukebox.

"Since she was smiling at him," Olivia asked, "you think she could be a girlfriend? It makes sense he would have one. He told us he was planning on divorcing Savannah."

I gave her a subtle nod. "Not trying to sound sexist, but no way. Whether you like him or not, you have to admit that Levi is one of those tall dark and handsome guys. This woman was maybe five foot four and two fifty. Not exactly his type."

"I see your point, but knowing how manipulative Levi is, it's no telling what he could get a woman like that to do for him. All he'd have to do is flash his smile at her."

"Yeah, and I could see him doing something like that," I said twirling my glass on the table, "it's just one more thing about this case that will keep me up at night."

We sat there in that dark bar in silence for over an hour, sipping our scotch, wondering about the mysterious woman. At the same time, we were both trying to calm the churning feelings deep inside our guts and stop the voices yelling in our heads telling us that we might have just helped a guilty man...get away with murder.

13

BUSTER

Following Father Alvarez's advice, for almost a year, each morning and each night, Ariel got down on her knees and prayed to God to give her memory back, but so far he hadn't answered those prayers. She also prayed for patience and faith, because she was struggling to keep both.

Everyday when she would wake up, look into the mirror and see that stranger's face, she had to fight back her anger and she constantly questioned her faith.

Why would the loving God, the nuns constantly talked about, if he really existed, do this to her? What terrible thing had she done to deserve this?

She wished she had Father Alvarez's unquestioning faith, that what happened to her was all part of God's plan, but she didn't. She had grown tired of hearing that explanation, because it didn't help her.

In the last month, she had given up. She had stopped praying to get her memory back, instead, she had been praying about the man in her dreams. *Please God, tell me who he is. Tell me why it hurts so much when I see his face, and why I cry so hard when he touches me. Who is he God? And who is the young boy standing next to him, the one with the beautiful blue eyes? Please God, either stop the dreams, or at least reveal that much to me. That's all I want...that would be enough. Please God...I beg you.*

∽

When Ariel finished work at the clinic, she was exhausted. It had been an unusually busy day.

The town of Tecolutla was the center of a large rural agricultural area as well as a busy commercial fishing port. The farms grew and harvested corn, peppers, oranges, grapefruit, and vanilla. The fisherman harvested common bass, crabs, shrimp, oysters, shad, and sea bass. The farm hands and the fisherman were the usual visitors to the clinic, needing stitches from their cuts and scrapes. The municipality also had 40 km (24 miles) of beaches along the Gulf Of Mexico; the Santa María del Mar and Barra Boca de Lima. Those were the closest beaches to Mexico City and usually had warm waters with gentle motion, drawing tourists to lazily float and swim in the ocean, but on that day the currents washed a bloom of jelly fish near the shore and they had invaded the shallow waters. The clinic soon became crowded with sunbathing tourists in need of help to doctor their stings and in some cases large whelps.

She was too tired to eat, so she skipped dinner, told the nuns goodnight and slowly walked to her room. When she opened the door, instead of plopping down on her bed like she had planned, she screamed with delight. The small room, including her bed was covered with stacks of framed blank canvases. Leaning against the headboard was a wooden easel and on her dresser were three large tubes of oil paint; one red, one yellow and one blue. There was also a small bucket full of brushes.

"Those are the only colors she gave me. I'll see if I can find more if you want me to. Is everything else OK? Do you like it?"

She turned around to see Father Alvarez standing behind her, surrounded by four nuns and they were all smiling wide.

"Oh yes!" she shouted, "where did you find all of this?"

He grinned. "There is a small art gallery in Tecolutla that sells our local artists work. I'm a good friend of the owner, who is a great artist herself. Have you ever heard of Lecitia Perez?"

Ariel shook her head. "No, I don't think so."

"She's very famous here in Mexico. I showed her a few of your drawings and she immediately started loading my car and told me to give them to you."

She picked up a small flat pallet and motioned toward the tubes of paint. "These are the three primary colors and all I'll need. I will mix these on this pallet to get the other colors. How much did all of this cost?"

"Lecitia, told me that all she wanted from you was one painting a month to pay her back. She said she would give you 50% of anything you sell."

Ariel's turquoise eyes sparkled with her smile. "And I will give that money to you Father, to help pay for everything you have done for me, and for letting me stay here."

She walked toward the easel, placed a blank canvas on it, and selected a brush from the bucket. "I guess I better get to work then."

∽

I finished my drink and stood up. "What do we do now?" I asked Olivia.

She lifted her eyes. "Travis, I know you're angry and think you need to do something, but right now, today, there's nothing you can do. For your sake and for mine, I think we need to leave, go back home and try to put this behind us."

I nodded. "I know you're right, but I'm not sure I can do that. Honestly, I could give a shit about what happens to Levi from here on, but the same reason he's free right now is why I just can't simply walk away and forget this."

I took her hand and helped her up to her feet, "It's what you said in your closing. I'm just like those jury members. I know it's improbable, but in my heart, I'm not convinced that Savannah is dead. Olivia, I know this isn't what you want to hear, but until I know for sure, I can't just simply walk away and move on with my life."

She raised up on her tiptoes and kissed me gently on the lips. "I know you can't," she said softly, with tears in her eyes, "but I also know that even though I love you...I can't wait any longer...it's time to move on with my life."

∽

We didn't talk much on our drive back to Austin. We both knew there was really nothing more to say.

When I dropped her off at her house, she kissed me on the cheek and said, "I hope someday I will meet someone that loves me as much as you love Savannah. And I sincerely hope that you find her...or at the very least...find some kind of closure. I do love you Travis and I'm sure I always will. Promise me that you won't give up until you find the happiness that you deserve."

∽

There were many changes in my life over the next year. The breakup between Olivia and I had not destroyed our friendship, as you might have expected. Instead our friendship was closer and stronger than ever. Two months after we broke up, the Governor Of Texas visited our office and while he was there, he encouraged Olivia to run for a state court judgeship that was opening up in Austin. She jumped at the chance, ran a great campaign, and won by a landslide. She still dropped by the office on occasion, but spent most of her time overseeing her court every week, as the Honorable State Court Judge, Olivia Bachman. I've even had the honor to represent several cases before her.

We still talk every few days, usually at night when we're going over our case notes in bed. Her new boyfriend, Jeb Hamman, a successful local architect, didn't seem to have a problem with our long talks and often joined in on our conversations. Olivia seemed very happy and content

"So what about it?" Jeb yelled into the speakerphone, "I promise, she's a real looker."

I sighed. "Maybe some other time," I said, "I'm just too wrapped up in this case..."

"Yada yada yada," Olivia said, with a chuckle, "that's all BS and you know it. Travis, you need female companionship. It would do you good."

"She's got some major ta ta's and you could bounce a quarter off her ass," Jeb shouted, "are you sure you want to pass on this one?"

"That's the most sexist thing I've ever heard you say!" Olivia yelled.

"I didn't make it up," Jeb yelled back at her, "I was just quoting a few lines from my favorite movie, Top Gun."

I could almost feel Olivia's eyes rolling over the phone. "Break it up you two, " I said, "Jeb, she sounds nice, but I think I'll pass this time."

"Ok, your loss," he said, "but I'm telling you, she has legs all the way up to Alaska."

I could hear the smack Olivia gave him through the phone. "Don't hurt him," I said laughing, "he's just trying to help."

"One more crack like that and I'm going to have him arrested," she giggled, "seriously Travis, will you at least think about dating again?"

"I promise, as soon as I wrap this case, I'll start looking around for someone," I said lying.

∽

On the one year anniversary of Savannah's disappearance, more for Alexander's sake than mine, Kelly and BJ held a memorial service for her.

"You need to be there, for Alexander," Kelly told me, "Travis, it's been over a year. It's time for him to give up this obsession of finding his mother alive and get some kind of closure. I don't expect you to stop 'your' search, but don't you think it's time Alexander did? He's graduating high school in three months and you know how BJ and I feel about him. We both believe he needs this closure, so he can move on and have some kind of chance at a happy life."

I *did* know how they felt about Alexander. It was like he was their own son, because he had been living with them for almost a year.

When Levi was acquitted and got out of jail, it didn't take long for his creditors to seize all of his assets, including his car dealerships and his beach house. He somehow arranged to keep his 36 foot Sea Ray, so he moved onto the boat, but it only had one small cabin and there wasn't enough room for Alexander, so he moved in with BJ and Kelly.

Being around automobiles his entire life, Levi had become a good mechanic. To buy food, pay his boat note to the bank and his monthly slip fee, he earned money working on the commercial fishing boats in the marina. On his days off, he backed out the Sea Ray and searched the coast line looking for Savannah's body. Of course, he never told anyone that's what he was doing, but everybody knew. Without her body, or body part, he couldn't collect on her insurance policy for at least 5 more years. That was the common gossip being spread in the barbershop's, nail salons and coffee houses around Matagorda. And the more he searched, the more the entire town talked, becoming more and more convinced of his guilt. Because of that, he had become a pariah in Matagorda. Even Alexander had lost a little faith in him and wasn't sure he was innocent any longer.

When Levi walked into the church at Savannah's memorial, the chapel fell quiet and everyone turned and glared at him.

Alexander slid out of the pew and we all watched as he walked up to him, towering over him several inches. "Dad, I don't think you should be here."

Levi frowned. "Why not?"

Alexander sighed and looked down at him. "This is for mom, not you."

"I was her fucking husband. I should be here," he growled.

"Please Dad, this is a church, watch your language. I know you may want to be here for this...but there's a lot of people that think...well you know."

Levi moved close to Alexander's face, glaring up at him. "I don't give a shit what anyone else thinks. What do 'you' think?"

Alexander didn't move and stood his ground. "That's not gonna work," he leaned closer, nose to nose, staring directly into Levi's eyes, "I'm not that little kid anymore. You don't scare me and I'm not afraid of you. To tell you the truth Dad, I don't know what I think anymore. But I 'do know' that I don't want you here tonight and I'm asking you nicely to leave. Now!" He shouted.

Levi's expression fell and his shoulders dropped. He backed away from Alexander and looked around the room at all the angry faces staring at him. When he saw mine, he lifted his eyebrows, shrugged, turned around and stormed out.

Ignoring what had just taken place, the preacher began the service. When he finished, several of her friends stood up and told stories about the wonderful times they had spent with Savannah.

I think everyone there expected me to speak, but I didn't. I had thought about it, but couldn't find the words that might explain my true feelings about her, so I just sat there quietly, listening to the others.

Savannah's memorial was a beautiful thing to have experienced, especially for Alexander. Hearing so many loving stories about his mother from so many of her friends, helped him more than he realized.

Although, I didn't want to admit it to myself, Savannah's memorial had changed me as well.

∼

When I got back to Austin, I called the two private detective agency's I had hired to search for her and told them to stop. I even removed her framed picture off my office desk and put it in a drawer. At home, I took the larger one off the wall of my trailer and held it in my hands. Staring at her beautiful face I lost control and broke down and began to cry. Wiping the tears from my eyes, I forced myself to accept the truth. It was finally time to ignore my gut feelings that she was still alive and face the facts that Savannah...was gone, she was dead.

For some reason after that, living in my trailer began to bother me.

The walls seemed to start closing in on me and the cramped spaces seemed to grow more irritating every day.

My case load at the firm had continued to grow, as well as my bank account, so one Saturday morning, on a whim, I took a drive through a few of the upscaled subdivisions in Austin. After viewing a few of the homes with the 'open house' signs in front, I decided to get serious about it and stopped in a realtor's office. I spent the rest of the weekend looking at houses and finally decided on a beautiful 4 bedroom ranch with a great pool, a hot tub, outdoor fireplace and an amazing outdoor kitchen. I even had a large RV carport in the back yard to put my trailer.

The office threw me a huge housewarming party and their gifts helped me fill my new kitchen cabinets with new dishes, glasses and my drawers with new silverware.

When Olivia and Jeb showed up and saw the almost empty house, they immediately went into decorator mode, dragging me all over Austin from one furniture store to another. Jeb had an amazing flair for fabrics, colors and interior decorating. Watching him work left no doubt to why he was such a successful designer and architect. Before they left, two days later, I was several thousand dollars poorer, but my house looked amazing. It was perhaps a bit more of Olivia's taste than mine, but when I complained, she rolled her eyes at me, put her hands on her hips and said, "You spent most of your adult life living in a friggin' camp trailer, what the hell do you know about this?"

She had me there, so I kept my mouth shut from then on and just signed the credit cards. The only time I spoke up and made a decision on my own, was when they took me to a gallery to select some art for my walls.

I saw it the moment I walked in. It was hanging on the back wall and the second I saw it my heart skipped in my chest. I ran up to it and inspected the artist's signature. It was signed, "Ariel."

"That's beautiful," Olivia said, "but don't you think it's just a bit too big? Where would you hang it?"

The store owner walked up, smiling. "It's exquisite isn't it?"

"Where did you get this?" I said abruptly and a bit too loud

Startled, the store owner took a step back. "Ahh," she stammered, "I bought it from an Art dealer. Why? Is there something wrong with it?"

Realizing my rude aggressiveness, I held up my hands and tried to smile. "No, I'm sorry. I didn't mean to shout at you. It's just that this mural reminds me of someone else's art. What do you know about the artist?"

She relaxed and returned my smile. "Unfortunately, I don't know much. The dealer told me that he had discovered it in a small art gallery in Tecolutla."

"Mexico?" Jeb asked.

She nodded. "Yes, Veracruz Mexico. Apparently the artist is a young Mexican woman who is a local. I'm not sure, but I seem to remember something he said about the local Catholic Church. It's possible that she could be a nun. The shop owner told my dealer that there would be more coming, because she had commissioned one painting a month from the artist. This was her first work of that commission," She turned and looked at the mural, "it's remarkable, isn't it?"

"Yes, she's very talented," Olivia said. "will they all be large three piece murals like this?"

The gallery owner shrugged. "I have no idea, but I can't imagine her creating something this large in only a month."

"Travis, if you really like this artist," Olivia said, "we can come back and see more of her work later and get a smaller painting, something that will fit in your house."

I shook my head, staring at the mural. "No. I want this one. And I want to hang it in my bedroom."

Of course, Olivia and Jeb were right. Once the three sections were delivered and hung, It was obviously too large for the room and looked out of place, but I didn't care. When Olivia and Jeb saw it on the wall, they just smiled and shook their heads. They didn't understand why I had to buy it, and I never told them.

That night in my bed, staring at the three piece mural on my wall, I drifted back to my childhood. Instead of seeing a 12 year old artist's attempt at a landscape with out of proportion misshaped trees and leaves, I was looking at an almost photo realistic painting of grey steel train railroad tracks gently curving through golden, fallen leaves through beautiful trees in lush green woods.

It was the exact scene of the tracks that ran through the woods behind my house when I was a kid, the exact scene Savannah had painted on those three pieces of plywood and shoved through my window when she was 12.

The only difference between this mural and Savannah's, was the addition of a beautiful woman staring at the tracks with her blonde hair blowing in the wind. You couldn't see her face, just her back, but that was enough.

There was no real way to explain it, it made no sense, and is exactly why I didn't tell Olivia, but when I first saw the mural hanging on the wall in the gallery...when I looked at the curving tracks and the woods, and then at the beautiful woman...I felt warm and happy for the first time in years.

∼

A few months later, one more totally unexpected change took place in my life as a result of a legal case, when one of my clients died.

Although he had three children, he had named me as the executor of his will. So when he died, it was my job to oversee the distribution of his assets to his family. It was a very large estate. In fact, John Willy was one of the wealthiest men in Texas. He had made billions in the oil business and even more with his real estate investments. I had spent almost three weeks with him several years earlier finalizing his will, so dividing up the assets, his cash, stocks and real estate holdings, was relatively easy, because it had been preplanned well.

However, I discovered that we had overlooked something important when I drove to his lakeside ranch, overlooking Lake Travis, to read the will to his children. When I finished they all were smiling and seemed satisfied.

"What about Buster?" his daughter asked, "what are we supposed to with him?"

"Who is Buster?" I asked.

"It's his dog," she said, "we all begged him not to keep him, but you couldn't tell dad anything."

I held up the will. "He didn't make any arrangements for a dog. How long has he had him?"

"He picked him up a year or so ago." His son said, "He's really ugly, some mutt he found somewhere. We've all talked about it and none of us want him. I guess we could get someone to take him to the pound."

"Where is he now?" I asked, but none of his children seemed to know, or care.

On my way out, I asked the housekeeper if she knew where Buster was. "Yes sir, I do. He's in Mr. John's office."

"What's he doing in there?" I asked.

Her expression dropped. "He's so sad. He's in there waiting from Mr. John to come back."

When she opened the door, I saw him. He was standing in a dark corner with his head hanging down, pressed against the wall. When I walked in the room, he didn't move, but started trembling.

I walked up slowly and sat down on the floor next to him. "You must be Buster," I said, softly, "what are you doing in here with your head stuck in the corner?"

He cowed away, pushing his head further into the wall. I reached out slowly and petted his head. "You look so sad," I whispered, "I bet you're wondering where John has gone. Are you thinking that he abandoned you?"

He slowly raised his head and looked at me. "That's better," I said smiling at him.

In my entire life, I had only made one snap decision, the day I left Savannah and that turned out to be a disaster, but without even thinking about it, I picked Buster up into my arms, walked to my car and drove away.

I slowly drove the few miles down the gravel road to the family cemetery and stopped. I picked up Buster and carried him to John's grave. The large, marble stone marker was surrounded with wilting flowers, overlooking the fresh turned earth that outlined where John's casket was buried.

When I put Buster down, he looked up at me. "This is John's grave," I said.

I had no idea if it would work, but I had heard stories and seen pictures of dogs laying on their masters graves. No one had any real explanations of how the dogs knew it was their graves, but somehow they did.

Hoping he might understand me, I looked down at him and said, "He didn't abandon you, he died."

Buster slowly walked toward the grave, sniffing the dirt and the wilted flowers. In the center of the fresh turned grave, he made a few circles and laid down with his head against the dirt.

After a few minutes, he absolutely broke my heart, when he let out a long, sad whine.

I sat down next to him and gently petted his head. "It's going to be alright".

He looked at me, laid his head on my leg and whined again. "I'm so sorry buddy. I know you're hurting and I know exactly how you feel. I lost someone too. Maybe we can help each other get over our heartbreak."

He never once raised his head off the seat to see where we were going on the drive back to my house. When we got there and I opened his door, he slowly crawled out of the seat, jumped down to the driveway and followed me into the house.

I dug out a bowl, filled it with water and sat it down next to him. He was apparently thirsty, because he drank it all, so I filled it again. After he drank half of that bowl, I took him outside and showed him around. It didn't take him long to figure out what I wanted him to do, so he started sniffing the trees and eventually took care of business.

Back in the house, I cooked up some hamburger meat and put it in a bowl, but he just looked at it, walked away and plopped down in the corner of the kitchen looking up at me with those sad eyes. Not knowing what else to do for him, I opened my leather satchel, took out a brief I was working on and walked outside to my patio, leaving him there alone in the kitchen. About twenty minutes later, I felt something nudge my leg. I looked down to see Buster staring up at me.

I guess he 'was' a little ugly. He had one ear that stood straight up and one that flopped down to the side. His coat was a light dirty brown with random black spots and patches. He had one black foot and a black tail. His face was a blend of light brown with a dark, almost black chin, and he had the biggest, saddest brown eyes I'd ever seen on a dog.

I reached down, picked him up and set him in my lap. He seemed happy there in my lap and soon fell asleep, so I went back to work as he snoozed.

~

It didn't take Buster long to get settled in my new house and steal not only my heart, but everyone else's at the Bachman Turner Lee and Associates law firm.

James Bachman, the founder and senior partner of the firm, frowned and gave me a stern look when I took Buster to work with me that first day.

"What kind of dog is that?" he asked.

"I'm not sure. I'm guessing mostly terrier. He's a mix, just a mutt."

Staring disapprovingly down at Buster, he asked, "Where did you find him?"

"He was John Willy's dog," I said smiling down at Buster, "his children didn't want him, so I took him home with me."

Buster walked up to James, sniffed his leg, sat on his butt and looked up at him with those sad eyes. "What's wrong with him?" James asked, "why is he looking at me like that?"

"I don't know, but I think he likes you."

"Why does he look so sad?"

"I'm sure he's missing his master. Maybe you remind him of John, but I can tell he likes you a lot by the way he's looking at you."

"I've never been a dog person," James said, "I hope you are not planning on bringing him here every day. When you do, keep him upstairs in your area. This is a law office, not a kennel."

I tried to keep Buster upstairs with me most of the day, but he slipped down the stairs when I wasn't looking and found James's office. I am not exactly sure what happened after that, but it didn't take James long to change his mind about him.

The next day he walked in with four large dog bowls and two fluffy dog beds. He handed me two of the bowls and one of the beds.

"Thanks, Buster will love this," I said grinning at him, "but what are the other bowls and bed for?"

He raised his head and frowned. "I thought since he keeps insisting on disturbing me in my office, he could at least be comfortable and have something to eat and drink while he was there."

"I thought you weren't a dog person."

"I'm not," he said gruffly, turning and walking away with the bowls and the fluffy dog bed under his arm.

After that, when I couldn't find Buster, I always knew where to look. He was usually laying in James's lap or in his new fluffy bed, next to his desk, sound asleep.

I took him out for a short walk every few hours, so he could do his business. When I was in court, Judy my legal secretary took care of him. The day I realized that Buster had finally become an official member of the firm was when I had forgotten the time and heard a noise outside my window. When I looked out, I saw James Bachman, one of the most successful and respected attorney's in the country, walking back from the park across the street with Buster on a leash. He was smiling wide. From three floors up, I could hear him praising him. "You know Buster, I've never been a dog person, but you are very intelligent, not some typical dog. I think you make a fine addition to this firm."

That year, Buster made his first appearance in the official Firm Christmas card.

"Merry Christmas from the
BUSTER, Bachman, Turner, Lee & Associates law firm."

14

SILVERADO

Although the two private detective agencies I had hired to track down Savannah's whereabouts had been unsuccessful finding anything about her disappearance, one of them had located the mysterious woman I had seen at Levi's trial.

The information the agency had dug up, verified my suspicions of the part she had played in Levi's scheme. Her name was Helen Craft. She was five foot one, 215 pounds and had worked at the Corpus Christi Medical Center as a nurse for the past seven years. Although it wasn't her job to input the hospital's procedures into the patients medical files, I assumed she knew some one who could, or knew how to access them herself. It would have been easy for her to delete Savannah's psychiatric stays from her medical records. And since the removed records had already been paid by the insurance company, there would be no reason for anyone to pull them up and check on them again.

Unfortunately, the detective agency hadn't discovered any connection between Helen and Levi, but I was sure there had to be one somewhere.

I leaned back in my chair, put my feet on my desk and let myself wonder what that connection might be. I also wondered about what might have happened if the D.A. had discovered Helen before the trial.

Then I smiled, remembering what my drill sergeant used to yell in our faces when one of us jar heads would say, "If. If I had just done this or if I had done that."

It didn't matter what it was, he always instantly responded, "If a frog had wings he wouldn't bump his ass every time he hopped, but he doesn't, does he? There's no *IF's* in the Marines! That can get you killed! Now go back and do it right this time."

I guess my old drill Sergeant was right, because that *IF* the D.A. and everyone else including Olivia and I had missed, helped Levi Cruz get acquitted and probably got Helen Craft killed.

Three weeks after Levi was released from jail, they found her body. She had washed up on the beach, just north of Padre Island. The autopsy showed that she had drowned. The bastard had done it again.

Although there was nothing legally anyone could do to Levi now, I took the file to Jerry Johnston, the Bay City D.A. anyway.

He wasn't exactly thrilled to see me. "Mr. Lee," he said with a frown, "I'd hoped I'd seen the last of you. What can I do for you?"

I spent the next thirty minutes showing him Helen Craft's file, filling him in on what I had discovered and telling him about my suspicions.

"What makes you think this was Mr. Cruz? It doesn't make any sense. This Helen woman could have come to me and made a full confession and I couldn't have done anything to Mr Cruz. He's protected by double jeopardy. Even if she was involved like you say, he had no reason to kill her."

"You're right," I said, "but I've been thinking about that on my drive here. If she agreed to do this, I don't think she did it just to be with Levi. I don't care how handsome he is, she did it for the money."

He shook his head. "You're probably right."

"But that was the part of their plan that blew up in their faces and I'm sure neither one of them ever anticipated that could happen.

I am now convinced that Levi knew about the insurance policy and threw Savannah overboard. He and Helen both expected her to drown and her body to wash ashore, but something prevented that from happening. Savannah didn't wash up on the beach like they planned. And no body, means no money...for years. And I bet Helen wasn't very happy about that."

"After going through all she'd been through, risking her job getting caught, you know she wasn't." He said with a chuckle.

"You know...and *I* know that there's no way around double Jeopardy," I said, "but what if Levi and Helen *didn't* know. Levi is flat broke and has no money to keep her quiet."

I looked him in the eyes. "Jerry, think about it. If Levi really did all of this just for the money...what do you think he would do to Helen, if she was blackmailing him, threatening to go to the police?"

He nodded. "I've been doing this job for years and it still amazes me what people will do for money," he shook his head, "It's the root of all evil, right?"

"You want to hear the worst part of my suspicions? I think Levi threw Helen overboard in the exact place he threw Savannah. He did it so he could test to see where she washed up. I'd be willing to bet he's searching that Padre Island coastline for Savannah right now."

The D.A. picked up the photographs and studied them again. "This poor girl had no idea of the evil she was playing with. I may not be able to get this bastard for what he did to Savannah, but maybe, just maybe...I can get him for what he did to Helen."

We both stood and shook hands. "Travis, thank you for bringing me this file, I'll look into it," he said, "but promise me, if I can connect Mr. Cruz to Helen, you and Olivia won't be his attorneys. That Olivia is one smart, tough cookie and she had my number. I don't ever want to go up against her again."

∼

"I hope you haven't blown all your money on that fancy new house." Kelly boomed in my ear, "because I may need a little of what you've got left."

I hadn't talked to him in a few months, since my house warming party. "Hey, Kelly, what's up?" I shouted, "did BJ finally kick your ass out and take all your money? Do you need a loan or something?"

"Not yet," I heard BJ's voice and her laugh over the speaker phone, "he doesn't have enough money, but as soon as he does, he's out of here!"

"You let me know when you do that. I'm looking for a rich girlfriend," I said. "So, I've got both of you on the phone. This must be important. What's going on?"

"It's about Alexander," Kelly said, "and it *is* important. We've got a problem and we're not exactly sure what to do about it."

"A problem with Alexander? Really?" I was shocked, "I can't imagine, he's such a good kid. What'd he do?"

"What did he do?" Kelly said, "you're not gonna believe it. He came home yesterday and handed us two letters to read."

I sighed. "From his school? Oh no, what did they say?"

"There was only one from his school, and it said that he was graduating salutatorian," BJ was almost in tears, "second in his class."

"That's fantastic!" I shouted, "what did the other letter say?"

"It was from the University Of Texas," Kelly said, "he's been accepted."

"That's amazing, good for him!" I yelled, "I thought you were calling to tell me some bad news." There was a long pause on the phone. "You guys still there?"

"Yes, we're here," Kelly said, "I'm just trying to figure out how to say this."

"Just spit it out."

"Travis, you know how much we love Alexander and we're thrilled with everything he's accomplished, but..."

"But what?"

"We have three kids of our own that we have to get through college. The facts are...Levi is broke and doesn't have any money. We *can* afford to pay for Alexander's tuition, but if we do that, we have to take that money out of our own kids college savings fund. That's why we're calling. What do you think we should do?"

"Any chance of scholastic scholarships?" I asked, "with his grades he should easily qualify."

"Yeah, we've applied for a few and we're sure he'll get one or two, but the tuition at U T Austin is about 25,000 a semester."

"It wouldn't be right for you guys to take money out of your children's college fund. Don't worry about it, I'll pay for it," I said.

"Travis, we're not asking for you to pay for it all," BJ said, "but maybe you could kick in a little to help."

"Guys, listen to me. Wherever Savannah is, dead or alive, I know she would be overwhelmed with everything you have done for Alexander. You are both amazing people and have been great friends to her. Please let me do this. I need to do this...for Alexander, but even more for Savannah."

∼

The night Alexander graduated from high school, even though he gave his father a hand written note with the invitation asking him to come to the ceremony, Levi didn't show up.

It had been over two months since Alexander had seen or talked to his father. He had tried, but Levi hadn't returned any of his calls and wasn't there when he had dropped by the marina to see him.

His marina slip neighbors told him that Levi had been working a lot on the fishing boats, but they weren't ever sure which one he was working on the days he dropped by to see him. Alexander had taped the graduation invitation to the steering wheel, so he knew he had gotten it, but he didn't come.

It was obvious that Alexander was disappointed, but torn at the same time; wanting his father to be there to see him in his cap and gown, with his honor ribbons hanging around his neck...watching him walk across the stage to receive his diploma, but at the same time, glad he wasn't there causing a scene, reacting to all of the glaring, hateful eyes in the crowd.

∼

We decided to split Alexander's graduation present between us, with BJ and Kelly picking up half and me paying the rest.

"Are you serious?" Alexander protested, "you want me to wear a blindfold like a little kid at a birthday party?"

"Only if you want your graduation present," I said, "but if you don't want it, that's OK with us. We can always take it back."

He instantly tied the scarf around his head and adjusted it to cover his eyes.

We led him outside to the driveway. "Are you ready?"

"Yes!" He was breathing hard with anticipation.

"OK, take off the blindfold." BJ said excitedly.

When he saw his present, he actually leaped into the air screaming, "Is this for me? This is mine? Really?"

He ran to BJ and lifted her up off the ground, swinging her around in a circle. "Thank you! I can't believe you did this for me!"

"Hey!" Kelly yelled, "what about us? We don't get no love?"

He put BJ down and threw his arms around Kelly and me. "You guys are awesome!" His eyes were glistening from his tears, "Thank you Uncle Kelly and Uncle Travis. I don't know what to say?"

I handed him the keys. "How about, would you like to go for a ride?'"

He ran to the bright red vehicle and carefully removed the giant white bow. "How did you know?" He yelled back to us, "This is what I've dreamed of, exactly what I've always wanted."

That part wasn't very hard to figure out, because every time he saw one drive by, he would always point and say, "Some day when I get out of college and get a good job, that's what I'm going to buy!"

You might be thinking that we had to take turns to fit into his fancy two seater sports car, but you'd be wrong, because it wasn't a sports car. It wasn't a car at all, it was a pickup. A bright red, brand new Chevy Silverado 1500.

Of course, it didn't make any sense for an 18-year-old boy going to college to have a pick up truck, but that's what he wanted and he was over the moon ecstatic about it.

So he could get acquainted living in Austin a few months before he started his first semester, the next day, we loaded Alexander's new truck with all of his belongings and with him driving his new truck, following me, we headed to Austin. Before we headed out of Matagorda, I turned and drove to the marina.

"I thought you might want to say goodbye to your father," I said, "you won't get a chance to see him again for a while."

He nodded. "He's probably not here, but I'll go check."

A few minutes later, I saw them walking up the ramp from the marina together.

"Isn't it cool?" He yelled, pointing at his new truck.

"It sure is," Levi said, walking around it, "but why the hell would you want a pickup truck? You're gonna look like some redneck driving around the campus!"

Alexander shrugged his shoulders. His smile was gone. "I don't know, but I've always wanted a pickup, a red Silverado."

"He's going to the University Of Texas," I said trying to lighten the mood, "I'd be willing to bet he won't be the only cool guy driving a pickup there."

"Yeah, I guess so," Levi said.

Then he turned and made eye contact with me. "I'm going to pay you and Kelly back someday for all of this. I really appreciate what you're doing for my boy."

I nodded. "No need for that. He's a great kid and deserves it."

I noticed Levi looking past me, frowning. I turned to see a dark colored car sitting in the parking lot with two men in black suits sitting inside watching us.

"You know anything about that?" Levi asked, "they have been following me for a couple of weeks."

"Are you sure they're following you?"

"Oh yeah," he said, with a smirk, "they show up every where I go. Fucking cops!"

I shrugged. "It can't be about Savannah's case. You were acquitted of all of that. They can't do anything to you. Just ignore them."

He wrinkled his forehead. "Why can't they?"

"It's something called 'Double Jeopardy.' You can't be charged or arrested for the same crime twice."

"Really?" He seemed shocked.

"Yes, really," I said, "unless you've committed another crime, you don't have anything to worry about. They can't touch you."

I studied him carefully when I said that. His eyes didn't break contact with mine, but he started nervously shifting his feet and cracking his knuckles.

I wanted to laugh, or at least smile, to let him know that I knew what he'd done to Helen Craft, but I didn't. Instead, I just said goodbye and drove away with Alexander following behind me in his truck, leaving Levi standing in the parking lot with his mind spinning about what he'd done to Helen Craft under the watchful eyes of the two homicide detectives.

~

I was hoping that with Alexander living there with us, Buster would cheer up a little, but he didn't. He apparently liked Alexander, because he followed him around the house a lot and let him pet him, but he remained sad and quiet, lying in his bed most of the time.

"Does he ever bark or play?" Alexander asked.

"He'll retrieve a ball if you throw it, and he seems to like his chew toys, but he never does much of anything, but lay in his bed. He's still grieving I guess."

I decided to buy a ski boat, so we could all have some fun that summer on Lake Travis. On one of our weekend ski trips, I noticed a realtor sign about a lake front lot that was for sale.

The lot was perched a couple hundred feet in the air over-looking Lake Travis. It had never been cleared and developed, so it was overgrown with thick bushes and trees. Using a machete, the realtor hacked a path from the road to the edge of the property, so we could see the view.

"Wow!" Alexander yelled, "This is awesome!"

It was much more than awesome, it was breathtaking. From the edge of that property, I could see hundreds of sailboats and speedboats floating and racing along the sparkling blue-green waters of Lake Travis. It curved through the winding canyons below the lush green Texas hill country for miles. We followed the realtor back to his office and I bought the lot.

Two weeks later, we hooked my Airstream up to Alexander's truck and pulled it to the property. I had hired a local company to clear an 8 foot wide path from the road to the edge and cover it with iron oar. I had also had an electrician run power to the site and a plumber to run the water line. It was a bit difficult to maneuver, backing the trailer in, but we eventually got it in place and set up near the edge overlooking the lake.

The following day, the septic tank company showed up and a few hours later, we were all hooked up.

It was late July and Alexander only had a few more weeks left before he started college. After filling the refrigerator in the trailer with food, I gave him some cash, a credit card and the keys to the trailer. I also gave him the keys to the ski boat that was tied up in a slip, in the Lakeway Inn Marina a few miles a way. When I knew he was all set up, I left him there alone to enjoy the rest of the summer and headed back to Austin.

He was a good kid, calling me almost every night letting me know that he was OK and having a blast.

"Are you making some new friends?" I asked him.

"Yes sir, lots of em'," he said, "there's always a bunch of U. T. students waterskiing on the lake."

"Is the boat running OK?"

"Yeah, it's great. Uncle Travis, have you ever heard of Hippie Hollow?"

∼

In the 1960's, before Woodstock, Hippies began to gather at a remote, rocky area of the shoreline along Lake Travis called McGregor County Park. Due to the remoteness and the cultural changes sweeping across America in those times, the Hippies began to take off their clothes to sunbathe nude on the large limestone boulders and swim naked in the lake. It didn't take long for the word to spread and soon this area became known as Hippie Hollow, and the shoreline became crowded with boats full of curious onlookers idling by slowly to get a good look.

At first, the adjacent land owners complained, but the local law enforcement decided they had more important things to do than arrest a bunch of naked Hippies, so they just ignored the infractions.

In 1983, the land was leased to Travis County and after some major cleanup and renovations and the addition of new signage at the entrance advising visitors that nude swimming and sunbathing may be encountered, it was officially reopened in 1985 as Hippie Hollow Park. Today, it remains clothing optional and is one of the most popular boating destinations on Lake Travis.

∼

"Hippie what?" I asked, "did you say Hippie Hollow? No, I've never heard of it."

Of course I had, but I wanted to hear what he had to say. "What about it?"

"Ahh, never mind, it's nothing," He stammered, "It's just a cool place to go on the lake. Are you still planning on coming here next weekend?"

"Yes I am. I'm bringing Buster with me, and I think Olivia and her boyfriend Jeb are coming too. They're staying at a resort close to us for the weekend. Make sure you clean up your mess before we get there."

"You don't have to worry about that Uncle Travis," He said, "I keep it cleaned up all the time."

I laughed. "Yeah I bet," I said skeptically, "but we'll see soon enough."

I paused for a beat, then said, "Alexander, one more thing; when you anchor close to the shore at Hippie Hollow, be careful not to get the anchor stuck. There's some large boulders on the lake bottom that can trap your line. And make sure you put some sun block on your tallywacker. I hear that can be a painful sunburn."

He was trying to tell me that he didn't get naked when I hung up the phone laughing.

That Friday morning I packed a bag, loaded Buster's toys and his food in the car and headed to Lake Travis. The night before, Olivia, Jeb and I had planned our trip. We decided to meet up along the way at the County Line restaurant. They're famous for their BBQ, so I bought a small rack of ribs for Buster. When he got his first taste, he perked up and almost wagged his tail...almost.

The night before I had apologized to Olivia and Jeb ahead of time for what we might encounter once we got to the trailer. I had assumed that leaving an 18 year old boy, alone for six weeks to party with his new friends, the trailer would be a complete wreck, but two hours later when I pulled into the path leading up to the trailer, I was stunned.

Instead of empty beer cans and trash laying all around the front steps, there wasn't a speck of anything in sight. Actually, the flimsy front steps had been replaced with a large wooden 10 x15 foot deck, with solid 2 x 12 steps with two hand rails leading up to it.

When Alexander heard us pull up, he opened the door, stepped out onto the deck and waved.

"Where'd this come from?" I said, pointing at the new deck.

"I built it," he said smiling, "pretty cool, huh?"

"It's way cool!" I yelled, "you did a great job on it."

"Where'd you get the lumber and nails?" Jeb asked, inspecting the deck.

"There was a lumber yard in Round Rock that was advertising for help. I took the job and they gave me the lumber and nails I needed in return."

I frowned at him. "So, instead of playing and waterskiing with your new friends, you've been working all this time?" I asked.

He shook his head and grinned. "It was only a few hours a day. I liked the work and the owner was cool. He said I could work there next summer on my break if I want to."

Alexander had also cleared back the woods around the trailer, planted some flowers and had built a circular fire pit out of cinderblocks. Leading from the fire pit to the edge of the cliff overlooking the water was a line of concrete block pavers.

He saw me staring at the pavers. "That leads to the rope ladder." He said.

I followed the path to the edge and looked over to see a large 2 inch thick rope with a big knot tied every few feet, leading down to the water.

"That's not a ladder," I said smiling, "that's a two hundred foot rope with knots in it."

"It works great!" he said, holding it between his legs and scaling down the cliff with ease.

When he made it to the bottom, he looked up at me and yelled, "Come on Uncle Travis, try it, it's easy."

I took the rope and yanked it hard to make sure it would hold my weight. Then I backed over the cliff and slowly began making my way down the rope. The second I had touched the rope, I flashed back to my Marine Corps boot camp training. During those very difficult 12 weeks, I had repelled down much higher cliffs than this one, hundreds of times. For two of those weeks, every morning and every afternoon I repelled out of a moving helicopter, but that was 20 years and 15 pounds ago.

"I told you it was easy," Alexander said, grinning.

I nodded. "Going down is always easy," I said, with a chuckle, "it's climbing back up is what I'm worrying about."

Alexander walked to the shoreline and pointed. "See the floating Clorox bleach bottle out there."

"Yeah, what's that for?"

"It's a mooring buoy," he said, "it's about 20 feet deep there. I swam down and hooked a chain around a huge bolder. I tie the boat to it. It works great!"

Like a monkey up a tree, Alexander flew back up the rope and looked down at me. "Come on Uncle Travis. You can do it, it's easy," he said smiling.

I laughed, grabbed the rope and began to climb. I made it, but on the way up, I felt every day of those past 20 years and every single ounce of those 15 pounds.

When I caught my breath, I turned and waved for Olivia and Jeb to come look at the view.

"Jeb," I said in between my gasps, "You think you could design something I could build here, so old guys like me can make it up and down to the water without needing oxygen?"

He looked over the cliff and studied it for a moment. "Are steps allowed?" He asked.

"I think so," I said.

I'll sketch out something tomorrow," he said already designing in his head, "It needs to be redwood, so they'll last."

That night we drove over to the other side of Lake Travis to the Oasis Restaurant and Bar to watch the sunset, eat dinner together, and listen to Alexander excitedly fill us in on everything he'd been doing for the last 6 weeks.

"Did you meet any cute girls?" Olivia asked him.

His face flushed bright red. "Yeah," he said shyly, "I met a few."

"Anybody special?" I asked.

He shook his head. "No, not really."

"Have you heard from your father?" Olivia asked.

Alexander frowned and lowered his head. "Only once, but it wasn't a good phone call."

"I'm sorry about that, but you need to understand that your dad is going through a lot these days. You need to cut him a little slack. He called, so he was thinking about you." I said trying to comfort him.

Alexander pushed his plate away and leaned back in his chair. "He wasn't thinking about me, he was thinking about my truck."

I glanced over the table at Olivia. "Your truck?" she said, tilting her head curiously.

"Yeah, he wanted me to let him use it. He said that he needed it for his boat repair business and that I could get a bicycle to get around campus."

Trying not to show my anger I calmly asked, "What did you tell him?"

"I told him that I would have to clear it with you and Uncle Kelly first, since you two bought it for me."

Jeb started laughing. "Now that's some quick thinking! I bet he didn't like that answer, did he?"

Alexander nodded. "No sir. He started yelling and cussing, so I hung up in his ear. That's the last time I've heard from him."

He leaned forward in his chair and looked over at me, "Uncle Travis, do you think he really needs my truck? I don't need it, I could walk to my classes..."

I raised my hand to stop him. "Alexander, we bought that truck for you, not Levi."

"I know, but he said..."

"I don't care what he said. He's not getting that truck!"

I couldn't hold back my anger any longer. I slid my chair back and turned to face him. "Do you remember what I said about your father when you walked in to my office two years ago? I told you that I had never liked your father. Do you remember that?"

He nodded. "Yeah, I remember."

"What I didn't tell you was why. You were only 16 years old and too young to understand, but you are 18 now and very mature, so I think you're old enough to hear this."

I took a sip of my water and looked over at Olivia, who was giving me a subtle nod of approval. Looking Alexander in the eyes I said, "I never liked your father, because he was, and still is a jerk. He is a master at manipulation and he learned that as a child."

I took another sip of water pausing, trying to come up with the right words. "Through all of this, the trial and everything else, I've tried my best to keep my true feelings about your father away from you. The last thing I want to do is influence you in anyway when it comes to your feelings for Levi. He *is* your father and he always will be. That's why I've bit my lip and forced myself to keep quiet, but this is the last straw, he's crossed the line and I can't sit by quietly and watch him do this to you any longer."

Alexander looked down at the table. "I think I already know. You don't have to say it."

"No you're wrong. It's time you know the truth. I just pray you won't hold it against me when you hear it."

He lifted his head and smiled. "Uncle Travis, there's nothing you could say that would change what I feel about you. I know you think I've only known you for two years, but that's not true. I've known you and who you are my whole life. You are everything mother told me you were. I hope you know that I love you. I wish you were my father, because that's the way I think of you...like a father."

He sat upright in his chair and slid it close to the table. "I've known for a long time that dad was guilty. He killed mom. But what I can't figure out is...how did he do it...and how can I make him pay for it?"

15

SEPARATION ANXIETY

It was almost midnight when Levi stopped at the last buoy, untied the Kayak that had been trailing behind his boat and lifted it over the side. With it secured to the deck, he cranked the engine and slowly idled into the entrance of the marina. He was exhausted, his arms were burning from paddling the Kayak and he was frustrated. It had been another unsuccessful search for Savannah's body.

∽

When he had gotten out of jail, he had searched the beach shoreline all the way from Matagorda to Harlingen, but after a few months he had given up on that. He knew that if any part of her was going to wash up on the beach, it would have already washed up by then. Now he was searching the miles and miles of marsh trails, only accessible by kayak. It was like searching for a black rose at midnight, but he couldn't give up, not now. All he needed was a finger, a foot, a lock of her hair, anything to prove she was dead and he would be sitting on a tropical island with two million in the bank.

He was especially drawn to search when the wave patterns and weather was the same as it was the night he hit Savannah on the head with the boat hook and watched her fall over the side, with her blood streaming in the water as she sunk beneath the surface.

"Fucking sharks!" He yelled out loud, every time he gave up his search and headed back to the marina. Her body being consumed by sharks was the only explanation he could imagine.

Why did I hit her so hard? He thought to himself. *It was the blood that drew the sharks. Why didn't I just slug her and push her over the side? Why couldn't she have just floated to shore like that fat bitch?*

When he had hit Helen he had used his fist, not the boat hook, and she didn't bleed. She just screamed, fell over the side and floated, like a cork, face down on top of the water all the way to Padre Island. He floated a few hundred yards behind her body for several hours to see where the current would take her. At first he didn't understand why she was floating on *top of* the water and why Savannah had quickly sunk and disappeared *under* the water.

When he figured it out, he cranked the engine and headed back to the marina, because he knew he was wasting his time. They wouldn't wash up at the same place, because Savannah was thin with very little body fat, but Helen had several layers of it and would float like a beach ball miles down the coast.

There was only one other possibility that kept running through his head. What if somehow, Savannah had survived, maybe swam to shore, or was picked up by a fisherman. If that was it, then where was she? He knew that was the most remote possibility of all, but it was one more reason he kept searching.

∽

When he pulled into his slip he saw two men dressed in dark suits standing on the dock waiting for him. He didn't recognized them. They were not the same two men who had been following him.

They stood there quietly watching him secure the boat to the slip. When he finished, one of them said, "Are you Levi Cruz?"

He looked at the man and rolled his eyes. "You know damn well who I am. What do you want?"

"May we come aboard, we would like to talk to you."

"No you may not come aboard," Levi snapped, "you can talk to me from there. What do you want?"

The man turned on a flashlight and lit up the badge he was holding in his hand. "I am Detective Jenkins and this is Detective Anderson. We are homicide detectives working out of the 14th precinct in Corpus Christi."

"You're a little out of your jurisdiction aren't you?" Levi smirked.

"No sir, we are working in coordination with the Bay City Police Department." He held up a photo of Helen Craft and shined the flashlight on it. "We are investigating the death of this woman, her name is Helen Craft. Do you know her?"

Levi glanced at the picture and shook his head. "Sorry, but I've never seen her before. She's not my type. I'm not into chubby chasing. I like them tall, thin and blonde."

The detective smiled. "Yeah, that's what we hear. Kinda like you're missing ex-wife. Did you have any luck finding her body out there tonight?"

Levi glared back at the detective. "It's late and I'm really tired, is there anything else I can help you with?"

"Yes," The detective said, "could you tell us where you were the night of May 22nd? Your neighbors seem to remember that you were with a rather large woman that night, and that you took your boat out. Can you tell us what you were doing out there?"

Levi smiled, stepped aboard his boat and opened the companionway door. "Officer, I told you I'm not into fat women. My neighbors must be mistaken. I *am* into astrology. So if I did take my boat out that night, I'm pretty sure that's what I was doing...watching the stars. Have a nice night." He slipped down the companionway stairs, closing the hatch behind him.

Levi sat on the edge of his bed. He was breathing hard, sweating with his heart racing in his chest. He knew the detectives were bluffing about his neighbors seeing Helen on his boat, because she had never been there, he had picked her up in a marina in Corpus. That wasn't what was bothering him. The problem was that they somehow knew about her and were trying to connect her death to him. How could two homicide detectives from Corpus Christi possibly know anything about him?

He thought for a moment trying to remember what they had said. They were working in coordination with the Bay City Police Department. Why would they need to do that? He wondered. Was the Bay City Police Department still working his case...even after he had been acquitted? Could they do that?

∼

When my phone rang, I fumbled around the nightstand to turn on the light and find my watch. It was 3 am.

I lifted the receiver and listened as Levi ranted into my ear. "No they can't do that," I said with a gravelly voice, " I don't know why but it sounds like they're trying to harass you. Just ignore them."

I held the phone to my ear for a long time listening. "Levi, I don't want to hear any of that. I am no longer your attorney. There's nothing I can do for you. If you think the police are harassing you, find another attorney and sue them, but please stop calling me in the middle of the night. Do you understand?" He slammed the phone down in my ear.

I reached for the light switch to turn it off, but noticed something out of the corner of my eye, it was Buster. He was standing up on his hind legs looking over the rail at me in the bedroom doorway.

The idea of a dog sleeping in my bed had never appealed to me. To prevent this, I installed a small metal gate in the bedroom doorway. Because of this gate, Buster had never actually been inside my bedroom.

I got out of bed, walked over to Buster at the gate and petted his head. "What's wrong buddy did the phone call wake you up?" I picked him up and carried him back to his bed in the kitchen and laid him down. "Go back to sleep. I'll see you in the morning."

Unfortunately Levi's phone call had woken me up as well, so I walked to the refrigerator, found some milk and cold fried chicken. After I ate the chicken and drank the milk, I walked back to the bedroom and tried my best to go back to sleep. For almost an hour I laid there with my eyes closed trying to force the sleep to come, but it never did.

I gave up, opened my eyes and stared up at the ceiling, frustrated. The room was dark, but gradually my eyes began to focus and I could see outlines of shapes as I looked around the room. When I looked in the doorway, I saw something. Squinting my eyes, I eventually realized what it was. It was Buster. He was standing up on his hind legs looking over the rail at me again.

I didn't move or say anything to him. I just laid there quietly, watching Buster, watching me. Occasionally he would go back down on his all fours, but then stand up again and look over the rail.

Eventually, I drifted off. When I woke up the next morning, he was in his bed, sound asleep.

The next night I left a light on in the hallway, so when I opened my eyes in the middle of the night, I could easily see if Buster was back at the rail watching me. And every time I looked, he was there, looking over the rail watching me sleep.

Over the next week, when I would roll over, I would peak at my doorway and he was always there. Apparently, Buster didn't actually sleep at night, only during the day. It was very weird.

About a week later, I was working especially late in my office, prepping a new case when James Bachman walked in my door carrying Buster in his arms.

"I'm leaving now and thought I would bring him up here to you," he said, "he seems especially tired today. He's been sleeping all afternoon."

"James, have you ever noticed that that's really all Buster ever does. He sleeps...all day."

He nodded. "Yes, I've noticed that he's not the most active dog I've ever seen."

"I think I know why. He doesn't sleep at night."

"What do you mean?" James took a seat in front of my desk, "if he doesn't sleep, then what does he do?"

I told him about him watching me sleep, standing there on his hind legs peering over the gate.

"I know it sounds strange, but every time I look he's there and I'm not sure what to do about it. I don't think it's healthy for him."

James furrowed his brow and thought for a moment. "I have a client who is a veterinarian that claims that she is also a dog psychologist, like a dog whisperer," he shrugged and smiled, "I've always thought that sounded sort of ridiculous, but maybe that's exactly what Buster needs."

" A dog psychologist, really?" I said laughing.

"Well, if the poor little fella can't sleep at night maybe she can help him. What could it hurt to try? I'll give her a call and see what she says."

The next day, James loaded Buster into his car and drove him to the vet.

I was in court all day and didn't get back to the office until 7 pm. When I walked in, James met me at the door.

"It's separation anxiety," He said with wide eyes.

I had forgotten about the pet psychologist. "Who has separation anxiety?"

He scowled at me. "Buster of course. He's been diagnosed with separation anxiety. The poor little guy is afraid to go to sleep, because he's afraid you won't be there when he wakes up."

I frowned. "How could she know that?"

"She said it's very common. Was he asleep when John Willy died?"

I shrugged my shoulders. "I don't know, maybe."

"I bet he was. What do you know about his first owner, the one that abandoned him before John Willy found him?"

I shook my head. "I don't know anything. His kids told me that John found him somewhere, but I never really checked that out."

James turned and started walking toward his office. "Juanita his housekeeper used to work for us," he said, "I know her very well. I'll give her a call."

I was exhausted and wanted to go home, but James seemed to be obsessed with Buster's separation anxiety diagnosis, so I followed him to his office, sat down on his couch and listened to his one sided conversation.

"So Buster *WAS* asleep when he died? That's what I thought. OK... now where did John find him?"

When he finally hung up. He sat there frowning. "Buster was a rescue dog. John got him from a dog shelter, but they can't remember which one."

I shrugged. "Does it really matter that we find it? What could they tell us that could help Buster? "

"I have no idea, but I'm going to find it. You look tired. Why don't you go home. I'll call you if I find something." I stood up and whistled at Buster to follow.

"Oh yeah, I almost forgot," James said, "you're supposed to take down the gate and let Buster sleep in the same room as you."

I frowned. "In the same bed with me?"

"No they didn't say that, just put his bed in there. That should be enough. She said he needs to be in the same room with you when he sleeps."

When I got home, I found a screwdriver and with Buster watching me carefully, I took down the gate.

"Go on in," I said to him, "go check it out, but stay off the bed."

I took the gate and the tools to the garage and put them away. When I got back, Buster was staring up at the mural on the wall.

"You like that?" I said petting his head, "I think it's beautiful."

He slowly walked from one end of the painting to the other, staring up at it. Then he plopped down on his butt and barked.

I actually jumped when he barked, because it was the first time he'd ever done that. "What's wrong?" I asked him.

He turned and looked at me, then turned back to the painting and barked again. But this time when he barked, he wagged his tail. I couldn't believe it. He was actually wagging his tail and barking like a real dog.

I sat down next to him, reached out and touched the painting. "You like this scene?"

He barked and wagged his tail more. I picked him up and held him closer to the painting, but when I held him near the woman, he whined loud and started wagging his tail so fast, I could barely hang onto him.

When I put him down, he looked up at me, still wagging that tail, but his eyes were different. I'm not sure why, but all of that sadness was gone. His eyes were bright and, I think...he was smiling at me.

A few weeks later, James located the dog shelter where John had found Buster. There he found out that Buster's first owner was a young woman who had returned him, because she was going away. She was in the army and was going to Iraq. Her parents didn't want him, so she gave him a sleeping pill and took him to the shelter.

"So he woke up abandoned." I said.

"Yes, then John died when he was asleep," James added, "no wonder he's afraid to fall asleep at night."

"Let me guess. His first owner, the young woman...she was a blonde, right?"

"How did you know that?" James asked.

"It's a long story. The next time you're at my house, remind me to show you something in my bedroom."

∽

For the next several months, our lives fell into a routine. Buster was finally sleeping at night, Alexander was doing well in college and my case load continued to grow, keeping me busy.

Almost every month, Alexander, Buster and I would spend the weekend at the lake at the trailer. Following Jeb's plans, we began building the steps that led from the water and zigzagged up the side of the cliff to the trailer. It was difficult work, but a nice break from Alexander's studies and my cases. While we worked, Buster would lay near the edge, looking down at us, watching our progress.

A few times a week I would get an e-mail from Kelly, filling me in on the latest gossip in Matagorda and about once a month I would hear from Jerry Johnston, the D.A. in Bay City on the progress of the Helen Craft case.

Apparently, Levi had covered his tracks well, because after three months the detectives hadn't found anything that connected him to Helen's death.

On his last phone call, Jerry reluctantly told me. "I'm sorry Travis, but we can't find any connection. None of her friends or family recognized Levi, and none of her colleagues working at the hospital, remember seeing Levi even talking to her. I'm afraid we're at a dead end on this one. I've got to call it off. I just can't justify the man hours any longer."

"I guess he's smarter than all of us," I said, dejected, "the bastard is gonna get away with two murders and there's not a damn thing anyone can do about it."

16

THE DREAM

Time flew by and before I knew it, it was December and Alex was off from college for a few weeks for the Christmas holidays.

"You have any plans for Christmas?" I asked him.

"I've been invited to go to Colorado for a skiing trip with some of my friends," he said, "but I don't know how to snow ski and I'm not sure if I really want to go. What about you?" he asked.

I shrugged. "I have no real plans. I think Olivia and Jeb are going to Europe, to Switzerland. Now that's a snow skiing trip," I said laughing, "if you're going to Colorado, I guess I'll just decorate the house a little and spend Christmas here with Buster."

"Could we go to Matagorda?" he asked with bright eyes, "It would be so awesome to spend Christmas at Aunt BJ and Uncle Kelly's beach house with everyone. Kind of like a big family Christmas."

I lifted my eyes. "Are you sure you'd rather do that than go to Colorado and hang out with your friends?"

"Oh yeah! I'd rather go deep sea fishing with you and Uncle Kelly than snow skiing with my dumb friends any day."

"I didn't know you liked to fish."

"I love it! Uncle Kelly used to charter a boat and we would go out all the time."

"In December? You can catch fish in December?" I asked.

He rolled his eyes at me. "Sure you can! We'll have to go out a long way, but there should be King Mackerels and Bull Redfish everywhere!"

"Ok, but won't it be sort of cold out there?"

He put his hands on his hips and grinned at me. "Uncle Travis, I thought you were supposed to be a big tough Marine?" he said laughing.

"I just said I was *in* the Marines. I never said anything about being tough. I hate the cold. Are you sure you don't want to go to Colorado with your friends and leave me and Buster here alone by my nice warm fireplace?"

∼

The Christmas festival was the largest holiday for the town of Tecolutla. All the hotels were booked solid and the town went all out decorating the storefronts and hung twinkling lights all along the streets.

It was also an important time for Capilla Del Sagrado Corazon (Chapel of the sacred heart). For over two weeks, when she wasn't working at the clinic, Ariel helped the nuns scrub the floors and walls of the chapel, getting ready for all the visitors. Father Alvarez told her that during the Christmas holidays every pew would be filled for every single mass.

It was a very critical time of the year for the church, because the donations raised during those two weeks paid to help keep the church open for almost six months.

It was also the busiest time of the year for the art gallery. The owner had requested four new paintings from Ariel and promised to give her 75% of the sales if she could meet the deadline.

Over the past six months, to her surprise she had sold several of her paintings in the gallery and had been able to give Father Alvarez almost $5000.

For inspiration for the new paintings, she had taken the bus to the beach and had set up her easel and stool in the sand near the dunes, next to the tall sea oats a few hundred yards from the breaking waves.

The beach was almost empty, with only a few tourists strolling along the shore. The wind was up and the water was too cold for swimming.

While she sat there, watching the waves crash on the beach, a strange feeling came over her. It was like she had been there before, this exact spot, next to the sea oats, looking across the white sand at the ocean.

Was it déjà vu, or an actual memory? She wondered. It had to be, because she had never been to the Tecolutla beach before.

She had always wanted to, but had been cautious to go by herself on the bus. She was afraid her Spanish wasn't good enough to communicate with the locals, but after working in the clinic for almost a year, speaking nothing but Spanish to the patients, she felt confident to make the trip.

She got off the stool, and slowly walked toward the ocean. As she walked she realized that it wasn't here she was remembering, but it 'was' a beach somewhere.

Suddenly she had the urge to sit down on the sand. Once she was there, she felt a stronger urge to lay on her back and stare up at the sky.

Lying there, watching the white fluffy clouds drift slowly by, felt very familiar. Somehow she knew she had done this too...many times before.

Then, as clear as the sound of the wind, she heard a voice. "Someday, when I am a big-time lawyer, we will live on the beach in a beautiful house overlooking the water."

She raised up on her elbows and looked around, but the beach was deserted. There was no one there, but her.

She laid down again and stared back up at the clouds. "We will have three kids," The voice said again in her head.

Her eyes filled with tears as she remembered the rest, and whispered softly, "Two boys and one girl."

She laid there a few minutes more, then got up and walked back to her easel and began to paint a beautiful sea scape with huge waves crashing on the beach. A few hundred feet from the ocean was a lush green sand dune with tall Sea Oats blowing in the wind.

Her turquoise eyes sparkled in the bright sunlight as her long blonde hair danced in the wind behind her shoulders as she painted. Never once did she look up at the white sandy beach and the white foam floating on the azure blue ocean water in front of her, because she wasn't painting that scene. She was painting the magnificent beach and ocean she was seeing, in vivid detail, inside of her head.

∽

On Christmas Eve morning, we packed the car with our luggage and Christmas presents, and the three of us, Alexander, Buster and I, jumped in and headed for Matagorda. Alexander had been out late to a Christmas party the night before with his friends and immediately fell asleep. A few minutes later, I heard Buster snoring in the back seat. With no one to talk to, I drove the speed limit, listening to the Christmas carols on the radio, trying to force myself not to think about the dream.

The dream had started several months ago, coming once or twice a week, but now it came almost every night.

I hadn't told anyone about it, not even Olivia, or should I say, especially Olivia, because...well to be honest I didn't want to hear it.

"Savannah has been missing for 18 months! When are you going to admit to yourself that she is dead and not coming back?"

I wasn't just hearing that chant from Olivia, but from everyone, and I mean everyone I knew had joined the choir. Even James Bachman had lectured me for over an hour about it.

"Travis," he began, "it's illogical for you to even consider the possibility. You are too smart to continue believing in this fantasy any longer. I just don't understand. Olivia tells me that you are convinced this Levi fellow killed her. Is that not correct?"

I shrugged my shoulders and gave him a subtle nod. "Yes, I know he did it, or at least tried."

James tilted his head, confused. "Tried? Travis, the woman has been missing for almost 2 years. It's obvious to me that Levi surely did more than just try. How can you not see that?"

I sighed and leaned back in my chair. "I know he did something to her, but whatever that was must not have killed her instantly. Otherwise, why would he continue searching night and day for her? Why would he do that if he knew for sure she was dead?"

James frowned and shook his head. "I've read the transcript for this trial. I know about the insurance money."

He sat up erect in his chair and adjusted his tie. With his blue eyes peering over his readers into mine, he said, "Travis, Olivia has told me everything. I know you have loved this woman your entire life. And I can understand how you can not accept her death without absolute proof, but son...you are frantically clutching at straws and ignoring the obvious. I'm not saying this to hurt you. I'm here because I care about you and want to help you see the truth. And that truth is...if Savannah is alive, where the hell is she? Come on Travis, you know in your heart that if she was alive, she would have shown up by now."

He took a deep breath and let it out slowly. "You know what Levi did out there. He threw her overboard into the ocean. He may not have waited around to watch her drown, but Travis it's time you accept the fact that Levi Cruz is not looking for Savannah. He is looking for Savannah's body. He absolutely knows that she's dead. He just hasn't located her corpse. And he will continue searching for it, night and day...because it's worth two million dollars to him."

He stood and walked to my door. "Please Travis, for your own good and for the good of this firm, I would like you to see someone about this, someone you can talk to, a professional. I believe a good psychologist could help you get through this, stop living this fantasy and accept the difficult truth that Savannah is gone."

He lifted his eyebrows and gave me a small smile. "I'm serious Travis. I think you need some help with this. It's time for you to find someone else to give all that love you have. If Savannah loved you half as much as you love her, she would want you to be happy, to move on and find someone else to love."

~

My respect for James Bachman was absolute. He not only had a brilliant legal mind, he had the most logical thought process of anyone I had ever known.

At that moment, there was no question in my heart of what I had to do. For me to keep believing that Savannah could still somehow be alive was not only an illogical fantasy, it bordered on delusional thinking. I 'was' too smart for that. It was time to put it all behind me and move on.

On my drive home, I had a good cry and finally accepted the truth that it didn't matter how much, and how long I had loved her...Savannah was gone...and she was never coming back.

When I pulled into my driveway and walked into my house, I was exhausted. Not physically, but mentally. I could barely think straight. It was only 9:30 pm, but all I wanted to do was get Buster fed and go to bed.

I actually let Buster sleep with me in the bed that night for the first time. I was hurting, sad and miserable and needed someone to hold. The minute my head hit the pillow I fell asleep.

~

I felt something crunch under my foot. I looked down to see dark green grass, covered with fallen golden oak leaves. I was barefoot and could feel the ground vibrating under my feet. The train was coming and I knew it wouldn't be long before I would hear the loud whistle and see the bright light of the engine coming around the bend. I reached in my pockets for a quarter to put on the track, but they were empty.

"The train is coming," I heard a woman's voice say softly, "can you feel it?"

I looked up and saw her, but she was turned away, hiding her face.

I could only see her back. She was wearing a blue jean jacket over a long flowing dress. Her blonde hair was blowing in the wind, dancing on her shoulders and down her back.

"It will be here soon," she said, "hurry, put the quarters on the track."

"I don't have any quarters," I said.

"Of course you do, look in your hand."

When I opened my hand there were two quarters in my palm. I bent down and placed them side by side on the track.

"Who are you?" I asked.

"You know who I am. Don't give up on me, the proof is right in front of you. All you have to do is look."

The woman turned around, but her face was hidden in dark shadows. I heard the train behind me and looked back to see the bright light of the Engine coming around the curve.

When I looked back at the woman, her face was glowing from the light, but it was so bright I couldn't make out any features, but I 'could' see her eyes. They were glistening in the light...and they were turquoise.

She held out her hand to me. "I am alive, but I am lost," she said, "find me Travis. I'm waiting for you."

When I reached for her hand, it disappeared. She was gone.

∼

Far away in the distance, I heard someone shouting, "NO, DON'T GO! COME BACK!"

As I slowly woke up, I realized that the shouting was coming from me.

I opened my eyes to see Buster standing over me, "Woof," He barked.

"Sorry buddy," I said, petting his head, "I must have been dreaming. Did I wake you up?"

"Woof, woof," He barked again. Then he jumped down on the floor and laid down in his bed under the mural.

"Well, excuse me. Sorry to have interrupted your sleep," I said smiling at him, "so much for that separation anxiety crap."

That was the last time Buster ever slept in the bed with me, but it was only a week later that my shouting woke him up again.

I wanted to call Olivia to tell her about the dream, but I knew if I did, she would've told James. I did consider calling a psychologist to make an appointment, but never did. I knew what he or she would tell me and I didn't want to hear it. I wasn't delusional, the dream was real and I couldn't just ignore it.

On the nights I had the dream, when I woke up, I would flip on the light and stare at the mural, searching it for something I might have missed, some kind of hidden clue, but I never found anything.

When I first found the mural in the art gallery, it wasn't the woman in the painting that had attracted me, it was the scene. The railroad tracks winding through the woods, reminded me of my backyard growing up. But what attracted me the most, and why I had to buy it, was how close it was to the crude landscape mural Savannah had painted when she was 12.

When I insisted on buying it I knew that Olivia thought it was because the woman in the paining reminded me of Savannah, but honestly, she didn't remind me of her at all, because when I saw Savannah in my mind's eye, I saw a little girl, not an adult. But now, because of the dream, when I look at the woman wearing the blue jean jacket, with the long blonde hair blowing in the wind...I see Savannah.

∽

"Where are we?" Alexander asked, yawning and stretching in the seat.

"We just passed Bay City," I said, "we're almost there."

BJ and Kelly's beach house looked like a miniature Disneyland, with giant eight foot tall blowups of Santa Clause in his sleigh being pulled by Rudolph. There was also Mickey Mouse, Minnie Mouse and a 12 foot tall Pluto, all blowing in the strong sea breeze, pulling hard against metal hooks that were anchoring them to the sand.

When they appeared in the doorway, I pointed at Micky Mouse and said, "I bet this embarrasses the hell out of your kids. They're way too old to think this is still cool."

Kelly burst out laughing. "It doesn't make any difference how much money you make, a red neck is a red neck. And yeah, my kids hate it, that's why I do it."

Inside their house, the Christmas decorations continued. "This is beautiful," Alexander said, hugging BJ, "it reminds me of mom. She loved Christmas. I used to help her decorate."

"I remember," BJ said, "she had an amazing eye for decorating. In fact, your mother helped me pick out most of this."

It has always amazed me how fast kids grow, especially when you haven't seen them in a while.

One by one their children walked up and welcomed us. Rodney, (11) their youngest had grown at least six inches in the last year. Walter, (13) was beginning to fill out, he wasn't that skinny little kid I remembered. But Rebecca, (18) had changed the most. She had developed into a beautiful young woman with high cheekbones framing her beautiful face. And had inherited her mother's hour glass figure.

When Rebecca walked into the room, Alexander lit up brighter than the Christmas tree. "Hey Rebecca," He said, nervously shuffling his feet, "it's really good to see you. You look real pretty in that dress."

She smiled and batted her long eyelashes at him. "Thanks," she purred, "I wore it just for you."

I shot a look at Kelly and raised my eyebrows. He grinned and whispered in my ear. "It's been going on a while. He calls her almost every night. Now you know why he passed on that ski trip to Colorado."

"Hey Alexander," I said grinning, "look up."

They were standing in the doorway to the living room. When they looked up and saw the mistletoe hanging above their heads, both of their cheeks flushed, instantly turning bright red.

"Sorry guys," I said, "it's a tradition. You've got to kiss her."

They both shook their heads. "I can't kiss her in front of them," Alexander protested, pointing at BJ and Kelly.

"Sure you can," Kelly said, smiling, "but no tongue."

"KELLY WAYNE SMITH!" BJ shouted, whacking him on his arm, "be nice!"

He raised his hands in the air. "All I said was no French kissing under the mistletoe."

"OMG Dad!" Rebecca yelled, running away, pulling Alexander down the hall behind her.

It was Christmas Eve, so that evening we all got dressed up and I took everyone out to dinner. Of course, when the check came I almost had to arm wrestle Kelly for it, but I eventually got it paid. After dinner we went to church.

Throughout dinner and in church I had worried a little about Buster being in a strange house all alone. I hoped that he wouldn't freak out and chew up the furniture or poop in the floor. But he was good. When we got back he was sound asleep in his bed and there were no little surprises anywhere to be found.

I hooked him up to his leash and Kelly and I took him for a walk down the beach.

Kelly started laughing. "What's so funny?" I asked.

"You are," he said, smiling, "when I conjure up an image of Travis Lee in my mind, I see a football player running touchdowns or maybe a marine dressed in combat camouflage, or even a lawyer dressed in a fancy suit standing in front of a jury, but this is an image I don't think I would have ever imagined."

I frowned. "What are you talking about?"

"You *do* know how silly you look with your suit pants rolled up, in your bare feet, holding on to that purple leash, walking behind that ugly ass dog."

"Hey, Buster's not ugly," I said, "I like to think of him as ruggedly handsome."

"Don't get me wrong, he's a good dog and I like him," Kelly said, reaching down to pet his head, "like the old saying, 'beauty is in the eyes of the beholder', but in my eyes, that is one butt ugly dog."

Buster looked up at me with his crooked ears, wagging his tail. "Don't pay any attention to him," I said, "he was the ugliest kid in school. What does he know about beauty? You can bite him in the ass if you want to ."

We both laughed and continued walking down the beach. "So how's Alexander handling college?" he asked.

"Great. He seems to love his classes and he made good grades this semester."

"That's great," Kelly said, "he's a smart kid. We thought he'd do well."

"To be honest, I was a little worried about his social life, because all he does is study. He never talked about girls and wasn't going out with his friends. But this trip explains a lot," I said, "how long has this thing between him and Rebecca been going on?"

"You know BJ and I were talking about that last week. When he was living with us, that entire year, he treated her like a sister. We never saw anything romantic, not even a spark between them. But when he moved out, she moped around the house for months. We didn't know what the hell was wrong with her, until he called one night. She lit up like a candle and has been dancing around the house ever since."

I grinned. "Funny, he never mentioned Rebecca to me once."

"Same thing here, we had no idea. I honestly don't think they knew it either, until Alexander moved out and they were apart for few months."

"What do you and BJ think about it?"

"To be honest with you, BJ was happy about it right away, but it was a little weird for me to comprehend at first, because I think of Alex like he's one of my children. But he is a really good kid. I guess I need to quit thinking of him that way, he's a grown man now. If things work out between Rebecca and him, I don't think she could do much better than Alexander."

When we got to the end of the beach, at the channel, we turned around and started walking back toward the house.

"But I will admit that I was worried a little about their future," he said, "or rather, their future with Levi Cruz in it. I'm not sure I'd want him around my grandchildren, and you know he would try. But there wouldn't be a damn thing I could do or say about it."

I nodded. "I was thinking about that too."

"Be honest with me Travis, do you think he did it?"

"Kelly, since I was 11 years old, all I've ever wanted to be, was a lawyer. Somehow I just knew that was what I was supposed to do with my life. I love what I do and I'm good at it, but without a doubt the biggest regret I'll ever have is agreeing to represent Levi Cruz."

Buster was panting and needed a rest, so we stopped and sat down on the beach looking at the waves rolling on the shore. The moon was waning, but the sky was clear, so we could see the white foam from the breakers shining a hundred yards or so away.

"I wasn't sure, when I took the case, but I'm convinced now. He played me like a fiddle and for a while I believed his lies."

I turned to look at Kelly. "I know he tried to kill Savannah...and I'm pretty sure he killed someone else to cover it up."

"Are you talking about that nurse?" He asked.

"Yes, Helen Craft. I think he killed her too, but it looks like he's gonna get away with that one as well."

Kelly picked up a hand full of sand and let it slide through his fingers. "We can't let him get away with this. There's got to be something we can do."

I stood up and knocked the sand off my butt. "Unfortunately, there's nothing that connects him to Helen and we can't touch him for anything he did to Savannah, but...I do have an idea that I believe he's overlooked. But to pull it off, I'm gonna need your help. It won't put him in jail, where he belongs, but it will ruin his day and all of his plans."

"Oh really? I'd love to ruin his day. How can I help?" Kelly's eyes were bright and he was smiling wide.

"It's Christmas Eve. It's very involved and I don't want to talk about this now. I'll tell you about it later, but trust me, you're gonna like it." I helped him up off the sand and we walked back to his house.

After the kids and Alexander went to bed, BJ, Kelly and I settled around the table on their deck, drinking eggnog, listening to the

Christmas carols playing on their stereo. It was a beautiful night with a clear sky. For a few minutes we didn't talk, we just sat there sipping the eggnog admiring the beautiful reflection of the moon on the calm ocean water.

"So what's wrong?" BJ asked.

I tilted my head and looked back at her. "Nothing," I said, "everything is great in my life."

"Travis, we've both known you since you were six years old. You can't fool us. Something is bothering you. Kelly and I both noticed it when you got here this morning. So spill it."

I stretched out my legs and leaned back in the chair. "Are you sure you want to hear it, it's pretty weird."

"It's about Savannah, right?" Kelly asked.

I shook my head and smiled. "Yes and that's why I didn't want to tell you."

"Why not?" BJ asked.

I shrugged. "Because both of you believe that Savannah is dead and I'm not sure I want to get lectured by you too!"

They looked at each other. "When have we ever lectured you about anything?" BJ asked.

"You're right, that was unfair of me. You guys have always been willing to listen."

"That's better," she said smiling at me. "OK...we're listening."

I told them about the mural I had found in the art gallery that reminded me of the train tracks in the woods behind my house.

"Kind of like the one Savannah painted on your wall in your bedroom?" Kelly asked.

"Exactly like that, but this one was done by a professional artist. The detail of the trees and the leaves are absolutely amazing. The weird part is that it is the exact same scene Savannah painted all those years ago. The only difference is that this mural shows the back of a woman. She is looking down the railroad tracks, into the woods."

Then I told them about the dream, how the painting comes alive and exactly what the woman says to me."

"Look!" BJ said, holding out her arm, "that gave me goose bumps."

"Is the painting signed?" Kelly asked.

"Yes. It's signed simply, Ariel."

BJ raised her head. "Like the mermaid Ariel? In the Disney film?"

"I haven't thought about that before, how is it spelled."

"I think it's spelled A R I E L."

"Yeah, that's how it's spelled on the painting."

We sat there quietly sipping our eggnog for a long time.

"You were right," Kelly said, "this is weird as hell. What do you think she means by, 'The proof is right in front of you, all you have to do is look'?"

"I don't know, I've searched that painting inch by inch...there's nothing there."

"How often do you have the dream?" BJ asked.

"Almost every night for the last four months."

"What do you think it means," Kelly asked.

I shrugged my shoulders and held up my hands. "I have no friggin idea. Of course, I'm praying that it means that Savannah is alive. That the dream is my subconscious mind trying to tell me something. Maybe it knows what she's talking about and understands clues I'm not seeing. All I know is that I believe it has to mean something, and I also believe that the damn dream is not going to stop until I figure it out."

17

TURQUOISE EYES

Buster and I slept in the living room, him in his bed I had brought from my house, and me on the couch. The next morning, Christmas morning, I woke up to the aroma of coffee and bacon and could hear it sizzling from the kitchen.

"Good morning," BJ chimed musically, smiling. "The coffee is ready. Did you sleep OK?"

I poured myself a cup and took a sip. "Ahhh, the nectar of life," I said.

"No dream?" BJ asked as she flipped the bacon.

I shook my head. "No, thank goodness. Actually, I slept like a log."

After breakfast, still in our pajamas, we gathered around the tree in the living room and opened our presents.

Everyone seemed to love their presents, especially me. Kelly, BJ and the kids gave me a Penn Squall Level fishing reel, and Alexander gave me the rod.

It was top-of-the-line gear. "I'm feeling a little bit like Ebenezer Scrooge. You guys out spent me just a bit."

Kelly laughed. "Well, Ebenezer, no surprises here, you always have been a squeaky tight bastard with your money."

It was a terrific morning, filled with screams of excitement and laughter, but the mood changed quickly when the doorbell rang.

When Kelly open the door, Levi Cruz was standing there smiling, holding a present in his hand.

"Is Alexander here?" He asked.

Kelly glanced back at me not knowing what to do. I walked to the door. "Yeah, he's here but I'm not sure that he wants to see you."

"It's OK," Alexander said, jumping up, "I asked him to come."

Alexander grabbed a present from underneath the tree, walked out the door and closed it behind him.

They walked down the steps together and stood next to Levi's car in the driveway. Kelly and I kept a close watch on them looking through the glass in the door. They talked for almost an hour, before Levi got back in his car and drove away.

Rebecca had also been watching through the window and ran to the door to meet him. When he opened it, she threw her arms around his neck. "Are you OK?" She whispered.

His eyes were red and his face was flushed, but he wasn't crying. He hugged Rebecca back and said, "Don't worry, I'm fine."

It was apparent that he didn't want to talk about it, so Kelly and I didn't press him and let him walk back to the living room, holding Rebecca's hand.

After we picked up the empty boxes, ribbons and torn wrapping paper off the floor, I hooked Buster up to his leash and took him outside to take care of business and then I took him for a short walk on the beach.

When we made it back to their house, I saw Kelly and Alexander walking along the shoreline. Kelly waved at me to join them.

"Hey what's up?"

Alexander smiled at me. "I was just telling Uncle Kelly what dad and I talked about earlier."

"And what was that?" I asked.

He shrugged. "I know I should have said something to you about it before I did it, but I wanted to talk to Rebecca first and he showed up before I could tell you."

Kelly raised his eyebrows and shot me a serious look. "So, don't keep me in suspense, what did you say to him?"

"I told him that I was legally changing my name to Alexander Walters, to mom's maiden name, and that meant that I was no longer his son."

I lifted my head shocked. "Are you sure you really want to do that?" I asked him.

"Yes sir. I want him out of my life and I don't ever want to see or talk to him again."

He paused and stared into my eyes, "What would you do if he killed *your* mother?" He shouted, "you wouldn't want him around either."

I put my hand on his shoulder. "Alexander, we don't know that for sure. It is possible that he is innocent. You are taking a drastic step based on rumors. Are you sure you want to do this?"

"Yes. I've been thinking about it a long time. I don't trust him and I can't have him in my life anymore. When I graduate from college, I'm going to marry Rebecca and I don't want him around her, or around our children. If I don't put an end to it now, you know he won't leave me alone...and I'm not sure what I might do to him if he doesn't."

There wasn't much else for us to say, so we walked back to the house.

That night after dinner, Alexander surprised of us all once again, when he got down on his knees and proposed to Rebecca in front of all of us.

"Rebecca, depending on my grades...will you marry me in three or four years?"

We all burst out laughing and cheering. Soon everyone was hugging, laughing and crying at the same time.

∽

Heeding Olivia's advice, I took four seasick tablets before I stepped onto the deck of the fishing boat the next morning at 5 am.

"You can't fish at noon?" I asked, grumbling to Alexander and Kelly as I walked on board, carrying my new rod and reel in my hand.

Fortunately, the ocean was smooth and the long hour and a half ride was not rough. When we reached the oil rig, the captain killed the engine, the crew pulled out a few buckets of bait and the three of us began casting and slowly reeling the line back.

After an hour of no one catching anything, the captain cranked the engine and we took off again stopping an hour or so later at another oil rig.

At noon we broke for lunch and after being out on the water for seven hours Kelly had caught two Bull Redfish and about five trash fish, as he called them, that he threw back. Alexander had caught one very large King Mackerel that had put up quite a fight. And I...well...I hadn't even had a nibble.

"Hey Alexander, be sure to let me know when this starts being fun," I said, eating my sandwich.

"Just wait," he said grinning, "you'll catch something soon and that's when it gets fun!"

I yawned and stretched, patting my mouth with my hand. "I hope so, because so far it's been about as much fun as watching paint dry."

Alexander shook his head and grinned. Then he continued his conversation with the Mexican crew, speaking fluent Spanish.

I smiled at Kelly. "The kids just full of surprises, isn't he? I didn't know he could speak Spanish."

Kelly nodded. "Well these days in Matagorda it's sort of a requirement. There's about a 75% Hispanic population in the schools. He's helped me several times with my customers. I speak a little but nothing like him, he's fluent."

That afternoon, I finally landed two Bull Redfish and I had to admit to both of them that it had been fun.

On the long ride back, Alexander hung out with the Mexican crew on the forward bow of the boat. He seemed to be in deep conversation with them. When we finally made it back to the marina and stepped off of the gangway, he had a strange, troubled look on his face.

"What's wrong with you," Kelly asked, "did you get seasick on the way back? You look like you don't feel so good."

He shook his head. "No, I feel fine. I'm just trying to process something."

I glanced at Kelly and smiled. "Process something? That sounds very cerebral. OK professor, what could be so difficult to process about a fishing trip?"

He grinned. "I heard something from the crew I think I need to tell you about. I'm just trying to figure out how to tell you without sounding...well, naïve or crazy."

"Alexander," Kelly said with a chuckle, "you're only nineteen, Uncle Travis and I already think that most of what you say is naïve or crazy, so don't think so hard about it. Just say it. What did they tell you?"

He rolled his eyes. "Ok, just blow this off. As weird as it may sound, every one of them believe it."

Kelly held up his right hand. "We promise not to blow it off. So spill it."

"Three of the crew guys were telling me about a mermaid they caught off shore last year."

Kelly laughed. "A mermaid? They said they actually saw a mermaid?"

Alexander's eyes were wide. "They didn't just see one, they swear they actually caught one in their net."

"How much tequila had they been drinking at the time," I said laughing.

"That's what I asked them too, but they all swear they were sober, working on a shrimp boat, pulling in the net when she fell out onto the deck."

"Yeah sure they were," Kelly said, "come on Alex, they're just yanking your chain."

"NO, I don't think so. It wasn't a joke to them."

"If that's true, then what did they do with her? Where is the mermaid? Don't you think something like this would have been all over the news?" Kelly said, "let me guess, they threw her back into the water, right?"

"No they didn't! And I don't think they are just messing with me. They said they thought she was dead at first, but when she started coughing and moaning they knew she was alive. She was bleeding from a gash in her head, so the captain took her down to the galley and bandaged it. Then they took her back with them to a clinic in Mexico, someplace called Capilla Del Sagrado Corazon. I think that's a catholic church because that means chapel of the sacred heart.

"Wait," I said, "They actually told you that they found a mermaid, a woman with fins in a shrimp net?"

"No she had legs, not fins."

"Then why did they think she was a mermaid and not just a woman?"

"Because she didn't drown in the shrimp net. She was alive. They're very superstitious and believe it was a miracle. They believe her fins changed to legs when they caught her in the net and pulled her out of the water."

"Ok," I said, "so...they bandaged the mermaid's bleeding head...then they took her to a clinic at a Catholic church in Mexico. Where in Mexico?"

"I don't know, I didn't ask them that.

"Come on Alexander, that's about the biggest fish story I've ever heard." I said, "Why would you believe something like this?"

The captain stepped off the boat laughing. "Are they still telling that mermaid story?"

"Yes sir," Alexander said, "and they really believe it too. Three of them claim they were there, on the shrimp boat when it happened."

"Oh yeah, I've heard all about it," the captain said laughing and shaking his head, "The blonde mermaid with the turquoise eyes."

I instantly spun around. "What did you just say?"

He lifted his eyebrows. "Say about what?"

"Did you say turquoise eyes?" I asked, breathing hard.

"Oh yeah. The legend is that this mermaid had long blonde hair and she had these beautiful piercing eyes the color of turquoise."

I locked eyes with Alexander. "Is this why you believe them?"

He nodded. "I don't believe the mermaid part, but Uncle Travis, blonde hair? Turquoise eyes? It's too much of a coincidence to ignore." he said.

"Where was she found?" I asked, "do they know the approximate longitude and latitude?"

The captain shook his head. "It's just another bullshit story, you guys don't really believe it, do you?"

I stared at him. "Do you know what happened to Savannah Cruz?"

He shrugged. "No, I don't think I've ever heard of a Savannah Cruz. I've only been here in Matagorda a few months. Did she get lost at sea or something? Did she drown somewhere in these waters?"

I frowned and shook my head. "That's what everybody thinks, but the truth is no one knows for sure what happened to her. Her body was never found."

The captain's eyes widened. "Are you saying she might be this mermaid? The woman these shrimpers found?"

"Who knows? But Savannah had long blonde hair and her eyes were a very unique color...turquoise."

I looked at Alexander, "Go find the crewmen who were on that shrimp boat," I said, "tell them I'll pay them. I want to know more about the mermaid with the turquoise eyes. We need to know exactly where they found her. And the name of the town in Mexico where they took her."

∽

Levi slowly opened his eyes and looked around the cabin. His head was pounding.

He swung his legs over the side of the bed and pulled himself up. He was dizzy and the cabin began to spin around him, still a little drunk from the two day drinking binge that he had started on Christmas Day.

He could smell the stench of odor reeking up from his body. He tried to remember the last time he had bathed, but couldn't recall it inside his foggy brain.

Slowly he got to his feet and stumbled to the companionway ladder and slid open the hatch. The cold December air rushed in, hitting him in the face and reviving him a little.

He made some strong coffee, stepped up the stairs and plopped down behind the steering wheel in the cockpit.

As his mind cleared, the memory of the last two days came back.

"I know you killed her." He heard Alexander's voice say in his head, "You have fooled everyone, but you can't fool me any longer. I didn't want to believe it, but now...I know you did it and I know why. It was all about the money."

Levi shook his head hard, trying to force Alexander's words out of his head. He climbed back down the steps and refilled his coffee cup, but added rum to it this time.

Back behind the wheel, sipping his Caribbean coffee, he heard Alexander's words again.

"You had it all planned out, didn't you Dad? And although it hasn't worked out exactly as you planned, you still believe you're going to get that money, don't you? But pretty soon you're going to find out that you are wrong."

"Last night I overheard a conversation between Uncle Kelly and Uncle Travis. And guess what Dad, you made a big mistake. All Mom's medical records you had the nurse erase from the computer at the hospital were copied to Uncle Kelly's computer in his office. Once the life insurance company sees them, they will deny coverage and you won't get a penny."

Levi finished his coffee and sat there behind the wheel quietly, replaying the last words Alexander had said to him.

"Remember how much Mom loved to read poetry to me? Probably not, because you always thought it was boring and you hated it when she would do it. But ironically one of her favorite poems was by Robert Frost and it has a line that is a perfect description of you now.

"The best laid schemes of Mice and Men often go awry,
And leave us nought but grief and pain, For promised joy!"

"I don't know how or when, but someday, some how, you will pay for what you've done. Until then, I don't want to talk to you or see you again. You are out of my life and no longer my father."

Levi walked back down the steps, picked up the bottle of rum and took a long swig. "We'll see about that kid," he said with a dark smile.

~

Olivia answered the phone on the fourth ring. "Hello?" She whispered in a gravelly voice.

Travis's excited voice boomed in her ear. "Slow down!" she yelled, picking up her watch from the end table, "Travis, do you know what time it is here? I was sound asleep."

"I'm sorry, no, I have no idea what time it is in Switzerland, but I really need to ask you something. It's very important or I wouldn't be calling."

She sighed. "Ok, but hang on a second, let me wake up a little.

"Is that Travis?" I heard Jeb ask in the background, "What's happened?"

"I don't know yet," Olivia said, "OK Travis, I think my brain is awake. What do you need to ask me?"

"Something very bizarre has come up. I'll explain it all to you later, but right now I need to know if by chance you or Jeb remember the name of the town in Mexico where the art dealer found my painting?"

"A town in Mexico?" Olivia asked, "what painting? What on earth are you talking about?"

"The mural on my bedroom wall. The woman at the Gallery said that her art dealer had found it in a small fishing village in Mexico. Do you remember her saying that?"

"Yes, tell him I remember," Jeb said, in the background.

"Put Jeb on the phone," I said.

"Travis I remember her saying that the artist was possibly a nun," Jeb said, "Is that right?"

"Yeah," I said, "I remember her saying that. But do you remember the name of the village or town?"

Jeb thought for a moment, then asked Olivia. "I'm sorry Travis, neither one of us can remember. What's this all about?"

"Does Tecolutla, Veracruz sound right?" I asked, "could that be what she said?"

Jeb repeated it to Olivia. "Gee, Travis we don't know. Neither one of us have ever heard of Tecolutla."

"Ok, I understand. It was worth a shot," Travis sighed dejected, "I have all the information at my house in Austin, but I'm in Matagorda and didn't want to have to go back there. OK, I'll call you back later and fill you in."

"Wait!" Olivia shouted, "You can't hang up like this. You called and woke us up in the middle of the night to ask us a stupid question, and now you're just gonna hang up and not tell us what it's all about? No damn way! We're both wide awake. What in the hell is going on?"

Reluctantly, I spent a lot of money on overseas phone charges the next hour explaining everything to them.

"What can we do to help?" Olivia said, when I finished, "We could catch a plane in a few hours and be home by Tuesday."

"NO, don't do that! I don't want to spoil your vacation. This is probably just a wild goose chase anyway."

"Travis," Olivia said, "you know I've always been very skeptical and never believed that Savannah was still alive, but this is beyond coincidental. How many women with long blonde hair with turquoise eyes could have been in the water on that exact day? You have to go there and check this out. It makes sense. It's possible that she was picked up by a fishing boat and that would explain why they never found her body."

"I know, but I'm trying not to get my hopes up. And I'm especially playing it down for Alexander's sake," I said, "I don't think he could survive losing her again if this turns out to be wrong."

"I understand, but I'm convinced you have to at least follow up on this to the end. Is there a private air strip in Matagorda? When we hang up I'm going to call my father. You need to take his plane. It will be a lot faster."

"That would be great," I said, "I just realized that I don't have my passport, so I have to go back to Austin to get it, so could you ask your father if I could use his plane and pilot tomorrow morning?"

Alexander and I jumped into my car and headed back to Austin. When we arrived at my house I ran to my home office, located my passport and Alexander dug through his files and found his birth certificate.

When I walked out of my office I saw Alexander and Buster standing in my bedroom staring at the mural. "Do you think Mom painted this?"

I shrugged. "I don't know, but look at the signature."

"Why would she sign it Ariel?" he asked.

"I'm not sure, it's just another part of this whole mystery, but if she *IS* the mermaid they're talking about with the turquoise eyes, calling herself Ariel sort of makes sense."

I handed him a sheet of paper. "Read this."

It was the bill of sale for the mural. On the bottom it said: Product: Three section mural.

Title: Tracks in the Woods.

Artist: Ariel.

Location: Tecolutla, Veracruz, Mexico.

Alexander turned, looked at me and shouted. "Oh my God!"

∽

The next morning I left Buster in the care of James Bachman, and Alexander and I boarded the small plane at 9 am on our way to Tecolutla.

The closest airport was El Tajín National Airport in Poza Rica de Hidalgo. There were no rental cars available and although it was only 30 miles from Tecolutla, it took us over two hours to get there, riding in a small, old, over crowded city bus.

The bus dropped us off at the Hotel Balneario, the highest rated hotel my legal secretary could find in the area. After we checked in, we walked down the narrow main street of Tecolutla. Although Christmas had been over for four days, all of the decorations and sparkly lights were still up and twinkling as the sun began to set. The street were lined with small shops all selling hand made trinkets and clothing. There were several of these shops that seemed to be selling the exact same things. There were also several small restaurants, so we picked one and had dinner.

Alexander wanted to rush straight to the church to see if we could find Savannah, but I wanted to find the art gallery first and see if we could discover more about the artist called Ariel.

"We need to know more about her and this church before we barge in asking questions," I told him, "we don't even know where it is, and if this is just some mythical fish story, and if it's Savannah or not. We don't want to scare them. Let's just take it slow and see what we can uncover and where it leads us."

When our waitress brought our meal, Alexander asked her something. "¿Hay realmente una sirena viviendo en Capilla del Sagrado Corazón?"

She smiled wide and said, "Sí, ella vive allí con las monjas católicas. Ella es muy hermosa."

Alexander smiled. "¿Ella tiene aletas como un pez?"

She shook her head and laughed. "No, ella tiene piernas, no tiene aletas."

"What did you say to her?" I said.

"I asked her if there really was a mermaid living in the church and if she had fins."

I laughed. "Why did you ask if she had fins?"

He smiled. "If she said that she did, we'd know that this was all just some mythical folk legend."

"What did she say?"

"She said that the mermaid had legs, no fins, was very beautiful and that she lived in the church with the nuns."

"When she comes back ask her if the mermaid has a name and also ask her where the art gallery is." I said.

When she brought us our tea, Alexander asked, "Señorita, ¿La sirena tiene nombre?"

When she answered, I didn't need a translator. "Si, es Ariel."

The small art gallery was only a few store fronts down from the restaurant on the opposite side of the main street, but unfortunately, it was closed.

We knew we were at the right place, because there were three beautiful ocean/beach landscapes displayed in the window. They were all signed…Ariel.

While we were looking in the windows, a small Mexican woman walked up to us on the sidewalk. "¿Estás interesado en comprar una pintura?"

Alexander smiled at her and said, "Si estamos muy interesados en el artista Ariel"

I looked at Alexander. "What did she say?"

"She wanted to know if we wanted to buy a painting."

"What did you tell her?"

"He told me that he was very interested in the artist named Ariel." The woman said, in perfect English.

I smiled. "I'm sorry I didn't realize that you spoke English."

She reached into her purse, pulled out a key and unlocked the door. "Apology accepted," she said, "come in. Would you like some coffee or tea?"

We both shook our heads. "No thank you."

"I am Lecitia Perez and this is my gallery."

I lifted my head and raised my eyebrows. "*THE*, Lecitia Perez?" I asked.

She smiled. "Yes, are you familiar with my work?"

"I just bought one of your pieces for my house and my partner's fiancé owns several of your landscapes. He is a huge fan of yours."

"A man with very good taste," she said smiling, "I would like to meet him some day."

"What can you tell me about this artist?" I pointed at one of Ariel's paintings, "I understand that she is a nun? Is that correct?"

She was staring at my face, as if she was studying me. "May I ask why you are so interested in Ariel? How do you know of her? She is not famous like me."

I wasn't sure if we could trust her, but Alexander spoke up before I could stop him.

"I think she's my mother." He said, "she's been missing for over a year."

She lifted her eyebrows and thought for a moment. Then she turned and looked me in the eyes. "Is he telling me the truth? You are here searching for his mother?"

I nodded. "Yes. Her name is Savannah. We're not sure if Ariel is the same person, but that's what we came to find out."

"Come with me," She said, walking to the back of the shop. She opened another door and walked into the room, motioning for us to follow her. The room was obviously her warehouse where she kept paintings that were not on display. Leaning against the walls were stacks of canvases. She started looking through the stacks. When she found what she was looking for, she pulled a small painting out and put it up on a wooden easel.

"If this is you, then I believe you have come to the right place. Have a look."

When Lecitia stepped out of the way, I immediately saw my face on the canvas. "Oh my God Uncle Travis, that's you!" Alexander shouted.

I walked to the canvas and studied the painting. It was signed by Ariel, but it was definitely me, but a much younger me and I wasn't smiling. It was a portrait of me frowning, looking down, wearing my Marine Corps Dress Blues and it was not a normal perspective for a portrait. This was very unusual, as if the artist was laying on the ground looking up at me.

My heart started racing and pounding in my chest when I realized what I was seeing. It was exactly Savannah's view the day she was crying on her knees in my mother's driveway the last time I had seen her...and the last time she had seen me."

18

SHARKS ONLY EAT THE FLESH

Alexander pulled out his wallet and held up a picture of Savannah. "Miss Perez, is this Ariel?"

Lecitia looked at the photo. "Is this your mother?"

"Yes, does she look like Ariel?"

"I'm sorry my child," She said, "but I've never actually met Ariel. I've only dealt with Father Alvarez. He has told me that she is very shy and introverted."

"Really?" I said, glancing at Alexander, "That doesn't sound like Savannah."

"Is the church close to here?" Alexander asked.

"No, it's not close," Lecitia said, "It is over 11 kilometers away, a very long walk from here. It is too late to visit there tonight anyway, everyone will be asleep. Are you staying in a hotel?"

"Yes, we are staying at Hotel Balneario." I said.

"Very good. I will meet you there in the morning and take you to the church," she said, " I will call Father Alvarez in the morning and let him know we are coming."

The next morning we were awakened with a knock on our door. When I opened it, I saw a tall, young, handsome priest standing there.

When he saw my face, his eyes widened and he smiled. "Hello, I am Father Alvarez from the church, Capilla Del Sagrado Corazon. Lecitia tells me that you have come to meet with Ariel. Is that correct?"

"Yes father. My name is Travis Lee and this is Alexander Cruz. We believe that Ariel, as you call her, is actually Savannah Cruz, Alexander's mother and my good friend."

He looked at Alexander and smiled. "May I come in?"

"Yes of course."

He took a seat at the table across from Alexander and I sat down on the edge of the bed.

"I hope you will forgive me for being so cautious, but Ariel is very precious to me. I would like to know a little more about you before I take you to her."

"Sure," I said, "what would you like to know."

"To be honest, I've never really done this sort of thing before, so I don't really know. I guess perhaps, could I see some form of identification?"

I showed him my passport and Alexander's birth certificate. "I'm sorry father, but that's all we have with us. I am an attorney, a partner in a law firm in Austin, Texas. Alexander is a college student at the University Of Texas. He lives with me there in Austin."

Father Alvarez raised his eyebrows. "So Ariel is from Austin?"

I shook my head. "No, she is from Matagorda."

"If you are from Austin and she is from Matagorda, how do you know her?"

"I grew up in Matagorda. We have been friends since she was a child."

He nodded approvingly. "I understand you have a photograph. May I see it?"

Alexander pulled out his wallet and showed him the pictures. "There's several. The one behind this one is of both of us. Does she look like Ariel?"

Father Alvarez flipped through the pictures, nodding his head subtly. "Yes, there is no doubt that this is our Ariel."

Alexander's chair fell over as he jumped to his feet. "I knew it! She's alive," he yelled, "hurry Father, let's go. I want to see her."

Father Alvarez glanced at me and then looked up at Alexander. "Soon my son, I promise, but first we have much to talk about."

He stood and held out his hand to Alexander. "I am hungry. Walk with me, we can talk at breakfast."

Holding Alexander's arm, they walked together through the large lobby to the restaurant. On the way, everyone seem to know Father Alvarez and bowed to him, respectfully. Some, ran up to him and kissed his hand.

"You are very popular. How long have you been the priest here in Tecolutla?" I asked him as we sat down at our table.

He smiled. "Only a few years."

"Are you from this area?"

"Yes, I grew up on a vanilla farm only a few hundred kilometers away. It's a very small village called, Poza Larga."

"I'm surprised," I said smiling, "you speak with no discernible accent. Where did you learn to speak English so well?"

"When I was seven years old, my father took me to San Antonio to live with his brother. That's where I graduated from high school. From there I went to seminary and after many years of praying, I was finally allowed to come back home to Tecolutla. I am very blessed. I love it here."

I ate my breakfast slowly and sipped my coffee, trying to be patient. "Father, you said we had much to talk about. Could we begin? We have been searching for Savannah for a long time and we are very anxious to see her."

He put down his fork and wiped his mouth. "I was the one who came up with the name Ariel. It seemed appropriate. She was brought to me by two fisherman who said they had caught her in their shrimp net. They believed she was a sirena."

"A sirena?" I asked.

"That means mermaid." Alexander said.

Father Alvarez raised his eyebrows. "You speak Spanish?"

"Yes sir." He said shyly.

"Very good, very good. I believe all young people should speak Spanish. It will serve you well in your life."

"When the fisherman brought her to the church," I asked, "was she hurt or injured in anyway?"

"Yes, she was in bad shape. She had a severe laceration on the back of her head. We have a small clinic at the church and the nuns had to put several stitches in to stop the bleeding. Truthfully, she was barely alive and I had my doubts that she would survive, but she did."

"Was that her only injury?" Alexander asked.

Father Alvarez frowned and shook his head. "It was her only *physical* injury, but..." he paused, raised his head and looked Alexander in the eyes, "I don't really know how to say this to you. The blow on her head was severe and...well...it caused your mother to have amnesia. She has no memory of her past."

Alexander slowly lifted his head and looked across the table at me. His eyes were red and full of tears. "We finally find her and she may not know who we are? Really?" He wiped his eyes with his sleeve and looked at Father Alvarez, "Is it permanent? Will she ever get it back?"

"I'm sorry my son, but we don't know. I had a doctor, a specialist from Mexico City come and examine her. He said there was no way of knowing for sure. Normally trauma induced amnesia is temporary, but it has been almost 18 months. That's why we needed to talk first, before you saw her."

I looked across the table at Alexander's sad face. "Alex, I've read a few articles about this for one of my cases. When we first see Savannah we need to be careful and take it very slow. It *is* possible that when she sees you, it may spark something and her memory may come back, but you need to be prepared and not act disappointed if she doesn't know who you are. We will be strangers to her and we don't want to frighten her."

"You won't be complete strangers to her," Father Alvarez said smiling, "She may not know your names, but I'm sure she will know your faces."

I tilted my head and looked at him. "Why do you think that?"

He stood up. "Before I take you to her, you need to see her room. When you see it, you will understand."

When we walked into the chapel and all the nuns saw us standing behind Father Alvarez, their faces lit up, excited. They broke into wide smiles and were almost giddy, whispering and laughing to themselves. I knew Alexander understood what they were whispering about, but he didn't tell me, he just looked at me with a strange expression I couldn't read. But when father Alvarez opened the door to Ariel's room, it all became clear to both of us.

On the wall in front of her small bed, she had painted the exact same mural of the railroad tracks winding through the woods, but in this painting, she had added something else.

Walking up the tracks toward her, was me, wearing my Marine Corps dress blues. Walking beside me, holding my hand, was Alexander.

The other walls were covered with three sketches of Alexander's face and five of mine. On the wall behind her bed was a painting of an even younger me, not in my uniform. I was maybe 15 or 16 laying on the beach with the ocean waves crashing behind me. I was propped up on my elbows, looking down at a smiling Savannah.

"Do you understand now?" I heard father Alvarez's voice say behind me,

I turned and nodded. "Yes I do."

Father Alvarez walked to the mural and touched the painting of the tracks. "I knew who you were the second you opened the hotel door, but I wasn't sure how to tell you about this. She painted these tracks and the woods last year," he slid his hand over to our images, "but your pictures are new. A few months ago, it was like she had an inspiration and started painting them. I may be wrong, but I believe she's beginning to get a few flashbacks. And at this point, those woods, the railroad tracks, that beach and your two faces are the only things she remembers."

∼

"Kelly, wake up," BJ shouted, shaking him, "Someone is knocking on our front door."

"What?" He growled, rolling over.

"Wake up damn it! It's 3 am and someone is pounding on our door," She yelled louder.

Kelly jumped up and slipped on his jeans. When he opened the door, two police officers were standing on his porch. The blue lights from their police cruisers in his driveway were flashing in his eyes.

"Mr Smith, there was an explosion at your office."

"An explosion?" He said, still half asleep, "at my office? What kind of explosion?"

"We don't know sir. The fire department is there now, but it looks like a total loss."

"Would you like us to take you there?"

Kelly thought for a second, trying to clear his head. "No, let me get dressed, I'll follow you there."

He heard BJ walk up behind him. "What's going on?"

"My office is on fire!" He yelled, running back to his bedroom.

She looked at the police officers. "On fire? What happened?"

"We don't know, but it was a large explosion."

Kelly ran past her, out the door and down the steps. "I'll call you when I get there," he yelled.

Two hours later, he pulled back into his driveway and slowly walked up his steps. He was covered in black soot. BJ was waiting for him when he opened the door, but didn't say a word. Instead, she wrapped her arms around him and burst into tears.

After he showered, she handed him a beer, then they walked out to the back deck and settled around the patio table.

"Is it all gone?" she asked, "Everything?"

He took a long sip, staring out at the ocean. "It burned to the ground. There's nothing left but ashes."

"Everything? All of your awards and trophies too?"

"I don't care about any of that, but I lost all the pictures of the kids on my desk, the ones of them growing up, and all my work files are destroyed. All the computers melted like butter."

He took another sip and shook his head. "Do you remember that fire proof room I built to protect the main frame and all my critical records?"

"Yes," she said, "Did it work?"

"Not worth a damn," he said smiling, "Fire proof my ass!"

"Do they know how it happened?"

"The fire chief told me that he suspected it was just an accident, probably caused by a gas leak."

BJ grabbed the beer from his hand and took a sip. "I didn't know you had gas in your office."

He lifted his eyes and stared at her. "I don't. This wasn't an accident. Some one did this on purpose."

"Who would do something like this?"

He shrugged. "I don't know, but whoever it was did a damn good job."

Trying to blend in with all the other spectators who had gathered behind the police barricades to watch the fire, Levi smiled, admiring his work.

Medical records? What medical records? He said to himself.

~

The next morning, Levi filled his old car up with gas and drove to Houston. Using a fictitious name, he had made an appointment with an attorney. It was one of those sleaze ball lawyers that was always advertising on TV. He wasn't actually planning on hiring him, but he needed some serious legal advice and he knew better than to call Travis Lee.

As he had expected, the lawyers office was in the center of an almost empty run down strip mall shopping center. Covering the entire front glass on each side of his door, were large blowups of the esteemed counselor's smiling face. They were snap shots from his tv commercials, touting his ridiculous slogan, "Sometimes you need a real fighter on your case! Hire me, The Pit-Bull and I will go for their throats!"

Levi had seen his commercials a thousand times and had always wondered who on earth would hire a clown like that to represent them. But he had a few questions to ask that a *real* lawyer may think were not ethical to answer, so...he called the "Pit-Bull."

Wearing dark glasses and a baseball cap, Levi got out of his car and walked through the door.

Apparently the relentless late night television ads were working, because almost every seat in the waiting room was filled.

"Are you Mr. Jones?" The young girl sitting behind the desk asked.

"Yes, that's me," Levi said.

She smiled. "You are right on time. You can go in. The Pit-Bull is waiting for you."

He had to bite his lip not to laugh. He wanted to say, "Are you serious? Did you actually just say, "The Pit-Bull is waiting?" But he didn't, he just returned her smile and opened the door.

"Mr Jones, please come in and have a seat," The lawyer with the familiar face boomed loudly, "What can the Pit-Bull do for you today?"

Levi frowned, sat down in the chair facing him and glared across the desk. "Can we cut out the Pitbull crap? I am not one of your typical red neck idiot clients wearing a neck brace trying to fake an accident claim. I am here to talk to you about a two million dollar life insurance policy in which I am the sole beneficiary. So can we please stop with the bullshit?"

That got his attention. "Of course, Mr Jones, call me Larry."

"Ok, Larry, for this first meeting, you can call me Mr. Jones, which I assume you realize is not my real name. I am here to ask you some hypothetical questions. If you give me the answers that I am looking for, then we will take the next step together and I will tell you my real identity. You will have to trust me, but if we do go to the next step, it will be well worth your time. Is that clear?"

The Pitt-Bull nodded. "Very clear. So what are your hypothetical questions."

Levi smiled and sat up right in his chair. "Ok, but remember this is just hypothetically. What if someone arranged to have some critical medical records disappear, so the underwriters of a life insurance policy could not find them. And, again hypothetically, what if the insurance company overlooks these medical records and approves a two million dollar policy," He paused, making eye contact, "Are you following me so far?"

The Pitt-Bull nodded his head. "Yes, I believe I am, and I think I already know what your next hypothetical question will be."

"Oh really? And what is that?"

"You want to know what would happen if this hypothetical insurance company discovers these lost medical records...your question is...could they then deny coverage? Am I correct?"

"Exactly," Levi said grinning, "So, what's the answer?"

The Pitt-Bull leaned back in his chair and put his feet on his desk. "Mr. Jones there is no simple answer to that question. Technically whoever this person was that hypothetically arranged to have those medical records disappear has committed a felony fraud and he or she could possibly go to jail for it. But on the other hand, a two million life insurance policy had to have been thoroughly investigated by a team of underwriters to be approved. It's my legal opinion that if the beneficiary of this policy could not be connected in any possible way to those missing medical records, I believe he would have a very strong case against the insurance company. After all, it wasn't his fault that the insurance company missed the records and put the policy in force."

He lowered his legs off his desk, leaned forward and looked Levi in the eyes. "Just to be clear, for let's say...50% of all funds collected from this insurance company, my firm would be very interested in representing this hypothetical person."

Levi smiled. He had come to the right place. " I was thinking more like 30%."

"Let's split the difference, how about 40?"

"35 sounds better to me."

"Agreed. Do you have any cash on you?" The Pitt-Bull asked.

Levi raised his eyebrows. "A little, why?"

"Give me $20."

Levi pulled out his wallet and handed him the money.

"I am now your legal representative, your lawyer. Anything you say to me is confidential and I am bound by the laws of the United States judicial system to never repeat them."

He leaned back and pushed a button on his phone. "Judy, could you bring in some coffee, and tell everyone out there waiting to see me to come back tomorrow."

When he hung up, he smiled at Levi and said, "Now, Mr Cruz, why don't you stop beating around the bush and tell me exactly how I can help you."

Levi jerked his head up, shocked. "You know who I am?"

"Mr Cruz, your murder trial was very high profile covered extensively by all the local and national media, so yes, I am very familiar with your case and I knew who you were, the minute you opened my door. So, tell me more about these missing hospital medical records. I assume they were your wife's, correct?"

"Yes. Savannah had tried to commit suicide a few times, but I don't think we have to worry about those any longer."

"May I ask why you think that?" Larry asked.

"Unfortunately, the person that erased the records from the hospital computer drowned last year."

"That was convenient," Larry said.

"Yeah," Levi said, with a smirk, "it was a real tragedy. But I discovered a few weeks ago that my health insurance guy had copies of these medical files in his office."

"How did you find that out?"

"From my son, but that doesn't matter, because his office blew up yesterday and they were all destroyed."

Larry frowned and sighed. "That was a stupid thing to do. Apparently you are not exactly computer literate, are you?"

Levi glared at him. "What are you talking about?"

"Is there anyway you can be connected to that explosion?"

"No, I was very careful. The dumb ass didn't have any security at all. It was easy. Two stolen propane tanks in his office with their valves open and a fork in the microwave in the kitchen and boom! No more medical records."

Larry shook his head and ran his hand through his hair. "No more medical records in that office, but what about somewhere else? Where do you think he got them in the first place?"

"I don't know. Do you think there's another copy of them out there somewhere else?"

"Mr. Cruz, I'm assuming that when your wife attempted suicide, she was hospitalized for psychiatric treatment, correct?"

Levi nodded. "Yeah, those are the records I didn't want the life insurance company to see."

"I understand," Larry said, "but your health insurance company paid for these medical treatments, right?"

"Yes."

"Are you really this dense? Of course there is another copy of these medical records out there. They are in your health insurance companies files. That's what they used to pay off the claims. The files that you just blew up were a copy that they had sent him for his records."

Levi didn't respond. He just sat there in silence.

"Are you sure they can't connect you to this blast?"

He shook his head. "No way."

"You better hope they can't," Larry said, "Ok, let's move on. Is your wife still officially missing, or have they recovered her body?"

"No, that's why I am here. In the trial they said it could be 5 to 7 years before they would declare her dead and I could collect on the policy. Is there anyway to speed that up?"

Larry lifted his eyes. "I can try, I will file some motions but I doubt we will be successful. More than likely it will be at least a five year waiting period. How long has it been?"

"Almost two years, 18 months," Levi said.

The door opened and the receptionist walked in carrying a tray. "Would you like cream or sugar?" She asked.

"No thanks," Levi said, reaching for a cup, "I'll take it black."

When she left, Larry leaned back into his chair sipping his coffee, thinking. "Are you absolutely sure your wife is dead? If she shows up somewhere, that would be very expensive for both of us."

Levi leaned forward and set his coffee cup on the desk. "There's no way that she could have survived. I'll never understand why she hasn't washed up somewhere. I've searched for her body for two years, even in the marshes, but she's not there."

Larry stared at the ceiling, rocking his chair. "That's exactly what's bothering me. If she is really dead, someone would've found her by now. Or at least a body part. Sharks only eat the flesh, not the bones."

Levi shrugged his shoulders. "I know. That's why I keep searching for her."

"Wait," Larry said, "You were acquitted of her murder without prejudice, correct?"

"I don't know what *without prejudice* means, but yes I was acquitted."

"You didn't cut any kind of a deal with the D.A. did you? It was a jury acquittal, right?"

Levi nodded. "No, there was no deal, the jury acquitted me."

Larry leaned back and chuckled. "Then we have nothing to worry about, even if she does show up alive."

Levi tilted his head, confused. "And why not?"

"It's called Double Jeopardy. Have you ever heard that term before?"

"Yes," Levi said, "My last lawyer told me about it. He said that it means the police can't come back and arrest me for Savannah's murder again."

"Exactly!" Larry said, "it's a small, unfortunate loop hole in our justice system. I'm not saying it would be pleasant, but since you've gone this far already…"

Levi wrinkled his forehead and looked him in the eyes. "Not pleasant? What the hell are you trying to say?"

"Mr. Cruz, your last lawyer didn't tell you everything, he left out a very important part. Now, you didn't hear this from me, but if your wife shows up tomorrow, alive…you could kill her again in front of the police station and the cops couldn't do a damn thing. They couldn't even arrest you."

19

THE MAN IN MY DREAMS

The clinic was small with only six hospital beds lined up in rows of three on each side of the room. She was standing next to the last bed on the right, wearing a yellow sun dress made of soft gauze material, like the ones displayed in the windows in the downtown shops. It was long, almost touching the floor, hanging just inches above her leather sandals. Strands of her long blonde hair were laying softly over her left shoulder, the rest pulled back and tied behind her head with a yellow ribbon. She was smiling, leaning over an older woman, talking to her in Spanish, wrapping her hand with a bandage.

"Ariel," Father Alvarez said softly, "you have visitors. They have come all the way from Texas to see you."

Although the room was dim, only lit from a few lamps and the rays of sun streaming through the small windows, when she turned to look at us, her brilliant turquoise eyes seemed to glow, sparkling and twinkling in the sunlight.

Alexander made the first move, walking toward her slowly. When she saw him, her eyes widened, she gasped and put her hand over her heart.

"Do you recognize me?" he said softly.

She opened her mouth to speak, but no words came out. After a few moments with tears building in her eyes, she said, "I don't know your name, but I know your face."

"I'm Alexander," He said, "I've been looking for you for a long, long time."

She studied his face, wiping away her tears with her hand. "Alexander?" She whispered, "Your name is Alexander?"

Tears were rolling down his face too. "Yes. I am your son. Do you remember me?"

She looked at Father Alvarez. "I...I have a son?"

He nodded, giving her a gentle smile. "Yes, you do."

She looked back at Alexander and held out her arms. He ran to her and they cried together as they hugged.

I was standing in the doorway, so I took a few steps closer toward them. When she heard me, she raised her head and gasped again. She fell to her knees and made the sign of the crucifix across her heart. Then she slowly lifted her head and stared into my eyes. "Eres el hombre en mis sueños."

I looked over at Alexander. "What did she say?"

He wiped his eyes with his hand and grinned. "She said that you are the man in her dreams."

She stood up and took a few small steps toward me. "I've seen your face in my dreams almost every night," She whispered, reaching out her hand, "What is your name?"

When I took her small hand in mine, my heart began to pound in my chest and my emotions took over. Tears were rolling down my face and I could barely speak. "I'm...Travis, Travis Lee."

Her wet eyes were glistening, as she slowly repeated my name. "Travis...Lee...Travis...Lee" She whispered softly, "How do you know me?"

I reached out and wiped a tear from her cheek. "I've known you my whole life, since you were seven years old."

"Really?"

"Yes. You moved into the house next door."

She lifted her head and her eyes widened. "Were there woods in the back yard and a railroad track?"

I smiled. "Yes, and a big treehouse. Do you remember the treehouse?"

She shook her head. "No...no I'm sorry, I don't remember that."

"We used to play in that treehouse all the time. That's where I fell in love with you."

She parted her lips to say something, but stopped and looked away. Finally, she turned back, lifted her beautiful turquoise eyes up to mine and said, "Did I love you too?"

I reached out and gently touched her face with my hand. "We were very much in love."

"Are you my husband, Alexander's father?"

I squeezed her hand. "No, I'm not. That's a very long story I will tell you about later. I know this may be overwhelming, so we're going to take it very slow. I think all you need to know now is that we are here to take you home. Your real name is Savannah, Alexander is your son and although I am not your husband, I've been in love with you since the first time I saw you. You are...and always will be...the love of my life."

∽

When Levi returned from Houston, he found a note taped to the door of his boat. It was from one of the commercial fisherman. It was an emergency. One of the engines on his boat was not running. The captain had a charter early the next morning and he needed Levi to come and repair it as soon as possible.

Levi was exhausted from his trip but he needed the money so he grabbed his toolbox and walked down the dock.

"Thank God you're here," Captain John Irwin yelled when he saw Levi standing at his gangway, "the damn number two engine won't crank. I hope you can get it running, I've got a large group charter tomorrow morning."

Levi glanced at his watch. "You better pray that it doesn't need any parts, I will never get them by tomorrow morning."

"I already called Willie, he said he would meet me at the store later if you needed any parts."

Levi nodded, stepped aboard, opened up the engine hatch and went to work.

Two hours later, he crawled out of the engine hatch, wiping his hands. "Try it now." he said.

Captain Irvin, climbed up to the steering station and turned the key. The engine fired up instantly. "Alright!" He yelled. "Thank you. You saved my life."

"Leave it running a while," Levi shouted up to him.

Captain John lowered the RPMs to a slow idle and climbed back down to the deck. "What do I owe you?"

Levi thought for a moment. "Would 400 work?"

"Sure, that sounds fair," he said, "but I'll have to write you a check. I don't have that much cash here on the boat." He slid open the door to the cabin, "Come on in. Let me get my check book."

Levi took a seat at the table in the salon and John sat on the other side filling out the check.

"Alexander Cruz is your son, right?"

Levi shook his head. "Yes he is."

"He sure turned out to be a fine young man. I understand he's going to the University of Texas?"

Again, Levi nodded. "Yes, he is just starting his second semester. How do you know Alexander?"

Captain John frowned. "He didn't tell you? He was on my charter last week with Kelly Smith and Travis Lee. I'm surprised he didn't tell you all about it, especially with all the crazy talk about the mermaid."

Levi lifted his head. "Mermaid? What the hell are you talking about?"

"It's just one of those crazy folk legends. It's all a bunch of crap if you ask me, but you know teenagers. I had three Mexican hands on the charter and two of them claimed that they were working on a commercial shrimp boat last year when they caught a live mermaid in their net," he said laughing, "your boy Alexander was all over it. Even

Travis Lee got all worked up about it. By the way, your boy speaks really good Spanish."

"Yeah he does, he learned it from my parents. Why was Travis Lee so excited about this mermaid story. He's supposed to be some big shot lawyer. He's way too smart to believe something like that. What was he saying about it?"

"At first he didn't believe it, and was laughing about it too, but when I told him they called her the blonde mermaid with eyes of turquoise, he got real excited. He had Alexander go find the crew and he asked them a bunch of questions."

It was Levi's biggest fear, but if Savannah had been picked up by a shrimp boat, it explained everything. And if it was true, he had to find her fast, before Travis did, so he could finish the job.

"What did the Mexican hands say they did with the mermaid?" He asked.

"Ah come on Levi, you don't believe in that crap too?"

"Of course not, but it's an interesting story. I was just curious about what they claimed they did with the mermaid."

"They all swore that they took her back to Mexico with them."

"Where in Mexico?"

He thought for a moment then shook his head. "Sorry, I don't remember. It was a strange name I'd never heard of before. Ask your boy, I bet he'll remember. All these hands were from Veracruz and they said they scooped her up about 20 miles off shore. If they were really on a shrimp boat working these waters, it couldn't be too far away. They said that their captain cut the trip short so they could take her back. Normally those large shrimp boats stay out 30 to 45 days at a time. I figure it's some small fishing village on the gulf coast or maybe along the Yucatán Peninsula."

Captain John paused, trying to recall what they had said, "I think they claimed they took her to a Catholic church that had a clinic or hospital. Something like that. To be honest with you I didn't pay that much attention to what they were talking about."

Captain John ripped the check out of his checkbook and handed it to Levi, "Here you go and thanks again. Tell Alexander I said hello.

I'm sure he can tell you more about it," he laughed, "it was the biggest fish tale I ever heard."

~

"When will you be leaving?" Father Alvarez asked.

I shrugged. "I'm not sure. My firm is trying to find out if Savannah will need proof of citizenship to re-enter the US. I think she will. If that's the case, we'll have to go back and get a copy of her birth certificate."

"I'm not leaving her alone," Alexander said, "I'm not gonna take the chance of losing her ever again. If you have to go back, I'm staying here with her."

As I had expected, Savannah *did* need some proof of her citizenship, so I left Alexander there and accepted Father Alvarez's offer to drive me to the airport. I called James and he sent his pilot and plane back to the El Tajín National Airport to pick me up.

It only took us a little over an hour to drive from Tecolutla to the airport in Poza Rica de Hidalgo, but it took several hours for James's pilot to get the clearance to land there. Since I didn't speak Spanish, Father Alvarez thought it would be better if he stayed there with me until the plane arrived, so we found a table at a small restaurant inside the airport to wait.

"Travis, I am very confused. The love you have for Savannah is very obvious," Father Alvarez said, "the way you look at her, talk to her...touch her. And yet, you say you are not her husband and not the father of her child. How could that be?"

I dropped my head. "I made a terrible mistake when I was young. Savannah did something that I couldn't forgive her for and I walked away. I have regretted it for twenty years."

"We all make mistakes in our lives, but only a fool makes the same mistake twice. I will pray for you."

I nodded. "Thank you Father, I'm praying too. Praying that she will remember the love she once had for me, so we can finally be together."

"Even if she doesn't get her memory back, and honestly I'm not sure she ever will, don't give up on her. She has survived a terrible thing, no doubt it was God's hands that kept her alive through it all. None of us knows why he does these things, but I believe he has a purpose for her life that she has yet to accomplish and that purpose has something to do with you. I believe she is supposed to forget her past, so she can have a future with you. If that's true, perhaps you need to forget some of your memories as well, especially the bad ones. The past holds all our bad decisions and mistakes that are sometimes best forgotten. The future is full of our dreams and God's plans for us. All we have to do is follow down the right path."

"I understand Father," I said, "but sometimes finding that right path is difficult."

"Oh yes, it can be very difficult for some, but I believe everyone knows what is right and what is wrong, but because most people are guided by the wrong human emotions like greed, selfishness, anger, jealousy, lust or fear, they take the wrong path. But if they would use the emotion God's words teach us to use...which is love...the correct path is crystal clear."

I smiled. "How old are you Father?"

"I just had my 38th birthday last month."

"We are close to the same age, but you are so much smarter than me. You are wise way beyond your years."

He grinned. "No, I'm not any smarter than you, I've just had a better teacher."

We both laughed.

His expression changed and he gave me a serious look. "May I ask you something that may be unpleasant to talk about?"

"Of course." I said.

"I may be wrong, but I believe you know the truth about how Ariel, excuse me, Savannah wound up in the water that day. Am I correct?"

I lifted my eyes and nodded. "Yes, unfortunately I do. It's a very long story, but the short version is...her husband, Alexander's father...tried to kill her. I believe he hit her on the head and threw her overboard."

Father Alvarez recoiled in shock. "Why would he do such a horrible, evil thing to such a sweet, gentle person?"

"It was for one of those wrong human emotions you were talking about. It was greed. He did it for money Father, a lot of money."

∼

I had the pilot fly me directly to Bay City, so I could go to the county records office and get a certified copy of Savannah's birth certificate. Unfortunately, there had been a fire 15 years earlier that burned the court house to the ground and all of the birth records had been destroyed.

30 minutes later, I was back on the plane heading to Austin, but we didn't arrive in time. The government offices were closed, so I went back to my house and planned on being at the state courthouse when they opened the next morning.

On my way home, I thought about dropping by John's house to pick up Buster, but I would have to take him back there in the morning, so I changed my mind and drove straight to my house.

I ordered a pizza and settled around the island in the kitchen to wait. The house seemed too quiet and lonely without Buster and Alexander. It made me realize how much I loved having them there and how much my life of living alone had changed for the better.

When the pizza arrived, I grabbed a beer out of the fridge and walked outside to my patio. It was a cool night, so I lit my outside fireplace, pulled up a chair and put my feet up on the brick hearth.

"Oh my God!" Olivia screamed over the phone, "you found her? She's alive!"

"Yes she is," I said, picking up my third slice out of the box, "I apologize for chewing in your ear, but I'm starving. It's been a very stressful and long two days."

I finished my pizza while filling them in on all the details.

"Is it total amnesia?" Jeb asked.

"Yes, pretty much. She recognized Alexander's face and mine, but she doesn't know our names. She also remembers the woods and the train tracks that were behind our houses where we grew up, but that's the extent of it. She has no memory of Levi or anything else in her life."

"What about her short-term memory," Jeb asked, "Is she having any problems with that?"

"No, she has total recall from the day she woke up in the church clinic 18 months ago."

"I think that's a good thing," He said, "it's a good sign that she doesn't have any actual brain damage."

"So you still don't know if she jumped or if Levi actually did it," Olivia said.

"No she has no memory of what happened to her, but something hit her on the back of the head hard enough to split her scalp wide open. It took 18 stitches to close it. Either someone hit her or she got it falling out of the net onto the deck of the shrimp boat. My money's still on Levi."

My phone started beeping in my hand. "Hold on guys, it's Kelly Smith calling, I'll be right back."

"Wait!" Olivia shouted, "just add him to this call. I haven't talked to him in a while, I'd like to say hello."

It took me a few minutes to figure out how to patch him in, but eventually I got it. "Hey Kelly," I said, "I've got you tied in with Olivia and Jeb."

They all said hello. "So what's up?" I asked him. I was with Alexander, when he had called him from Tecolutla, so he already knew about Savannah.

"I got a strange phone call today I thought you might need to hear about." Kelly said.

"Oh yeah?" I said, "from who?"

"From Captain John Irwin. Remember, he was the captain of our fishing boat last weekend."

"Sure, I remember him. what did he want?"

"He wanted to know if we thought the mermaid might have actually been Savannah. When I told him yes, he got very upset, because he thinks he may have made a terrible mistake."

"Mistake about what?" I asked.

"A few days ago one of his engines quit running, so he called Levi to come fix it. Apparently he wasn't around during Levi's trial and didn't know that he had been arrested for Savannah's murder. He had just found out when he called me."

"So what's the problem?" Olivia asked.

"The problem is that he told Levi about the mermaid and how excited we all got when we were talking to his crew. He's afraid that Levi has put the pieces together and now knows that Savannah could be alive. I'm at his marina now, his boat is gone and no one has seen him in two days."

"Oh God," I said.

"I don't understand the problem," Jeb said, confused, "what difference does it make if he knows she's alive?"

"It makes a lot of difference, if she's alive, he won't be able to collect on that two million dollar insurance policy," I said, "and if we're right, and he tried to kill her for it, she's in real danger if he finds her."

"You don't think he'd try to kill her again, do you?" Jeb said.

"Olivia, what do you think?" I asked.

"I think you need to get her out of there, fast!"

∽

Levi studied the chart and decided to take a chance on a small town called La Pesca. He had planned on stopping much further down the Mexican coast at Tampico, but the current had been strong and he was low on gas. He slowly pulled his boat up to the fuel dock, killed the engine, jumped off and tied the deck line to the old wooden post.

There was no one there to help him fill his tank, so he walked down the dock to the marina office.

"Bienvenido señor, necesita combustible?" (Welcome sir. Do you need fuel?) A man behind the desk asked him.

Levi smiled. "Sí, tomas dolares americanos?" (Yes, do you take American dollars?)

Levi followed the man down the dock to his boat and leaned casually against a tall post watching the man fill his tanks.

"¿hay una iglesia católica por aquí (Is there a Catholic Church around here?) Levi asked.

"No señor, solo tenemos una capilla muy pequeña (No sir, we only have a very small chapel.) The attendant said.

Levi had assumed that he had not gone far enough and wasn't surprised at his answer.

"Estoy buscando a la sirena con los ojos color turquesa. Entiendo que ella está viviendo en una iglesia aquí en México (I am searching for the mermaid with the turquoise eyes. I understand she's living in a church here in Mexico.) Levi said, "¿Alguna vez has oído hablar de la sirena de los ojos turquesa?" (Have you ever heard of the mermaid with the turquoise eyes?)

The man looked back at him with bright, wide eyes. "Sí, ella es muy famosa. Ella está en la capilla del Sagrado Corazón de Tecolutla" (Yes, she is very famous. She is in the Chapel of the Sacred Heart in Tecolutla.)

Smiling, with his tanks full, Levi pulled out the chart and plotted his course for Tecolutla.

∼

"Kelly, did Captain John tell him exactly where it is?"

"No, fortunately he didn't remember, but he did tell him that they had taken her to a Catholic Church in a small fishing village on the Gulf coast."

"Do you know exactly when he left?"

"No, I talked to his slip neighbor and all he knew was that he hasn't been there in at least two days. How far is Tecolutla down the coast?"

"I'm not exactly sure, but I think it's about 550 miles south of Harlingen."

Kelly thought for a moment, calculating in his head. "Matagorda is about 300 miles north of Harlingen. That would make it 850 to 900 miles by boat. If he's doing 25 or 30 knots," he paused, calculating in his head again, "Travis, he could be there by now."

I hung up the phone and immediately dialed the pilot's number and told him that he needed to take me back to Mexico.

"Travis I'm not sure I can get a landing clearance this late at night," he said, "all of the immigration offices are closed. Let me check, I'll do my best. I'll call you back in a few minutes."

I sat there impatiently waiting for over 20 minutes before he called back. "I'm sorry Travis, but there's no way to get the clearance this late at night. I'll try again first thing in the morning, but I figure the fastest I can get you back there will probably be sometime tomorrow afternoon."

I walked back into the kitchen, grabbed another beer and stood by the phone on the counter. My brain was spinning, trying to come up with an idea, anything that could get me back to Tecolutla fast. On a whim, I picked up the phone, dialed information and got the number for the Corpus Christi Naval base.

When the base answered I said, "This is Lance Corporal Travis Lee, 1st Battalion 8th Marines of the 2nd Division calling. This is an emergency, I need to talk to your commanding officer. Tell him I need his help desperately. Tell him I'm calling in that favor he promised."

I knew it was a long shot and probably a stupid idea. It had been over 17 years since I'd talked to the CO of that base and I wasn't even sure he was still there, more than likely he wasn't, but I couldn't think of anything else to do. The day the CO had put me on that jet to Washington to meet the plane carrying the caskets of my fallen platoon members, he told me that if I ever needed anything to call him night or day.

"As long as I'm the CO here," he said, "anything you need son, if it's within my power, you've got it."

The base operator took down my number and told me that he would try to contact the commanding officer and give him my message.

While I waited, I pulled out my wallet and found the small piece of paper where I had written Father Alvarez's private number. After 10 rings, I hung up and tried again. When there was no answer the second time, I checked my watch and called Alexander's hotel. It was six o'clock in Tecolutla and I assumed that they may have all gone out to dinner and couldn't hear the phone. I dialed Father Alvarez's cell again.

"Answer your danm cell phone Father?" I yelled.

I jumped when the phone rang on the counter. Breathing fast, I jerked up the receiver and held it to my ear. "Hello?"

"Matador, is that you?" A voice I didn't recognize asked on the other end of the phone.

"Yes, this is Lance Corporal Travis Lee, who is this?"

"It's Kansas, from boot camp, do you remember me?"

I racked my brain, thinking back. "Wait! Are you that real ugly guy that couldn't shoot for shit on the range?"

"Yes sir, that was me sir," he said laughing.

"It's good to hear from you Kansas. It's been years. Why are you calling? What can I do for you?"

"Well, actually I'm calling, because I think there's something I need to do for you. I'm the officer on duty here at the Corpus Christi Naval Base and I just got this weird call from my operator with your number."

"You're an officer? What the hell has happened to the Marine Corps?"

Kansas laughed. "If you stay in long enough, they either kick you out or promote you. I'm a Major now. Seriously, the operator said that this was some kind of an emergency. So what's up Marine?"

"To be honest with you major, I haven't been active for 17 years, but I'm still a Marine. I didn't know who else to call. I need a long range helicopter and I need it fast."

"What do you need it for?"

"To invade a church in Mexico to save someone's life. Someone I love desperately."

There was a long pause on the phone. "Kansas, are you still there?"

"Yes, I'm just trying to figure out how to do this without getting my ass in a world of shit. How long range? Where are we going in Mexico?"

"Tecolutla. It's about 650 miles from you." I paused and took a breath, "Kansas, I love this woman and she is in grave danger. If I don't get there soon, she'll die."

"Matador, where are you now? Could I land a chopper in the street?"

"Yeah, I live in a cul-de-sac. There's plenty of room."

"Is this an American citizen we're rescuing?"

"Yes. Actually there's two. Her son is there with her."

"We've got an old Jayhawk we use for Search and Rescue. I haven't flown one of those in years, but it's got about a 1,500 mile range. Is there an airport near Tecolutla where we could refuel?"

"Yes, there is an international airport about 30 miles north of there."

There was another long pause. "Well, Lance Corporal Lee, this might be the end of my military career, but this sounds like a search and rescue mission to me, so screw it!

Oorah Marine! I'll be at your front door in one hour. I'll have you in Tecolutla by eleven. Sooner if we have a tail wind!"

20

BLOOD TYPE

It was almost sunset when Levi pulled into the small marina at Tecolutla. He found an empty slip near the fuel dock, tied the bow and stern deck lines to the cleats and walked to the small marina office. The office was an empty room, except for an old Mexican man sitting in a chair behind a folding table in the corner.

"¿Cuánto costaría remolcar mi bote aquí por una noche?" (How much would it cost to tie my boat here for one night?) Levi said, pointing toward his boat.

The old man thought for a moment, then said, "Tres cientos pesos." (300 pesos, 12 dollars.)

Levi handed him a 20 dollar bill. "Puede quedarse con el cambio" (You can keep the change.)

The old man's eyes opened wide "Gracias Señor." (Thank you sir.)

'¿A qué distancia está la capilla del Sagrado Corazón desde aquí?" (How far is the Chapel of the Sacred Heart from here?)

The old man stood, walked to a map of the city hanging on the wall and pointed. "Tú estás aquí y la iglesia está allí. Se trata de una hora de caminata" (You are here and the church is there. It is about an hour walk.)

Levi studied the map a moment, then walked back to his boat and checked his dock lines. In his cabin he lifted his shirt, put the gun inside his belt behind his back, pulled his shirt down over it and checked his reflection in the mirror. No one would notice the gun. He thought to himself.

Purposely, he didn't hurry and walked slowly through the streets of the small town on his way to the church. He didn't want to draw any extra attention to himself. He was just another tourist looking in the shop windows.

He was alarmed to see two heavily armed police officers, carrying military style automatic assault weapons standing on one of the corners and three more patrolling the streets.

He stepped inside one of the shops and pretended to casually browse through the store.

"Good evening. Are you looking for something special?" A smiling Mexican woman behind the counter said to him cheerfully, in perfect English.

He smiled. "No, not really. I'm just looking around. You speak English well."

"Thank you. You are not a local, so I was hoping you spoke English. A lot of the tourists do, and I need the practice."

He picked up a tee shirt with Tecolutla printed in gold letters across the back. "How much is this?"

"Ten dollars US or 200 pesos," She said.

He pulled out his wallet, found a ten and handed it to her. "Has something happened? There seems to be a lot of police around and they are carrying machine guns."

She frowned as she took the money and rang up the sale on the cash register. "So far the drug cartels have not come this far and we do not want them. The government has increased the size of our police to help prevent that. Don't worry about them, they are here for your protection."

Levi smiled and shook his head. "That's good to hear. I understand that the chapel of the sacred heart is a beautiful building, I would love to see it while I'm here, is it far?"

The woman wrinkled her forehead and looked at him. "It is not that beautiful. It's very old and in need of some repair. Do you want to see it tonight?"

"Yes. I will be leaving early tomorrow morning."

"You won't be able to see much. There are no street lights there, but I'm sure the chapel will still be open if you want to see inside. Just follow this street. It's about a 30 minute walk."

Darkness and a 30 minute walk away from the armed police officers was exactly what Levi wanted to hear.

35 minutes later, he found the church and stood silently across the street from the entrance. The stained glass windows were glowing, lit by the bright lights inside. There was a small overhead light in the arch of the doorway illuminating the two large wooden doors in the entrance as well as the street where he was standing. High above the building, on a tall steeple, was a large golden cross shining brightly, lit up by four spot lights.

He checked his watch, it was ten PM. He had no real plan, so he stood there quietly for a long time trying to think of one.

He didn't want anyone else to get hurt. All he wanted to do was find Savannah, shoot her in the head, then escape back into the darkness. When it was over, he would slip back to his boat, crank it up and head back to Matagorda.

Thirty minutes later, he heard the doors begin to creak, so he moved further back into the darkness. When the doors opened, he saw Savannah standing there. She was smiling at a man in front of her. His back was turned, so he couldn't see his face. Then she leaned over and hugged the man and told him goodnight.

Levi reached behind his back, pulled out the gun and started walking toward the door, pointing it at Savannah.

When he walked into the light and the man turned around, he froze. It was Alexander.

When Alexander saw Levi with the gun, he jumped in front of Savannah. "What are you doing here Dad?" he yelled.

Levi lifted the gun and pointed it at him. "Move!" He growled. "I don't want to hurt you son. Get out of the way!"

"RUN MOTHER! RUN AWAY!" Alexander yelled, pushing Savannah back inside the door, "RUN! NOW!"

Frightened and confused, Savannah started running through the chapel screaming. "HELP! SOMEONE PLEASE HELP!"

Alexander reached for the door and started pulling it closed, but Levi ran up, stuck his foot in the way and put the gun against Alexander's head. "Let go of the door and back away!" He growled, "Don't make me shoot you!"

Alexander let go of the handle and backed into the church. Levi kicked the door open and walked inside pointing the gun at Alexander's head. "Where did she go?" He yelled.

"What's going on here?" Father Alvarez yelled, running toward them through the chapel, "who are you and what do you want?" Several of the nuns ran into the chapel behind him.

Levi waved the gun. "GET BACK! ALL OF YOU!" he shouted. "I'M ONLY HERE FOR HER. I DON'T WANT TO HURT ANYONE ELSE!"

"Why are you doing this?" Father Alvarez asked, "here in my church?"

"I'm sorry about this Father, just give her to me and I will leave."

"Who are you talking about?" Father Alvarez asked, taking a few steps closer, "Who are you?"

"He's my father," Alexander shouted, "He's here to kill my mother."

"Why would you do such a thing?" Father Alvarez said, moving closer, "here in your Holy Father's house? Have you no decency, have you no soul?"

Levi laughed. "Father, I'm not sure I've ever had one of those, but for two million dollars, I'd kill her in my mother's house," he snarled, "So where the fuck is she?"

"We have hidden her well, you will never find her. We have also called the police and they will be here soon. Please my son, don't do this. For your own sake, drop the gun and leave us."

Father Alvarez was standing only a few feet away from Alexander. "Please, just go away, before the police come."

Levi pointed his gun at a nun, who was standing close by. "Come here. What is your name?" She walked up to him slowly.

"I am Sister Maria."

He pointed the gun at her head. "If you don't tell me where Savannah is, I will kill Sister Maria and all of the rest of them, one at a time until you tell me. You have five seconds."

He started counting. "Five, four, three..."

"Who are you and why do you want to kill me? What have I done to you?" Savannah said stepping into the lights from the shadows.

Levi turned and glared at her. "Who am I? Are you friggin' kidding?"

"She's lost her memory," Alexander said, "she really doesn't know who you are, she has amnesia. Please Dad, don't hurt her."

"Don't worry son. I'm not going to hurt her, I'm going to kill her."

Suddenly the church began to vibrate and a deafening noise echoed through the chapel and off the walls.

Distracted by the noise, Levi lowered his gun and looked behind him. When he did, Alexander lunged at him, knocking him off his feet to the ground, slamming his fist down on his face, then he grabbed his arm. Levi rolled over and they began to wrestling and fighting for the gun.

A loud explosion filled the room and Alexander's body slumped and became still on the floor.

Levi jumped to his feet, waving the gun in the air. "OH MY GOD! WHAT HAVE I DONE, WHAT HAVE I DONE?" He screamed, looking down at Alexander's bleeding body on the floor.

Savanna ran up to Alexander, falling to her knees, cradling his head in her lap.

Levi slowly raised the gun and aimed it at her head. "See what you made me do. I killed Alex. You worthless bitch!"

"Forgive me Father," Father Alvarez said, as he swung the large metal cross with all his might.

When the cross connected with the back of Levi's head, he dropped like a sack of sand on the floor. Father Alvarez took his foot and nudged his body, but he was out cold. Then he reached down and picked up the gun.

~

The building was still vibrating, but the noise was gradually getting softer when Kansas and I ran through the door. Behind us in the street, with the blades winding down, was a H.H.- 60 Jayhawk helicopter glowing in the lights.

When I ran in and saw Levi and Alexander both laying on the floor bleeding, I was frightened and shocked. "What the hell happened?" I yelled.

"Alexander has been shot," Father Alvarez shouted back, "help us get him to the clinic."

I bent down and picked Alexander up in my arms. "Keep an eye on him," I said to Kansas, motioning to Levi, laying on the floor, "Don't let him go anywhere."

Savannah and the nuns pushed me out of the way as soon as I had laid Alexander on the bed and they went to work.

There was nothing more I could do there, so I walked back to the front of the church where Levi was laying in a puddle of his blood.

"Is he still alive?" I asked.

"Yeah, he has a pulse," Kansas said, " Is this the guy, the killer?"

"Yes, that's the sorry bastard."

I bent down and picked up the cross on the floor. It was mangled and broken. "What happened to this?" I turned and looked at Father Alvarez, "Did you break this Father?"

He shrugged and gave me a small smile. "The cross has always been a mighty weapon against evil."

When the local police arrived, Father Alvarez told them what had happened and they arrested Levi for the attempted murder of Sister Maria and Alexander.

They didn't seem too concerned about his gushing head wound when they jerked him off the floor, slammed him against the wall and handcuffed him. He was barely conscious and still bleeding when they dragged him out the door, down the street and stuffed him into the back of their car.

Kansas grinned as they pulled away. "I was in a Mexican jail once. Got the shit beat out of me almost every day. Gringos are not real popular there. I'm pretty sure he's not gonna like jail much."

I nodded. "Especially when the other prisoners find out that he tried to kill a nun."

When we walked back into the church, Savannah was there talking to Father Alvarez. When she saw me she said, "Where is the man? Alexander's father?"

"The police just took him away, why?" I asked.

She turned back to Father Alvarez. "Call them. Tell them to bring him back, Alexander has lost too much blood, he needs a transfusion."

I frowned. "You're his mother, why can't you give him some of yours?"

"I have type A. and that's the wrong blood type. We just checked Alexander, he has type O. We need his father's," She said with frightened eyes. "Please Father, call the police and tell them to hurry!"

When they brought him back, Levi had stopped bleeding from his head, but was barely conscious when they laid him on the bed next to Alexander's.

When the nun stuck the needle in his arm, he moaned and said, "What's going on?"

I walked to his bed and leaned over him. "Alex needs a transfusion and we're taking some of your blood."

He rocked his head side to side. "NO!" He shouted.

I grabbed his chin to stop him from moving. "Alexander needs blood or he's going to die. So shut up and be still!"

"NO, NO!" He yelled, "Don't give him my blood. It will kill him."

"Stop moving!" I yelled, "You're his father and he needs your blood! It's the only way we can save him!"

He tried to sit up, but the two police men slammed him back down on the bed. "NO, NO, NO!" He screamed, "Not my blood! It will kill him! It's the wrong type!"

I looked at Father Alvarez. "How long does it take to get someone's blood typed?"

He looked at the sisters and asked them, "¿Cuánto tiempo tomará obtener un tipo de sangre?"

"Ten or fifteen minutes." Savannah said, "But I'm not sure we can wait that long."

"Please do it, check my blood," Levi mumbled, barely conscious, "you'll see."

Ten minutes later, Sister Maria walked into the clinic holding the results of the blood test in her hand. She was shaking her head side to side. "El tiene apretado B este hombre no es su padre."

Savannah gasped and sat down on the edge of Alexander's bed, "Oh my God," She whispered.

"What did she say?" I asked.

She looked up at me with sad eyes. "This man is not Alexander's father. We can't use his blood."

"No!" I yelled, "That's not true, he *IS* his father. There must be some mistake."

She shook her head. "There is no mistake. I have A, he has O. It's impossible for his father to have A.B."

She looked down at Alexander and stroked his hair. "We have very little time left," She whispered. She looked at me and Kansas. "Do you know your blood types?"

Kansas unbuttoned his shirt, pulled out his dog tags and read them. "I have type B," He said.

I shook my head. "I'm sorry, but I can't remember what mine is."

Levi shifted his body on the hospital bed. "It...will work," He mumbled softly.

I leaned over him. "What did you say? What will work?"

He coughed and opened his eyes. "She...couldn't go...through with it." His eyes closed again.

I shook him, hard. "Wake up you bastard. What are you trying to say?"

He moaned loudly, reaching his hand up, touching the cut on the back of his head. Then he opened his eyes and made contact with mine.

"There...was...no abortion," He coughed again and closed his eyes, "you...are his father, not me."

∼

I tried to revive Levi several more times to wake him back up, but he was out cold. More than likely he had received a concussion when Father Alvarez smashed him upside the head with the cross.

And although he had tried to kill her, Sister Maria wouldn't let the police take him away until she had cleaned and bandaged his head. She begged them to leave him there in the clinic until he woke up, but they wouldn't do it. They picked him up by his arms and feet, dragged him back to their car and hauled him away.

To make sure, they tested my blood, and it *was* type O.

We carefully carried Alexander to the chopper and did the transfusion on our way back to Texas. Kansas put his military career on the line for the second time when he set the Jayhawk down, unannounced, in front of the Valley Baptist Medical Center in Harlingen. The second we landed, he started yelling orders at the doctors and nurses like he was flying in an injured combat soldier.

Without any hesitation, they followed his orders, loaded Alexander onto a gurney and rushed him into the emergency room.

After they rolled Alexander away, Savannah threw her arms around Kansas's neck and hugged him. "Thank you Kansas," she said, "you saved my son's life."

"I sure hope so ma'am," He said smiling, "I'm planning on meeting him someday when he's feeling better."

I held out my hand to shake his, "What can I say?" I said. He pushed my hand away and hugged me instead.

"Matador, I sure hope you have a big house, because if they kick my ass out of the Marine Corps for this, I'm moving in with you!"

"Oorah!" He yelled as he climbed into the chopper and cranked the engine.

The sun was just beginning to rise in the black sky, glowing golden and orange on the horizon. As we stood there, watching Kansas lift off and fly away toward the sun, Savannah reached down, took my hand and gently squeezed it.

When the loud thumping of the rotors had faded, we ran into the emergency room to check on Alexander.

The doctors had rushed him to surgery. They said that he was stable, but critical. For the next three hours, Savannah and I held hands and prayed. Finally a doctor pushed through the double doors and walked up to us.

"Are you the family of the gun shot victim?"

"Yes, this is his mother," I said.

"And who are you?" he asked.

"I'm his father," I heard myself say. I started to say something else, but stopped. Suddenly the reality hit me. So much had happened so quickly, my only thoughts had been about saving Alexander's life, the truth had not yet registered. I was Alexander's father.

"So, it was you that gave him the blood?" the doctor asked.

"Yes," I said.

"The bullet nicked an artery in his stomach. We found it and closed it up. No doubt he would have bled out if it hadn't been for the transfusion. You had to have given him a lot of your blood. I think we need to check you in as well and get some fluids in you."

"I don't care about me!" I yelled, "How is Alexander? Is he going to live?"

The doctor smiled. "He's going to be fine. He's young and strong. You don't have to worry about him, you need to worry about yourself."

Before I knew it, they had me lying on a hospital bed hooked up to an I.V. receiving someone else's blood. I must have been weaker than I realized and soon I fell asleep.

∼

On his way back to the Corpus Christi Naval base, Kansas had called my law office and told them what it happened and where we were.

Against my wishes, Olivia and Jeb had caught the next plane out of Switzerland and had just landed when called.

Olivia called Kelly, then she and Jeb boarded her father's plane and Kelly, BJ and Rebecca jumped in their car.

When I woke up and opened my eyes, Olivia was standing over my bed.

"Olivia?" I asked, "is that you. You're supposed to be in Switzerland?"

"Yes, it's me. We got back this morning. How are you feeling?"

"Ok I guess. How long was I out?"

"I'm not sure. We got here at noon. It's 4 o'clock now."

"What? It's 4 o'clock?" I raised up on my elbows, "where is Savannah?"

"She's with Alexander." She said.

"How's he doing?"

"He's great. He woke up hungry an hour ago," She said laughing.

"Thank God," I said, laying back on the bed.

"I really like her," Olivia said softly.

"You met Savannah?"

"Yes. We've been talking all afternoon. She's even more beautiful than you described."

"What have you two been talking about?"

She laughed. "What do you think? We've been talking about you."

An hour later they let me get up, put my clothes on and visit Alexander. When I walked in his room he was sitting up in bed, smiling and eating with his right hand. Rebecca, smiling widely, was holding his left.

"Hey Uncle Travis," He said, "how are you doing?"

I laughed. "I'm doing great. You're the one that got shot. How are *you* doing?"

"I'm ok, a little sore, but the doctor said I'm gonna be fine."

"That's what I hear, but you sure scared the hell out of us."

He put down his fork and looked at me. "Mom told me what you did. Thank you sir...thank you for saving my life."

∽

Olivia had booked us all rooms at the Courtyard Marriott, so after we said goodnight to Alexander, we caught cabs to the hotel. After we checked in, we all met for dinner at a small restaurant a few blocks away.

"So, where is he now?" Kelly asked.

"I'm not sure," I said., "but I suspect he's sitting in a jail cell in Tecolutla."

Olivia shook her head. "No, he's not. I talked to the local police there this morning. They moved him to a prison in Cereso Poza Rico."

"Already? Without a trial?" I said, "they have him in a prison?"

She smiled. "It's Mexico. They do things a little different down there."

"What about his boat?" Kelly asked, "it has to be there."

"They will confiscate it as soon as they find it." Olivia said, "it's gone."

Savannah had chosen to sit between Rebecca and BJ, and other than talking to them casually off and on through the evening, she didn't join in the group conversation at all.

When we got back to the hotel, she asked me if we could talk for a while in the lobby, so we said goodnight to everyone and found a comfortable couch by the fireplace.

Savannah turned and looked at me with concerned eyes. "I know you are probably wondering, but not sure how to ask me, so I thought I would just tell you to get it out in the open."

I lowered my eyebrows. "Wondering about what?"

"My memory," she said softly, "wondering if all of the horrible, frightening trauma we had just lived through over the last 24 hours might have brought it back," She dropped her head and stared at her hands, "it didn't."

I didn't react. I wasn't sure exactly what to say. I couldn't imagine what it must've been like for her to have someone try to kill her and have no idea why.

"He was your husband. His name is Levi Cruz and you've known him most of your life. Sadly, this was all about money. A lot of money."

She nodded her head. "I know. Olivia told me who he was. She also told me about the insurance policy...and about the trial."

"What else did she tell you?"

"That he's been trying to kill me for a long time. That's why I was in the water the day the shrimp boat found me."

"Yes, we think he hit you with something and threw you overboard."

She sat there silently staring at the fireplace a long time. "Travis, what did I do to him to make him hate me so?"

I shrugged. "I don't know, but I've thought about it a lot. I believe his hatred for me had a lot to do with all of this."

She lifted her head. "Really? How?"

"It goes back to our childhood. He was obsessed with you, because you were my girl. He had no friends, no one liked him and he wanted what we had desperately. So he did everything he could to break us up, but when he succeeded and realized that you could never love him the way you loved me, his obsession changed and that love he had for you, turned to hate. Not just for you, but for me as well. I believe that's when he started planning to kill you. In his twisted jealous mind, he believed that he had to kill you, so we could never get back together."

"Is he really that evil?" She asked.

I shrugged again. "I don't know if he's really evil, but I *do* know that jealousy makes men to do unthinkable things. The Bible warns us about the evil of jealousy. Levi let it take control of him and it ruined him."

We sat silently, not talking watching the dancing flames in the fireplace.

"May I ask you about what something Levi said?" she asked.

"Sure, what do you want to know?"

She shifted nervously in her seat. "He said there was no abortion. You...thought I had an abortion?"

I lowered my head. "Yes, I did."

"That's how he broke us up, and why you left me?"

"Yes."

"Because you thought it was his baby and I had betrayed you. And that broke your heart."

I shook my head. "It shattered it."

Her eyes filled with tears. "Olivia told me that you two had dated," she whispered softly, "but she broke it off, because she knew that you still loved me. She said that after all these years...even though I had crushed you...you never stopped loving me."

I smiled, staring into her beautiful wet eyes sparkling, reflecting the flames from the fireplace. "I've loved you every minute of every day of my life."

She reached out and gently touched my face with her fingers. "I wish I could remember that love. It must have felt wonderful."

I kissed her hand. "How does it feel now?"

She pulled her hand away and dropped her head. "Truthfully?"

"Yes, please," I said, "You can always tell me the truth. I need to know what you're feeling."

She thought for a moment trying to find the right words. "Having you love me so much, but not knowing you, not knowing anything about you, is very...confusing. I want to love you back, but..."

I put my arm around her shoulder. "Please, don't worry about that. I understand."

"I know you do, but I don't," She leaned against my shoulder and began to cry. "What if I never remember. And if I don't...what if I'm not the same woman you fell in love with back then?"

"Savannah, I'm not the same guy you fell in love with back then either. So it really doesn't matter if you remember the past or not. All that matters now is that we are together and have the chance to fall in love with each other again."

I wiped a tear from her cheek and smiled. "Remember? I told you we were going to take this very slow, and we are. I'm not going anywhere. I know you are confused and scared, but there is nothing to fear."

She lifted her head, smiling with her beautiful eyes. "Thank you Travis," she whispered, "Olivia said you were amazing. I can't wait to get to know you."

"Me too," I said.

She looked so beautiful in the soft glow of the fireplace. I wanted to lean over and kiss her, but I knew that she wasn't ready for that.

"You want to hear what Father Alvarez told me?"

She lifted her eyes. "Yes."

"He believed that God saved you from drowning because you have something else to accomplish in your life. He also believes that I am supposed to be part of that."

Her turquoise eyes sparkled as she grinned. "Father Alvarez is a very wise man. And what do *you* think?"

"I agree with him. I believe that one day you will either get your memory back, or you will simply realize that right here, in my arms, is where you have always belonged."

21

THIRTY-SEVEN

When I got to my room I took a long hot shower, crawled under the clean crisp sheets and stared at the ceiling for hours. My body was aching, I was completely exhausted, but my mind was wide awake, trying to process everything that had happened in my life in the last twenty four hours. My mind kept jumping from one thing to another.

Savanna was alive, Levi was in a Mexican prison...and Alexander was my son.

Was it really true? Or was that just another one of Levi's lies? But if it was true, how could I not have realized it before?

I thought back, trying to remember the exact date I saw Savannah and Levi at that abortion clinic. It was in the summer, because I was working for the florist delivering flowers. I was 18 and we had just graduated from high school.

How old is Alexander? I asked myself. "19, he's 19," I whispered. In my head, I did the math; 18 plus 19 equaled 37.

I picked up the phone and dialed the front desk. "I need Olivia Bachman's room number please."

"She's in number 383, would you like me to put you through?"

"No thanks, that's just down the hall. I'll go bang on her door."

When she jerked the door open, she wasn't smiling. "Damn It Travis! Don't you ever sleep?"

Ignoring her, I ducked under her arm that was holding the door open and walked into the room.

Jeb squinted his eyes when he saw me. "Travis?" he asked, fumbling for his glasses on the night stand, "is that you?"

"I'm sorry to wake you up guys," I said pacing in front of the bed, "but I need to talk to someone."

Olivia walked back to the bed, fluffed her pillow, pulled back the covers and crawled back in, sitting up against the headboard. "Ok, we are listening," she said, "So talk."

"How could I have been so stupid?" I yelled.

Olivia glanced over at Jeb. "Do you want to take that one?"

"Nope," he said, "I'm not gonna touch it."

"Ok, I give up," she said, "Stupid about what?"

"18 plus 19 is 37," I ranted, "Don't you see? I'm 37!"

Again, Olivia looked over at Jeb. "I thought he was much older," he smirked.

"Stop pacing!" Olivia yelled, "You're driving us crazy. Sit down and tell us what the hell you are talking about."

I plopped down in the chair behind the desk, leaned over with my elbows on my knees and whispered. "I'm Alexander's Father."

Olivia and Jeb didn't respond. They just stared back at me smiling.

"Did you hear me?" I shouted. "I'm Alexander's father!"

"Stop yelling," Olivia said, "it's 2 am. Of course we heard you."

"Well?"

"Well what?"

I jumped up and started pacing again. "I tell you that I just found out that I have a son and all you can say is well what?"

Olivia pointed at the chair. "SIT!"

I sighed and plopped back down.

"Travis, are you serious? Are you telling me that you've never suspected this before? You've never added it up before now?"

"No," I said, running my hands through my hair, "I thought it was Levi's child she had aborted. That's why I left. It wasn't until we interviewed Levi and he told me, that the child she aborted was mine. But remember, he said that she had gone through with the abortion. It never crossed my mind that she had backed out. I never knew that child was Alexander."

"Travis, have you ever really looked at him?" Olivia asked, "I've known from the first day he walked into your office. I always thought you knew it too, but kept it a secret for his sake."

I leaned back in the chair and wiped my eyes. "I didn't know. I swear I didn't know."

"What about Alexander? Does he know?" Jeb asked.

I shook my head. "I don't think so."

"Travis, you have to tell him, he needs to know," Olivia said, "I think it will answer a lot of questions he has in his heart."

∽

The next morning my phone rang at 7 am.

"Mr. Lee, this is Lieutenant Anderson from the Harlingen Police Department. I apologize for the early phone call, but we need to talk. Would it be OK if I swing by your hotel this morning?"

"Of course," I said, "I'll meet you in the lobby in 30 minutes."

When I hung up I called Olivia and told her about the meeting. Thirty minutes later we met at the elevator and rode it down to the first floor together.

Lieutenant Anderson was waiting for us in the lobby, so we found a table in the breakfast area, grabbed some coffee, and settled around it.

"Lieutenant, this is Judge Olivia Bachman, she is a state court judge from Austin. I am an attorney from the firm, Bachman, Turner, Lee and associates, also from Austin. We assume you are here to talk about Alexander Cruz?"

He stood and reached out to shake Olivia's hand. "It's nice to meet you Your Honor," he said politely. Then he smiled at me and shook mine. "Nice to meet you too sir."

He sat back down and took a sip of his coffee. "Is Alexander the name of the boy in the hospital...the one with the gut shot?"

I nodded. "Yes, that's him," I said.

He pulled out a small note pad and wrote down Alexander's name. "What relationship is he to you?"

"He is my son." I heard myself say, but the words sounded foreign.

He raised his eyebrows. "I thought you said his name was Cruz?"

"It is. I'm his biological father, his mother was married to a man named Levi Cruz."

"What is his mother's name?" He asked, "And where is she?"

For the next twenty-five minutes, Olivia and I took turns telling the Lieutenant the entire story. After the first few minutes he stopped writing in his pad, leaned back in his chair and just listened.

When we finished, he shook his head and leaned forward. "Where is Savannah now?" He asked.

"She's here in the hotel, upstairs," Olivia said.

The lieutenant sat quietly, staring at his notes, sipping his coffee for a few minutes before he spoke. "I guess the first thing we need to do," he began, "is to get all of you cleared through immigration. After that, if you don't mind, I would appreciate it if you would talk to my chief," he said with a grin, "maybe he can figure out what to do next."

I tilted my head confused. "What to do next?"

The Lieutenant smiled. "Well Mr. Lee, the problem is...you flew across the Mexican border, got into a gun fight, and then flew back carrying an undocumented passenger. I'm afraid in doing that, you broke a few laws...International laws. And to be honest with you, that's just a bit above my pay grade."

Fortunately the local judge was an old friend of Olivia's father and in a matter of minutes everything got settled. All we had to do was promise to fax the judge a copy of Savannah's birth certificate and all would be forgotten.

To clear up the legal mess had taken most of the day. On our way that morning to talk to the police chief, we had dropped off Savannah at the hospital. When Olivia, Jeb and I finally made it back we were all shocked when we met Savannah and Alexander walking down the hallway together. She had her arm around his waist, helping to support him.

He was bent over holding onto a rolling IV unit, but smiling. "Hey!" He yelled as he saw us.

"What the hell are you doing out of bed?" I said, "Aren't you the guy that got shot yesterday?"

"Yes sir, that's me," he said with a chuckle, "but they told me the sooner I get up and start walking, the sooner I get out of here."

Against the doctor's wishes but bowing to Alexander's insistence, we were allowed to load him into James Bachman's airplane and fly him back to a hospital in Austin.

It was a six passenger plane but after we secured Alexander's gurney to two of the seats, the only place left for me to sit on the three hour flight back was in the small head. It was the longest and most uncomfortable three hours of my life.

∾

After we got Alexander checked into his room at the St. David's Medical Center, we all took a cab to my house.

Savanna had been very quiet most of the day, only talking, when talked to. I wasn't exactly sure what was wrong, but it was obvious that something was troubling her.

Jeb and I grabbed a beer and settled around my patio table by the pool, while Olivia gave Savannah a tour of the house.

When they got back, I noticed that Savannah's eyes were red and she had obviously been crying. "What's wrong?" I asked, glancing at Olivia.

Olivia gave me a slight shrug and a look that told me that she had no idea why she was so upset.

"Savannah, what's wrong?" I asked softly, "Why are you crying?"

She wiped her eyes and looked away. "I'm sorry, it's nothing. We can talk about it later."

"No," I said, "let's talk about it now. I think it's important for you to know that you can talk about anything in front of Olivia and Jeb. Even if it's about me. You have to be all jumbled up inside right now, scared and confused. The only way any of us can help you is for you to tell us what's going on inside your head. So please...tell us why you're crying."

She pulled out a chair and sat down at the table. "I don't really know why I'm crying. I just can't seem to stop."

She smiled and looked around the table at us. "I know you are all incredible, wonderful people and that you care about me. I know you want to help me, but you are strangers to me. Do you understand that?"

"I nodded. "Honestly, I don't think any of us can fully understand what you're going through. That's why you need to talk to us, tell us what you are feeling, so we *can* understand."

"I'm crying because I'm angry," she whispered, "And I know that makes no sense."

Olivia took her hand. "Angry about what?"

"I'm angry that I have a child in the hospital recovering from a gun shot wound that he received trying to save me. A child I don't remember raising. I'm so angry that this young man risked his life to save mine and I don't have any idea who he is.

She wiped her eyes with her hand and looked at me. "The mural on your wall...where did you get it?"

"From an art dealer here in Austin," I said, "but when I bought it I didn't know that you had painted it."

"Then why did you buy it?"

I smiled. "Because it reminded me of you."

"That's what I thought," She broke down, crying hard.

I reached for her, but Olivia held up her hand and glared at me. "She needs to cry," she said softly, "to let all this out."

For about twenty minutes, no one said a word. We just sat in awkward silence listening to Savannah cry.

When she stopped, Olivia, acting like nothing had happened said, "Do you have any decent food in this house? I'm starving."

She stood up and looked at Savannah. "Do you remember how to cook?"

Savannah shrugged. "I don't know."

Olivia took her hand and pulled her up. "Well let's go find out."

Savannah discovered that she remembered how to cook, so

together, using whatever they could find in my freezer and refrigerator they prepared an amazing meal. She also discovered that she preferred white wine over red that night.

∼

Not wanting Savannah to feel uncomfortable being alone with me in the house, I convinced Olivia and Jeb to stay, Jeb and Olivia in one of the guest rooms, and Savannah in the other.

When I woke up the next morning I found a note from Olivia on the island in the kitchen.

Travis,

I'm sorry, I had to leave early. It's Monday and I am presiding over a case that's scheduled to start at 9 am. Just give Savannah some space and time. I'm sure she will adjust soon.

P.S. If my case gets settled and doesn't go to trial, tell Savannah I will be picking her up after noon to take her shopping. She needs clothes, shoes and everything else.

Love,

Olivia

When I looked up from the note, I saw Savannah standing there. She was wrapped in a towel and her hair was wet.

"Do you have any tea?"

"Yeah, I think so," I said opening the cabinet door.

While I was searching for the tea, she found a tea pot, filled it with water and put it on the stove.

I grinned at her. "I didn't know I owned one of those," I said pointing to the pot.

She laughed. "I found it last night when Olivia and I were cooking."

I poured a cup of coffee and sat on a stool at the island. "I'm a coffee guy, I've never liked tea much."

When the tea pot started whistling, she poured the hot water over the teabag in her cup and sat on the stool next to me. "I don't suppose you have a spare toothbrush do you?"

I smiled. "As a matter of fact I do. My electric toothbrush came with four different heads, you can use one of those."

She followed me into my bedroom, to the master bath. I found the new brush head, snapped it on and handed it to her. Then I walked back to the kitchen and started cooking breakfast while I waited for her, but she never came back.

When I checked on her in my bedroom, she was standing in the middle of my closet. "What are you doing in here?"

She started laughing. "I'm trying on some of your clothes. My dress is covered in blood and I can't walk around in a towel all day."

I wiggled my eyebrows. "I wouldn't mind that."

Those words slipped out of my mouth without thinking. I instantly cursed myself worrying that I may have crossed a line, but she didn't appear offended at all.

She put her hands on her hips. "I'm sure you wouldn't," she said laughing, "maybe you better take me back to the church."

It was the first time I'd heard her laugh in years. It sounded like music to my ears. I was hoping it was the first sign of her opening up and feeling comfortable around me.

Eventually, she found an old pair of my skinny jeans that fit her perfectly and a sweatshirt. When she walked into the kitchen barefoot, with her hair pulled back into a ponytail, she looked maybe 18, exactly like the girl I had remembered in my dreams.

While we ate breakfast, I tried, but I could not keep my eyes off of her.

"You're doing it again," she said smiling, "Stop it. You're making me nervous."

"I'm sorry, but I don't think I can. You are just so beautiful."

She slid back her stool, stood up, and walked up to me. "Stand up," She said.

I slid back my stool and stood. She wrapped her arms around my waist and looked up into my eyes. "I'm following Olivia's orders. I don't know if this is too soon or not," She whispered, "but *She* thinks we need to kiss."

"What do *you* think?" I asked.

She gave me a shy grin. "I think we should follow her orders."

I'm not sure how *she* felt, because she didn't say anything. She just smiled and pulled me back down and kissed me again.

But when I leaned over, that first time, took her face in my hands and gently kissed her lips, my heart skipped a beat and my knees almost buckled.

∼

At noon, the doorbell rang and Olivia walked in holding a pair of flip flops. "Put these on for now," she said to Savannah.

Then she walked up to me, held out her hand and said, "Credit card please. We'll be back very late. Have a nice day."

When they left, I took a shower, got dressed and headed to the office. when I walked in, Buster almost knocked me down, he was so excited to see me. When he finally calmed down a little, I stuck my head in James' office to say hello.

"I hope Buster wasn't too much trouble. I really appreciate you looking after him."

He looked up at me over his readers. "he's a real pain in the ass sometimes, but I survived." he said, "He sure missed you though. He's been spending most of his time hanging out in *your* office waiting for you."

After I went through the large stack of messages on my desk, I took Buster for a walk and called the hospital to check on Alexander. He was in great spirits and told me that the doctors said that he may be released soon, possibly later that evening or first thing in the morning.

"Uncle Travis, Rebecca's here. She drove up this morning. If they let me out tonight or tomorrow, would it be OK if she stays with us at the house for a few days?"

"Of course," I said, "but she's not staying in your room, understood?"

"Yes sir," he said a little disappointed.

When I hung up I sat down on a bench in the park and watched as Buster did his business.

Thinking about my conversation with Alexander made me smile. He was going to be fine and for the first time in my life, I had acted like a father.

In my head, I replayed what I told him. *But she's not staying in your room, understand? Maybe a cool uncle would have let him get away with it*, I thought to myself, *but not a father*.

At 5:30, Olivia called to let me know that she was taking Savannah out to dinner and that they would be back late, so when I left the office I stopped at a hamburger joint, bought two burgers for me and Buster and drove to the house.

After we ate our hamburgers, although it was only 8:00 pm, Buster seemed exhausted from all the excitement of the day, so he walked into my bedroom, crawled into his fluffy bed, and fell asleep.

A few minutes later Alexander called to tell me that they were releasing him in the morning at 8 am. I promised we would be there to pick him up.

∽

There are only two things I know for sure about women. Some love to shop and some don't. Olivia was the first category. If there was a professional shopping league, she would be the quarterback. She loved shopping for clothes, especially shoes more than any woman I had ever met. It was her true passion.

I wasn't sure about Savannah, because all I knew about her was when we were young, and back then she was very poor, like me. The holey jeans we wore to school were not considered cool, just a sad sign of our poverty. But when the girls finally made it back and I saw the smile on Savannah's face and the twinkle in her eye, I had my answer.

It took them two trips to unload the car, carrying all of the boxes and shopping bags to Savannah's bedroom. When Olivia handed me back my credit card, she grinned and said, "Don't ask, you don't want to know."

For the next hour I was forced to sit in a chair in Savannah's bedroom, nodding my approval, watching the two of them, giggling like little girls, hold up pants, blouses, belts, skirts, dresses, matching shoes, and purses, and on, and on, and on...

They had also apparently spent a few hours trying to clean out the shelves of Victoria's Secret. And with no signs of embarrassment except for mine, they boldly held up skimpy thongs and ornate bras of every color of the rainbow.

While they were organizing and hanging the clothes in Savannah's walk-in closet, I walked into the kitchen and opened a bottle of Chardonnay. When I popped the cork, Buster was standing there looking up at me.

"What's wrong buddy, did all the giggling and laughing from the girls wake you up?"

"Woof," he said, plopping down on the floor on his belly.

When Savannah walked into the kitchen and saw Buster, she dropped to her knees and said, "Who is this?"

Buster looked up at Savannah and his tail immediately started wagging at hyper speed. Then he jumped up and ran out of the room. A few seconds later, he ran back into the kitchen barking like crazy. Then he took off again, still barking.

"What in the hell?" I said, following him.

He was running back and forth between my bedroom and the kitchen, barking and whining like he was trying to tell us something. When he took off again, we all followed him into my bedroom to see what he was barking about.

He was standing under the mural looking up at the woman in the painting, whining. Then he ran up to Savannah, jumping up with his paws on her knees. His tail was wagging so fast, it looked like he was dancing with his hips swaying back and forth.

Since I had picked him up that day at John Willie's house, I'd never seen him this excited. It was obvious that he wanted Savannah to pick him up, so she bent down and lifted him up into her arms.

As Savannah laughed, Buster barked, wiggling in her arms with over the top excitement, licking her face.

It was very strange, but somehow Buster knew that she was the woman in the painting and apparently loved her as much as I did.

It was an instant bond for Savannah as well, love at first sight. I believe it was something that both of them needed at the time. Buster's sad face disappeared, never to be seen again and Savannah's seemed happier too. She stopped obsessing about her memory loss and began to relax and open up to me. Somehow Buster's unconditional love seemed to help her heal, helped her laugh and made them both happy. From that day on, Buster never left her side. He was either sleeping in her lap, laying at her feet, or following her around the house. They were inseparable.

∼

It took two weeks before Alexander felt strong enough to go back to college. Because he had missed almost three weeks of the second semester, we weren't sure if they were going to allow him to attend, but after my boss, James Bachman, one of UT's major benefactors, made a few threatening phone calls to the Dean, they allowed him to start, and they also instructed his professors to catch him up on what he'd missed with special, private make up classes. After a few months, Alexander had caught up and fell back into his regular routine. In return for keeping the pool clean and the landscaping up, I agreed to fly Rebecca back and forth from Matagorda to Austin once a month, so they could spend a few days together.

Against everyone's advice, I didn't tell Alexander the truth about me being his father. I can't really explain why, but there never seemed to be an appropriate moment to bring something like that up. So he continued calling me Uncle Travis.

∼

After doing some research, I took Savannah to the Houston Medical Center to meet with the best doctors I could find. They did multiple tests, from CAT scans to MRIs trying to discover the cause of her memory loss. In the end, they told us that there was no obvious brain damage caused from the blow to her head, and they couldn't find any physical reason for her amnesia.

They recommended that she begin weekly sessions with a psychiatrist, to see if her memory loss was caused, not necessarily because of the blow on her head, but from the mental trauma of the experience she had lived through.

All of the doctors were brutally honest, explaining that because of the length of time that had passed, there was a real possibility that she would never regain her memory. Each time a doctor would tell her this, Savannah did a great job of hiding her true feelings. She would just smile and pass it off, but later that night, I could hear her crying in her room.

My personal relationship with Savannah was moving forward slowly. We spent a lot of time talking. Interestingly, she didn't want to hear much about our childhood growing up in Matagorda, and never wanted to hear anything about her father or Levi.

When I brought them up, she would stop me and say, "I don't want to know about the bad things, just the good ones."

What seemed to intrigue her the most was hearing my stories about my years in the Marine Corps and the years in college, and in law school.

My caseload was growing and my work was piling up. But instead of working late in my office to catch up like I had always done before, I brought it home to work on it there, so I could spend the time with her.

A few times a week, we would go out on a date. I would take her out to dinner and a movie. We also spent time with Olivia and Jeb. Almost every weekend we either went to their house, or they came to ours.

During the days, when I was at work, she spent her time swimming in the pool, taking Buster on long walks, visiting with

Alexander when he was home, or sketching in the art notebook I had bought her.

She seemed to be happy, but at the same time distant and sometimes she was very quiet.

As far as any romance between us, I had decided that was going to be up to her. The last thing she needed was to feel any sexual pressure from me. I wanted her love, not anything else.

I wasn't sure, but I thought that if she was going to fall in love with me again, being her friend, her true, trusted friend, was the best way to get that started.

I will admit it was difficult sometimes, especially when she would surprise me. Often she would come sit in my lap and kiss me. I wasn't ever sure if that was all she wanted, so I always held back, hoping she would make the next move, and for the first six months, she never did.

~

Although my house was only one story, the Attic over the garage was tall enough to stand. I told Savanna that I was building a home office and hired a contractor. I had the room insulated and air conditioned, installed two big skylights in the roof, and two larger windows on each end. When it was finished and the circular stairs were installed, I filled the room with a large wooden easel, a padded stool, a large supply of oil paints of every color, brushes of all sizes and a couple of dozen blank canvases.

"Where are you taking me?" She said laughing.

"You'll see. No peeking," I said adjusting the blindfold covering her eyes.

I carefully led her up the circular stairs with Buster following us close behind.

"OK, you can take it off now," I said, excited with anticipation. When she took off the blindfold and saw her new studio, she screamed, and ran around the room looking at her easel, paints and brushes. Then she ran up to me, jumped into my arms and kissed me for a long, long time.

That night, I heard my door open. A few seconds later, Savannah pulled back the covers and slid her warm, naked body next to mine.

My heart was pounding in my chest. I could smell her hair and her perfume, as she wrapped her smooth, long legs around me and whispered in my ear, "You are the man in my dreams, and I've been dreaming about this for a long time. Make love to me Travis. I want you...I need you...now."

22
THIS IS NOT OVER

On the weekends when Rebecca would fly in from Matagorda for her visits, and the weather was good, we usually drove to Lake Travis for some fun on the water, skiing or just cruising up and down the lake. In the evenings we would light a fire in the pit and watch the sun set together. Buster seemed to especially love the new stairs Alexander and I had built that led down to the water. He constantly ran up and down them until he wore himself out and plopped on his belly next to the fire pit.

With every monthly trip, it became more obvious that Rebecca and Alexander were madly in love with each other. Watching their young love reminded me of how I had once felt about Savannah when I was their age. It was wonderful to see, but at times it made me a little melancholy and sad realizing how much time with Savannah I had missed in my life.

And although I realized the Savannah I knew now, wasn't the Savannah I had fallen in love with, my feelings for her had not changed. In fact, they had grown. I loved everything about her, her laugh, her smile, the taste of her lips, her smell, the look in her beautiful eyes when we made love...

As far as I knew she had not regained any of her memory. If she had, she had kept it to herself and not told me. Her past was something we rarely talked about.

~

On the one year anniversary of the day I had found her in the church, I surprised her with a road trip back to Tecolutla. Father Alvarez and the sisters were very excited to see her again. We spent an entire day there with them catching up.

The next morning, we stopped in to see Lacitia Perez, at the art gallery, and Savannah gave her three of her new paintings to sell and promised to send her more in the future.

That afternoon we drove to the ocean and walked hand-in-hand along the beach talking about the times she would come there to paint. It was a fun trip that Savannah seemed to love.

On our way back we drove along the coast through Padre Island and Corpus Christi to get to Matagorda.

It was Savannah's first trip back home. I wasn't sure if it would spark any of her old memories, but I was hoping it would.

When we pulled into town, I turned down the road that led to our old houses. There was a for sale sign in front of mine, but they were both run down and looked abandoned.

When I pulled into the driveway and turned off the engine, Savannah looked at me and asked. "Is this where Kelly and BJ live?"

I laughed. "No, they live in a beautiful beach house on the Matagorda Peninsula. This is someone else's house."

I got out of the car and looked in the windows. The house was empty. When I wiggled the front doorknob, I smiled, it wasn't locked.

"What are you doing?" She yelled from the car.

I waved for her to follow me, opened the door, and walked inside. A few minutes later, I heard Savannah's voice echoing from the living room. "Travis? Where are you?"

"I'm in here, in the bedroom on the right. You need to come see this."

"See what?" She said walking into the room.

"See that." I said pointing at the old faded mural still hanging on the wall.

When she saw it she gasped. "Was this your house?"

"Yes," I said, "And that's your painting."

She walked up to it and gently ran her hands over the surface. "How old was I when I painted this?"

"You were 12 years old."

She stood there silently staring at the mural for a long time. Her eyes suddenly widened. "I pushed these panels through there." She said, pointing at the window, "Why did I do that?"

I smiled. "I was real sick. It was my birthday and you brought it to me. It was your present."

She stared off into space trying to remember. Then she shook her head and smiled. "Did you like it?"

"I loved it and I still do."

Suddenly, she jerked her head up. "Did you hear that?" She ran out of the room.

I ran after her, following her around the house to the back yard. The train appeared around the bend just as we ran up. When she saw it, she turned and smiled at me. Then she held her hands up covering her ears, seconds before the engineer blew the loud whistle.

Suddenly, I was 10 years old again watching my beloved Savannah laughing and giggling, holding her hands over her ears, as the train blasted its whistle and rumbled by.

The old treehouse wasn't there any longer, but I pointed up at the limb where it used to sit and told her about it anyway. When we got back to the car, I dialed the number on the for sale sign and asked what they wanted for the old house. I really didn't want the house, but I wasn't going to take a chance on losing that mural again.

On the way to Kelly and BJ's, I had to drive past the beach house that Savannah and Levi once owned. The second I turned onto the beach road, her expression dropped and her smile disappeared.

"Did I used to live there?" She asked pointing at the house.

"You remember that?" I asked, slowing down.

She shook her head slowly, staring at the house. "Yes." She said, clinching her jaw, "Please don't stop. Get me out of here!"

She was perspiring and her face was pale. I pressed on the excelerator and sped away. "What do you remember about that house?"

She pursed her lips together and frowned. "Pain," she whispered, "I remember pain."

"Pain?" I asked confused.

She shook her head. "I remember standing on that deck, looking at the ocean, feeling pain."

"Where did you feel the pain?"

She touched her hand to her face, "Here." She turned and looked at me, "He hurt me…beat me, didn't he."

"Yes," I said softly, "So bad you had to have three plastic surgeries to reconstruct your face."

She stared out of the window at the ocean, gently touching her face. Then she turned and looked at me. "I've been having dreams. Nightmares."

"About what?"

She dropped her head. "About him."

I pulled over and stopped. "Savannah, look at me. Tell me about these dreams."

She slowly lifted her head. Her eyes were filled with tears. "This is not over. He's coming again…to kill us all this time."

I tried to explain that Levi had been found guilty of attempted murder and was never gonna get out of that Mexican prison, but it didn't seem to calm her down at all.

She was so distraught, I called Kelly to tell him that we were just too tired after our long drive from Tecolutla to stop by, and drove back to Austin.

The next morning she seemed OK, but wouldn't talk about the dreams again. But the next night, she woke up screaming, hyperventilating, drenched in sweat.

When I asked her about it, she whispered, "It was him again."

I held her in my arms until she fell back asleep, but for the rest of the night I stared at the ceiling and worried.

When I had set up Savannah's sessions up with the psychiatrist, I had her sign a medical power of attorney that allowed me to see her medical records and to talk to her doctor about her progress. When I got to my office, I called him and made an appointment for that afternoon.

"Yes, we've talked about the recurring dreams," the doctor said, "They started a few months ago. They are very violent and graphic."

"What do you think it means?"

He lifted his eyebrows and shrugged. "Sigmund Freud believed that dreams are the royal road to the unconscious. But today that theory is not widely accepted and is controversial. Some psychotherapists, still believe that dreams are a key to unlocking and liberating repressed memories of past traumatic experiences. On the other side are neurobiologists who argue that dreams are just byproducts of electrical activity -- random firing of brain circuits during sleep that cause bizarre images and weird associations."

"What side are you on?" I asked.

He smiled, "The jury is still out for me. Usually, I don't include a patient's dreams in my evaluations, but when they are recurring, especially with the vivid detail in dreams like Savannah's, it's hard not to at least consider them. Unfortunately, there is no hard science for me to refer to when evaluating them, but I suspect it may have something to do with her memory loss. I believe the dreams may be memory flashes of something she's experienced in the past. Was her husband physically abusive?"

I nodded. "Yes, he beat her up. He broke her arm, her leg and shattered her cheek bone. We also believe that he hit her on the head with something hard enough to cause the memory loss."

The doctor frowned. "Is this man in jail?"

"He's in a Mexican prison and hopefully will never see daylight again."

"Are you sure about that?" He asked, "Because Savannah is convinced that he will be coming for her again, and soon."

I left the psychiatrist's office confused and frustrated with no real answers that might help me with Savannah. The only idea I had that I thought might help her, was to somehow absolutely prove to her that Levi was in a maximum security prison with no possible chance of release and no way for him to escape. To do that, I knew I would have to go there and see for myself.

The next day I called the Mexican Consulate and filed the official paperwork to visit Levi at Cereso Poza Rico, the Mexican prison where he was being held. Three days later, they called and told me my request had been denied, because Levi refused the visit. Next, I got Olivia involved and she made an official request through the Mexican judicial system. That was also denied.

Finally, I got the approval when James Bachman had one of his golfing buddies, who just happened to be the FBI Special Agent in charge of the State of Texas, to make the request.

Since it was a formal FBI request, I was accompanied there by two local FBI Special Agents to make it appear official. The story was that Levi was a suspect in an ongoing FBI case and they needed to interview him.

We flew there in James Bachman's plane and we were met by a local police officer who drove us there.

We could not believe the location and condition of the prison when we arrived. It was surrounded by what I can only describe as a shanty town. There were hundreds of small shacks, all filled with poor impoverished Mexican families. Small barefoot children, dressed in rags filled the streets playing and there were skinny stray dogs everywhere. In front of many of the shacks were fires burning in barrels I assumed being used for cooking and for heat.

The prison was much smaller than I had envisioned. The building was constructed of gray unpainted concrete blocks with rusted steel bars that were lined up a few inches apart, filling every opening or window. Inside, the walls and floors were filthy and the stench of urine and human feces hung in the air. It was overwhelming and sickening.

We showed the guards at the gate our paperwork and after a few minutes a very large man dressed in an ill fitting suit walked up to us.

His white shirt was frayed at the cuffs and the collar squeezing his ample neck was more yellow than white.

In surprisingly understandable, but broken English he said, "My name is Augusta Raul Martinez. I am warden here. May I see your badges?"

The two FBI Special Agents held up their credentials, "Is the prisoner ready?" The agent asked, "We are on a very tight schedule."

Fortunately, the warden didn't seem to notice I wasn't holding up anything. "Si," He said gruffly, "Follow me."

We followed him into a small room just inside the main door and took a seat behind a metal table. A few minutes later, the door opened and two guards brought Levi in and slammed him down in the chair facing us. But it wasn't Levi.

"Who is this?" I yelled at the guards, holding up his picture on the paperwork, "This is not Levi Cruz!"

The guards began talking back at us in Spanish, but neither of the two agents understood Spanish any more than I did. We had no idea what they were saying.

"Warden!" I yelled, "Get the warden!"

When he walked in and I showed him the picture and told him that the prisoner was not Levi Cruz, he immediately turned and ran back out the door yelling at the top of his lungs. Seconds later, alarms began going off with deafening volume. We were quickly escorted out of the room and out the large steel front door, that was slammed and locked behind us.

Soon the streets began to fill with Mexican army vehicles, and heavily armed soldiers quickly piled out, and surrounded the building, holding their machine guns at the ready.

An hour later, the warden finally reappeared at the door. "He is not here," he said.

"Where is he?" I yelled in his face.

He backed up and glared at me. "Cruz has escaped."

I stepped forward and yelled in his face again, "When did he escape? How long has he been gone?"

The warden looked away and shrugged. "I don't know."

We rushed back to the airport. When we took off, I had the pilot connect me with the phone at my house. Alexander answered.

"Where is your mother?" I asked, trying to remain calm.

"She's outside by the pool, why?"

"Alexander, I don't have time to explain this, but Levi has escaped and I need you to get your mother out of there. Now."

"Oh no," he said, "I understand. I can get her out of here, but where do you want me to take her?"

I thought for a moment, trying to think of some place Levi wouldn't know about. "Take her to the trailer at Lakeway. I'm on my way there now. I should be there in three or four hours."

"OK, I'll go get her now." He said. I could hear a tremble in his voice.

"Alexander you need to keep it together. Stay calm. Now listen carefully, this is very important. Under my bed there is a large metal container. Don't look inside, just load it into your truck and take it with you inside of the trailer when you get there. Did you get that?"

"Yes sir, I'll get it."

∼

Sitting in a stolen van, backed into a driveway of a vacant property, four doors down from Travis Lee's house, Levi watched Alexander load a large green box in the back of his truck. He smiled when he saw Savannah walk out the front door with a small dog on a leash and slide into the passenger seat.

Following a few cars back driving down the Southwest Parkway, Levi kept a close watch on the truck as it pulled on to Highway 71, headed north and sped away.

23

TO KILL A SNAKE

I knew that all it would take would be for Levi to do a quick online search of the Texas Bar Association to get the address of my office, but my home address and the lot on Lake Travis were not listed there. And even if he did a property search and found the address to my house, they weren't there. They were safe in the trailer on Lake Travis.

Even if he did discover the lot, there was no physical address. All it would say would be, Lot 275, Lakeshore Point, Lago Vista, Texas. There wasn't a mailbox or any markings to identify it, and it was in the middle of acres and acres of raw undeveloped land. If you didn't know where it was, even if you had the lot number, you'd never find it.

On the flight back from Tecolutla, after hearing the entire story, Special Agent Ronald Green looked at me and asked, "Do you really think he's that stupid? To come back to Texas? If I'd somehow figured out how to escape that prison, and spoke Spanish, I would disappear to some Mexican beach, never to be heard from again."

I shook my head and frowned. "Levi is not stupid, but now, more than ever, he's full of rage and revenge. He's been insanely jealous of me his entire life and knowing that Savannah is back with me...stupid idea or not...I know he's coming for us."

On our flight back, Agent Greene contacted the FBI field office in Austin and requested to stay with me to give me some backup, but because it was a local police matter and out of the FBI's jurisdiction, his request was denied.

"Travis, when we land in Austin, I'm officially off the clock," he said, "you go to the lake house and make sure your son and Savannah are safe. It's none of the FBI's damn business what I do with my off time, so I'm going to do some unofficial surveillance of your office and your house. If I see anything, I'll call you on your cell."

~

Levi didn't turn into the iron oar road behind them, instead he drove past the entrance a few miles and parked the stolen van off the road deep in the woods, hidden by the thick bushes and trees.

Three days before, he had slipped across the Texas border on foot, a few miles west of Reynosa and had stolen the old van off a ranch in Hidalgo. It was sitting there for the taking, behind an old hay barn, with no one around for miles. It had only taken him fifteen minutes to hot wire it and crank it up. His next stop was a local convenience store. He pulled up to the pump and filled the tank with gasoline. The attendant inside obviously recognized the old van and walked outside to talk to him. The second he walked up, Levi attacked, leaving the old man lying in a pool of blood behind the van. Then he nonchalantly walked inside the store and filled three sacks full of beer and food. After he cleaned out the cash register, he walked to the van and drove away.

Seventeen miles north in McAllen, he found a small gun shop on the out skirts of town. He parked across the street from it and watched the activity around the shop for several hours, then he drove to a truck stop on the highway and bought a pair of work gloves, a sweatshirt with a hood, silver duct tape, and a roll of paper napkins.

Back across the street from the gun shop, he waited patiently until he saw the owner turn off the lights, lock the front door and drive away.

He cranked the old van, drove down the highway about a mile and parked it.

He took the paper towels and rolled it around his face, just below his eyes several times, then took the duct tape and did the same to secure the makeshift mask to his head. He slipped on the gloves and the sweatshirt, pulled the hood over his head and slowly walked along the dark road back to the gun shop.

He assumed the gun shop would have an alarm system and video surveillance, but he also assumed the response time of the local police wouldn't be that fast. He knew he would have 10 or 15 minutes at least before they arrived, plenty of time to grab a gun and some shells and walk away in the dark.

When he smashed through the back door, he didn't hear an alarm, so he assumed it was silent, dialing the police directly. Quickly he ran to the rack of rifles and broke the padlock open with the tire iron he had found in the old van. Standing there in the low light, he stared at the row of rifles but didn't recognize any of them. It had been years since he been hunting and had no idea which gun to choose, because he wasn't sure what kind of ammunition it would use. Then he saw a Winchester model 70 with a scope. It was the same gun his father had taught him to shoot when he was a kid. He knew it held 30-06 shells, so he pulled it out of the rack. Behind him he smashed the glass case where the shells were stacked. He grabbed two boxes of Remington 30-06 shells, put them in the pockets of his sweatshirt and ran out the back door. A few hundred yards away, he stopped running, slid the barrel of the rifle down inside his jeans next to his right leg, pulled the sweatshirt down to cover the stock and slowly walked back down the dark road to the van.

When he cranked the van and slowly pulled out on the highway, he realized that he had been wrong. It had been well over 20 minutes since he'd smashed through the gun shop door and he could hear no police sirens. There wasn't a silent alarm, apparently there was no alarm at all.

At a rest area a few miles down the road, he stopped and removed the makeshift mask, pulled off the hot sweatshirt and drove away, on his way to Austin.

Six hours later, a few miles south of the Austin city limits, he found a cheap roadside hotel and checked in. In the phonebook by the bed he looked up the address of the Austin public library. It took him almost an hour to locate the building and another ten minutes to find a place to park. Using the Libraries computer, he typed Travis Walker Lee, attorney at law in the search bar. In a few seconds, the page filled with a link to the Bachman, Turner, Lee and Associates website.

"You're kidding me," Levi said, using his best southern accent. "I just talked to him two weeks ago and he told me to give him a call if I was ever in Austin. So here I am and you're telling me he's out of town? When will he be back?"

"I really don't know, sir," The young receptionist at the law firm said, "he hasn't checked in this morning."

"Don't that beat all. I haven't seen him since high school and I don't get here but about twice a year. And when I show up, he ain't here. Damn, I sure wanted to see him and Savannah while I was in town. Is she gone too?"

"No, I don't think so. She didn't go with him. She's probably at their house."

"Really? Boy I would sure love to see her. Where do they live?"

"I'm sorry sir, but I'm not supposed to give out his home address."

"I know, I know, but that's for strangers and such. I grew up with him and I've been one of his good friends from high school. I've known Savannah since she was just a little girl. Come on now, I'm not a stranger, you can give it to me. It'll be alright."

∽

When we landed, I said goodbye to my new FBI Special Agent friends, jumped in my car and drove as fast as I could through the heavy traffic to Lake Travis.

When I arrived, I saw that Alexander had followed my instructions well. His truck was backed in, twenty feet from the entrance, pointing at the road, so he wouldn't have to turn around to make a quick getaway if he had to.

When he opened the door, I could see the fear in his eyes. "Do you think he'll come here?"

Savannah was sitting on the couch behind him and looked up with worried eyes waiting for my answer. "No, I don't think he could find this place. It's not marked anywhere. I'm pretty sure he's going to make his move at my house."

The large green metal box I had asked Alexander to get was laying in the floor. I sat down next to it, undid the padlock and opened it.

I removed the folded American flag that had been given to me by Brenda, Hags fiancé after his funeral and carefully set it on the coffee table. Then I reached in and pulled out a gun.

"What is that?" Alexander asked, "I've never seen a gun like that before."

I held it up and started wiping it down with a rag. "This is a M249 Squad Automatic Weapon. We call it a S.A.W. in Beirut. It was brand new back then. It wasn't widely used until 1984. We were the first to test them."

"Why do you have it? Weren't you supposed to turn that back in?"

When my barracks in Beirut were blown up, they shipped me what was left of my personal belongings in this box and this was in it. I'm not supposed to have it."

"If you're so sure Levi isn't coming here, why did you have Alexander bring that box?" Savannah asked.

I lifted my head and gave her a small smile. "Just in case. There's no weapons here and I wanted it just in case I was wrong. But don't worry, Levi doesn't know where this place is...he isn't coming here."

"But what if he does?" Savannah said in a strained urgent voice,

"We're isolated out here, with no one around to help us. I don't feel safe here."

∼

As quiet as he could, being careful not to step on any leaves or branches, Levi slowly walked down the iron ore drive toward the trailer past Alexander's truck and Travis's car.

When he got to the opening where the trailer was setting, he slipped into the thick bush and slowly worked his way through until he had a clear view of the large front window and door. He had loaded the Winchester rifle with five rounds and he had one in the chamber.

Three of them, two shots each, he thought to himself as he placed the barrel in the Y of a small tree limb to steady his aim.

Placing the end of the gunstock against his right shoulder, he leaned in and looked through the scope. Twisting the ends of the lens, he focused the scope until he could see Savannah's face clearly. He raised the barrel a few inches above her turquoise eyes, placing the black cross hairs in the center of her forehead and carefully put his finger on the trigger.

Before he could squeeze it, the scope blurred. He looked up over the scope at the trailer and through the window he could see Travis's back. He was standing in front of Savannah, blocking his shot.

I guess I could take him out first, he thought, but then they would all start to scramble and duck out of the way. "Just relax," he whispered, "stick to the plan. Savannah first, then Alexander...then Travis."

Shifting his weight, he took a step back breaking a small fallen limb under his foot, making a loud cracking sound. Instantly he heard the dog start barking inside the trailer.

∼

Suddenly Buster started barking and ran to the door. He barked again and jumped up on it.

"Not now Buster," I said, "I'll take you out later."

Savannah jumped up off the couch. "Do you think he heard something outside?" Her eyes were wide open, obviously frightened.

I hadn't told them that I was only there to check on them and wasn't going to stay, but looking into their panicked eyes made it very clear that I couldn't leave them there in the trailer alone.

"He probably heard a squirrel or maybe a possum. Don't worry, there's nothing out there," I wrapped my arms around her and kissed her on the forehead, "I realize you are scared. Would you feel better if I took you to a hotel? They would have security and there would be lots of people around. Would you feel safer there?"

She shook her head and whispered, "Yes I would."

"Ok then, let's go."

Savannah picked up her purse and Buster's leash. She bent down to clip it to his collar, but before she could get it hooked, I opened the door and he immediately ran out.

"No Buster! Come back here!" I yelled, stepping down onto the first step.

"Buster!" I heard Savannah yell, as she rushed into the doorway.

In slow motion, I heard a shot ring out. Then I heard Savannah yelp and fall backwards into the doorway.

Recognizing the unmistakable sound of a bolt action ejecting and reloading a new round in the chamber, I jumped back inside the trailer slamming the door behind me. I landed next to Savannah and immediately started looking for blood. When I found it, my heart sank in my chest. It was a head shot and she was bleeding severely from the temple.

I ran to the green metal box in the floor and found the medical kit. It had never been opened it the entire two years I carried it in my pack patrolling the streets of Beirut, but thanked God they had packed it in that box and it was there.

I ripped open the sterile bandages and wrapped them tight around Savannah's head, praying the pressure would slow her bleeding.

I looked up at Alexander who was standing behind the door, frozen like a stone. "We need to get her to a hospital!" I yelled, "We can't get out the door, he'll shoot us, but there's another way out. Help me carry her to the bedroom."

Instead of bending down to help me, he jerked opened the door and yelled, "Dad, mom is hurt. I'm gonna carry her to my truck and take her to the hospital. Don't shoot! You might hit me. You wouldn't shoot your own son would you?"

I lunged forward, pulling Alexander back just as the bullet shattered the doorway above his head.

"YOU ARE NOT MY FUCKING SON!" Levi screamed.

I had pulled him down on top of me. He scrambled up off the floor to his knees and looked at me. "What? I'm not his son?"

I jumped up, ran to the door and slammed it. The third bullet barely missed my hand.

"We have a lot to talk about," I said, "but not now. Take her feet and help me move her."

We carried her to the bedroom. I took hold of the bed and lifted it up, exposing the storage area underneath. Then I dove into the space and unlocked the exterior door and crawled out.

"Alexander," I whispered, "Put her in the space feet first, but be careful with her head."

We slowly worked her limp body through the storage door and I laid her down on the ground. When Alexander made it out, I lifted her up and carefully placed her over his shoulder in a fireman carry.

"Wait until you hear me start firing. Then run to your truck and take her to the hospital."

He was blank faced staring off into space. "Alex!" I said, shaking him, "Do you understand?"

"Yes, sir," he said softly.

I crawled back through the storage space and ran to the living room to the box. I grabbed some rope and my knife and strapped it to my leg. Then I snapped the full clip into the SAW, kicked open the front door and sprayed the woods with bullets. When I heard Levi yell, I jumped down to the ground and ran into the thick brush.

Once I was hidden, I stopped and listened for Alexander's truck to crank and speed away.

When I heard it, I yelled, "Hey Levi! Did you hear that? That's Alexander's truck and he's on the way to the hospital. You barely nicked her, she's gonna be just fine. Just so you know, Savannah's living with me now and I'm gonna keep her this time.

"Sorry to mess up your big murder plan, but this time you really fucked up! You should have shot me first. It's just you and me now...and you are in my element. I was trained for this shit. I'm gonna hunt you down and cut your throat. You know what they say ole buddy, 'To kill a snake, you've got to cut off it's head!'"

24

CLOSE ENOUGH

Alexander slammed on his brakes, skidding to a stop in front of the emergency room doors. "PLEASE HELP! My mother has been shot!" He screamed, "PLEASE SAVE HER!"

The medical team ran out, quickly loaded her onto a gurney, and rolled her away.

They wouldn't let him follow the gurney through the door, so he ran up to the front desk. "Can you get the police on the phone? I need to talk to them."

When the police arrived, Alexander told them what was going on and offered to drive them to the lot, but they said they knew where it was. "You need to stay here with your mother. We'll take care of this."

With their blue lights flashing and the siren blaring, they sped away, leaving Alexander standing alone in the emergency room driveway. He walked back inside and asked if they knew anything about his mother's condition, but they didn't, so he found a chair in the waiting room and sat down wiping his tears away from his cheeks with his sleeve.

∽

My lake front property had never been cleared, except the 10 foot wide road from the highway to the trailer I had bull dozed. The rest of it was covered with dense Ball Moss plants, Bluewood Condalia, Bald Cypress, and Anacua trees. It was so thick, you couldn't maneuver through it quickly and you had to keep a close watch out for diamondback rattlers, copperheads, and coral snakes when you did.

"You might want to watch out for rattlesnakes and copperheads," I yelled, "there's a bunch of em' living out here in these woods."

"FUCK YOU TRAVIS!" Levi yelled back, "I'M NOT AFRAID OF SNAKES!"

The voice came from behind me from the south. I was hoping he would say something, so I could start tracking him.

There was also a lot of bull nettle or stinging nettle on the property. That's a nasty small plant covered with tiny hairs that when it comes in contact with your skin, it feels like a bee sting. It grew wild in the Texas Hill country and I had found that out the hard way several times when I first walked around my property.

Since he was moving south, he was trying to escape and was working his way through the woods. I knew the first thing I needed to do was find him, so I started slowly working my way toward him. On my way, every 50 yards or so, I would set up a nettle trap. Using small lengths of the rope, I tied it to the nettle plant, bending it back and secured it to a small twig. If Levi walked into the rope, the twig would break and the nettle plant would fly up and hit him in the face. I had set about 20 of them before I spotted him.

He was easy to track, since he was moving as fast as he could, crashing through the thick bushes breaking the limbs and plants along his way.

∾

When I had yelled at Levi that I was trained for this, I wasn't kidding. When I was in the Marines, they woke us up one night at 1 am and loaded us into the back of a troop carrier vehicle. We were driven to the air strip and loaded into an airplane. Four hours later, we were loaded into the back of another troop carrier vehicle. In case you're wondering, there were no seatbelts, so for several hours, sitting on a hard metal bench, we hung on for dear life bouncing in the back of that truck. When we finally stopped we were in the middle of a thick jungle. There were 20 of us sitting in the back of that truck, 10 on each side.

When the back canvas flap opened, our Platoon leader climbed in with us. As he walked between the row, he handed each one of us a numbered green canvas bag. "Listen carefully, I will only say this once," he began, "You will find four items in your bag; a canteen full of water, a map, a compass and a knife. On your map, marked with a grease pencil, will be the area in which you must stay within. Do not cross this border. The compass will guide you and the knife will protect you. Make no mistake Marines, you are in severe danger. This jungle is full of poisonous snakes, frogs, spiders and wild animals. You could die here, so don't fuck up. You will be in this jungle for the next 48 hours, so if you get hungry, kill something.

This bag is to be worn over your shoulder with the number displayed. The map inside will mark the exact location in these woods where you will be dropped off. Fifteen miles due east of us, there is another platoon of 20 Marines being dropped off as we speak. They will also be issued a numbered bag with the same content. Are we clear so far?"

"Yes Lance Corporal!" We all yelled in unison.

"Very good," he said, "The mission of the other platoon will be to track you down, capture you and bring you back to his drop off location. Not all of you as a group, just the one who is wearing his number. Your mission is not to embarrass this platoon. You will not be captured! Do you understand me Marines!"

"Yes Lance Corporal!" We yelled again.

"This is just between us, none of the big brass knows this. Your mission is supposed to be to allow them to capture you, but I think that's a bunch of bullshit. My mission for you is to evade these hunters and turn the tables on them. I want *you* to capture *them* and bring them back to your checkpoint. When you succeed at this...and you will succeed...it is going to severely piss off the brass on the entire base and I will probably get busted back down to a private. But I say...FUCK EM'! ARE YOU WITH ME?"

We were dropped off exactly one mile apart and our mission began. We found out later that we were in South America, near Panama. I will save you the gory details, but only three of the 20 in my platoon were captured. I found my guy 23 hours later, it was an easy capture. I heard him yelling and watched him take off running when he almost stepped on a huge snake. After he surrendered, we found the snake, killed it, built a fire and ate it. Maybe it was because I was hungry, but it was delicious and tasted like chicken to me.

The point of that dangerous mission was to teach us how to survive in deadly situations. It was not fun by any definition of that word, and I hope I'm never in that situation again, but somehow I survived it and learned well.

∼

Slipping quietly through the thick prickly bushes and trees of the Texas hill country was nothing compared to that dense jungle in South America, so it was easy for me to slip by Levi and get below him.

I wanted to force him to move back toward the trailer and hopefully into a few of my nettle traps, so when I heard him coming, I fired a few quick rounds into the ground.

"In the Marines we called this gun a SAW, because it can cut down a tree," I yelled at him, "So I wouldn't come this way if I was you." I heard him cussing and running back.

Every few minutes, I would yell something at him and duck to the ground, hoping he would fire his rifle and use another bullet, but he never did. I had heard him rack the bullet into the chamber after he shot Savannah, so I knew he had some kind of a bolt-action rifle. I figured that gave him five or six shots before he had to reload. He had shot three times, so he had at least three more rounds.

As I worked him back I heard him scream with pain when he

walked into one of my Nettle traps. "What's wrong?" I yelled, "Did you find one of my traps? Sorry about that. Be careful there's a lot more out there. I bet that hurts like hell."

When I worked him back close to the trailer, suddenly I heard Buster barking and snarling. I had actually forgotten about him running through the door and that he was out there with me. I heard another shot and Buster yelp. The bastard had shot him!

That was it, I had played with him long enough, it was time for me to make my move, but unfortunately, when I had fired the rounds into the ground to move him back toward the trailer, I had emptied the clip, I was out of ammunition. My only weapon was the knife strapped to my leg, but Levi didn't know that, so I rushed him, knocking him off his feet to the ground. I had hoped he would have dropped the rifle when I tackled him, but somehow he hung on to it. He jumped back up to his feet and fired at me, but he missed. *That was five*, I counted in my head.

He pointed his gun at me and I pointed my empty gun back at him. "A Winchester model 70," I said, "That's a nice gun, too bad you can't shoot for shit."

I raised my gun and smiled. "Me on the other hand, well I don't like to brag, but I've earned three marksmanship medals. I don't miss, so if I was you, I would lower that gun. It's over Levi, there's no way out this time."

He lifted his head and smiled. "Travis, I know how much you hate me, I can see it in your eyes. You want to kill me for all the things I've done to your precious Savannah," he laughed, "And I don't blame you, if someone was fucking my girlfriend behind my back, I'd want to kill him too. But what did you do? You tucked your chicken shit tail between your legs and left town. You didn't kill me then and I know you're not going to kill me now. You could have taken me out easily in those woods, but you didn't and I know why. You stopped shooting thirty minutes ago. I figure that means you are out of bullets. And just in case you've been counting," He pulled back the lever, injecting the bullet casing and loaded another one in the chamber.

"As you can see, I'm not out of bullets," He said with a grin, "Of course, you still have that knife there on your leg, but to use it you'd have to get real close to me. Every one thinks you're a big tough Marine, but I know better. You don't have the balls to actually kill someone up close and personal like that, but you don't know what you're missing. I've done it several times and it's quite a rush."

He took a few steps backwards, still pointing the gun at me. "I guess what we have here is what is called a Mexican stand off. Pardon the pun," he laughed out loud, "So let me tell you what is going to happen next. I'm not gonna kill you now, I'm going to save that for another time when I come back for that bitch Savannah and my dumb ass step son. And trust me, I *will* be back to finish the job." He turned and started walking away.

I knew he was walking toward the edge of the 200 foot Clift, so I just stood there and let him go.

He was only a few feet from the edge when he stopped. "Are you really going to just stand there and let me walk away. On second thought, I think I'll kill you now." He lifted the gun and fired.

I felt the bullet hit me in my left shoulder, knocking me backwards to the ground. I heard him rack back the bolt action again, but before he could fire, I reached for the knife strapped to my leg and threw it.

Levi looked down with wide, shocked eyes to see the handle sticking out of the center of his chest. He stumbled backwards a few feet, cussing and coughing up blood. He reached his hand up to wipe his mouth, staring at his bloody hand. Slowly he raised the rifle and growled, "Die you bastard!"

Out of the darkness, Buster suddenly flew by me, snarling and growling. He jumped up on Levi's chest, knocking him backwards. The gun fired into the air as I watched them both tumble out of sight...over the edge of the cliff.

Far away in the background, I could hear police sirens. I crawled to the edge of the cliff and looked over. "Buster!" I yelled, but he didn't bark back.

I slowly pulled my self up off the ground and sat with my legs dangling over the side of the cliff, calling his name over and over. But the only thing I heard were the sirens echoing through the air, getting louder and louder.

∼

"Don't move," I heard someone say behind me. I looked around and saw four county sheriffs standing there with their weapons drawn.

"What is your name, sir?" One of them asked me.

"Travis Lee. This is my property," I said.

"Is your son's name Alexander?"

I nodded, staring down over the cliff. "Yes," I whispered.

"He told us that there was a shooter here. Where is he?"

I pointed down over the cliff. "He's down there…with my dog."

The county sheriff walked to the edge and shined his flashlight. I could see Levi's body laying face up at the bottom of the stairs, but his legs and arms were mangled, angling out, twisted in the wrong directions. But there was no sign of Buster.

I got up and walked to the fire pit and sat down in one of the chairs that surrounded it. About ten minutes later, the EMT's arrived, took one look at the bullet hole in my shoulder and loaded me on a gurney. But as they were rolling me away, I heard Buster's bark.

"Wait!" I yelled, "That's my dog!" A few seconds later, his beautiful ugly face appeared in one of the sheriff's flashlights.

"I see him," he yelled, walking down the steps. A few minutes later, he brought him to me on the gurney. When he sat him down close to my face, he looked at me and whined. "I'm going to be alright. Thank you Buster. You saved my life. You're eating nothing but steaks from now on."

"Woof," he said, licking my face.

"He's bleeding," the sheriff said, " "Looks like he's been shot. Don't worry, I know a good vet not far from here. I'll take him there now."

Another sheriff walked up. "Is he stable?" He asked the EMT's, "I need to talk to him before you take him away."

"Yes, he's stable," The EMT guy said, "he's not bleeding too bad. It looks like a through and through, but we need to get him to the ER soon."

"I'll just be a second," he told them.

He held up my knife. "I assume this is yours?" He asked.

I shook my head. "Yes, I threw..."

"Wait," he said stopping me," I know you are in severe pain and don't feel like talking, so just answer yes or no. OK?"

I nodded.

He held up the knife again. "Is this your knife?"

"Yes."

"Marine issue?"

"Yes."

He smiled. "I thought so. I'm an old jarhead myself. I understand that the dead man at the bottom of the stairs is Levi Cruz, an escaped convict from a Mexican prison. Is that correct?"

"Yes."

"OK, so I can fill out my report, I want to make sure I have all the facts correct. Are you with me Marine?"

"Yeah, I understand." I said.

"The way I'm figuring it, is that this Levi guy shot your wife and tried to shoot you and your son. Is that right?"

I nodded. "Yes."

"Some how your son got away and drove his mother to the ER. And I'm also figuring, that this Levi character some how got a hold of that Marine Corps issue M249 Squad Automatic Weapon we found over there in the woods. I know that it couldn't have been your weapon, because that would be against the law to have one of those. Isn't that correct?"

"Of course. I'm a lawyer and and officer of the court, I would never break the law."

"Yep, that's exactly what I was thinking. So you decided to go after this guy, being and ex marine and all, armed only with this knife. Am I right so far?" He said with a grin.

"It's almost like you were here," I said.

"OK, so I figure what happened next was that during your scuffle with this Levi guy, he slipped and fell down those stairs and somehow on his way down…he fell on your knife. That's what I want to write in my report. Now, that *is* the way it went down, right Mr. Lee?"

I smiled. "Close enough."

25

RAMBO

They loaded me into the ambulance and rushed me to the same hospital emergency room Alexander had taken Savannah.

To be honest, it didn't hurt that much when they rolled me into the ER, but after the x-rays and all the digging, and prodding, and cleaning the wound, it was killing me.

They wanted to check me in to the hospital for overnight observation, but I refused, so they shot me full of antibiotics, bandaged it up and let me go.

I found Alexander in the waiting room. When he saw me, he ran up and hugged me. "Ouch!" I yelled, "be careful with that shoulder, I got shot."

"I know," he said, "Sheriff Oliver just left and told me what happened."

He backed up and looked me in the eyes, "Is he really dead?"

I shook my head. "Yeah, he fell down the steps. They said that it must have broken his neck."

A woman doctor dressed in green scrubs walked into the waiting room. "Is anyone here waiting for Savannah Cruse?"

I turned and held up my hand. "We are. This is her son."

She walked up to Alexander. "We've done all we can do for your mother here at this facility, but she needs emergency surgery. I have called for Life Flight to come and transport her to the Houston Medical Center."

"What kind of surgery?" I asked.

She frowned. "The bullet fragmented and some of the pieces lodged in her brain. We need to get her to a neurosurgeon...a good one...and fast.

Although we tried, they wouldn't let us ride in the helicopter with Savannah on the ride to the Houston Medical Center. Before they even took off, I had called Olivia. She promised me that she would do what ever it took to track down the best neurosurgeon in Houston to do the surgery.

Alexander and I stood side-by-side and watched the blades of the life flight chopper spin faster and faster until it slowly lifted off the pad and disappeared into the dark sky.

We stared at the sky until we could no longer see the flashing green and red glow of the helicopter lights.

When I looked over at Alexander I was surprised. He wasn't crying like I had expected. "How are you holding up?" I asked.

"I'm OK, I guess. I kind of feel numb." He dropped his head. "She said there's fragments in her brain. She...She's not gonna live through this...is she?"

I put my arm around his shoulder. "I'm not gonna lie, it's not good, but at least she is still alive and fighting. I guess it's in God's hands now."

He slowly shook his head. "I guess so. Does it hurt bad?" He asked, pointing at my bandaged shoulder.

"Actually, I don't feel anything now, they've got it all numbed up. Ask me again in a few hours when it wears off. I have a feeling it's gonna hurt like hell.

We walked to his truck and I jumped in the passenger seat. "Let's go back to the trailer and see if they'll let me take my car."

"Why wouldn't they let you take it?"

"It's a crime scene. They probably won't," I said, "but let's just check anyway."

Usually at a crime scene, especially when someone has died, the entire area is blocked off until the forensic team has finished. Collecting forensic evidence is a very slow process and usually takes several hours, but when we pulled into the drive, there was no yellow tape in sight. Slowly, we drove up the drive to the trailer, but saw none there either. Except for the shattered front door frame where Levi missed Alexander with his shot, nothing looked out of place.

"Well, I guess this case is over," I said, "I'm going to go check on Buster, I'll meet you back at the house. We need to pack a bag. We may be in Houston a while."

"OK," He said, "But before you get out, could I talk to you about something."

I shook my head. "Of course. What do you want to talk about?"

He was looking forward, through the windshield. "Do you remember when I first met you and I told you about that scrapbook that mom had made?"

"Yes. You told me that you guys looked at it a lot."

"That's an understatement, we looked at it almost every single day when I got home from school."

I wasn't exactly sure why, but he was getting emotional, fighting back tears. "What I wanted to tell you was...when we would look at all that stuff about you being a hero in the Marines and then all that stuff about college and law school...I never told mother, but I used to wish that you were my father instead of Levi."

He turned his head and looked at me. "If Levi is not my father...is it you?"

I wasn't sure how to respond, so I just nodded yes.

He lowered his eyebrows and looked away. "Did you know?"

"Alexander, look at me."

He turned his head and made eye contact.

"You know me. If I had known about you, I would have been there. I've missed so much of your life...but she never told me. I found out that night in Tecolutla. I wanted to tell you then, but didn't know how. I'm so sorry you had to find out this way."

Alexander turned his head and looked back out of the windshield, but didn't say anything.

"So now that you know the truth," I said, "what do you think about it?"

He started crying, but truthfully I couldn't tell if he was crying or laughing, but when he turned his head and I saw his wide smile, I knew it was both. Eventually he stopped, wiped his eyes with his sleeve and said, "It would have been cool if I'd known you were my father sooner, but I know now...and I think it's awesome!"

∽

Buster must've heard me or smelled me when I pulled into the vets driveway, because when I opened the door I could hear him barking from inside

Fortunately, when Levi had shot at him, he only nicked his ear, the one that was always sticking up. I started laughing when I saw him. His entire head was bandaged with that one silly ear wrapped tight, sticking up in the air even further than normal.

He was too doped up to walk, so I carried him to the car. On the drive to my house, I called James Bachman and asked him if he would look after Buster, once again, while I was in Houston.

"I had already anticipated that," he said, "I just got off the phone with Olivia and I am on my way to your house now."

When I arrived, my house was full. Somehow my neighbors already knew about Savannah and were there to offer their help, comfort, and love.

When Olivia walked in and saw my bandaged shoulder, she burst into tears. "Who the hell do you think you are, Rambo? You could have been killed."

I hugged her. "Naw, only the good die young." I said, smiling.

"It's not funny! I am so angry at you," she said, "Why didn't you call the police?"

"You would have had to been there, but I'm glad you weren't. There wasn't much time to do anything but duck. I don't want to talk about that anymore, did you find a doctor?"

"Yes," She said, "I just got off the phone with Dr. David Baskin. He's at the Houston Methodist Department of Neurosurgery. He's supposed to be the best. Savannah should be arriving there any minute now."

James offered me his plane and it was tempting to get there as quick as possible, but I knew there was nothing that I could do, and probably wouldn't be able to see her for several hours, so I decided to drive.

When we arrived, three hours later, as I expected, she was in surgery and had been there for two hours. No one would tell me or Alexander anything about her condition or how she was doing in the surgery.

"How long does something like this usually take?" Alexander asked the receptionist.

She gave him a concerned look. "I know you're worried about your mom, but there's just no way of knowing on this kind of surgery. I've seen them go on for hours."

I walked up and stood beside Alexander at the desk. "Is there a hotel close to here?"

A nurse walked up behind the counter to get some paperwork. "Yes, there are several within a few blocks of here," she said, looking down at the paper. When she looked up at me, she pointed at my shoulder and said, "What happened to you?"

By this time the pain medicine had long worn off and my shoulder was throbbing with each heartbeat. "I got shot."

"I can see that. Before you take off for that hotel, I think you need to come with me."

"Why?" I asked.

"Because you're bleeding through your bandage."

She smiled at Alexander. "Have a seat over there, young man. This won't take long."

She took me to the back, peeled off the bandage and carefully inspected my wound.

"When did this happen?" She asked.

I had to think about it to calculate the time. "Ahh, I think about seven hours ago."

"Seven hours!" She shouted, "Why aren't you in a hospital bed somewhere? Who do you think you are, Rambo?"

I started laughing.

"What's so funny?"

"That's the second time I've heard that today, but no, I'm not Rambo, I'm a lawyer, but if I told you where I've been and what I've been through the last two days, you wouldn't believe it. I'll be honest with you, this is hurting like hell and I wish I could be laying in a hospital room right now, but my son's mother and the woman I love with all my heart is upstairs having brain surgery. My son is frightened and he needs me here beside him, and I need him beside me as well. So I guess I'll have to deal with this later."

She looked around the room, reached into a drawer and pulled out a package of Tylenol. "Take four of these now and four more in 8 hours. Will you be here tomorrow?"

"I guess that depends on how the surgery goes, but I think so."

"This is not an ER and I'm not supposed to be doing this, but if you're here tomorrow, I'll look at it again for you," She said with a smile, "Are you a good lawyer?"

"Yes I am."

"Could I ask you something?"

"Of course, do you need a lawyer?"

"Honestly I don't know, but maybe."

I grinned, leaned in and read her name tag. "I'm Travis, may I call you Louise?"

She smiled. "Yes you may."

"Alright Louise, tell me why you *maybe* need a lawyer."

"It's kind of silly I guess, but two years ago I splurged and leased a brand new Cadillac. It's the prettiest thing you've ever seen. But about a month after I leased it, the emergency brake light started coming on while I was driving down the road at 60 miles an hour. Thank goodness the emergency break didn't actually engage, but the light kept coming on. Honestly it scared me to death when it would happen. What if the brake did engage? Can you imagine what would happen to me out there on the freeway if it did?"

I nodded in agreement. "What did they say at the Cadillac dealership when you took it back?"

She frowned. "Which time? I've taken it back to them and they've supposedly fixed it over ten times, but it keeps coming back on. They just can't seem to fix it. So last week I asked to talk to the General Manager and told him I wanted a different car, but he said all he could do was put me into a brand new car with a new lease. He wanted $3,000 down and the new payments were $75 more a month. I can't afford that. Do you think I need a lawyer?"

I leaned back in the chair and thought for a moment. "Have you ever heard of something called 'The Lemon Law?'"

She shook her head. "No, I've never heard of that, but even if that law could help me, I can't afford to hire a lawyer. That's my problem."

"Tell you what, I'll make a few phone calls and see what I can do about your car on one condition. They won't tell us anything out there. I need to know about Savannah Cruz, about how the surgery is going and about her prognosis if she survives. And I need to know the truth. Will you go back there and find that out for me? Do we have a deal?"

30 minutes later Louise met us in the coffee shop. When I saw her, I studied her face, but her expression was blank. "What did you find out?" I asked, "Is she out of surgery?"

"Not yet, but I don't think it will be too much longer. When he's finished, she'll be in the ICU and I can find out more. I'm sure the doctor will come out and talk to you about the surgery and what he did removing the bullet fragments, but he won't be able to tell you much else."

Alexander raised his head. "Why not?"

"Because she will be in a medically induced coma, to help her body heal and until she is out of that, he won't know anything."

She wouldn't look me in the eyes. Every time I tried, she looked away. "What are you not telling us. You know something, don't you? Please Louise, tell us. We need to know everything, even if it's not good."

She sighed. "I'm a surgical nurse, but I'm not on Dr. Baskin's team, I work with Dr. Ball. I've assisted on hundreds of surgeries like this." She took a deep breath and looked at me, "It's the location of the bullet fragments that worries me."

"What about the location?" I asked.

"The fragments were lodged in her left Temporal lobe. This area of the brain controls the ability to understand language, memory and hearing. One of the larger pieces was in the Broca's area. Depending on the damage, she may have difficulty moving her tongue or facial muscles to produce the sounds of speech. She could still read and understand spoken language but may have difficulty speaking and writing, forming letters, and words. This is called Broca's aphasia."

Alexander leaned forward. "You mean she'll understand what we're saying, but won't be able to talk?"

She shook her head. "No, I'm not saying that. No one knows what's going to happen to her. I'm just telling you that from the location of those fragments...it's possible.

~

We didn't hear from the doctor for three more hours. When he walked into the waiting room, I instantly knew it was him. I can't explain it, but he looked exactly as I had envisioned. He was maybe late 40's early 50's, a little shorter than me, 5 foot 11ish. He was still dressed in his surgical scrubs including the hat and booties over his shoes. When he looked at me, not smiling with those piercing, intelligent black eyes, you could almost see how brilliant he was.

As Louise had warned us, all he could really tell us was that he had been successful removing all the fragments from her brain and that Savannah would be in a medically induced coma for the next 48 hours.

"I realize you are anxious and want to know something," he said, "but until she is out of this coma and fully conscious, and I can run some tests, I won't have any idea of what she may have suffered as a result of the gun shot trauma, or the surgery. Normally by this time I could tell you more, because usually the patient is awake during surgery allowing me to communicate with them. Throughout this communication, symptoms and problems can be identified, but your mother was unconscious when she arrived. So again, until the induced coma that's keeping her in this state is reversed, and she regains consciousness…we won't know anything."

"Can I see her?" Alexander asked.

"That's always the first question and the answer is yes, but I wish you wouldn't."

Alexander shot me a concerned look. Then he looked back at the doctor and asked. "Why?"

"Because she looks," he paused trying to find the correct words, "well to be blunt, your mother looks terrible. You wouldn't recognize her. There is a lot of swelling with this kind of surgery."

"I don't care what she looks like," he said, "I want to see her."

The doctor put his hand on Alexander's shoulder. "Son, I'm not saying this is going to happen, but the odds are not in her favor. If your mother doesn't make it, trust me, the way she looks now is not how you'll want to remember her."

Alexander's eyes teared up. "That's why I want to see her. I want to at least hold her hand and tell her that I love her…one last time."

∽

Dr. Baskin would only allow a five minute visit and only one of us at a time, so Alexander went first. Because it was the Neurology surgical ICU, (Intensive Care Unit) we had to wear sterile hospital scrubs, including the booty's over our shoes, the hat and the mask.

When Alexander walked back to the waiting room after his visit, he was in a state of shock. His eyes were wide open and he was white as a ghost.

"How is she?" I asked.

He shook his head slowly, but didn't answer. I let him walk on by me and sit down.

A few minutes later the nurse came to take me back. When she led me to the foot of Savannah's bed, It took me a second to realize what I was actually seeing. She was surrounded with machines connected to wires and tubes monitoring her vitals and respiration. The only exposed skin on her entire head I could see was the tip of her nose and her lips around the ventilator tube. The rest of her head, including both of her eyes were covered and wrapped in white gauze bandages. From her nose up, her head was the size of a basketball. The sound of the beeps and alarms coming from the machines were so loud, it was overwhelming and actually made me nauseous. I wanted to touch her and say something, but instead I turned and rushed out. The doctor was right, I wish I hadn't seen her that way.

When I changed out of the green scrubs and walked out of the doors I saw Olivia, Jeb, Kelly, BJ, and Rebecca walking through the entrance doors together.

When Rebecca saw Alexander in the waiting room, she burst into tears and ran to him. The rest of them ran to me.

When they surrounded me, I lost control and cried for the first time. Our group hug lasted for almost five minutes.

When they let go, I begged them not to go back to see her, so they didn't.

They had made reservations at the same hotel, so I rode back with them and let Alexander take my car so he and Rebecca could have some private time.

After they checked in, I met Kelly, BJ, Olivia and Jeb in the lobby bar to talk. Alexander and Rebecca stayed in the room.

Kelly took a sip of his beer and set it down on the table. "What did the doctor say?"

I shrugged. "Not much. He got all of the bullet fragments, but he doesn't know the extent of the damage."

No one said anything for a few minutes. We all just sat quietly sipping our drinks trying to think of something to say, but there just wasn't anything *to* say.

"Who is the nurse you were talking to right before we left?" Olivia asked.

"That was Louise Black," I said, "She's one of the surgical nurses that I have made friends with. She wasn't on Savannah surgical team, but she knows a lot about it and is keeping me updated as best she can."

"What was she telling you?"

I sighed, letting out my breath slowly. "Please don't tell Alexander this, but she told me that if Savannah had any family...I should probably contact them."

"Oh God," Olivia whispered, squeezing my hand, "This can't be happening...not now. You two just got back together."

Again we all stopped talking and sat there in awkward silence, listening to the music playing in the background.

"Have you eaten today?" Olivia asked breaking the silence.

I shook my head. "No, but I don't have much of an appetite."

What about Alexander?"

I looked over the table at her. "No, he hasn't eaten either."

Taking control as usual, Olivia said, "Travis, you know Alexander and you know he has to be starving. And I don't care if you don't have much of an appetite, you need to eat. If I order some pizzas will you at least try?"

When the pizzas arrived, Rebecca and Alexander joined us. I was surprised to see him smiling and in a good mood. Apparently Rebecca was just what he needed to help get him through this.

For the rest of the evening, purposely, no one talked about Savannah's current plight. Instead, Kelly started telling old stories about the three of us growing up together.

"She could throw a football further than me or Travis," he said.

"Really?" Alexander said, "How far could she throw it?"

Kelly laughed. "I can't remember exactly how far, what do you think Travis?"

"She could throw a perfect spiral almost 50 yards," I said with a chuckle, "I was never any good at that, but she sure was."

"Has she always been an artist?" Rebecca asked, "When did she start painting?"

I smiled. "Since before I knew her. All her life, I guess."

That was the first of three nights we all gathered together after dinner telling old stories, trying our best not to let our worry about Savannah show.

26

AND I'VE NEVER STOPPED

Remarkably the swelling on Savannas head had gone down considerably by the end of the 48 hours. She was still hooked up to the numerous machines with wires and tubes, but they had removed most of the bandages and I could actually recognize her face again. And although they had shaved off her long blonde hair and she was bald...she was still beautiful to me.

The first big step, was to disconnect her from the respirator to see if she could breathe on her own and she could. Then they slowly turned off the anesthesia, removed the drainage tube from her head and waited for her to hopefully regain consciousness. Unfortunately, she didn't.

For the next five days, Alexander and I sat on each side of her bed, praying she would wake up, holding her hands, watching her breathe, until the visiting hours were over and they kicked us out.

Olivia had to return to her court and Kelly had to get back to his business, so after the 48 hours was over and Savannah did not wake up, they left and went back home, leaving Alexander, Rebecca and me there to wait it out.

The hotel was in the center of the Houston Medical Center, a few miles south of Rice University. The beautiful neighborhood that surrounded that area had narrow tree lined streets that crisscrossed through large old historic homes, reminiscent of the Antebellum mansions you might find on the old plantations in Louisiana and Mississippi. After the fourth long day of sitting and pacing in the hospital waiting room, I needed to go for a run. Running had always been my tranquilizer, my solace.

My shoulder was healing well, Louise had kept a close watch on it and had changed the bandages regularly and I thought that if I could run with a smooth gait it would be OK, but I was wrong. It only took a few hundred yards to realize it, so I stopped running and walked through the beautiful neighborhood, admiring the houses and thinking for about an hour.

Along the way, I passed a small Baptist church. There was nothing unique about the structure but it reminded me of the very first church I had gone to. I was nine years old and I had gone there with Savannah and her mother. I remembered that I really didn't want to go, but Savannah had insisted.

My mother didn't go to church, or, if she did she never told me. She never talked about God and as far as I knew there wasn't even a Bible in our house.

Growing up I had wondered what it was all about and had seen my friends, all dressed up walking to the churches on Sunday morning, but until Savannah moved in next door and forced me to go, I had no idea.

Walking back from the church that first day, I looked at Savannah and asked, "Who is this Jesus guy they were talking about?"

That afternoon, in the tree house she told me the whole story, from the day he was born to the day he died and was resurrected.

I can still remember the look she had on her face that day. I'd never seen it before and I can't really describe it, but it was more than just a simple smile, much more. And her turquoise eyes seemed to glow as she told me the story.

I will admit that believing in an invisible man in the sky was hard to comprehend and accept for my nine year old brain, but I didn't tell Savannah that and never missed going to church with her once, but my skepticism remained. The first Sunday I missed was the Sunday after I boarded that bus and left town.

After losing Savannah and then all my friends in that explosion in Beirut, it became more and more difficult for me to completely believe in God. Because I had learned the gospel from Savannah and all those years of going to church, I didn't completely deny his existence, but I could never convince myself to completely cross over and dedicate my life to him either.

When I got back to the hotel, I saw Rebecca and Alexander eating breakfast in the restaurant, so I joined them.

"Where have you been?" Alexander asked.

"I went out for a walk. There is a great neighborhood behind here with some beautiful old historic houses."

"Are you going again tomorrow?" He asked.

"Yeah, I think I will. With all that sitting around the waiting room I need the exercise," I said.

"Wake me up in the morning, I want to go with you."

In the five days we had been hanging around the surgical neurology waiting room, we had met several families with loved ones in the ICU, but unfortunately for most of them, they had not received good news and they had come and gone. Every day hearing about their tragic stories and learning of the eventual outcome of their loved ones was difficult to deal with, but in a way I believe it also made Alexander and me realize and accept the impossible odds we were facing and helped us prepare for the worst.

After the sixth long day of waiting, I kissed Savannah on the cheek, told her I loved her and drove back to the hotel.

The next morning Alexander was waiting for me in the lobby, so we headed out for our walk. When we passed the old church, Alexander walked up to the door and pulled on the handle. When it opened, he waved at me to follow him, then he walked in and let the door close behind him.

Reluctantly, I walked up the steps and opened the door. I saw Alexander walk down the center isle and take a seat in the front row. Slowly, I walked down the isle and took the seat next to him.

He bowed his head and began to pray silently. I didn't pray. I just sat there watching him. When he finished he looked up at me and smiled.

"I've been wanting to find a church around here," he said, "The chapel at the hospital is OK I guess, but it's nothing like this."

"You've been going to the chapel?" I asked.

"Yes, every day."

"What are you praying for?"

He smiled. "Nothing really. I just want him to know that I still believe in him."

I was stunned by his answer. "You're not praying for your mother to get better?"

He shook his head. "I don't believe that's how it works."

He turned in his chair and stared into my eyes. "Are you a Christian dad?"

My heart swelled in my chest when I heard that word...dad. I could feel the emotions building up inside of me. Fighting them back I said, "I like that. It feels good."

"What feels good?" He asked.

"You called me dad for the first time. Thank you. I am so proud to know that you are my son."

"I've been thinking about that a lot," he said, "about what I should call you. I liked saying it. I just hope you know how proud I am to be your son. But you didn't answer my question. Do you believe in God?"

I sighed and leaned back in my chair. "I'd like to tell you yes, I do, but I never want to lie to you, so to be honest, I don't know what I believe. Truthfully, I have trouble believing that if there is a God, he would let something like this happen to your mother."

He smiled. "He didn't let it happen. I believe he is as sad about mom as we are."

I frowned. "You really believe that?"

"Yes I do. I learned it from Mom. In the Bible it tells us that God wanted us to have the ability to love, but to do that He had to give us free will. That free will allows us to decide to believe in Him, or not to believe. I chose to believe and knowing that no matter how tragic, hard, and difficult my life here on earth may be, His rewards to me in heaven will out weigh anything I have lived through here."

He reached in his back pocket, pulled out a small New Testament and began flipping the pages. "He tells us in John 16:33, 'I have told you these things, so that in Me, you may have peace. In this world you will have trouble. But take heart! I have overcome the world.'"

He lowered the book and looked at me. "Dad, He didn't say *we might* have trouble, He said, *we will*. I'm not mad at God for this, I'm mad at Levi. He did this to mom, not God, but because of my faith in Him, no matter what happens...I'll be alright."

He looked me in the eyes again. "What about you?"

~

On the eighth day after Savannah's surgery, we'd just made it back to our hotel when my cell phone rang. It was Louise.

"Travis," She said, "You need to come back to the hospital."

My heart was pounding. "Why? What's wrong? Did something happen?"

"I don't know. I just got here and I heard Dr. Baskin's nurse calling him at his home telling him he was needed for Savannah Cruz. Just come back to the hospital, now."

We rushed back there, but when we arrived, Dr. Baskin was with her and they wouldn't let us back to see her. As usual, they wouldn't tell us anything.

I asked for Louise, but she was in surgery, so we found a seat in the waiting room. Although it was only about a 20 minute wait, it's seemed like hours before Dr. Baskin walked into the room.

With the same somber, expressionless face and concentrated black eyes, he looked at us and said. "She's awake."

"What!" I screamed, "She's awake?"

"Yes, she opened her eyes about 45 minutes ago."

"She woke up?" Alexander shouted, excited.

Dr. Baskin smiled for the first time since we'd met him. "Yes son, she did. Would you like me to take you back to see her?"

"Yes!" He yelled, running toward the doors.

Dr. Baskin looked over at Rebecca and me. "Would you like to come too?"

They had moved Savannah out of ICU into recovery. Rebecca and I held back a few feet and let Alexander walk up to her first.

From where I was standing, I could see her image clearly in a mirror, but a curtain blocked her view, so she couldn't see me. The back of her bed was raised up. She was sitting upright, lying with her head on a pillow with her eyes closed. The large bandages were gone, as well as all the machines and vitals monitors. She was only hooked up to one tube, the IV connecting to her jugular vein in her neck. Her head was covered with a blue silk scarf. When she heard Alexander walk up she opened her eyes and they glowed and sparkled in the light.

"Hey mom," He said softly, walking up to her, "how are you doing?"

The doctor hadn't told us anything about her condition, only that she was awake. We had no idea if she could talk or recognize us.

When she looked up at Alexander, her eyes widened and she gasped. "Alex? Is that you? Oh my gosh, you're all grown up."

"Do you recognize me?" He shouted, leaning over hugging her, "Do you know who I am?"

"Of course I do," she said, "What kind of question is that?"

He looked back at me and yelled, "She knows me!"

Rebecca walked up next. "Rebecca? Is that you?"

Before she could answer, I walked around the curtain. When she saw me, her mouth flew open. "Hi there, do you remember me?"

She stared for a long time, studying my face. "Travis?" She said softly, "Your eyes...you have wrinkles...and your hair...it's graying."

I laughed and took her hand. "Well, it's good to see you too."

"No," She said, giving me her beautiful smile, "I didn't mean it that way. You look great, but..."

I squeezed her hand and smiled back. "It's OK, you haven't seen me in a long time."

I knew she was confused, but I couldn't resist leaning over her bed and kissing her. When she didn't resist, I kissed her again, longer, savoring the taste of her lips.

When I pulled back, her turquoise eyes were glistening in the light. "Oh Travis, I've missed you desperately." She whispered.

"I've missed you too."

She opened her mouth to speak, but stopped, let go of my hand and pulled away glancing around the room. "Where is Levi?"

I smiled and nodded. "I know you must be very confused. We have a lot to talk about, but we can do that later. For now all you need to know is that you are in a hospital and you're going to be fine. Just rest and get better, we'll talk later."

"No. Please tell me now," She said, "I need to know, where is he? Where is Levi?"

I glanced over at Alexander and made eye contact. He shrugged, "You want me to tell her?"

"Tell me what?" She asked.

I looked down at her. "What is the last thing you remember?"

She stared past me with a blank expression, trying to remember. After a few moments, her frightened eyes, filled with tears, looked up at me. "He...he hit me...in the head," She whispered, "I was in the water...he was trying to kill me."

I wiped away the tears rolling down her face. "I know."

She broke down and cried, covering her face with her hands. With a Kleenex I wiped away the tears from her cheeks and stared down into her beautiful wet eyes.

"Savannah, Levi is dead, it's all over."

He's...he's dead?"

I nodded slowly. "Yes, but I'm here now."

I sat on the edge of her bed and pulled her into my arms. "Savannah, I fell in love with you the first day I saw you...and I've never stopped loving you. I was a fool to leave, but I will never leave again. You are safe now, here in my arms, where you've always belonged. And I promise...no one will ever hurt you again."

27

GOD'S WORK

They released Savannah six days later, after running a barrage of tests checking her physical and mental capacity. When the tests were completed, Dr. Baskin walked out to the waiting room, shrugged and shook his head. "Everything is normal. She is showing no signs of any brain damage at all, physically or mentally," He handed me a business card, "This is one of my colleagues in Austin. I talked to him this morning and he is well informed. He will take it from here. I have set up an appointment for Savannah to see him in two days, to change her bandages and to check her healing progress from the surgery.

He turned to walk away, but stopped and turned back toward Alexander and me. "Mr. Lee, I've been doing this for 23 years. I've done hundreds of surgeries very similar to the one I did on Savannah," He paused and shook his head, "But in all those surgeries I've never seen a 100 percent recovery like hers. There is no medical explanation for it."

I smiled. "They said you were the best. Thank you."

He shook his head and smiled back. "I'm very good at what I do, but I didn't do that. That was God's work."

They put Savannah in a wheel chair and Alexander pushed her to the elevator. When we got to the lobby, I left them to go get the car from the parking lot. When I pulled up to the entrance, I saw Louise Black standing there talking to Savannah.

When she saw me, she waved and gave me a big smile. "What did you say to them?" She asked.

I smiled back. "Did it work? Did you get a different car?"

"Not just a different car, a brand new Cadillac," She said with a wide grin, "They were falling all over me, offering me coffee and donuts, and it didn't cost me a dime, nothing down and the payments are actually $50 lower a month. I'm not sure what you did, but it sure worked."

She ran up and gave me a hug. "Travis, I can't thank you enough."

"A deals a deal, right?" I said, "I'm glad I could help."

Actually, when I called I didn't have much luck, the general manager of the dealership was a real jackass and just blew me off, but when the law firm representing the Cadillac division of General Motors received a call from a Texas State Court Judge, the Honorable Olivia Bachman and she explained how concerned she was about her good friend Louise Black's defective car, and the very expensive potential liability General Motors was exposed to...that seemed to get their attention.

∾

The other unexplained mystery was Savannah's returning memories. Dr. Baskin had no idea how that could have happened.

"I have studied images of her brain extensively," he said, "There is nothing wrong with it. I can't even explain why she may have lost her memory to start with, let alone having any medical explanation of why it came back."

Actually, Savannah didn't get all of her memories back. Interestingly, she had no memory of the last two years. She had a vague memory of being on the boat with Levi, and of him hitting her, and falling into the water, but nothing else until she woke up from her brain surgery, wondering where she was and how she had gotten there.

She had no recollection of being rescued by the fisherman, or any memory of the years she had spent in the church in Tecolutla.

"Father Alvarez?" She asked.

"Yes, Father Julio Alvarez," I said, "He is a wonderful man. And I'm pretty sure he saved your life. When the fisherman brought you to his church, you were in bad shape, barely alive, bleeding from your head. You needed blood and fortunately he had the same type, so he gave you some of his. When you got better, he paid to have a doctor come check on you from Mexico City. After that, he fed you, taught you Spanish and convinced you to paint again."

"Really? I spoke Spanish?" She asked with wide, amazed eyes.

I nodded. "Yes you did," I said, "You spoke it well."

She tilted her head and wrinkled her forehead, thinking. "All I can remember is, ¿Cómo se llama? What is your name? But I learned that in high school."

I laughed. "Well, you were fluent in Tecolutla."

"Where is Tecolutla? Could we go there some day?"

"It's a small village on the Gulf Of Mexico about 500 miles south of the border. And yes, I think we *should* go there. They will be so excited to see you again."

~

You would think that after all of the years of loving each other and fantasizing about being together, when it finally happened, it would be easy and natural for us, but it wasn't. Actually it was awkward and difficult at first.

There was no question in my mind that I loved her and I'm sure there was no question in her's that she loved me, but in reality the love we felt for each other was based on who we were as children. Although now we could both remember those magical days of our youth, we were not those innocent children any longer, we were adults and almost complete strangers.

In my fantasies, I had assumed that if Savannah and I ever got the chance to get back together, we would simply pick up where we left off, like nothing had ever happened, but I soon realized that fairytale endings to love stories are just that...a fantasy. In the real world it wasn't that easy.

The realization that I didn't know Savannah at all, happened when we arrived at my house after the long drive from the hospital and she met Buster for the first time.

Naturally, he went absolutely nuts when he saw her, spinning in circles and barking. But when he ran up to her, instead of reaching down and picking him up, she screamed and jumped back, frightened. Of course, poor Buster didn't understand and kept barking and jumping on her anyway.

"GO AWAY!" She screamed.

Fortunately, Buster understood her scream and negative body language and backed off, but he was confused and heartbroken by her reaction.

"That's just Buster," I said, "he doesn't bite. Actually, he loves you."

"Well, I don't love him! I don't like dogs!" She said abruptly, "Please, take him away."

I didn't argue with her and took him outside. When I hooked him to the chain, he looked up at me with his sad face. It had been a long time since I'd seen it, but it was back.

When I looked up, I saw her watching me through the kitchen window, frowning.

"He won't bother you anymore," I said when I walked back inside, "I'll get some lumber tomorrow and build him a dog house. I won't let him inside again."

"Do we have to keep him?"

I sighed and looked at her. "Buster is a sweet loving dog. He's been abandoned twice in his life and I'm not going to do that to him again. So, yes we have to keep him."

I was surprised and angry. I wanted to ask her how could anyone not like dogs, but I didn't. Instead, I bit my tongue and smiled at her. "Would you like the 50 cent tour of the house?"

"I'm sorry I acted that way about your dog," she said, giving me a small smile, "Levi had a dog, a pit bull and he hated me. He bit me two times. Ever since then I've been afraid of dogs."

"I understand, Pit bulls can be mean, but not all of them. It really depends on how they are trained. All I ask is that you give poor Buster a chance," I looked through the kitchen window at him looking at me, "If you will, I think he'll steal your heart."

"I doubt that, but for you I'll try," She said, "Now how about that tour? What I've seen so far is beautiful."

I laughed. "I can't take any credit for it, Olivia and Jeb picked out all the furniture and the decorations. I just signed the checks."

"Olivia and Jeb?" She said confused, "Who are they?"

That's when it hit me like a brick. We were back at ground zero. It wasn't just *us* that were strangers, as far as she knew, she had never met Olivia and Jeb, or anyone else in my life. So once again, I started over.

I slowly walked her around the house, pointing out the different art pieces and paintings that Olivia and Jeb had picked out. She was very impressed with their choices, but when I showed her a painting signed by Ariel, she did not recognize it.

"You did this one." I said.

She studied it closely. "Why did I sign it Ariel."

"That's what Father Alvarez called you, but that's a long story I thought I would let him tell you when we go visit him."

When I showed her the art studio I had built for her, she was overwhelmed and started to cry. "I've always wanted a studio like this."

"Well, now you have one."

Although it had only been a week since we had slept together in my bed and made love, I showed her the guest room. Fortunately, she hadn't moved into my bedroom completely and had left all her clothes and makeup in the guest room.

"Who's are these?" She asked, when she walked into the closet."

"They're yours. You and Olivia picked them out."

She slid back the hangers looking at the clothes. "These are mine, all of them?"

"I nodded. "Yep, all of them. Do you like them?"

"Yes, they're beautiful. I can't wait to meet Olivia, she has amazing taste."

The next morning, I loaded Buster into my car and we drove to Home Depot to buy lumber for his new dog house.

With Savannah and Rebecca swimming in the pool, Alexander and I went to work building Buster's new home. It was bigger and a bit fancier than most dog houses, but he deserved it.

When it was finished, I crawled inside and laid down with him. "I'm sorry buddy, but she doesn't remember you. You're just gonna have to make her fall in love with you again."

"Woof," he said, looking at me with that sad face.

The next morning, I took Buster with me to the office, so he wouldn't have to stay outside all day. Alexander took a few more days off from college, so he and Rebecca kept Savannah company while I was at work. I was glad he had decided to do it, so Savannah wouldn't be alone at the house, it was going to take her some time for her to adjust to her new environment and her new life.

I was anxious for her to meet Olivia and Jeb, but she was very self conscious of her looks with her bald head and didn't want to meet anyone for a while.

"That's ridiculous," Olivia said when I told her, "We don't care what she looks like, we just want to see her again."

"I know, I know, but she's embarrassed about her shaved head." I said.

We were talking in Olivia's chambers on a lunch break from her trial. When she finished her sandwich, she tossed the sack in the trash and stood up. "As a woman I understand, but she is so beautiful, if anyone could pull off bald, it would be her."

"You're right, and I've told her that," I said, "but she's not buying it. Just give her a few more weeks for the incision to heal. Her new doctor told her that when it was completely healed, she could start wearing a wig until her hair grows back."

"OK, but I still think she's being ridiculous."

Olivia lifted a glass off her desk and took a sip of her iced tea. "Have you asked her about the two million dollar insurance policy? Did Levi force her to do it? Is that why she drove all the way to Corpus Christy to sign the papers alone?"

I frowned and nodded. "As it turns out, she thought Alex was the beneficiary. That's why she was happy to drive all that way to sign it. As usual, Levi lied to her. He told her that it was a joint insurance policy he had already signed, so if anything happened to him, or her, Alexander would get the money."

Disgusted, she shook her head and opened the door of a small closet behind her desk. She took her black robe off the hanger and slipped it on. "Travis, I know this is none of my business, but have you talked to her about her suicide attempts? I'm not trying to bring up unpleasant memories for her, but if she truly has regained her full memory...then she rememberers that too."

"No, we haven't talked about it." I said.

"Why not?" She shouted, "Travis, you just can't ignore that part of her past! She was suicidal and It's important for you and her to know why."

I nodded. "I know, I know. But how do you bring something like that up? 'Savannah, how's your steak? And oh, by the way, why did you try to kill yourself three times?'"

She scowled at me. "Just set her down and ask her. She won't like it, but it needs to be discussed," She said, glancing at her watch, "I have to go back, but I'm telling you, it's important for her to talk about it and to get it out in the open."

Reluctantly, that night after we cleaned the kitchen after dinner, I poured her some wine and asked her to join me on the patio.

"I would like to talk to you about something." I said, handing her a glass, "It's...it's important."

We sat around the patio table. "You look so serious," She said, smiling, "What's wrong?"

"Do I?" I said, nervously shifting in my chair, "Sorry, I've never been good at hiding my emotions, but this *is* kind of serious and I'm not sure how to bring it up."

"Just say it," She said with a grin, "That's usually the best way to start a conversation."

I took a long sip of my wine and looked her in the eyes. "I know this may be difficult for you to talk about, but...I need to know...what made you try to kill yourself? I realize that living with Levi had to have been horrible, but you had Alexander to think of. If you had committed suicide he would have been devastated and it would have damaged him for life."

She wrinkled her forehead and frowned at me. "I guess you really don't know me at all, do you?" Her eyes filled with tears, "I may not look like that girl you knew when we were children, and I know I have changed some, but deep down, I'm still that same little girl who you sat next to in church every Sunday. I may have lost you, but I never lost my faith. I'm a Christian and you of all people should have known that I would never do something like that."

"But Alexander told me he found you...hanging in the shower...and you told him you did it, because you wanted to die. Was he lying to me?"

"No," she said wiping her cheeks, "he wasn't lying. That *is* what I told him."

"Why would you tell him that if it wasn't true?"

"He was just a little boy, only seven years old...a little boy who idolized his father. How could I tell him the truth?"

I took her hand and squeezed it gently. "I understand. So, what *was* the truth?"

She looked away and stared down at the table. "When you left, I was lost and so devastated. I know now I should have told you instead of Levi, but I just couldn't. No one knew I was pregnant, so when I started to show he offered to marry me. You know how it was back then, nice girls didn't get pregnant before they were married. It would have been such a scandal for my mother to live through...so I agreed.

"He knew I didn't love him, but I guess he thought that someday I would. I tried, I really did, but...I was in love with you."

I lifted her chin with my hand, leaned over and gently kissed her. "So what happened that day Alexander found you in the bathroom?"

"I was tired of living a lie, so when Alexander left for school, I told Levi that I was moving out and wanted a divorce. When I told him, he went crazy yelling, 'It's Travis isn't it? You still love him, right?' When I said yes, he hit me for the first time, knocking me to the floor. I jumped up and ran to the phone to call the police, but he jerked it out of my hand and slammed it down. I'd never seen him like that before, he was in a rage. I was wearing a scarf around my neck. He grabbed it and started choking me with it, yelling, 'I'd rather see you dead than with him again!'"

She reached for her glass and took a sip of wine. "I'm not sure what happened after that, I blacked out. The next thing I remember I was on the bathroom floor with Alexander leaning over me crying."

"Why didn't you call the police then?" I asked.

"When Alex found me, he ran to the phone and called Levi. He was there before I could do anything. He told me that if I ever told the police what he'd done, or ever tried to leave him again, he would kill Alexander."

"I sighed and nodded. "That's why you stayed with him and always bailed him out of jail, to protect Alexander."

She shrugged. "I had no choice. I couldn't let him hurt Alex."

"I'm so sorry I forgot who you were back then. If I had just stopped and thought for a second I would have realized you could never have betrayed me and could never have an abortion. But I was so hurt and jealous when I saw you walk in to that clinic with him that day..."

"I didn't go there to have an abortion, I went there because it was a free clinic that would treat you anonymously."

I dropped my head. "I was such a fool. I never once considered that. I'm so sorry."

"Travis, it wasn't all your fault, it was mine too," She whispered, "I should have told you."

So all those other times, it wasn't you trying to hurt yourself, it was Levi?"

"Yes."

It took almost a month before the doctors told her she could start wearing a wig. That night when we had just gotten back from her appointment, our doorbell rang.

When I opened it, Olivia was standing there holding several boxes. Before I could stop her she walked around me and yelled, "Savannah where are you?"

I shrugged and said, "She's in her room."

Without knocking, Olivia opened the door, walked in and closed it behind her.

Through the door I heard her say, "Hi, I'm Olivia. I've got something for you. Come with me."

Thirty minutes later, the door opened and they walked out. Savannah was beaming with a huge smile. "What do you think?"

She looked absolutely amazing, with long blonde hair streaming down her shoulders. "Wow!" I said, "You look beautiful."

"You should see her in the short one! She looks like a friggin' supermodel!"

She hugged Savannah. "Got to go. Big case starting tomorrow." She said, "But we're on for lunch, right?"

Savannah smiled and looked at me. "Would that be OK?"

"I assume I'm not invited?" I said,

"Nope, just Savannah," Olivia asserted, "We've got some catching up to do."

When Olivia was gone, Savannah grinned and said, "I love her!"

From that day on, having Olivia as her good friend, to go shopping with and to talk to, Savannah began to change. She began to paint again and started singing around the house. She even began to warm a little to Buster.

She started allowing me to take him off his leash when we were outside, sitting on the deck.

I had picked him up and put him on my lap when she asked, "Are you sure he doesn't bite?"

I laughed. "Buster? No way. He's a lover not a fighter. Isn't that right boy?"

Slowly, she reached over and petted his head. Buster's tail started wagging and he smiled for the first time since she had yelled at him.

He jumped out of my lap and ran to his dog house. When he came back he had his pink Dinosaur chew toy in his mouth. He jumped up back into my lap, then leaned over and dropped the dinosaur in Savannah's lap.

"Woof," He said, smiling and wagging his tail.

Savannah laughed and picked it up. "Is this for me?"

"Woof," he said again.

She looked at me laughing. "What is he trying to say?"

I smiled and petted his head, "That's his favorite toy. I think he's giving it to you."

She leaned over and scratched him under his chin. "Thank you Buster. I will cherish it."

A few days later Buster moved back into the house and once again, Savannah and Buster were best of friends.

When the doctors released her completely and told her it was OK for her to travel, I booked us on a flight to Tecolutla. For the second time, we spent most of the day with Father Alvarez and the sisters, then walked through the village, then I took her back to see the ocean. But this visit was very different. This time, she was seeing everything for the first time, through new fresh eyes.

She instantly fell in love with Father Alvarez and the sisters. She tried her best to talk to them, but the fluent Spanish they had taught her was no longer there, but none of them seemed to care. With Father Alvarez translating for them, they giggled and laughed like little girls for hours. But when Father Alvarez told her the mermaid story and why he called her Ariel, she almost cried.

She absolutely loved the quaint small village of Tecolutla and instantly bonded with Lecitia Perez at the art gallery. They browsed through the stacks of paintings in the back store rooms for hours, talking about each of the different artist's techniques.

That night we joined Father Alvarez and Lecitia for dinner at a small outside restaurant just off the Main Street. The food was delicious and Savannah seemed to be having the time of her life, laughing at Lecitia's stories and even a few from Father Alvarez.

I didn't talk much that night, I just sat back, watching her have fun, looking at her beautiful smile and listening to her musical laugh. But the biggest surprise of the night happen when we got up to leave.

Savannah hugged Lecitia and promised to send her more paintings signed by Ariel. Then she turned and looked at Father Alvarez. "Father, when Travis and I get married, would you come to Austin and do the ceremony?"

He broke into a wide grin. "It would be my honor and nothing would make me happier."

I didn't say anything at the time, but that night when we got back to our hotel, I put my arms around her waist and stared into her eyes. "When we get married?" I said.

"May I come in?" She asked. "Sure," I said opening the door to my room

When she walked in, she kicked off her shoes and pushed me down on the bed. "Travis Lee, I fell in love with you the first day I saw you. I've never stopped loving you and I never will."

I smiled. "That sounds kind of familiar."

She leaned over and kissed me. "When you said those words to me in the hospital, it took my breath away, but I was so confused and overwhelmed, I didn't know what to say back. But I know what to say now."

"Oh yeah?" I said kissing her again, "and what's that?"

She sat up on the bed and took my hands in her's. "Travis William Lee...will you marry me?"

EPILOGUE

When I was in law school, one of my professors had a picture of Abraham Lincoln on the wall behind his desk. Below it, it had one of Mr. Lincoln's most famous quotes.

"In the end, it's not the years in your life that count. It's the life in your years."

It took me a several months to accept it, but when the reality set in that I actually had Savannah back in my life, I was determined to live the rest of it…guided by that quote.

Six Years Later

Kelly and I were dozing in lawn chairs on the deck of my new Lake house when she crawled into my lap and looked up. Her beautiful turquoise eyes were sparkling in the sunlight. Then she giggled and said, "Can we go boat ride Grandpa?"

Her name was Molly Ashley Lee. She had those unique beautiful turquoise eyes, inherited from Alexander and Savannah, with long golden blonde hair, and she had me wrapped around her tiny 19 month old fingers.

"Have we met?" I said with a grin, "Who are you?"

"I'm Molly," She giggled.

"And who am I?"

"Grandpa." She said with a smile that melted my heart.

"And who is that ugly guy over there?" I asked pointing at Kelly.

"Paw paw," She yelled with a giggle.

Alexander and Rebecca followed their plan and waited to get married until he had graduated from college. Two weeks after his graduation ceremony, they were married on the beach, behind BJ and Kelly's house on the Matagorda Peninsula. Eleven months later they had Molly.

I was ecstatic the day Alexander told me he wanted to go to law school. So with a little pressure from Olivia and James Bachman, he was accepted at Yale.

Kelly and I went together and bought them a small house near the campus and also shared the tuition costs and their living expenses. And the four of us had spent another small fortune flying back and forth to visit them in New Haven, Connecticut.

Because of what had happened with Levi, I never wanted to see my lot on Lake Travis and that trailer again, so I sold it and bought a new lot with a better view on the other side of the lake. I started building the lake house a few months after Savannah had gotten out of the hospital. From the circle drive to the back deck, Savannah, Olivia and Jeb had worked together with its design and had become inseparable friends in the process.

When it was finished, it was spectacular. Jeb, Olivia and Savannah had fought like cats and dogs with the interior decorating, but the result looked like something you'd see in Architectural Digest. The walls in every room had new paintings signed by the artist named Ariel. Savannah had kept the name, because her paintings had sold so well and had become a favorite of art collectors around the world. But the most prominent display of her work was above the fire place in the living room. Lit by two art lights was the three faded 2 x 6 plywood panels, the original mural of the curving tracks through the woods behind our house that Savannah had pushed through my bedroom window 35 years earlier.

⁓

That Christmas, started our new family tradition. From Christmas Eve to New Year's Day, everyone came to celebrate together; Olivia and Jeb, BJ and Kelly, and their two boys, Rebecca and Alexander and now of course, sweet Molly.

Christmas Eve we all went to midnight mass together and Christmas Day we opened the presents. After we cleaned up the mess, we started eating and didn't stop until we had our Black Eyed Peas on New Year's Day.

When we weren't eating, the guys played golf while the women went shopping in Austin or we all squeezed into the boat and slowly cruised up and down the lake. It was the five best days of the year for everyone, something we all looked forward to each Christmas.

Every year on Christmas Day in the afternoon, James Bachman and his wife Amelia dropped by to give Buster his Christmas present. This was the sixth Christmas in a row and every one was there.

While Buster was chewing on his new toy, James took his knife and clanged it against his wine glass. "Could I get everyone's attention for a second, I would like to make an announcement."

The room got quiet and everyone turned to look at James. "In the past few months, I've been in secret communication with a new associate for my firm," he began, "I felt I needed to work fast because this brilliant young legal mind has already received several very substantial offers from some of the largest law firm's in the country, as well as offers to clerk for a few prominent federal judges. So on this wonderful Christmas Day, I felt it would be an appropriate time to announce that I have been successful in convincing this brilliant young man to join my firm."

"That's great," I said, "Who did you hire?"

James lifted his glass and said, "Please lift your glasses and join me in a toast to our newest associate, Alexander Lee."

Savannah screamed and ran up to Alexander, almost knocking him off his feet with her hug. "My baby's coming home?" She bent down and lifted Molly up in her arms, "All my babies!" She yelled.

∼

On New Year's Day, when I returned from taking Rebecca, Alexander and Molly to the airport, I found Savannah sitting on the back steps of the deck petting Buster.

When she heard me in the doorway, she turned and looked at me. Her long blonde hair had all grown back and it was swaying gently in the breeze. Her eyes, those amazing turquoise eyes were glistening and sparkling in the setting sunlight.

She pat the step next to her. "Come sit with me and watch the sunset. Look at those clouds, it's going to be beautiful."

"I'm kind of enjoying this view," I said, grinning, "You are the most beautiful thing I've ever seen."

She patted the step again. "It's a little hard to kiss you when you're way over there."

I walked over and sat down next to her. "You keep saying things like that and you just might get lucky tonight Marine." She said with a grin, leaning against my shoulder.

I lifted her chin with my fingers and gently kissed her lips. "Yum, you taste good." I whispered in her ear.

"Are you happy Travis?" She whispered back.

"I'm much more than just happy," I said, "Honestly, I don't think there's a word that could describe the way I feel. How about you? Are you happy?"

"Ditto, I'm so much more than just happy," She said, "I guess you're right, there really isn't a word to describe it."

We sat there holding on to each other watching the sunset. She was right, that sunset was one of God's best paintings, with streaks of gold, changing to red, to orange to purple, glowing over the beautiful Texas hill country.

"You were right," She said.

"Right about what?"

"All the terrible things I've lived through are best forgotten. That was another lifetime ago, full of broken dreams and pain."

She lifted her head and kissed me for a long time. "I think I know the word that describes the way I feel."

"And what's that?" I asked.

"Blessed, I feel so blessed to have a chance to live another lifetime with you, but this one will be full of happiness."

I pulled her close and brushed her hair away from her face. I kissed her again and whispered, "And full of love."

The End

A NOTE FROM BEN

Thanks for reading *Another Lifetime Ago*, I hope you enjoyed it. People often ask me where I get the inspiration for my novels. Usually, I have an answer for that, because most of the time there is something that inspires the story, but for this novel there really wasn't one. I only know where the part about the turquoise eyes comes from.

I was sitting on my patio when my wife, Dana, came out to join me wearing a beautiful turquoise blouse. When she walked out of the door, the bright sun lit up her face and her eyes glistened. Of course, I'd noticed the unique turquoise color of her eyes many times before, but on this day...wearing that blouse...they almost seemed to glow.

I was holding my iPhone in my hand, so I pulled up my writing app and typed, "Travis fell in love with Savannah's beautiful turquoise eyes when he was only eight years old."

That's how it started and the story began to flow from my brain from there. I know where I got the name Savannah, but don't ask me where I got the name Travis, because I have no idea. I love writing that way, letting the story sort of tell itself as the characters appear out of nowhere, walking into the story. Perhaps I should seek some professional help about this.

Maybe someday I will, but for now I'll keep doing it this way, so I can be just as surprised as you are when something happens. I hope you liked the way *Another Lifetime Ago* turned out as much as I did. And again, thanks for reading my book.

ABOUT THE AUTHOR

Thanks for reading *Another Lifetime Ago*. I hope you liked it. This book is also available in print and audiobook format, on Audible.com, iTunes and Amazon.

If you enjoyed this book, I invite you to read my other novels, *An August Harvest, Sing Roses For Me, Serpentine Roses and Children Of The Band*.

My first novel, *Sing Roses For Me* can be downloaded for **FREE** on Amazon. Just search for *Ben Marney books*.

Sing Roses For Me is a suspense- thriller based on a true story that actually happened to me. I am very proud of this book. It's been downloaded to over 300,000 readers and has been ranked in Amazon's Kindle Free top 10 for Suspense, Thriller, Mystery and Romance categories since it's release in May of 2017.

My last novel, *An August Harvest* has been nominated for several awards including, Best Romance novel by the prestigious Mazy Awards.

One more thing... Writing is a lonely job, so meeting and getting to know my readers is a thrill for me and one of the best perks of being an author. I would like to invite you to join my **Private Readers' Group** and in return, I'll give you a **FREE** copy of *Lyrics Of My Life*. This is a collection of autobiographical short stories about my amazing life so far.

I really would like to meet you! Please join my readers' group here:

www.benmarneybooks.com

Printed in Great Britain
by Amazon